"When I see you, I don't see broken, and I sure as hell don't see ugly," he said, his voice rough.

"Don't," she whispered, but she didn't pull away when he landed a kiss on the smooth skin of her shoulder. His lips parted and he sank to his knees as he ran his lips and tongue across her back. He could feel her tremble, hear her breath speeding up as he slid his hands around her waist and kissed his way across to her right hip and followed the scar back up to her shoulder. He pulled her back against him and slid his arms around her waist. He nuzzled his face in her neck and whispered, "When I look at your scars, when I remember what you went through, it reminds me how brave you are, how loyal." He straightened to his full height and pulled the shirt back over her shoulders.

Talia let out a little sob and turned in his arms. "I'm just afraid—all I know is that caring about someone makes me weak, it makes me stupid." She sobbed against his chest. "The last time I was with someone, he ended up controlling everything. I'm afraid of letting myself be that way again, even with you."

Praise for
Jami Alden's novels

Hide from Evil

"4½ stars! Anyone who says that romantic suspense is no longer a hot commodity hasn't read Jami Alden. She's quickly making a name for herself as one of the top writers in the genre. Her latest novel continues her streak of excellent, gripping stories and brings captivating recurring characters along for the ride."

—*RT Book Reviews*

Beg for Mercy

"4½ stars! Top Pick! Alden's emotionally gripping *Beg for Mercy* makes readers beg for mercy, too...This is a high-caliber romantic suspense—exactly what the genre should be!" —*RT Book Reviews*

"An exhilarating investigative thriller...Never slowed down...Filled with action, but character-driven by the heroine, sub-genre fans will appreciate this taut suspense...and look forward to Slater's follow-up case."

—GenreGoRoundReviews.blogspot.com

"The chemistry between Megan and Cole was absolutely mouth-watering. You could *feel* the sizzle when they were in the same room...I'm really looking forward to the next book in the series." —Romanceaholic.com

RUN *from* FEAR

RUN *from* FEAR

Jami Alden

FOREVER

NEW YORK   BOSTON

Forever
Hachette Book Group
237 Park Avenue
New York, NY 10017
www.HachetteBookGroup.com

Printed in the United States of America

First Edition: March 2012

10 9 8 7 6 5 4 3 2 1

Forever is an imprint of Grand Central Publishing.
The Forever name and logo are trademarks of Hachette Book Group, Inc.

To my sweet boys.
Your fierce hugs and kisses are the highlight of my days.
Thanks for letting Mommy write her books,
even though you won't be able to read them
for at least ten more years.

And to Gajus. Without your love and unwavering
support, none of this would be possible.

Acknowledgments

As usual, I have to thank Monica McCarty for keeping me sane, talking me through the tough times, and helping me figure my way out when I write myself into a wall. Thanks for being MY reader :) I also owe tremendous gratitude to Kelley Murray. I'm so grateful you came into our lives. Thank you for loving and caring for my boys (including the furry one!) and for your willingness to go the extra mile when deadlines loom. You're the best! And last, but most certainly not least, I want to thank you, my fans. Your enthusiasm and love for the books are a constant reminder of why I love my job.

RUN *from* FEAR

Chapter 1

There was nothing to suggest that tonight was anything other than an ordinary Sunday night at Suzette's Bistro, but Talia Vega couldn't shake the feeling that something wasn't quite right.

From her position behind the bar, she scanned the room as though it would hold a clue to her uneasiness. Sunday was never the busiest night of the week, but tonight the crowd was heavier than usual. This first week of May, the spring rains had finally run their course, and with the nice weather and later sunsets, the citizens of this affluent corner of California were flush with spring fever and ready to go out and celebrate.

Tonight the bar was about two-thirds full, girlfriends catching a quick drink as they braced for a busy week ahead, couples having drinks and a light dinner, a few older students from the nearby university craving something a little more sophisticated than the college bars.

Certainly there was nothing and no one to account for the itchy, tight feeling high on her shoulders and the sense that something in her nice, normal life was about to go awry.

She shook the feeling off and fixed her face into

a friendly smile as she handed a blonde in her forties another glass of chardonnay across the bar.

She murmured "thanks" as the blonde slipped her a five and turned her attention to a man in his early fifties, his salt-and-pepper hair swept back from his lined forehead. He was a regular enough customer for Talia to remember the face if not the name.

She poured him a vodka martini and made small talk, and the feeling of disquiet faded further into the background as she settled into her rhythm. Chatting with customers, mixing drinks, oohing and aahing with the server whose table had ordered a five-hundred-dollar bottle of wine from the cellar.

It was all so refreshingly normal.

So far away from where she'd been. What she'd been. Terrified. A victim. Living underground in a series of safe houses in Northern California, always looking over her shoulder as she frantically tried to keep herself and her teenage sister safe from people who wanted nothing more than to see them suffer.

Now she and her sister, Rosario, were free—had been for two years.

After Rosie got her GED, they'd spent over a year traveling; then eight months ago they'd settled back down in Palo Alto, California, so Rosario could begin her freshman year at nearby Stanford.

Even though it had been almost a year, Talia still marveled. Her baby sister was going to freaking Stanford! Not bad for a girl who was mostly raised by a sister who was mostly clueless but did the best she could.

As for herself, she'd found a good job with people she liked, working as the bar manager at Suzette's, which didn't land her in the lap of luxury, but it was enough to pay her bills and help Rosie with the expenses her scholarship didn't cover. All in all, a very nice life, one she couldn't have even imagined just two years ago. And there wasn't a day that went by that she wasn't intensely grateful for it.

Even on nights like this, when old memories tried to creep back in, unwanted, unsettling. She moved to the other end of the bar to clear away two wineglasses and a picked-over plate of calamari.

"Talia!"

A smile stretched her voice at the familiar voice. "Rosie, you're early," she said, turning at the sound of her younger sister's voice. She wasn't hard to spot in a crowd. At five foot nine, Rosario Vega was a good four inches taller than Talia, easy to spot in the mostly seated crowd.

But even without the height, Rosie would have stood out from the crowd. At eighteen, she was finally growing into the huge brown eyes, long nose, and full mouth that had given her a mismatched look throughout her childhood. Now the bold features gave her a beauty that was as arresting as it was unique.

Something that didn't go unnoticed by a single straight man in the bar.

Except, Talia noted as she felt her smile fade, maybe by the boy-man standing to Rosie's left. Rosario's boyfriend had his hands stuffed in the pockets of his scruffy black hoodie, a look on his face that said everything in the entire world was crushingly lame. "Oh, and I see you brought Kevin," Talia said, trying to keep the acid from her tone but failing, if Rosario's warning look was anything to go by.

"Still cool if we have dinner here?" Rosario said as she plopped onto a bar stool. She motioned for Kevin to follow, who joined her with an eye roll.

It was on the tip of Talia's tongue to remind Rosie that the invitation to dinner on Talia's tab did not include shiftless twenty-three-year-old sixth-year seniors who should be out working for a living instead of sucking off his parents' seemingly limitless college fund while preying on hapless, wide-eyed freshmen.

Instead she bit out a sharp, "Sure." Sure, she'd forgo her share of tips tonight to pay for the extra forty or so dollars of food and drink Kevin would undoubtedly suck up. Sure, she'd do her best to ignore the way Rosario would ignore everyone and focus all of her attention on Kevin, bouncing around him like a puppy while he mumbled monosyllabic replies around a mouth stuffed with food.

Because two years ago, when the tightrope she'd been walking had snapped out from under her, Talia had promised herself, promised Rosario, that she'd make a normal life for them. A life where Talia didn't have to hide out in a safe house, away from Rosario, who was forced to live under an assumed name with a family of well-meaning strangers. A life that didn't include living under the protection of full-time paid bodyguards.

And plenty of normal college girls had boyfriends, often directionless, disinterested, unworthy boyfriends like Kevin. Part of being normal meant getting your heart bruised by a guy who didn't deserve a second of your time, a lesson Talia fervently hoped Rosario learned sooner rather than later.

And really, who was she to judge? Kevin might be a shiftless douche bag, but at least he wasn't the force behind an international criminal organization that had resulted in the suffering and deaths of countless innocent women. Talia still held the gold medal in the falling-in-love-with-the-absolute-worst-person-on-the-planet contest.

She swallowed hard and forced the memories of the threats against herself and Rosie from her mind.

He couldn't hurt them anymore.

She put menus in front of Rosario and Kevin and excused herself to fill an order for the main dining room. When she got back, she automatically put a Coke in front of each of them.

Kevin let out a little huff of disgust and pushed the glass back in her direction. "Can I get a bottle of Budweiser?"

"I don't think—" Talia started, only to be interrupted by her sister.

"God, Tal, why do you do this every time? He's legal, and you know it."

"You're not, and I don't think he needs to be drinking with you—"

Kevin started to stand. "Fine. I'm supposed to meet Sam at the Z-bar anyway," he said, referencing a bar across town that was popular with the students. A bar underage Rosario wouldn't be able to get into.

Rosie grabbed his arm in a vise grip. "No, she'll give you the beer!" As she spoke, she shot Talia a look that shouted, *Don't ruin this. You owe me. You owe me big-time*.

Talia knew she could spot Rosario's boyfriend a whole truckload of beer and it wouldn't make a dent in what she owed Rosie for bringing a monster into their lives. She grabbed a beer and *thunked* the bottle in front of Kevin and asked him sharply what he wanted to eat.

"What's up with you tonight?" Rosie asked after Talia returned from putting in their order. "You've got your major crabby pants on."

Despite her irritation, Talia couldn't help smiling at Rosie's description of her bad mood, one that stemmed from their childhood. It was on the tip of her tongue to snap that she'd been in a fine enough mood before Rosie brought Mr. Lazy Trust Fund in to mooch dinner.

Instead she shrugged and admitted the strange uneasiness that had dogged her most of the evening. "I can't explain it," Talia said. "But I just have this bad feeling, like something's about to happen."

Talia was grateful when Rosie pulled her attention away from Kevin and reached out to cover Talia's hand with her own. "No offense, but I told you to stop reading all that crap. How do you expect to feel when you've spent the last two days wallowing in it."

Talia's mouth pulled tight, but she didn't remove her hand from her sister's. "I wasn't wallowing," she said stubbornly.

Rosie rolled her eyes. "Call it whatever you want, but when I stopped by yesterday, I checked your browser history, and it shows that you looked up about fifty thousand articles about that old bitch."

"What are you talking about?" Mr. Personality asked, finally intrigued by something.

Talia was summoned by a server and left Rosie to do the explaining.

As she filled the order, she had to grudgingly admit Rosie was right. Margaret Grayson-Maxwell—the old bitch in question—had been released from prison earlier this week. When her involvement with her late husband David's less-than-legitimate business of trafficking in people, drugs, and weapons was discovered, Margaret had cut a deal. In exchange for a reduced sentence, Margaret had spilled everything she knew about an organized crime network that spanned the globe.

Now she was out after only eighteen months served, and her release sparked a fresh wave of press about David Maxwell and all of his sordid dealings.

And, of course, the stories never failed to detail Talia's role as the disgruntled mistress who helped to take him and his empire down.

Talia could have all the fresh starts she wanted, but she couldn't prevent her picture from appearing front and center of every newspaper in Seattle. She was alternately portrayed as the mercenary gold digger who looked the other way while her wealthy keeper used his monster of a nephew to murder high-class prostitutes, and as the victim who had barely escaped with her life when that same nephew, Nate Brewster—known better under his infamous moniker, the "Seattle Slasher"—had set his sights on Talia.

Despite repeated admonitions from Rosie and Talia's own common sense, from the moment Talia had heard about Margaret's pending release, she hadn't been able to stop herself from inhaling every news story about it that she could find.

At first she'd been afraid that people around here would recognize her, that customers would do the math and realize her connection to the whole sordid mess.

To her relief, what was big news in Seattle proved to be of no interest in bustling Silicon Valley. Sure, the revelation of Nate as the Seattle Slasher had been a national story two years ago when it resulted in the release of Sean Flynn from death row.

A few months later, it was revealed that David Maxwell, a man who had married into a family often referred to as Washington State's version of the Kennedys, had not only been the shadowy force behind the Seattle Slasher but had also run a criminal organization that netted millions of dollars and was linked to the Russian Mafia.

At that point, there had been magazine articles, front-page stories, even features on news programs like *48 Hours* and *Dateline*. Though Talia had refused to be interviewed, her involvement with David Maxwell meant her name was dragged through the mud with his, and for about a week or so there, her name definitely had been on the country's radar.

But news moved fast, especially in the Internet age. Though Seattleites had clearly reveled in the opportunity to rehash one of the few lurid scandals to hit their comparatively whitewashed city, as far as the rest of the world was concerned, Margaret Grayson-Maxwell's arrest and the nefarious activities of her dead husband were lost in the ether.

And as Rosie had so wisely pointed out, Talia should have let it stay lost, in the past, rather than spend all of her free time delving back into every lurid detail of the past she worked so hard to escape.

As she went back to the kitchen to retrieve Rosie's and Kevin's meals, Talia vowed that from now on, she would avoid any further information about Margaret Grayson-Maxwell, even if it meant she had to cut her Internet connection to do so.

What she'd done and the choices she'd made were all

in the past now. And she'd fought too hard to escape that past to let it ruin what had become a very nice present.

She'd no sooner had that thought than she turned the corner back into the bar and saw Rosie enthusiastically hugging a very large man. After a few seconds the man released her, and Talia's confusion morphed into shock at the first flash of recognition.

Jack.

She must have said it out loud, because his head whipped around even before the plates holding Kevin's burger and Rosie's chicken breast slipped from her suddenly nerveless fingers. The sound of shattering crockery was enough to jolt her from her stupor, and she felt her cheeks burn with embarrassment as she scrambled to clean up the mess. *Real smooth, Talia.*

What did she have to be embarrassed about? she chided herself. No doubt she'd looked clumsy and stupid, standing there with her mouth hanging open while the plates slipped out of her hands, but that wasn't the worst Jack Brooks had seen of her.

Not even close.

And after two years with no contact, suddenly he was kneeling on the floor next to her. "Let me help," he said, his voice a familiar rumble that tugged at something in her chest. Ignoring her protests, he helped her gather up shards of pottery and mounds of food onto the tray a busboy had helpfully provided.

Finally Talia stood, wiping her hands on a towel, her mind buzzing with a thousand questions as her tongue remained stubbornly glued to the roof of her mouth.

"Judging from your reaction, I probably should have called ahead," Jack said, flashing her a grin that softened the harsh lines of his face and warmed the glacial blue of those eyes.

"What are you doing here?" she blurted with absolutely no finesse. But who cared? It was too late to pretend his unexpected appearance hadn't completely thrown her for a loop.

She moved back behind the bar, partly because a customer was signaling her for a refill, and partly because she wanted the physical barrier between herself and Jack. It had been two years, another lifetime, and still she found herself overwhelmed by Jack's presence.

It wasn't just the way he looked, though at six-four, packed with hard muscle and a square-jawed face that was all planes and angles, to call Jack intimidating was the understatement of the year.

But it was more than that. It was in the way he carried himself, the way he could be perfectly still yet be ready to spring into action at a second's notice. The way he could scan a room and memorize every detail of every person and object in it.

Mostly it was the way he looked at you. Jack had a way of looking at a person that made you feel like he knew all of your secrets, even the ones you didn't know you were hiding. She'd felt it that first day he'd walked into Club One and looked her up and down. At the time she'd told herself there was no way Jack knew a damn thing about her, and she was keeping it that way.

Now, she supposed, Jack knew all of her secrets. The good, the bad, the horrifically ugly.

She held herself still as he did a quick scan of her face and body. Was he mentally comparing her to the vixen she'd once been and finding her lacking?

Or was he relieved to see she was no longer the bone-thin, pale shadow of a woman he'd last seen in a safe house less than twenty miles from here?

Whatever he was thinking, his expression didn't give a clue. Nor was there anything approaching attraction or appreciation, and Talia was shocked to feel a little pinch of hurt at the realization. She certainly wasn't the glammed-out man-eater who'd once had men salivating as she walked by, but she wasn't exactly a dog.

Stop it. She mentally slapped herself. *You should be grateful Jack doesn't want anything like that from you. If he did, sooner or later he'd be calling in favors.*

The thought made her a little queasy, and she filled herself a glass of club soda.

"You've been working out. You look strong," Jack said.

Talia nodded, unsure if she should thank him, unsure it was a compliment. There was a time, a lifetime ago, when she would have come back with something snappy, shown some attitude, run her hands over her body to make sure Jack got a good look at what she had to show.

All Talia could do was stare, tongue-tied, unable to make even the simplest small talk with the man who had saved her life.

Rosario was more than capable of taking up the conversational ball. "You never answered Talia—what are you doing here?"

Broad shoulders shrugged under his jacket. "I thought I'd stop by, make sure you were doing okay with all the noise going on with Margaret's release."

Talia's brows knit over the bridge of her nose. "You flew all the way down here to check up on me?" It was ridiculous to even consider, but Talia couldn't deny the tiny burst of warmth at the possibility.

A warmth that was quickly doused by Jack's reply. "Of course not," he said with a chuckle, and shook his head. "Sorry—I just wrapped up an assignment and have had about four hours of sleep in as many days."

Now that she looked closely, Talia could see the dark, faintly puffy circles under Jack's eyes, the weary lines around his mouth. It did nothing to take away from a face that was undeniably attractive in a chiseled, hard-jawed, sharp cheekboned kind of way.

"Danny just landed a new client and they needed me to come down to help out, so I'm relocating here for the next month or so." Jack managed the Seattle operations of Gemini Securities, a firm based in the San Francisco Bay Area that specialized in corporate and personal security. The firm was owned and operated by Danny Taggart, one of Jack's team members from his time as a Green Beret, along with Taggart's younger twin brothers. "I figured I'd save myself a phone call and come see how you were doing myself."

"As you can see, I'm doing just fine," Talia said.

Rosario rolled her eyes. "Except for the part where she's spending hours online reading everything she can about the old bitch's release and reading all kinds of trash about herself in the process."

Jack sighed and rubbed his hand over his face, his weariness almost palpable. "You shouldn't read that stuff."

"I'm a big girl, Jack. I can manage my own reading material. I don't need you to save me from myself anymore." Talia winced at her snotty tone. What was wrong with her? She hated herself when she got like this. But it was too much, Jack showing up unexpectedly after she'd spent the week rehashing the past. Suddenly she was back in that place where she was like a cornered cat, spitting and hissing in her desperation to get free.

Her rudeness seemed to bounce off his broad shoulders. "I know you can take care of yourself, and Rosie," he said with a nod to her sister. "I just don't like the idea of you reliving everything that happened. You barely made it through the first time, and I hate the idea of it still hurting you. You deserve to be happy, after everything that happened."

There was something in his voice, a fierceness that made her chest feel tight, her stomach feel wobbly. And the look in his eyes—there was an intensity there, a heat like she'd never seen before.

Out of the corner of her eye, she saw a customer flag her down, and another server handed her a long list of orders. Talia filled the orders as her mind churned over Jack's appearance tonight. He made it sound so casual, just checking up on her.

But there was something going on; she couldn't put her finger on it. And in her experience, nothing was ever casual with Jack.

As she moved back to his end of the bar, she heard him chatting with Rosie about her first two quarters at school. He nodded sympathetically as Rosie complained about the physics class that was kicking her ass.

"You can call me or e-mail me anytime for help, you know," Jack said.

"That's right," Rosie said. "You were a physics major at West Point, right?"

Talia frowned. She had no idea Jack had gone to West

Point, much less been a physics major. But apparently Rosie and Jack had talked enough for her to know all sorts of details about his life.

Talia busied herself wiping down the already immaculate bar, telling herself there was no reason to feel this stab of hurt over the fact that Jack and Rosario were apparently BFFs when the only contact she'd had with him in the past two years was a terse, one-line e-mail refusing any payment for the security services he and Gemini Securities had provided while keeping her and Rosario safe from David's reach.

Not that she wanted anything more, she reminded herself forcefully. Jack was a six-foot-four, two-hundred-plus-pound reminder of everything she wanted to leave buried.

And yet, seeing him here...it awakened something inside her, something struggling to dig its way through the rubble left over from the life she'd left behind.

"So are we ever going to eat, or what?" Kevin interrupted her thoughts in a tone she'd last heard used by a three-year-old. It was clear from his sidelong glare at Jack that Kevin was not happy with Rosie's very obvious case of hero worship.

Jack turned his steely blue glare at the boy as though he'd just noticed him. He looked him up and down and turned back to Rosie. "This is the guy you told me about?" he said, not bothering to hide the skepticism in his voice.

"Yes, this is Kevin, my boyfriend," Rosie said with a tentative smile.

Talia winced at the uncertainty in her sister's voice. She looked up and caught Jack's gaze. As their eyes met, she knew his thoughts echoed her own.

Douche bag. His mouth tightened in resignation, and in that moment she felt a little crack in the wall that had always existed between them, even after Jack had pulled her out of a basement and saved her from a psycho killer.

Kevin, so sullen his bottom lip was practically protruding, reluctantly reached out his hand to take the one Jack offered. His thin hand was swallowed up by Jack's massive palm, and Kevin winced as Jack gave it a firm squeeze.

"Kevin," Jack said, his voice scarier for its icy calm. "Let's get something straight, okay?"

Kevin nodded.

"These two have run into enough creeps for three lifetimes. I've taken it upon myself to keep an eye on them and make sure they don't run into any more. Got it?"

He released Kevin's hand, and the younger man glared sullenly as he absently rubbed his sore palm. "Yeah."

"Good," Jack said with a baring of white teeth that couldn't quite be called a smile. "I'm going to be in town for a few weeks, and while I'm here, think of me as their very big, very protective older brother who will come after you if I find out you're giving either of them any trouble."

Kevin gave a grunt and heaved himself up from his seat. "Yeah, that's cool and all, but I think I'm out of here. Rosario, I'll catch you at school. It's getting a little heavy in here."

"No!" Rosario grabbed her coat and purse and started after him, shooting daggers at Jack.

Talia went after her and grabbed her arm. "Rosie, let him go. This is one of the only nights of the week I get to see you—"

Rosie jerked from her hold. "Dammit, Talia, let me go! Jack, you're as bad as her, thinking everyone in the world is out to get us. Just let me live my life," she said, whirling dramatically as she stomped after Kevin.

"Be back at my place by midnight," Talia called to her sister's disappearing back. She sighed and turned to Jack, whose usual poker face had cracked to reveal a faint sheepishness.

"I'm sorry if that was out of line...," he began.

Talia waved him off as she went back behind the bar. The crowd was thinning out and it didn't take her long to refresh a handful of drinks. "It's okay. Kevin is a jerkoff but he's mostly harmless. But I do wish she'd find someone more motivated, not to mention someone who's actually nice to her," she said as she rejoined Jack where he was leaning against one end of the bar.

His full lips quirked into a rueful smile, revealing the flash of a dimple in his lean cheek. "Why is it the good ones always go for the assholes who don't deserve them?"

"I don't know." Talia sighed with a tired smile. "But with my track record, I'm hardly in a position to question her judgment."

Jack's eyes darkened. "You can't keep blaming yourself."

Talia felt like a snake was curling around her insides as the guilt, the shame over her own bad decisions tried to claw free from the dark corner where she had shoved them. "I really don't want to get into this right now," she said, shooting a smile at a customer a few seats down. God, five minutes in Jack's presence and she was already back there, scared, powerless.

Guilty.

"Shit, Talia." Jack reached out a hand, stopping short of actually touching her. "I didn't mean to . . . I didn't come here to upset you."

There was something in Jack's face that made her swallow hard and made her feel . . . something . . . she couldn't quite pinpoint. An ache, a curiosity—

"Hey, who's your friend?"

Whatever it was got pushed away in a wave of perfume and blond hair striding across the room, a glint of interest in her blue eyes and a toothpaste-commercial-worthy smile on her face.

"This is my . . . uh . . . This is Jack Brooks," Talia said. "And, Jack, this is Susie Morse, the owner of Suzette's and my boss."

Talia watched Jack's huge hand swallow up Susie's much smaller one. She grabbed a rag and gave the bar a vigorous wipedown so she wouldn't see the inevitable flare of attraction on Jack's face. Who could blame him? With her thick, honey-colored hair, blue eyes, and tall, athletic body, Susie was a dead ringer for Christie Brinkley in her *Sports Illustrated* days. Normally Talia didn't pay enough attention to her own looks to let the contrast bother her, but suddenly she felt like a small dark mouse in the shadow of Susie's blazing sun.

"Nice to put a face with the name," Susie said, though the way her eyes were raking up and down Jack's body, Susie was appreciating a lot more than just his face.

Something was odd, though. "Why would you know Jack's name?"

Something flickered across Susie's face that looked suspiciously like guilt, but then her smile was back in full force. "Oh, Alyssa told me all about you."

Alyssa Taggart was married to Derek Taggart, who worked with Jack at Gemini Securities. Alyssa and Susie were childhood friends, and when Talia had moved to Palo Alto, Alyssa had hooked her up with Susie, who happened to be in the market for a new beverage manager at her popular restaurant. While Talia hated feeling like a charity case, she'd been happy for the introduction and had worked her ass off to make sure Susie never regretted the decision to hire her.

"Last time she and Derek were in, she said I had to meet you the next time you came to town, and I can see exactly why she was so insistent."

In her time at Suzette's, Talia had come to like and respect Susie a great deal and counted her as one of the few people she trusted enough to call a friend. But right now, watching as Susie looked at Jack like he was a juicy piece of meat, Talia had to squash the urge to smack her friend's hand away from where it lingered in Jack's.

Talia wasn't sure in the dim lighting of the bar, but she was pretty sure Jack was blushing. "Uh, thanks, it's, uh, nice to meet you too," he said, and gently disengaged his hand.

"Dinner service is wrapping up," Susie said, "but I'm more than happy to set up a table for you and have the chef put something together—"

Jack silenced her with a raised hand. "Thanks, but I'm fine. I'll just sit here at the bar, if that's okay?" He quirked a thick brow at Talia as if asking for permission.

Which struck her as odd. In her short but intense interactions with Jack, he never asked her approval for anything. "Fine with me. What can I get you?"

"Beer is good," Jack said as he settled onto a stool. Talia slid the drink in front of him and saw another customer signaling her from the corner of her eye. "I need to—"

"Go right ahead," Jack said. "I'm good."

Talia got the customer his check, and as the crowd thinned, that sensation of being watched came back, ten times stronger now. But it didn't creep her out, having Jack's intense gaze track her. Instead of prickles on the back of her neck and between her shoulders, she felt a strange ache.

Oh, God, was she actually *attracted* to Jack?

No, it was ridiculous. Impossible. Still, as she gathered up glasses from an empty table, she heard Susie's tinkling laugh from the main dining room and felt a sudden burst of envy. For the easy way her friend was able to smile at Jack, toss her hair, laugh, and make her interest clear.

Talia had been like that once. Friendly, flirty, ready and willing to use what she had to attract the attention of any man she set her sights on. She'd been normal once. She knew she had. Able to talk and banter and be attracted to a man as gorgeous and compelling as Jack.

But when she tried to remember what that was like, it was like parting the curtains on some distant, foggy past that belonged to another person. She'd tried to reclaim that part of herself in the past two years. She'd dated a few nice, normal men who took her out to dinner and *didn't* expect her to sleep with them. But none of them had been able to wake her body from its apparent coma. No one made anything that felt remotely like attraction spark in her belly.

Until now.

Of course. Because no matter how much she longed

for a normal life, of course her fucked-up past and twisted psychology would make her yearn for the one man who knew exactly who she was, what she'd done, what had been done to her.

The one man who'd made it all too clear he didn't want a damn thing from her.

—⁓—

Coming here was a mistake.

Jack hadn't known what he'd expected to feel, seeing Talia in person for the first time in nearly two years. But he hadn't expected to feel like he'd been punched in the gut, dangerously close to being overcome with a whole mess of emotions that ranged everywhere from lust to need to admiration and went way beyond the realm of mere protectiveness. He knew he was making her uncomfortable, the way he tracked her every move as she worked, but he couldn't help it.

She was so fucking beautiful. Not that he hadn't known that before tonight—the first time he'd seen her, he'd experienced the same dizziness every straight male experienced on his first encounter with Talia Vega. Made-up, dressed to kill in a dress that hugged a body that had more curves than the Pacific Coast Highway, the Talia he'd met that long-ago night when he'd signed on as the head of security at the nightclub she helped manage was something to behold.

But this woman, with her dark, wavy hair brushing her jaw, skin so smooth and clear it didn't need makeup to mess with its perfection, and a tight, toned body that moved with a fluid grace as she made the rounds... she was infinitely more appealing than the man-eater she'd once presented to the world.

He was shocked by his immediate, visceral response, the sudden need to claim her when his plan in coming here was to finally let her go for good. Even though she didn't have the slightest clue he'd been hanging on.

He struggled to keep his turmoil from showing on his face and reminded himself of his purpose here tonight.

Closure. All he wanted was to confirm, in person, everything he'd known for the past two years. Everything Danny, Derek, and Ethan Taggart had reported back to him for the past eight months. That Talia and Rosario were settled into their life here, were healthy and safe and doing just fine and had no need for Jack to come riding on his goddamn white horse to save them from an evil troll.

That last bit had been from Danny, but Jack got the point. With Nate Brewster and David Maxwell both dead, Talia's dragons had been effectively slain, leaving her free to get on with her life, free of the violence and abuse she'd suffered in the past.

And leaving Jack free to abandon his two years of under-the-radar surveillance, keeping tabs on her through his own recon missions, the Taggarts' reports, and the occasional communications with Rosario.

No more need for the behind-the-scenes help he'd provided over the past two years. Help he knew Talia would have refused if she had any idea it was coming from him.

She didn't like owing him, he knew. Though he'd been careful to conceal how he really felt about her, he knew somewhere inside her she was just waiting for the other shoe to drop. She was waiting for him to call in her debt. And in her experience, men, even the ones she thought loved her, would expect payment in only one form, whether she wanted to or not.

Logically, he got it. But it still stuck in his craw, knowing on some level that she lumped him in with the other assholes who had used and hurt her. He wished he could get her to see him differently, that after everything he'd done—and hell, hadn't done—surely he'd proven beyond a reasonable doubt that of all people she could trust him not to hurt her.

But it would never happen, and any foolish hope he might have had that maybe enough time had passed to open up a little crack in her armor died a swift death at the look on her face at first sight of him.

Shock, followed immediately by wariness. A look that said, *Why is he here, and what does he want from me?*

So closure it was. Tonight he would say good-bye to her for good. Because Talia didn't need Jack to keep her safe anymore.

Chapter 2

They never saw him coming. No, scratch that. They never saw him, period. Growing up, Eugene Kuusik resented how unremarkable he was. How easily his average frame and face faded into the background. How easy it was for the girls he liked to ignore him in favor of the jocks or the tough guys or the artsy emo kids who dressed in black and pierced their faces full of holes. No one wanted to go out with the nerdy nobody whose only distinguishing characteristics were a foreign-sounding last name and a slight accent most people couldn't place.

Now his ability to go unnoticed was one of his greatest advantages. He imagined it had worked equally well for the other greats, like Dahmer, Gacy, and BTK.

As he'd studied them, learned their techniques, he'd been struck by a feeling of kinship. He, too, knew what it meant to walk through the world looking so very ordinary on the outside, knowing he was anything but.

Yet when he'd learned about Nate Brewster, dubbed the Seattle Slasher by the press, it was as though he'd been hit with a bolt of lightning. Even though Brewster was a pretty boy like Bundy, able to use his good looks to seduce his victims, as Gene read about the man shot down in his prime, he'd felt an electric shock.

When he'd learned that Brewster had filmed his kills and had watched the footage that had leaked onto the Internet, he'd realized the world had been robbed of a master. He watched the footage over and over, especially of Talia Vega, the victim who got away. And with every viewing, his certainty grew that it was his destiny to continue Brewster's work.

This was how he would make his mark. No one would ever think him unremarkable again.

He'd been perfecting his methods over the past months. Refining, experimenting, working out the kinks. Practicing to get every detail perfect. Pushing himself relentlessly to that final step.

Click clack, click clack. His ears pricked up at the sound of high heels echoing across the asphalt like a shark scents blood.

He was nearly there.

What if you mess up with this one too?

No. He was ready to go all the way.

He wouldn't fail again. With this one, he would be able to take the final step.

The woman didn't even see him ducked down between an SUV and a station wagon as she hurried by. Her keys were out and she was moving fast, confidently, and he could practically hear the script of some dumb self-defense class she'd taken.

Move with confidence. Don't act like a victim. Keep your keys out as a possible weapon.

Right. As if good posture and a two-inch piece of metal could really dissuade someone determined to take you.

He smiled into the dark. Someone like him. If she saw him, would she even remember him as the man who had passed her on the street twice on her way to the restaurant?

He ducked out of his hiding place and skirted silently through the shadows. Her phone rang, distracting her as she dug in her purse and pulled it out to answer.

He ducked down, less than ten feet from her. Close enough to hear her side of the brief conversation without any trouble.

"I'll be there in less than ten minutes."

He imagined himself melting into the inky blackness until his body dissolved, leaving only his shadow. A leather-gloved hand came up, so quietly she didn't even flinch until the syringe touched the curve of her throat and pierced her carotid artery.

By then it was too late.

———————

Talia woke up the next morning with an ache in her chest that she couldn't seem to shake. It was stupid for Jack's surprise visit to have such an impact on her. But the way he'd left, with that half smile softening his face as he said, "Take care of yourself," it was like there was a finality to it.

Like he was saying good-bye for good this time.

And so what if he was? she scolded herself as she shuffled into the kitchen to make coffee. It wasn't like he'd been such a huge presence in her life since she'd been able to live out in the open. But she'd always had that sense that he was out there somewhere, watching out for her even though she'd told him dozens of times that he'd done enough, that he didn't need to worry about her or Rosie anymore.

Based on his visit last night, it seemed like he was finally taking her word for it.

She should be happy. The last thing she wanted was for Jack, a living, breathing reminder of her past, to be front and center in her life. And yet it was still there, that pinch in her chest at the thought that Jack was right here, in town, and would be for several weeks—though he'd made it clear he wouldn't be making any effort to see her again.

Rosie padded into the kitchen, jerking Talia from her moping before it turned into a full-on pity party.

"You up for hitting the gym in about half an hour?" she asked.

Rosie shrugged. "I guess so." From her tone, she hadn't quite forgiven Talia for pissing off Kevin the night before. But maybe they could work it out in the ring.

It had become their tradition on Mondays, the one day Rosario didn't have class, for Rosario to join Talia for a training session at a nearby boxing gym. Talia trained there nearly every day with Gus Esperanza, a mixed martial arts fighter who had toured with the Ultimate Fighting Championship until he suffered a career-ending knee injury.

Talia had started training with him shortly after she'd moved to Palo Alto. With the thought that it would make sense for her and Rosario to brush up on their self-defense skills, she'd signed them both up for an "issues in women's self-defense" class through the continuing studies department at the university.

They'd stopped going after three sessions, when it became clear that more time would be spent in a circle listening to a bunch of privileged, navel-gazing girls in their late teens and early twenties cry about how frat boys "objectified" them and made them feel so "vulnerable."

After a plump little brunette with a bouncy ponytail and Kewpie-doll mouth complained that even seeing images of rail-thin models in magazines made her feel somehow assaulted, Talia had had enough.

For the most part, Talia tried to keep the past in the past. But sometimes she couldn't keep the pain and the anger that accompanied it from spewing out.

"You want to know when I felt vulnerable?" she cut in, ignoring the way Rosario winced and hid her face behind one hand. "I felt pretty fucking vulnerable when my boyfriend threatened to have my sister gang-raped by his goons if I ever tried to leave him. I also felt assaulted when a psychotic killer drugged me, tied me up, dragged me to his basement, and showed me videos of himself killing other women while he burned me with a cigarette and stabbed me."

She had stormed out, shaking, furious with herself and those snotty princesses who had no idea how lucky they were. She needed to learn to kick some ass, not give free voice to the fear that she'd finally managed to bury.

Thank God Susie had introduced her to Gus and his training program. A few years ago, right after Susie had opened the restaurant, she was mugged at knifepoint while walking to her car. "I never kidded myself I could take out a huge guy determined to hurt me, but I wanted to at least give him a run for his money. There was a lot of buzz when Gus opened his gym, so I gave him a try. And"—she'd leaned in as though delivering a delicious secret—"I'm wearing smaller jeans than I did in high school. That's saying a lot for someone who works in the restaurant biz."

In the past six months, Talia had reaped the benefits, too, physically and psychologically. Her aggressive training with traditional and Thai boxing, tae kwon do, Krav Maga, and Russian Sambo had tightened and honed her body, tempering her once outrageous curves with sleek muscles. More importantly, she reminded herself, if someone did jump her, she'd have a decent shot at fighting him off.

In addition to her twice-a-week workouts with Susie and her Mondays with Rosario, Talia found herself at the gym most other days of the week, even when Gus said she needed a day off.

Somewhere down the line, it had gotten hard for Talia to make it through the day without working up a hard sweat. Self-defense skills aside, it centered her, gave her a sense of strength and resilience that would help her get through anything.

Even things like having Jack Brooks show up and throw her entire existence out of whack.

She slipped on a pair of capri-length stretchy pants, a sports bra, and a high-necked tank top. Unlike Susie and, to Talia's dismay, Rosario, there was no way Talia was setting a foot in the gym with her abdomen on full display. Even if she could forget about her scars for minute, she wasn't comfortable showing off her body, the irony of which, given her past, wasn't lost on her.

If it were up to her, she'd wear an oversized T-shirt and baggy sweats, but Gus had told her straight up it wouldn't do. "Gotta see your form, *mija*. Can't tell if you're doin' it right if you're wearing goddamn clown clothes."

Talia had conceded, but she always wore an oversized T over the Lycra tank until the very last second.

Familiar sounds and smells greeted her as she pushed open the door to the warehouse on the corner of Industrial and Murphy. Grunts, huffing breath, and the occasional meaty *thwack* of a fist or foot connecting a blow echoed through the gym. The smell of salt and sweat permeated the air, and gangsta rap pumped through the speakers.

This was so much better than the three-hundred-dollar-a-month private club where she used to train in Seattle. Talia's muscles twitched in anticipation. She and Rosario made a quick side trip to the ladies' locker room, which was much more nicely appointed than the rest of the gym would have suggested. But Susie wasn't the only one to realize how well Gus's shredder classes worked to keep the pounds off, so he'd tricked out the ladies' locker room to rival that of any high-end gym.

She and Rosario ditched their stuff in a locker and went out to join Gus for a private training session. As he had them warm up with jump ropes, Talia's mind wandered back to Jack.

If last night was good-bye, why bother to come see her at all? In the six months she'd lived here, he'd never made an effort to see her when he traveled down from Seattle for business.

Talia had had reservations about moving here, specifically because she thought it would mean running into Jack more often than she thought she wanted. Though Jack ran the Seattle office, Gemini's headquarters were just up the road in Menlo Park, which, the connection to Jack aside, did turn out to be a lucky coincidence. Though Talia was all about self-sufficiency in this new life of hers, it was good to have people nearby who had shown their willingness and ability to help her out of a jam.

However, along with that reassurance came the trepidation that Jack might be popping in to say hi on his trips to the Bay Area. But it had never happened, and she knew from Alyssa, who came to Suzette's at least a couple times a month, that Jack had been here half a dozen times since she and Rosie had moved here.

Last night was the first, and apparently last, time Jack was planning to darken Suzette's doorstep.

"Ease up, this is just a warm-up drill," Gus said when she jabbed the focus pad hard enough to make him grunt. He took off the pads and motioned her and Rosie to follow him into the studio to spar.

She was glad, she told herself as she and Rosie circled each other. She didn't need Jack, with his cool, analytical stare that saw too much. Yet even as he unnerved her, she had to admit something happened to her whenever she got in the same room with him. After all this time, she felt safer with him than any other human being on the planet. She wished—

Rosario's gloved fist connecting with Talia's stomach jarred her back to reality.

"So what happened with you and Jack after I left?" Rosie asked, a little breathless as she bobbed to avoid Talia's return blow.

"He had a beer; we chatted at little bit. He said he was glad we were doing well, and he left."

"That's it?"

Talia used her forearm to block Rosie's kick. "What else would there be?"

"He didn't ask you out or anything?"

The question startled her, tangling her feet so instead of lightly dancing out of Rosario's considerable range, she staggered back and fell on her butt.

"Jack and I aren't like that." She took Rosie's proffered hand and let her sister pull her up.

"Okay."

"What?"

"Nothing. It's just that sometimes when I talk to him, the way he asks about you—"

"Wait, how often are you talking to him? What are you saying about me?"

"Jeez, Tal, calm down," Rosie said as they resumed the fighting stance. "When we talk, he asks how you are— that's it. I just thought—"

"Did you say something to make him think I wanted him to ask me out? Because, Rosie, believe me, after everything that happened, I don't really want to go out with anyone, especially not Jack."

"Why not?"

The reasons were endless, starting and ending with the fact that Jack had seen her at her lowest point, had pulled her naked and bleeding from that basement. And worst of all, he knew that it was her own fault, her own stupidity, her own bad choices that had landed her there.

He knew firsthand her ability to fuck up. Not just for herself, but for Rosie too. And a guy like Jack, who always tried to do the right thing, no matter the threat to himself, would never be able to forget that.

By some miracle, he'd actually seen something in her worth saving. Talia wasn't going to push it by asking for more. In answer to Rosie's question, she said simply, "It's complicated. But I don't want you bugging Jack anymore."

She lifted her hand when Rosie opened her mouth to protest. "I got the sense he came by last night to reassure himself we're doing well so he can feel okay about cutting us loose. Jack has done more than enough for us—we owe him our lives. He doesn't need to worry about us anymore."

—m—

Twelve hours later, Talia shot out of bed at the first screech of the security alarm. Her heart hammered against her rib cage with bruising force as she fumbled for the keypad next to her bed and entered the code that would silence the earsplitting din.

Ears still ringing, she grabbed her cell phone and started blindly for the bathroom, where she'd spent a week's worth of tips to install a steel-core door with a bolt lock, the best approximation of a safe room she could put together in her little rental house.

Rosie. She stopped herself just as she was about to throw the lock, and her adrenaline-drenched brain came to life and reminded her that her sister was staying down the hall. Alone. Vulnerable.

Panic propelled her to the hallway, where Rosario stood in the doorway in her pajamas, her own cell phone in one hand, rubbing her eyes with the other. "What's going on?" she mumbled.

"Something set the alarm off." As she reached for Rosario, a loud crash nearly made her heart burst through her chest, and holy Jesus it sounded like it was coming from somewhere in the house. "Come on!" She grabbed her sister by the arm and dragged her into the bathroom, slamming the lock home.

"It's going to be okay," she whispered shakily as Rosario sank to the floor and drew her knees up to her chin while Talia sat on the edge of the tub. "The police will be here soon, alerted by the alarm company," she said, as much to herself as to her sister. She tried to force her breathing back to normal, tried not to show Rosie the true depth of her terror. She had to be strong, had to make sure Rosie knew everything would be okay.

The ring of her phone nearly made her jump out of her skin, and she forced herself to take a deep breath as she answered. It was just the alarm company, calling to make sure the alarm hadn't been tripped accidentally.

"We'll make sure a patrol car is sent right out," the dispatcher said after Talia confirmed the alarm was set off by a possible intruder.

"Police are on their way," Talia said, closing her eyes as she prayed that whoever had broken in wasn't at that moment sneaking up the stairs, prepared to break down the door to get to them.

Rosario stood and reached for the lock.

"What are you doing?" Talia said, and batted Rosario's hand away.

"I can hear the sirens," Rosario said, gesturing to the barred bathroom window.

Sure enough, Talia could hear the sound of a squad car siren getting closer.

"Shouldn't we go let them in?" Rosie asked.

"We stay in here until we see the squad car pull up," Talia said. But that still meant she'd have to walk through the house to unlock the door or risk having it broken down.

It was going to be okay. The police—police who were on her side now—would be here soon.

Clearly her efforts to conceal her panic hadn't worked, because Rosie pulled her into her arms. "It's okay, Talia," she said in a tone suited for soothing a baby as she rubbed her back. "The police are coming. Nothing is going to happen."

"You're right," Talia said. Yet she couldn't escape the sensation that she was being sucked back into that dark pit, the terror that she thought she'd buried once again threatening to consume her.

She stood on shaky legs and forced herself off the floor so she could look for the police through the bathroom's tiny window.

She heard a tapping sound behind her, the familiar sound of Rosie on her phone. "Are you tweeting about what a head case I am?" she asked.

Rosie gave a little laugh but didn't answer. At least she didn't seem too scared, which was good. Though Talia tried to instill some caution into her sister, she was glad the months in hiding hadn't left Rosie with the unfortunate paranoia that Talia only mostly kept under control.

Yes, Rosario had suffered from the fallout, but Talia had done her best to keep her sheltered from the reality of her situation. And while the attack on Talia had scared her, Rosario had been kept away from her in her own safe house so she never saw the true horror the Seattle Slasher had inflicted on her.

Though Rosie was a lot more street-smart than most girls her age, thanks to the lessons Jack and his friend Danny Taggart and his brothers had drilled into her, she didn't have the instincts for danger that came from experiencing violence firsthand.

Talia hadn't done much right, but she'd kept Rosie out of harm's way.

She heard a car pull up outside and slid open the bathroom window. Since the house was all one level and all of twelve hundred square feet, including the garage, she could easily hear the footsteps falling on the flagstone walkway. Seconds later, there was a knock at the front door. "Ms. Vega? It's Officer Roberts from the police department."

"I'll be right out," she called through the window.

She kept Rosario behind her as she hurried through the bedroom to the front door, turning on every light in the house on her way. By the time she peeked through the peephole, the house was blazing with light, no shadows left to conceal any creeps who might be lingering. Outside, a uniformed officer stood illuminated by the floodlights that automatically came on when the alarm was tripped.

She unlocked the door, let the officer inside, and briefly explained what happened.

"So you heard something banging in the garage but didn't see anything?"

"That's correct," Talia said.

"And you were here, inside the entire time?" Officer Roberts asked Rosario.

"I was asleep," she replied.

"She got in a couple hours ago, right after midnight," Talia added. "I waited for her to get in to set the alarm."

The cop made a note on his notepad. "Okay if I take a look outside?"

"Of course." Talia nodded.

Talia could hear the crunch of gravel under the cop's feet and saw the beam of his flashlight as he moved around the side of the house. She went into the kitchen and was pouring herself a glass of water when she heard a knock on the door that led to the single-car garage.

Talia put down her glass and opened the door to Officer Roberts. "I think I know what the problem is."

But another voice, deep, male, and all too familiar, distracted her. "Where's your sister? Is everything okay?"

Talia turned to see Jack in her entryway, dressed in frayed jeans and a gray sweatshirt that proclaimed him property of the U.S. Army. His eyes were a little puffy and his short dark hair was ruffled as though he'd just rolled out of bed. Which, at just after two on a Tuesday morning, he no doubt had.

"What are you doing here?" she asked.

"I texted him from the bathroom," Rosario said.

"Rosie, we shouldn't bother Jack with stuff like this," Talia said tightly, even as her stomach did a little flip at the idea that he was willing to pull himself out of bed at this ungodly hour to make sure they were okay. "He doesn't need to deal with our problems anymore."

Jack's heavy footfalls echoed on the wood floors as he took the ten steps that led from the door to the small kitchen.

Talia turned to face him. "I'm so sorry, Jack. Rosie shouldn't have—"

"Of course she should have," Jack said, his eyes narrowing on her. "Why didn't you call me yourself?"

"It didn't occur to me," she said honestly. "Besides, the alarm company automatically calls the police. There's no reason for us to bother you with it."

She could see a muscle tighten in his jaw. "When are you ever going to understand that it's not a bother? I need to know you're safe for my own peace of mind."

Under his scrutiny, Talia suddenly became aware that she was wearing her pajamas, which consisted of a pair of soft cotton pants and a thin tank top that showed off every curve of her braless breasts. Her face heated and she crossed her arms over her chest.

It was silly to feel self-conscious—the man had seen her naked, for God's sake—but there was something different between them now, a weird charge in the air.

And it didn't help that snippets of her earlier conversation with Rosie kept popping into her brain. Making her wonder if her sister was right, that Jack did have a thing for her after all and had just been biding his time before he called in his favors.

Stop. Jack isn't like that and you know it, she told herself, giving herself a mental slap for even thinking it. After all that he'd done—and more to the point, hadn't done—Jack didn't deserve anything but her gratitude.

"I appreciate that you're concerned about us, Jack, but I'm sure whoever tried to break in is long gone. No need for you to lose any more sleep over it."

"Actually, I don't believe there was an intruder," Roberts broke in.

"Then what set off the alarm?" Jack said.

"Want to follow me?" He gestured them out to the garage, Jack following Talia so closely she could feel the heat rolling off his much larger body.

The overhead light was on, illuminating Talia's silver Honda Accord parked inside. Next to it, a plastic garbage can lay on its side. The bag inside had been dragged out and shredded, and bits and pieces of banana peel, coffee filters, and other assorted trash littered the concrete floor.

"Looks like the side door into the garage was left

slightly ajar," Roberts said, picking his way over a Styrofoam container dripping week-old noodles as he walked to the door. "My guess is raccoons pushed the door open, and when they did, they set off the motion detectors in here." Roberts took a curious look around. "Don't often see motion detectors in a house this small."

Especially not one full of secondhand furniture and cheap electronics. But it wasn't stuff Talia's moresophisticated-than-average security system was protecting.

She turned to Rosario, who was lurking in the door that led to the kitchen. "You told me you locked the door when you came in."

Guilt flashed in her sister's eyes as she grimaced. "I thought I did, but it's possible it didn't latch..."

Now she really felt like a jerk, having the police show up and dragging Jack out of bed because of a mishap with the neighborhood wildlife. "You need to be sure!" Talia snapped, her unease morphing into annoyance.

"I'm sorry, okay? Don't yell at me!"

Talia took a deep breath and bit back her temper. "I'm sorry I yelled. I know it was an accident. This is a safe neighborhood, but we still need to be careful."

Rosario nodded, but her mouth was still pulled into a slight pout.

Officer Roberts's radio squawked from his hip and he unclipped it to have a low-pitched conversation full of codes Talia couldn't decipher.

"Ms. Vega?"

Talia turned back to Officer Roberts. "Are you satisfied everything is okay around here? I have a possible two-sixty-one I need to respond to."

"What's a two-sixty-one?" Talia wondered out loud.

"It's sexual assault," Jack said quietly before Roberts could answer. "Right?" Jack asked Roberts as an afterthought.

"That's correct."

"Yes, we'll be fine, Officer. Thanks for responding so quickly," Talia said. As he walked away, talking into his radio, she heard something about "panic," and "raccoons."

As she looked at the garbage tossed around her garage, Talia suddenly felt very, very tired. "How could you not check to make sure the door was locked?" she said again as she took a garbage bag from the box on a shelf and gingerly picked up an empty pretzel bag.

"It was just a raccoon," Rosario said defensively. "It was nothing."

"This time," Talia snapped as she threw a bunch of rancid carrot tops into the bag. "But you heard him. He left to go investigate a rape. That could have been us. It could have been you—" Her voice choked on the thought.

"Don't get all paranoid again—"

"Your sister's right," Jack snapped, and knelt down to scoop up some stray papers. "You can't just think you lock the doors; you have to be sure—"

"This is exactly why I live in the dorms," Rosario snapped, and stomped back into the house.

Talia snatched a milk carton from Jack's hand. "You can go now," she said, wincing at her peevish tone. "I'm sorry," she added immediately, and sat back on her heels with a sigh. "I shouldn't talk to you like that. It's just, I thought I was past it, you know?" She pushed herself to her feet and held up her hand to show him how much it was shaking. "One minute I'm fine, sleeping like a baby, but all it takes is a wayward raccoon to send me into a full-blown freak-out."

Jack caught her arm, the warmth of his big palm seeping into her skin, making her suddenly aware of how cold the rest of her body was. She clenched her teeth to keep them from chattering as a shudder tumbled through her.

"Next time it might not be nothing. Don't beat yourself up for being prepared."

Talia let him pull her into the house. False alarm or not, the adrenaline rush of fear and the subsequent crash were real. And though she was loathe to admit it, it felt good to have him here, his strong presence, ready to spring into action at the slightest threat.

She closed her eyes. Jack was not her personal knight in shining armor, and she couldn't keep depending on him. She already owed him so much. She couldn't keep adding to the list.

—⁓—

Jack pulled Talia into her postage-stamp-sized kitchen and forced himself not to focus on the silky feel of her wrist under his fingers. Though she was trying hard to keep it together now that her intruder had turned out to be a furry bandit, she was clearly shaken up. She didn't need him to start fondling her arm like some sexually frustrated perv.

But it was damn hard to pull his hand away as he settled her into a spindly wooden chair. He gave her wrist one last squeeze, telling himself it was to comfort her, but it was just as much to savor a last quick feel of the smooth, milky, coffee-colored expanse.

"You should let me redo the system," he said. "Hook it back into the Gemini network so I get an alert when it goes off—"

She looked up at him, her eyes shadowed with fatigue, her full mouth pulled into a wry half smile. "Really? So you can come running every time a raccoon gets in my trash? Besides, the Gemini alarm system would mean retrofitting the house's phone lines. Even if my landlord let me do it, I can't afford to pay for it."

"I can—"

"Don't you dare offer to pay for it!" Talia snapped before he could even get the words out. "I'm sorry, I know I'm acting like a bitch, but you don't need to do anything else for us." She shook her head and huffed out a little laugh. "I know that sounds ridiculous given how much you've done for me and Rosie. But, Jack, it's been over two years. Whatever debt you think you owe me for what happened, believe me, you've made up for it. You can let go of your guilt and stop worrying about us."

Goddamn, if only it was that simple, he thought as he studied her. So different now than the almost savagely beautiful woman he'd met for the first time two and a half years ago. Back then she'd been tough as nails, slinking around Club One, ruling with an iron fist and a killer bod.

Or so he'd thought. It hadn't taken him long to see the cracks start to show, to realize she was in way, way over her head.

And with his usual—and sometimes misguided—sense of what his sister called old-school chivalry and what he called an idiotic hero complex, he'd decided Talia Vega was a damsel in sore need of rescuing.

But he'd drastically misjudged his opponent and nearly gotten her killed.

So, hell yeah, guilt had driven him, especially at the beginning. But as he'd gotten to know Talia, he'd seen firsthand her drive to protect her sister at any cost, her fighting spirit that helped her survive an attack that would have killed most.

Then he'd watched her these past two years as she picked up the pieces and built a new life for herself, and his admiration had grown exponentially.

Admiration and something else he wasn't quite ready to put a label on. In any case, whatever he felt for Talia was a lot more complicated than simple guilt. "I don't see why it's such a problem for me to want to help you out every once in a while." The truth was, he wanted a hell of a lot more, and a depraved part of him knew she'd probably give it if he asked.

But it would never be for the reasons he wanted. And he would never settle for anything less.

"So can you indulge me?" he asked softly. As he gazed into her dark, shadowed eyes, her beautiful face with the high cheekbones and full lips that gave her an exotic air, his hand itched to caress her cheek. Trail down her neck. Tangle in the thick tumble of near-black curls.

He curled his hand into a fist.

She nodded. "I don't want you to think I'm not grateful. For everything—"

"I don't want your goddamn gratitude," he said, harsher than he'd intended.

To her credit, she didn't flinch. "But I don't know why you feel obligated to bother with us, especially now that we're safe."

"But you don't feel safe, do you?"

"It's over," she said. "There's nothing to worry about anymore."

He wasn't sure if she was trying to convince him or herself, but the fear was still there, along with the scars that had faded but not disappeared.

And though he knew it would be torture to be around her while knowing he couldn't have her, at that moment he knew he was going to stick around for as long as it took him to banish her fear for good.

—⁓—

The light in the penthouse suite was dim, the heady scent of gardenias filling the air. The silk of her dress rustled against her skin as she gazed out the window at the Seattle skyline. She smiled as the strong hands looped the delicate chain around her neck. "It's beautiful," she breathed as she held the diamond-encrusted platinum rose charm between her thumb and forefinger so she could better admire it.

A deep voice rumbled in her ear. "I wanted to give you something to remind you exactly what you mean to me."

The voice sent a shiver of dread through her as the walls of the suite started to ripple. Suddenly the room changed, morphing from a luxurious hotel suite into a dank, cold dungeon. The scent of the flowers grew stronger, the sickly sweet scent threatening to suffocate her. The necklace tightened around her neck, digging into her throat, cutting through her skin.

She clawed at the chain, its razor sharpness slicing through her fingers as the chain sliced its way through her neck.

"Jack!" She tried to scream but nothing came out except a weak gurgle.

Talia jerked awake, her body bathed in a cold sweat, her breath coming in sharp pants. Her hand went automatically to her throat. Nothing. She let out a sound, half sob, half laugh.

Though her fingers and neck still tingled, there was nothing there. The necklace David had given her was long gone, taken from her body the day Jack had carried her, bleeding, from Nate Brewster's hideous torture chamber.

She breathed deeply, reassuring herself there was no trace of the cloying gardenia scent in the air.

She swung her feet to the floor, groggily shuffled to the bathroom, and tried to sweep away the lingering images of David Maxwell from her mind. She couldn't remember the last nightmare she'd had about him, but clearly last night's scare had called one of her primary demons from the depths of hell to torment her.

You don't feel safe, do you?

No. She hadn't from the instant she realized she'd given her love, given herself to a monster. And now, even with him dead, it seemed she would never escape the cloud of fear he'd cast. She resisted the urge to spend the day behind a locked door and forced herself to keep with her regular routine.

She'd come too far, worked too hard to get her life to some semblance of normal. No way was she going to let a stupid raccoon send her back to that place where she could barely go to the grocery store without having a panic attack.

It helped that Rosie didn't have class until the afternoon and had offered to hang out this morning. The fact that her sister was unfazed by the nighttime visitor made it easier for Talia to get herself out the door to the boxing gym.

And the fact that Jack Brooks was somewhere in the vicinity, ready to drop everything to come to her rescue at a moment's notice...

No, no way, you are not going there. Jack has done more than his fair share to save your ass. You haven't been a pain in his side for nearly two years and you're not going to start up again now.

Two hours later, Talia was feeling immensely better after an intense training session, energized from both the workout and the bucket-sized lattes she and Rosie had picked up on the way home.

But her postworkout euphoria vanished when she saw an unfamiliar car parked in front of her garage. Unbidden, irrational uneasiness consumed her. There was no reason to freak out, she told herself, just because there was a strange car in her driveway. Maybe the landlord sent someone over to do a repair, though he'd never sent anyone over unannounced before.

If that was the case, Talia would have to have a word. She didn't care that she was merely renting. She didn't like strangers, and she didn't like being caught by surprise.

She parked on the street and walked up to the car and peered into the driver's side window.

Empty.

"Who—"

She raised a hand and cut Rosario off as she walked up the path to the front door. Her stomach leaped to her throat as the door swung open just as she was reaching for the handle.

The realization that it was Jack, followed closely by a tall, muscular man Talia had met but whose name didn't immediately come to mind, didn't do much to quell the impending heart attack. She staggered back, hand up to her chest as Jack looked down at her.

"Shit. I was hoping to have this finished before you got back," Jack said.

"Have what finished? What are you doing?"

"Jack wanted to make a few modifications to the security system." His friend offered his hand with a flash of white teeth that might have charmed the pants off a normal woman. "I'm Ben Moreno. I don't know if you remember me," he said as his big hand swallowed the one Talia automatically offered. "We met a couple times at Suzette's, when I came in with Derek and Alyssa."

Talia nodded. "I remember now." Every female in the place—besides herself, of course—had been tittering and buzzing around the table. Immune though Talia was, even she had to admit that between him and Alyssa's husband, Derek, they'd provided quite the display of eye candy. "You work with Gemini, too, right?"

Moreno nodded and released her hand. "Since I just finished upgrading all of the employee residences, I told Jack I'd give him a hand with this."

Talia gave her head a frustrated shake and hurried up the stairs. Ignoring Ben, she tried to keep her tone civil as she said to Jack, "We talked about this last night."

Jack's square chin jutted out another inch. "You talked. I decided to upgrade."

"What, you thought I wouldn't notice when the security system I use every day has changed?"

"Actually," Ben broke in, "it's designed to work seamlessly with your existing system, so much so you wouldn't have noticed if—"

He broke off at Jack's icy glare. "Wow, I sure could use a cold drink."

"I'll get you something." Rosario rushed past her, her cheeks already flushed as she basked in Ben's lazy grin. Rosario wasn't the first woman between the ages of eighteen and eighty to fall under the spell of that sexy grin and dark eyes, and she wouldn't be the last.

Talia clenched her jaw. "I realize all of this is coming from a good place, so I'm trying really hard to stifle my inner bitch right now. But you had no right to go behind my back and do something like this without telling me."

Jack folded his arms across his massive chest, about as giving as a block of granite. "It needed to be done. You weren't going to let me do it. I found another way."

"You bulldozed right over me is what you did," Talia said. Her throat tightened at the thought of how he saw her—weak, afraid, easily controlled by someone bigger and stronger. "Did it ever occur to you," she said, choking past the lump in her throat, "that maybe going behind my back and installing a secret security system isn't the best way to make me feel safe?"

She held up a silencing hand when he would have responded. "I get it. I was in a bad place for a very long time and not far out of it the last time you saw me. But since David died, I've been taking care of myself and taking care of Rosie. I know you see me as someone who makes stupid decisions, but I'm not that girl anymore. You can't just go behind my back and go against what I want just because you think you know what's best for me." She thumped her finger on his chest for emphasis.

Jack flinched, his broad shoulders slumping under his jacket. "I'm sorry. I didn't think—"

But Talia was on a roll now, David's control over her fresh in her memory after the nightmare. "Obviously," Talia said, anger coursing through her. At Jack for going behind her back. At the way his presence brought everything bubbling back up to the surface, reminding her of the kind of person she'd once been. The kind of person he could never, ever see as an equal, worthy of his respect and lo–

She cut the thought off and lashed out. "What's next? You going to install cameras in my bathroom so you can watch me shower? Trust me, Jack. This"—she made a gesture to her body—"is not even close to what it used to be, all scarred up and—"

"Shut up," Jack bit out, his voice soft. He pressed his lips together and squeezed his eyes shut. When they opened, their familiar icy blue had given way to a stormy gray, dark and troubled. "I'm sorry. I never thought about it that way—"

"No, of course you didn't," she said, the anger draining out of her as she realized her arrow had more than hit its mark.

Jack didn't deserve this. It wasn't his fault she was damaged goods still trying to firm up her place in this new life of hers. "I'm sorry—that was a horrible thing to say. I had a really rough night after you left, and I shouldn't take it out on you. Especially when you're only trying to help. But you have to understand that all of this, being around you, having you do stuff against my wishes, it brings up stuff—"

"I get it," Jack said curtly. "I'm hard for you to be around." His face was carved in granite, and a muscle throbbed in his jaw. "As soon as I'm done, I'll make myself scarce."

Every cell in her body protested at the idea of saying good-bye again, but logically she knew it was for the best. She'd reached a good place in her life, a calm place. The emotional turmoil Jack caused just by showing up put all of that at risk.

Still, as she walked into the house, dropping her gym bag on the entryway floor, she couldn't stop herself from saying, "That's not what I meant. You just have to understand that I won't be dictated to, and I won't be walked over. No matter how much you've helped me in the past, you can't just ignore me when I ask you not to do something."

"You're right," Jack said as he followed behind her. "And I apologize. But—"

"No. You can stop at sorry." When he opened his mouth to speak, she put her hand up. "And you can remove the new system."

"Afraid that won't be possible," Jack said.

"Why not?" She turned to Ben. "Whatever you've done already, just undo."

"Well, it's not as simple as that," Ben said as he rubbed a broad palm across the back of his neck. "It's too complicated to explain, but if we rip out the new system, your entire system will have to be rewired. You'll have to buy and reinstall a new security system."

Talia could feel the muscles in her jaw throb. She was tempted to tell them to rip the entire thing out, but she knew it could take weeks for a new system to be installed. No way was she staying here without a working security system, even if the greatest threat to her security was the local wildlife.

"Fine. How much do I owe you?

"Nothing," Jack said.

"How. Much." She pinned Ben with a hard stare. When he didn't answer for several seconds, she reached for her cell phone. "Fine. I'll call Danny and ask him." Somehow she didn't think this was a sanctioned Gemini work order. "I'm sure he'd be more than happy to collect for the time and the equipment."

Ben and Jack exchanged a look, confirming her suspicions.

She'd met Danny only a couple of times, but on both occasions it had been clear that while he was more than happy to help Rosario, the innocent victim in the mess Talia had made of their lives, he was helping Talia only as a favor to Jack. *You'd better be damn careful, pulling him into this mess of yours,* Danny had said the first time they'd met. No way would he be okay with Jack throwing her any more freebies.

Ben's gaze darted between their matching glares. "Well, fully installed, this usually runs a few grand." A warning grunt from Jack made him sputter, "B-but since I had most of the equipment already—"

"Never mind," Talia said, and yanked her checkbook out of her purse and quickly scrawled out a check for five hundred dollars. The ripping sound echoed through the kitchen and she thrust it at Jack. "This is all I can afford right now. Have someone at the office get in touch and I'll set up a payment plan."

Jack crumpled the check in his hand.

"I swear to God, if that check doesn't clear by the end of the week, I'll rip out the system myself."

"Jesus, Tal, why are you being such a hardass?" Rosario said. "They're just trying to help us out."

Talia whirled on her sister. "Because it's not okay for anyone to come into my home and do things against my will and then tell me I should be grateful." She winced inwardly at her shrill tone, could only imagine that Ben must think Jack was crazy for wanting to help a bitch like her. But she'd spent too long being pushed around, her entire existence under the control of one man. Now everything inside her rebelled at the idea of being manipulated, having her needs and wants ignored, even if it was motivated by the best of intentions.

"I've never demanded your gratitude, Talia," Jack said quietly, his hand still fisted around the check.

Talia let out huff of laughter and felt her shoulders slump under an unexpected wave of sadness. "No, you don't seem to want anything."

For a second something flared in Jack's eyes, but it was gone as quickly as it appeared. "I know you're not happy with the way I did this," he said softly. He nodded at Ben, who left with a quick wave for her and Rosario. "But maybe you'll change your mind when you see the scratch marks on your garage door lock."

Talia's brow furrowed, a chill running through her as the impact of his words started to sink in. "It wasn't a raccoon?"

Jack's head gave a quick jerk to the side. "The lock was picked. Someone tried to break into your house."

Chapter 3

You can go ahead and file a report," the officer, who was not nearly as nice as Officer Roberts, said in a voice that managed to convey the emptiness of that gesture. "But your landlord admitted the lock is old and the house had been previously burglarized. There's no proof those scratches are from the other night—"

"They look fresh," Jack interrupted. "Had they been from the previous burglary, they would have been smoothed out—"

"So being a high-priced rent-a-cop makes you an expert in forensics?" the cop said, adjusting his belt under his hefty gut as he puffed his chest out.

Ben rolled his eyes and went back into the house. Talia was pretty sure that crunching sound was Jack biting on his tongue. "What else do you suggest I do, Officer?"

"Keep your doors locked and your alarm on," he said with a smirk, and left.

Jack muttered something under his breath.

"Tal, do you want me to stay with you for a little while?" Rosario asked, her hand on Talia's arm the only warm spot on her body.

Talia shook her head. "I'll be fine." Rosario loved

living on campus, and Talia would never take that away from her. And maybe she was being paranoid, but if someone was specifically targeting her, she wanted Rosie well away, safe in her dorm, protected by the university's own rigorous security protocols. "Just do me a favor—no missing any curfew calls this week. Deal?" When Talia had agreed to let Rosario live on campus, they'd agreed Rosario would call her every single night, no matter what, at eleven p.m. to let her know where she was. In the eight months since school started, Rosario had gotten a little lax. And try as she did not to overreact, nothing sent Talia into a tailspin faster than not being able to get ahold of Rosie. There had even been one humiliating—according to Rosario—incident involving her dorm RAs and the campus police.

"Deal," Rosario replied with a smile. "Eleven o'clock, on the dot, unless I go to bed early, and if I can't call, I promise to text." She gave Jack a quick hug good-bye and ran inside to get her stuff together.

"Talia—" Jack got cut off as his phone beeped. He let out a low curse. "I'm sorry, but we have to go." He nodded at Ben, who emerged from her house with his bag of gear. "We need to move it if we're going to make it on time," he called over Talia's head, then focused back on her. "I'm on a personal security detail over in Atherton—our client has been receiving death threats, so they're temporarily relocating from London. It's going to be twenty-four-seven, so the next few weeks—"

Talia held up her hand. "Jack, you don't have to explain to me that you have a job to do. I know you didn't come down from Seattle to see me. You don't have to babysit me. I'll be fine."

He cocked an eyebrow and looked meaningfully in the direction of her garage door.

Talia shrugged and said, "Like Officer Friendly said, that probably happened ages ago."

"You don't buy that bullshit any more than I do."

"Let's move," Ben said. "And I'm driving. You drive like a grandma."

Jack didn't budge. "The system is wired now to call Gemini headquarters and my cell phone if the alarm trips. I'll get here as fast as I can, but if I can't someone else will. And if anything else happens, you call me immediately. I'll have my phone on and with me at all times."

Talia rolled her eyes. "It was probably just some dumb kid looking to steal beer—"

"Immediately," Jack bit out. "And if I don't answer, you call Danny, Derek, or Ethan directly."

"Or me!" Ben interjected.

"Not Ben," Jack said with a smile so slight she wondered if she was imagining it. "He's an asshole."

Did the iceman just make a joke? "I promise," she conceded. "But don't expect to hear from me. And I won't expect to hear from you," she said. But she couldn't ignore the hollow feeling that washed over her as she watched Jack and Ben climb into the car and drive away.

It was stupid, she told herself as she walked back into the house, the way seeing him left her with that strange, hollow ache. A faint yearning for him to stick around, for her to unglue her tongue and figure out what to say instead of her halfhearted efforts to push him away. A wish that maybe they could have . . . something.

Right, like that was possible, she thought, and gave herself a mental kick. What she and Jack had, so oddly intimate yet so excruciatingly uncomfortable, could never be untangled enough to go anywhere good.

She drove Rosario back to campus and contemplated what to do for the rest of the afternoon. Maybe she should see if Susie was up for a movie, she thought, then quickly dismissed the idea. Talia was in a weird, melancholy mood and had no business inflicting herself on anyone.

Besides, she had only a few hours to kill before she had to work. Maybe she'd do some laundry. The house phone rang, cutting off her mental meanderings. She started to ignore it—anyone she knew would have called her cell. She picked up the handset to turn the ringer off, hesitating when she saw the number on the caller ID display.

Wireless caller. Her brow furrowed as she recognized the Washington State area code and Seattle exchange.

Without thought, her thumb pressed the TALK button. "Hello?"

"Talia Vega?" an unfamiliar male voice asked.

"Who's calling?"

"Is this Talia Vega?" he repeated.

Her grip on the phone tightened. "Who wants to know?"

The phone went dead.

Cold sweat filmed her forehead. *They'd found her.* Just like that, she was back down in that black hole of panic and fear, leaving the safe house only when necessary. Breath held, constantly looking over her shoulder, dreading the moment when he or one of his lackeys would snatch her from her bed or, worse, take Rosario and use her as bait to flush Talia out.

No, stop. She took a deep breath, reminded herself that David was dead, his organization blown to smithereens.

There was no more "they." No one had bothered to come after her in nearly two years. Why would they now?

But whoever called knew her name, knew her phone number.

It wasn't like she was in hiding, the rational, calming part of her brain argued. She'd kept her information unlisted, but she knew there were ways to find out that sort of thing if someone was motivated enough.

That last thought wasn't at all comforting. She picked up the phone and brought the number up on the caller ID. She knew it was overkill, but she could call someone back at Gemini's office and have them trace it. She didn't want to bother Jack—

The phone rang in her hand. It was him again.

"What do you want?" she asked sharply.

"Talia Vega?"

She didn't answer.

"Sorry about before. I went through a canyon and my cell dropped the call. I'm trying to get in touch with Talia Vega. Can you at least tell me if I have the right number?"

"And I'll ask you again," she said, irritation doing its part to chase away some of the fear, "who wants to know?"

"My name is Greg Fitzhugh," he said. "I'm working on a book for *Seattle Magazine* about the fallout from the Grayson-Maxwell scandal—"

"I have nothing to say on the matter."

"Please," he said, "if it hadn't been for you, no one would have ever connected him to Karev's operation," he said.

Talia wasn't sure if he was genuinely impressed or just kissing her ass.

"If it weren't for you helping Deputy PA Slater, the corruption would have gone unchecked, and none of those people would have been arrested."

Her fingers started to go numb at the tips. The last thing she wanted to do was remind all of those people of her existence and, worse, make it seem like she was bragging about her part in bringing them down. Hell, at one time she'd been as knee-deep in the shit as the rest of them. She had nothing to brag about.

"I know you took a bit of a beating in the press before," he said at her continued silence, "but you don't have to worry about how you'll be portrayed."

What, like they could somehow turn the mistress of a notorious criminal—who, among other things, had twisted her testimony to help send an innocent man to death row and stood numbly by while half a dozen women were butchered—into a heroine for justice? "I'm sorry, I'm afraid I can't help you."

She hung up and immediately unplugged the phone in case Greg Fitzhugh decided to call back, then realized she'd forgotten to ask him where he'd gotten the number.

You should have changed your name. Not for the first time, Talia questioned her decision not to change her identity. Jack assured her that as long as they held up their cover stories, he could create a cover for them that was all but bulletproof.

Everything in her had rebelled at the idea. David Maxwell had nearly taken everything from them. She wasn't going to let him take their identities. Most importantly, it wasn't fair to force Rosie to live this lie with her.

And deep in her heart, Talia didn't feel like she deserved to disappear into anonymity. Her own bad choices had gotten her into trouble, and part of her penance was living with that truth. For better or worse.

This, she supposed, was the worse part.

Nothing to do but move past it. What was done was done, and unless she wanted to turn her and Rosie's lives upside down all over again, she had to accept reality: If a person was motivated to find Talia Vega, there wasn't much to keep them from tracking her down.

—∞—

He'd failed.

He hurried into the house, ignoring his mother's demands to know where he'd been as he raced to his room. He slammed the door behind him and threw the bolt lock, the roaring in his head drowning out the sound of Mother pounding on the door.

He couldn't think over the twisting sickness in his stomach. He was a loser, an imposter, too weak to do what needed to be done.

Too weak to kill.

He'd hoped number three would be his first. He'd done everything right; everything went exactly according to plan.

Up until the very end, when he messed it up.

Like he always did.

He stripped off his clothes and jumped into the shower, scrubbing away the stink of abject failure. He dressed quickly, tried to quiet his mind. He needed to get a grip on himself—there was still so much to do tonight.

He'd left the experiment running at the campus lab, and he needed to get back in time to analyze the samples before they were ruined. But he couldn't go yet, not with his brain a scattered roar as he faced the reality of this latest failure.

He wasn't worried about getting caught. He was too careful for that. But it ate at him like acid that once the drugs wore off and she recovered from her wounds, the bitch would be walking around this earth, a living reminder of his weakness.

He gulped down a glass of cold water and flipped on his computer. He checked his e-mail, and the knot in his stomach twisted tighter when he saw he'd received a Google alert about a new article mentioning Nate Brewster.

He didn't want to read it, didn't want another reminder of how unworthy he was a successor. But he couldn't stop himself from clicking on the link that directed him to the article.

It was a long-form article for a Seattle-based magazine, focusing more on Margaret Grayson-Maxwell and her family's fall from grace; there was very little about Nate at all. He was about to close the window when another name caught his eye. He zeroed in on the single sentence that would change his life.

Talia Vega, who declined to be interviewed for this article, left Seattle after David Maxwell's death and now lives in the San Francisco Bay Area.

They say lightning doesn't strike twice, but he could feel it, blazing through him.

Of course.

She was to be his first. Why had he never realized it before? All along he'd been copying the master but never thought to look for the lone survivor. The woman whose image was burned into his brain, inspiring him all along.

A sense of peace settled over him, washing away the bitter taste of failure. He hadn't failed, he realized. The others were practice, necessary for him to get every last step correct before he moved to the next level.

Though her address and phone were unlisted, it took him less than an hour to find both.

She lived in Palo Alto. For the last eight months, she'd lived less than five miles from the Stanford campus where he spent 90 percent of his waking hours.

To find out she lived so close . . . it was like the hand of God steering him in the right direction.

A voice screamed in his head for him to go to her, tonight. He stifled it. He wasn't ready for her yet. He hadn't achieved perfection yet. And for her, he needed to be perfect.

—∿—

The next three days passed without incident, and Talia pushed aside the urge to call Jack. What could he do? Help her change her number? The horse had already left the barn with that one, but Talia had canceled the house phone service anyway, just in case Fitzhugh was inclined to keep bothering her.

As her life settled back into its soothingly predictable pattern, Talia pushed the phone call out of her mind. The fact that the reporter had tracked her down had nothing to do with the possible break-in. Nevertheless, when Rosie had called for her nightly check-in, Talia warned her about the guy just in case. No reason to dredge it all up again, she'd told her sister, and you could never rely on them not to twist your words into something you never meant to say.

Susie came in on a cloud of perfume and plopped herself onto a bar stool. Talia looked up from wiping glasses in preparation for the happy-hour crowd.

"Finally, a moment alone," Susie said, a little breathless. "Time for you to dish, sister."

Talia's eyebrows knit in confusion. "About what?

Susie opened her mouth in mock exasperation. "Hello? About that prime piece of man meat who was parading through here the other night."

"Jack?" Talia said.

"Of course Jack."

"There's nothing going on between me and Jack," Talia said forcefully as she turned to check the back bar supplies. "He helped me out of a really rough spot, but that's it."

Talia could see Susie's reflection in the mirror as her eyes narrowed under her perfectly arched brows. "So you're telling me there's absolutely nothing romantic between you."

"Not even remotely," Talia said firmly, ignoring the faint bitterness the words left in her mouth.

"Then you don't mind if I call him, try to get together when he's in town."

"Of course not," Talia said, pasting a bright smile on her face. Yet she couldn't suppress the curl of something— it wasn't jealousy, dammit!—at the thought of Jack's big, dark hands tangled in Susie's blond hair as he bent to kiss her… "He's not even my type!" Talia said, then snapped her mouth closed at Susie's speculative look.

"Oh, please, he's so much more your type than that nerd you were dating last winter."

"Just because he was a calculus professor doesn't make him a nerd."

"No, but the milky complexion and delicate girl hands did," Susie scoffed.

Talia rolled her eyes. "Whatever. In any case, the point is moot, because even if Jack were my type, I'm not his." Goddamn it, why did it have to hurt so much to admit that out loud?

Susie leaned back on her stool. A half smile quirked her lips and she shook her head. "Talia, Talia, Talia, can you really tell me you didn't see how he was looking at you?"

Talia froze in the act of reaching for a corkscrew as hot color flooded her cheeks. "What do you mean?"

"Well, if he'd been a cartoon, his tongue would have been hanging out and little hearts would have been floating around his head."

Talia's own heart started to thud inside her chest. Could he really— She stopped herself short. There was no way. "My relationship with Jack is complicated, to say the least."

Susie's expression turned serious. "I can only imagine, after what you went through, that it's hard to open yourself back up like that."

Talia nodded, her chest tight. When she had first started working here, Susie had made no secret of the fact that she'd Googled Talia and knew all of the details—the ones that were printed, anyway—of what had happened. "So you understand, given the circumstances of how we met, and what happened after, that doesn't really lend itself to any kind of romantic involvement. That's not something I'm ready for, with any man. Especially Jack."

"If you say so," Susie said, a little exasperated. "And if you're cool with it, I'm going to get his number from Alyssa."

"Go for it," Talia said, the words scraping her throat like sandpaper.

Why shouldn't Susie and Jack have some fun? she told herself as she watched Susie walk away. Better he hooked up with someone Talia knew and actually liked than some random skank.

But the thought of them together... She turned on the TV over the bar to distract herself.

As she finished stocking the bar, something the talking head on TV said penetrated her consciousness.

There are reports today of yet another victim of kidnap and sexual assault, and police believe the perpetrator is the same man who has raped at least two other women in the last month. The man abducted the victim in the parking lot on Broadway and took her to an unknown location where she was repeatedly assaulted.

Talia swallowed back a surge of bile and tried to force back the images of herself, of the other girls Nate had brutalized and murdered. *This has nothing to do with any of that*, she reminded herself. Nate's dead, over and done. But the world was full of evil assholes, and she couldn't let herself dwell on them.

Police are not releasing certain details about the crime, but the victim, who was found unconscious near her car in the same lot early this morning, sustained serious injuries and is currently listed in critical but stable condition. In a statement given earlier today, Lieutenant Kortlang of the Redwood City

Police warned area women to be on guard while out at night, to park only in well-lit areas, and to stay in groups of two or more if possible.

Talia grabbed the remote and snapped off the TV. "Creepy, isn't it?"

Talia gave a little shriek and dropped the glass she was holding as she spun around.

She held her hand to her heart to slow its pounding and recognized Frank Everett, one of their regular customers. A retired professor in his sixties, he and his wife came in several times a week for an early dinner and a glass of wine.

His dark eyes under bushy brows were full of apology. "I'm so sorry for startling you, Talia. I thought you heard me come in."

"No, I'm sorry," Talia said with a shaky smile. "I was distracted." She waved in the direction of the television.

"It's awful, what people are capable of doing to each other." Frank shook his head.

You have no idea, Talia thought. "Let me clean this up and then I'll get you something." She quickly swept up the glass shards.

"Don't worry about me, dear. I know you're not officially open yet." It was four forty-five and technically they didn't open for dinner until five. "But I was going stir crazy in the house and told Peg to meet me here on her way back from her gardening club meeting."

"No worries." Talia waved him off. Some patrons she would have kept cooling their heels until the last second, but Frank and his wife were a sweet couple, friendly and full of stories of all the places they'd traveled in their decades of marriage. And still so clearly in love with each other. Talia liked to study them like she was on some sort of anthropological mission to observe a foreign culture. "What can I get you? Cocktail? Wine?"

"You choose," he said with a paternal smile.

Talia pulled a bottle of red from behind the bar. "We just got a couple cases of this in. Technically it's not available by the glass, but I'll let you have it for the same as the house cab. Just don't tell," she said with a wink.

She didn't know what it was—the weird feelings she'd been having lately, the call from the reporter, the hideous news story—but for a split second, she flashed back to her old life.

The pulse of heavy techno music as she smiled and vamped for the high rollers. Scoring a thousand dollars in tips on a good night just by keeping the liquor flowing and the girls fawning. A smile on her face even as her feet screamed from the pinch of sky-high heels and her stomach churned at the prospect of *him* summoning her.

"You okay? You look dizzy."

Talia shook off the strange sense of vertigo and pulled the cork from the bottle. Instead of a slick executive or pro athlete who had money leaking out of their pores and women jumping to do their bidding, she was staring into the concerned, lined face of the pleasantly disheveled professor. Instead of a too-tight dress that put her centerfold-worthy body on display, she was wearing jeans, comfortable boots, and a turtleneck sweater.

She'd never make more than one hundred dollars in tips on her very best night. But she'd take this life over the old one, a thousand times over. The thought brought an odd sense of peace. All of the fear, the paranoia that dogged her for the last twenty-four hours, faded into the background.

Soon Peg Everett joined her husband. She greeted Talia warmly before turning to her husband. Frank greeted her with a kiss and asked how her day was like he really cared. Talia shook her head. She didn't remember much about her father—he'd left before her ninth birthday, right after Rosario was born—but she knew that drunk loser had never been half as nice to her mother.

The crowd filtered in, and Talia settled into a rhythm, filled with a fresh sense of gratitude that she had the life she did.

She'd been given a chance to escape, to start over in this nice community full of friendly people who smiled and tipped and wanted nothing more from her than a few drinks and bit of small talk. A place where she could call the cops if she had trouble, and a sense of security could be had with a new alarm system installed by a man who could turn her world upside down with a single look of his ice-blue eyes.

Rosario called at exactly eleven on the dot, and Talia listened with half an ear as she chattered about a trip she wanted to take with some of her dormmates after midterms were over. She cleaned up the bar and helped Susie close up.

That night, safe and secure in her house, armed with Jack and Ben's upgraded alarm system, Susie's thoughts about Jack came back to haunt her.

But the dream she had was anything but a nightmare.

She woke up late the next morning to dark skies and a steady stream of rain, typical for March in Northern California, unable to remember the details. Left with only foggy images and a restless ache, she hauled herself out of bed and forced thoughts of Jack out of her mind.

She met Susie for a training session with Gus, and shoved aside the surge of jealousy when Susie told her she'd called Jack and invited him to come in for a drink on the house. "I'll have to make sure he comes on your night off," Susie said as she wiped her face with a towel, "otherwise I won't have a snowball's chance in hell of holding his attention."

"Shut up," Talia said with a little laugh. No matter what Jack did or didn't feel about her, it felt good to have a friend who could bust her chops and add a little lightness to what had begun as a very heavy situation.

By the time she got to work later that evening, Talia was in a better mood than she'd been in all week.

"Hey, this came for you," Susie said as Talia stashed her bag in the office. Talia took the envelope. "Weird that someone would send it here," Susie said, not bothering to hide her curiosity as Talia ripped the envelope open.

Oh, God, oh, God. Talia's field of vision swooped and dipped and her body went numb with cold as the platinum chain tumbled into her hand.

"Talia, are you okay?"

The roar in her ears deafened her. Hands clasped her shoulders and pushed her into a chair. When she came back to herself, her head was between her knees and she was breathing in deep gasps.

Talia sat up and looked at Susie, perched on the edge of her desk, her face knotted in confusion as the necklace dangled from her fingers.

Platinum chain, with a square diamond pendant. "It's beautiful," Susie said, and held it out to Talia.

Talia jerked back like it was a snake.

"What's wrong? It's just a necklace," Susie said.

Talia just shook her head, her eyes glued to the diamond's wicked glimmer. It wasn't just any necklace. It was the necklace from her nightmare, the one that nearly sliced through her throat as it choked her. It was the necklace David Maxwell had given her after she'd testified against Sean Flynn.

The necklace she'd been wearing when Nate Brewster tried to kill her.

Chapter 4

He nursed his cup of coffee, his gaze flitting around the campus coffeehouse as he tried to contain his excitement.

As he waited, his thoughts were irresistibly drawn to what was waiting for him after this meeting.

Or rather, who.

Slim, with dark hair and dark eyes. Her skin dusky and buttery soft. When he'd left her this morning, she was still unmarked, the smooth expanse of her back bared to him as she huddled in the corner, her hands cuffed around a bar he'd installed just for that purpose.

He'd picked her up last night—too soon after the last victim to be safe, he knew. But he hadn't been able to resist when he saw her shopping alone at the grocery store. She looked so much like Talia.

In that instant, he'd known she would be the perfect canvas on which to practice.

He smiled faintly as he traced his finger in a pattern across the tabletop. In his mind, the burnished wood became caramel-colored flesh, splitting open, blood welling in the wake of his knife.

She would scream. She would scream and struggle

and try to get away. But the ties around her wrists and ankles would hamper her, and she wouldn't be able to hold him off.

As he daydreamed, he could feel the heat building low in his belly.

Tonight. Usually he liked to keep them for a little while. Experience had taught him that when a woman was locked in a dark, cold room, stripped naked, and bound in utter darkness for several days, she became much more pliable.

But he wasn't sure he'd be able to wait with this one. He curled his fingers into fists so no one would see them tremble in excitement.

The other hand went under the table and slipped discreetly between his legs. He grabbed his testicles and gave them a vicious twist. White-hot pain shot through him, so severe he had to swallow back bile.

Control. The pain served its purpose, dampening his excitement, reminding him that he couldn't let his excitement get the best of him.

He was so close; he couldn't let carelessness be his downfall.

He gave his balls another squeeze. He would wait with the new girl as he did the others. Now was not the time to let impulse take over. If he could control himself with her, if he could continue to improve, it would bode well for when he finally had Talia under his control.

He'd make it last days, weeks, until she was begging for him to kill her and put her out of her misery.

"Thanks for meeting me." A feminine voice pulled him from his reverie. "I really appreciate the extra time. If I don't get at least a B in this class, I'll be totally screwed."

He pasted a bland smile on his face, careful to conceal the excitement twisting his insides into knots. This was just a meeting between teaching assistant and tutor. Nothing out of the ordinary. Nothing at all. "It's my pleasure, Rosario." He smiled at the beautiful, dark-haired girl as she slid into the seat across from him. "I would hate to have you lose your scholarship because you're struggling with physics."

As she went to order herself a latte, he marveled again at his continued streak of good luck. Discovering that Talia lived nearby and that her sister was enrolled here at Stanford.

It had been laughably easy to get placed as a replacement teaching assistant for Rosario's Physics 43 study section. He was, after all, one of the top PhD candidates, his research in single molecule biophysics on the bleeding edge of the field. When Rosario's teaching assistant had suffered a bad fall down the stairs, the professor teaching the lecture series was only too glad to bring him on board.

And as though the universe felt the need to grant him yet another miracle, Rosario Vega was terrible at physics. The only way she'd pass the midterm, he'd explained after he'd graded her latest problem set, was if she met him regularly for extended tutoring sessions.

She'd smiled and nodded, so eager to please, so eager to do well, it actually made him feel bad about the suffering she'd no doubt feel when he killed her sister.

—ᴍ—

Jack could read the upset on Talia's face from across the bar, and for about the thousandth time he wished he could have gotten here hours ago. But Susie's call had come right as he was debriefing the Blankenthorns on the new security protocols he had developed for the entire family.

Every instinct had screamed at him to drop everything and rush to Talia's side, but he couldn't risk pissing off an important client for something that, according to Susie at least, might not be an emergency at all.

But he'd been assured Talia was safe, though shaken up. And judging from the look on her face when she caught sight of him in the crowd, none too excited about seeing him.

He wished he could say the same, he thought with a little inward sigh. Truth was, he'd found it hard to stay away these past few days. But after their discussion, he knew he couldn't even do one of his "stalker runs," as Danny Taggart called Jack's discreet missions where he got a long enough glimpse of Talia to reassure himself she was doing okay.

All of it, including the regular reports from Susie and Rosario, had to stop. Not because he would be okay not knowing how she was, but because after her reaction to the alarm installation, he knew she would be furious if she knew he was checking up on her behind her back.

From now on, any interaction with Talia had to be face-to-face. Problem was, he didn't trust himself to keep a lid on what was really going on inside him.

But goddamn, it was hard. Today's meeting aside, he'd had a lot of downtime this trip and it was driving him crazy, knowing Talia was a short drive away and knowing she wouldn't welcome him sniffing around constantly like a dog.

Even her frown at first sight of him tonight couldn't diminish the primal, idiotic feeling he got in his gut whenever he saw her. It hadn't started out this way with her, and he didn't know when the switch had flipped, but somewhere along the line, Talia had gone from being someone who aroused his deep-seated protective instincts to being much more...important.

And he could fantasize all he wanted, but the idea she would ever genuinely return his affections was a big fucking joke. And even if by some miracle she felt an inkling in that direction...

Where she came from and what was between them was too twisted and fucked up for her to ever open up to him the way he needed.

But he could do this at least, he thought as he strode up to the bar. Show up when called, her personal warrior to the rescue whether she wanted him there or not.

Talia gave him a grim nod while she filled drink orders. Finally she turned to him. "Please tell me Susie didn't call you." Though she strove for annoyed nonchalance, Jack could see the lines of strain around her mouth, her eyes.

He curled his fingers against the urge to smooth the line between her brows with his hand. "She said you got an interesting package, but she didn't have time to go into details."

Her dark waves rippled as she gave her head an irritated shake. "It's nothing, just like the break-in," she said. But her knuckles were stark white as her slender fingers curled around the stem of a wineglass. "I'm sure it's nothing," she said again, like she was trying to convince herself.

"Show me."

"We're really busy right now," she said, gesturing at the buzzing crowd.

Jack raised his hand and caught the eye of the other bartender on duty. "Hey, man, you mind covering Talia for a few minutes while we talk?"

"No problem, just don't be gone too long."

"Five minutes, Max," Talia said, and wiped her hands on a rag. "It's in Susie's office." She came out from behind the bar. Jack trailed a few feet behind, doing his best to keep his eyes off the rounded curve of her ass encased in tight jeans.

Eyes up, he scolded himself. She was scared, and after everything that had happened to her and between them, he had no business looking at her in a way that was remotely sexual. But he was a red-blooded man, with big appetites, and traumatized or not, she was beautiful, dammit.

He forced himself to lift his gaze, only to have it collide with Susie, who was looking at him like she knew exactly what he was thinking.

Jack gave her a quick wave but felt the heat rise in his cheeks. Susie had called him a couple days ago, making her interest clear. Jack knew he at least owed her a drink for giving Talia a chance at the restaurant.

And for keeping secret all this time the fact that Jack had made an anonymous investment in the restaurant to make sure Talia got the job.

Goddamn it, he hoped this didn't get messy.

He followed Talia into the office and closed the door behind him. She took her purse from a chair in the corner and pulled out an envelope. "This came in the mail today," she said, and held it out to him.

Jack pulled the envelope open with his thumbs. Inside he could see the glint of a silver chain. He reached in and pulled it out, along with the note that accompanied it.

I thought you would appreciate having this back.

"Do you recognize it?" Talia's voice sounded tight.

Jack felt choked with his own fury. Hell yeah, he remembered the silver chain and the diamond pendant. Imprinted in his brain as it lay against Talia's throat, sparkling coldly against her blood-splattered skin.

"I know I was wearing it when he took me," Talia said, "but I don't know . . . I don't remember—"

"You had it on when they put you in the ambulance," Jack interjected. He tried but couldn't banish the image of her, naked, bleeding, her glowing skin gone gray with shock, pain, and blood loss. Unlike most things, the trauma of that day didn't seem to fade in his mind, the memory growing more painful as time passed and his feelings for her grew.

Now, standing less than two feet away from her, knowing she was being buffeted by the same memories, he felt like he'd taken a sucker punch to the gut.

He read the note again. *I thought you would appreciate having this back.* No signature. Who the fuck would do something like this? There had to be a logical explanation.

"It's probably nothing, right?" Talia said. "Like the break-in. A stupid coincidence, but it doesn't mean anything."

Jack nodded. Of course there were several possible benign explanations. But in his experience with Talia, those benign explanations rarely panned out.

"I mean, if I was wearing it in the ambulance, and they

took it off me, maybe someone ran across it in storage or something and tracked me down. Right?" The note of desperation in her tone made Jack ache.

"I suppose anything's possible," he replied.

Talia stared down at the necklace clenched in Jack's fist. Her own hand came up to rub absently at her stomach, right below her rib cage. In the exact spot, he knew, where Nate Brewster's knife had penetrated, nearly causing her to bleed to death in his arms.

Against his better judgment, he closed the distance between them and his arms came up to wrap around her.

She froze, stiff against him, and Jack silently cursed himself. This was why he'd always been so careful not to touch her. After everything she'd been through, she didn't welcome the touch of any man.

Not even his.

But as he was about to release her, something miraculous happened. Instead of staying stiff and pulling away, Talia let out a sigh that came from the depths of her soul and sort of collapsed into him. Timidly her arms came around his waist.

Jack slid his palms up her back and molded her against him until she was so close even a sliver of daylight couldn't slip between them. God, she was so warm and soft against him and she smelled so good. Flowers and soap and woman.

His temperature went up about a dozen degrees and he felt heat gather heavily in his groin. Silky black hair tickled his nose and chin, and he wondered what she would do if he tilted her chin up and kissed her like he'd been dying to.

Her shudder and wet sniff brought him back down to

earth. Hard. She may have healed enough in the past two years to accept a comforting hug, but he knew better than to push it. She was only letting him touch her because she was afraid. Not because she wanted anything else.

He pulled her in tighter. Call him selfish, but he'd take whatever she could willingly give.

"I don't want to be scared again," she said, her voice muffled against his chest. She pulled her head away and tilted her face up to him. "Even if it's totally nothing, just somebody being nice, the fact that it can mess me up this much..." Her voice rose in pitch. "I thought I was over it. I thought all this was over."

Something told him she wasn't just talking about what happened tonight.

A lock of hair fell across her cheek. Jack reached up to push it back, and when his fingers brushed her skin, he swore he saw something besides fear flash in those night-dark eyes.

"Is everything okay?"

They both jumped back at Susie's voice.

"It's fine," Talia said. "I was just showing Jack the, uh, necklace." She gestured awkwardly to the chain still tangled in his fingers. "And I should show you the envelope." She looked around, flustered, and said, "Aha" when she spotted it on the floor.

"Here," she said, holding it out to him so their fingers barely brushed. "There's no return address, but if you look carefully, you can see it has a Seattle postmark."

"Mmm-hmm." Jack forced himself to study the faint smudge of ink, but it was hard to focus when the skin of his torso felt seared from where she'd been plastered against him. Christ, if he felt that intensely through their combined layers of clothing, he'd spontaneously combust if he ever rubbed up against her, naked skin to naked skin...

"So is there any way to find out where it came from?" Talia's voice was higher pitched than usual. But judging from the looks she was shooting Susie, it was more from embarrassment and maybe a little guilt than uncontrollable lust.

Jack pretended to examine the envelope as he brought himself back under control. "I can't read the signature, and with no return address, we're probably SOL." He looked at Talia, watched her nervously bite her bottom lip.

Wished he could bite it for her.

"I'll follow up with the hospital. I got you out of there in such a hurry and I never thought to see if they kept it. And I'll call Cole—maybe they took it as evidence and it turned up when they were cleaning it out."

"Thanks, especially for calling Cole."

Jack nodded and gave her a faint smile. While Talia had earned back some points with Detective Cole Williams and his wife, Megan Flynn Williams, when she'd given up David Maxwell as the mastermind behind the frame job they did on Megan's brother Sean, they were never going to be BFFs. Not after Talia's testimony had helped put Sean Flynn on death row for two long years.

He halfheartedly held out the necklace. "I don't suppose—"

Talia threw up her hands as though he'd offered her a poisonous snake.

Jack pocketed it. Maybe he could pawn it and give the money to a women's and kids' shelter.

"So....um...," Susie interjected.

Jack could see she wanted to ask about a million questions, but he appreciated her restraint as Talia's body language all but screamed she didn't want to talk anymore about the necklace or how it had ended up back in her hands.

"Talia, I'm still cool with you taking off early—"

"No, I'm fine. I want to work," Talia cut her off.

"In that case, I could really use you back out there."

Talia nodded and left. The office was so small she couldn't help but brush against him on her way to the door. Jack held himself still as every nerve ending went on high alert.

He started to follow, but Susie stopped him with a hand on his arm. "Be careful with her."

Jack frowned down at her. "Of course I will. I'll do whatever it takes to protect her."

She rolled her eyes. "I'm not talking about the necklace. I may have given her this job as a favor to you and Alyssa—"

"Which you better keep to yourself," Jack said, then winced at how harsh his voice sounded.

Fortunately Susie wasn't intimidated. "That's what I'm talking about. Talia is my friend, and I don't want to see her get hurt by anyone, even in the name of protecting her."

"I don't want to see her hurt either."

"Then like I said, be careful. This thing between you two . . ."

"There's nothing between me and Talia." Because *between* implied there was something on both sides of the equation.

Susie gave a little laugh and a knowing smile. "I've

seen you two together. If there's nothing now, there will
be soon. I guarantee it. And when it happens, just make
sure it turns out good for her."

Jack shook his head, wishing with everything in him
that what she said was true. Knowing with every fiber of
his being that it never could be.

—⁓—

Someone was watching her.

Rosario could feel the tickle between her shoulders.
She tried to brush it away, told herself it was nothing, just
a delayed reaction from the stupid thing with the raccoons
the other night.

And it *was* raccoons. She wasn't about to indulge
Talia's paranoia and believe it was something else. Admit-
tedly, Rosario had been terrified, too, when the alarm
started shrieking, which was why she'd called Jack. The
police might have been on their way, but there was no one
in the world who could make her feel safer than their very
own self-appointed bodyguard.

Talia felt exactly the same about Jack, even though
she tried to play it off like she was mostly annoyed when
Jack came around. Rosario knew that because of what
happened to her, Talia was pretty messed up about men.
Even so, she'd lay odds that whatever feelings Talia had
for Jack, annoyed wasn't near the top of the list.

Jack wasn't exactly indifferent either. Now whenever
the two of them got together in a room, Rosario found
herself wishing they would just do it already. The tension
between them was enough to give her a migraine.

Damn, she wished Jack were here right now. He was

in town, and he'd probably even come if she called, but he was doing his real job right now.

Besides, if she called him for something as stupid as a creepy feeling, she'd be even lamer than her sister.

She tightened her grip on her shoulder strap and picked up her pace, the rubber soles of her Converse All Stars making almost no sound against the pavement.

She did a low-key scan to the sides and over both shoulders. At eight-thirty on Wednesday night, downtown Palo Alto was buzzing with activity. Couples out for dinner. Students heading out for an early drink or to study at one of the many coffee places that lined the street.

It was impossible to pick out an individual giving her an unusually intense stare. It was two blocks to the shuttle stop that would drive her back to campus. Normally she would cut across the street and duck through the alleyway between the Chinese restaurant and the Turkish hookah bar.

But tonight she stayed on the well-lit street. Dammit, she should have asked Gene to give her a ride or at least walk her to the shuttle stop. But her physics tutor was nice enough to squeeze an extra session in with her before midterms, and he made it clear he was meeting a date at the restaurant after they were finished.

Besides, she reminded herself, this was a totally safe area, with lots of people around. No one was going to try anything on her as long as she didn't do anything stupid.

There was a group of students up ahead, five in all, boys and girls, who looked like they might be headed in the direction of the shuttle stop.

Rosario speed-walked until only a few feet separated them, close enough to look like she was part of the group to anyone passing by.

Safety in numbers.

One of about a thousand nuggets of advice Talia had pelted her with nonstop for the past two years.

The tingling grew more intense as they approached the shuttle stop. To her relief, the group stopped there, too, and Rosie hovered around their periphery as she kept a lookout. But there was nothing in the faces of the other people at the shuttle stop that should give her this creeped-out feeling.

She tried to shake it off, cursing herself and her sister when she couldn't. It was Talia's fault, so paranoid it had bled into Rosario until she couldn't walk down a street without wondering if someone was going to jump out and snatch her.

It was Talia's fault for getting them into a situation where the paranoia was justified.

Rosario felt a stab of guilt and shoved the horrible thought aside. Talia had never meant for there to be any threat to Rosario, real or imagined. Everything she'd done, she'd done so she could get custody of Rosario and keep her safe.

Rosario watched the streetlights stream by as the shuttle wound its way back to campus. As the creepy feeling eased, she reminded herself of all the reasons she loved her sister and why she should be thankful for everything Talia had done for her.

And she was. She truly was.

But as she stepped off the shuttle in front of her dorm, she took a cautious look around to see if anything was waiting to leap out of the shadows.

And wondered how it would feel to live without this fear, without the compulsion to always look over her shoulder. To be normal.

She'd barely completed the thought when a rough hand closed over her shoulder and wheeled her around. Adrenaline surged through her, lending her strength as she nailed her assailant with a hard elbow to the chest.

The man grunted and coughed. "What the hell, Rosie!"

Rosie pulled her punch, but not enough, when she recognized Kevin's voice. Her fist caught him with a glancing blow on the cheekbone.

She felt a split second of guilt as he staggered back.

"What did you do that for?"

She put her hand up to her mouth in horror. "I'm sorry. I didn't know it was you." Her sympathy quickly faded as she remembered how he'd ditched her to go get shitfaced at Z-bar after they left Suzette's Sunday night. "What the hell are you doing, jumping out of the dark to grab me?"

"You didn't have to punch me." Kevin held his fingers up to his eye and winced.

Wuss.

"How else am I supposed to talk to you when you won't return my calls or texts? I sent you, like, fifty messages on Facebook."

"Yeah, and I told you I don't think we have anything else to say to each other. Especially lurking outside my dorm waiting to give me a heart attack."

"Wait." Kevin grabbed her arm. She tried to jerk away. "Come on, Rosie, I said I was sorry."

"Sorry doesn't mean crap," she said. "I'm tired of chasing after you all the time just so you can treat me like shit."

"What, you think that nerd you met tonight is going to treat you so much better?"

The anger that surged through her gave her the strength to jerk away. "You were following me?" She shook her head. That explained the creepy tingle. "We're done, Kevin. You have no right to know where I'm going, who I'm meeting, and you sure as hell don't have the right to stalk me all over town." She grabbed her backpack from where she'd dropped it on the ground. "Asshole," she muttered. "Talia was right about you from the beginning."

"Yeah?" Kevin called as she stomped up the walkway to her dorm. "You better watch out, bitch. No one gets to treat me like this, not you or your cunt of a sister."

Rosario's back stiffened and she forced herself to ignore him. As she walked up to her room, she told herself it was nothing, just a bunch of smack talk from an idiot who was sky high and didn't like the word *no*.

It took her half an hour to stop shaking.

———⟋⟍———

Why? Why now? Talia wondered as she drove home with Jack's headlights glowing in her rearview mirror.

As expected, he hadn't even acknowledged her half-hearted protest that he didn't need to stay at the restaurant, quietly nursing a cup of coffee at the bar while he waited for her shift to end so he could see her home safely.

And in truth, Talia was more than happy to have him there. The appearance of that damn necklace . . . She shuddered and gripped the wheel harder.

It brought back too many memories. Of David's fingers fastening it around her neck. The way the delicate chain felt as heavy as a slave's collar.

Its coolness against her skin when she lay helplessly on

the floor, forced to watch Nate Brewster murder equally helpless women as his knife sliced through her own skin.

She hated to admit the weakness, but she needed Jack there, his strong, steady presence chasing away the darkness.

And, God, the way he'd held her. His hands so big and warm against her back, pressing her in close to that mile-wide chest of his.

His scent had flooded her senses, clean and woodsy layered over male musk. Chasing away the demons. Folding her in a cocoon so safe and warm that the bad guys would never be able to get to her.

There had been something else there too. A vibe, an energy, an awareness that was new for her.

If he felt it too, he gave no indication. There was nothing in the way he touched her that would lead her to believe that the hug was any different from one he might have given to his little sister.

Yet she couldn't get the feel of him, the scent of him out of her head. For longer than she could remember, she'd tolerated a man's touch with gritted teeth and reminders that it couldn't last indefinitely.

But tonight all those weird yearnings she'd started to feel around Jack were converging around a need. To be held. To touch and be touched, by a man who was big and tough and who had seen and done things that would bring a lesser man to his knees.

A man who would cut off his own arm before he hurt her, she knew.

Yet that didn't mean he felt anything more, she thought as she turned into her driveway and clicked the button to open the garage door.

Still, she couldn't stop herself from wishing as Jack pulled up behind her and parked in her driveway. He got out of the car and followed her in, waited while she disarmed the alarm and unlocked the door before following her into the kitchen.

Wishing she could go back, way back, to when she was just a normal young girl looking for love. Before she'd been stupid enough to fall in love with David Maxwell, too blinded by his charisma and grand romantic gestures to see the evil that lurked underneath before it was too late. Because if she was that girl, even if she wasn't sure about how Jack felt about her, she would have the guts to try.

Instead of awkwardly offering him a cup of coffee as he took up all the space in her kitchen, she'd lead him to the couch and pour him a glass of wine. Or something stronger.

She'd laugh and flirt and toss her hair like she used to do in high school. Get Jack to smile back and flash those dimples while they talked about anything else but Talia's safety and how she was getting along in the big bad world.

She'd tilt her head back, part her lips, make it obvious she was waiting for his kiss.

And she'd never have the memory of the way his eyes had darkened with revulsion the one and only time she'd made it clear she wouldn't turn down his advances.

"Do you want me to stay?" Jack asked around a yawn. "I can take the couch." Lines of fatigue formed around eyes that were nevertheless on high alert and full of concern.

And nothing else.

She shook her head and swallowed around the lump

in her throat as she watched him go. Even if there was a chance Jack's feelings might have changed, the memory of his total and complete rejection that long-ago night was enough to prevent her from ever making any kind of move.

And even if she did, she didn't think she'd ever be capable of following through.

Chapter 5

The flowers were waiting on her front stoop when Talia got home from work Friday night.

She didn't realize what they were at first when the glare of her headlights revealed an unfamiliar object on the small landing of her front door. Talia parked the car and entered through the garage as usual. She went to the door, trying to remember if she'd ordered anything recently that would have been delivered.

She flipped on the porch light, opened the door, and bent to look. She didn't need to look to know they were gardenias. They scent wafted up, strong, sweet, making her stomach clench with nausea. She slammed the door shut and swallowed back the bile.

When she was reasonably sure she wasn't going to heave up the gnocchi she'd had for dinner, she forced herself to open the door again. She scanned up and down her street, but at this hour her quiet street was deserted, the houses dark and buttoned up for the night.

She didn't want to bring the vile blooms into the house, so, breathing through her mouth, she knelt on the flagstone landing and felt around for a card. Nothing. She picked up the container and held it closer to the light, but she couldn't see anything to indicate where the flowers came from or who had sent them.

Just like the necklace.

Her legs went watery and the flowers tumbled out of her hands. The plastic container split, leaving a pile of dark soil and white flowers on the stone. Talia went back inside and slammed the door. She rubbed at her nose, but she swore the sweet stink was leaking through the door.

The smell had once filled her with such pleasure. Stupid girl that she'd been, she thought they were a symbol of true love from a good man, someone who was going to lift her out of the mess her dead mother had left behind and give her the kind of life and love she'd only dreamed about.

That was before she'd seen the evil truth behind the mask he showed to the rest of the world. Before the beautiful flowers he sent every week became yet another symbol of her captivity.

Who sent them? she wondered as she sagged down to the floor, one hand pressed against her chest to stop her heart's frantic pounding.

And did the sender realize the significance? How? The only person who knew about the gardenias was Rosario, who had never asked why Talia always threw away the flowers as soon as they arrived.

She went into the kitchen and poured herself a glass of red wine and tried to come up with a logical explanation.

But she kept coming back to the same place: the necklace David had given her and the same flowers he used to buy her showing up in the same week? It couldn't be a coincidence.

Unless...the scenario was so unlikely it was ridiculous.

But even as her brain screamed at her that there was no way Jack had bought her flowers, much less the same exact kind David Maxwell used to send, her fingers had dialed Jack's number before she could stop herself.

She tried not to be devastated when her call went straight to voice mail. *Idiot.* Of course Jack was busy, on a job. It wasn't like he was just sitting around waiting for her to call.

She considered calling the police, then dismissed the idea. All they would do was take her statement and file a report, something that could be just as easily taken care of in the morning after she confirmed what she already knew—they didn't come from Jack.

She set the phone down and sipped at her wine and thought about turning on the TV to distract her. But even as she tried to convince herself there was a nonsinister explanation for both the flowers and the necklace, she couldn't shake the idea that with the TV on she might not hear someone creeping around outside.

She picked up a magazine from the pile on her table and jumped, sloshing coffee everywhere when her phone buzzed to signal an incoming text.

Working, can't talk. What's up?

It was from Jack.

Talia quickly wrote back before she could think better of it. *Did you send me flowers?*

Why would I send you flowers?

The blunt question startled a laugh out of her, even as she felt a little pinch in the region of her chest. Why indeed? *That's what I thought.* She texted back.

WTF is going on?

Nothing to worry about. Will explain later.

R U SAFE???

She looked around the house, at the locked windows, bolted doors, thought of the state-of-the-art alarm Jack had installed. She wasn't sure.

Jack texted her again. *Coming over. 20 mins tops.*

Part of her wanted to let him, but she knew it was over-kill, not to mention unfair for her to make Jack abandon what was clearly a high-profile client. Whoever had left the flowers was gone. Talia was safe inside her house and no one was getting in without her knowing about it.

Not necessary. She texted back quickly. *Am fine.*

Stuck here all night. Do you want me to send Ben? Or Alex?

No, she didn't want either of Jack's old army buddies and now coworkers camping on her couch, no matter how creeped she was feeling.

I am fine, she reiterated. *Talk tomorrow.*

She turned off the ringer and stuffed the phone into her purse so she wouldn't hear it. She knew Jack, knew he would keep texting her, trying to get her to tell him what was going on.

But for months she'd managed to keep quiet about the identity of her sugar daddy while Jack had her tucked away in a safe house, despite his constant badgering. He could wait until tomorrow to hear about the flowers.

Talia could hear her phone vibrating in her purse as she walked up the stairs to climb into bed.

—∞—

By the time Jack tracked Talia down at Gus's gym the following afternoon, he was mad enough to throw a few punches himself. Talia had ignored all of his phone calls and texts, forcing him to do a drive-by after he'd left the Blankenthorns at two in the morning to make sure everything was okay.

He'd found her car in the garage, the house locked up tight, and the log from the alarm system indicating no one had entered or left the house since he'd received her text.

Still, he needed to talk live or, better yet, see her in person before he'd feel at ease. But she'd blown off his earlier phone calls, and by the time he finished a morning debrief with Danny, he knew he'd most likely find her here at the gym.

He had a few hours before he had to be back at the Blankenthorns' for an event, so he quickly changed into shorts and a T-shirt and joined Talia where she was doing push-ups on the mat.

Jack took a jump rope off a peg and started his warm-up. "Hey."

She was at the top of her push-up and barely looked up at his curt greeting. His irritation eased a little as he admired her form. Though slender, she was strong, the sleek muscles of her back shifting as she lowered herself to the floor and smoothly pushed herself back up. When she was finally done with the set, she rolled into a seated position and reluctantly took the hand he offered.

"How did you know I was here?"

He figured she wouldn't take it well if he admitted that he was as familiar with her daily routine as he was with his own. "Unlike you, Rosie doesn't ignore me when I call her. You want to tell me why you haven't called me back?" Jack asked, and resumed his rope work.

"I've been busy," she said, a little out of breath. Her

hair was damp around the edges and the neckline of her tank top was dark with sweat.

"Too busy to return three calls and half a dozen texts?"

"They don't like you to use your cell phone at the police station," she snapped.

Jack stumbled as his feet got caught in the rope. "What. Happened."

Talia looked around as though to make sure no one was listening.

"This is about the flowers?"

When Talia had texted him last night asking him if he'd sent her flowers, his immediate reaction was anger. Even though it was none of his business if Talia dated, the idea of another man trying to get in her pants made his blood simmer.

"They were at my house last night when I got home. No card, no name of the florist. Totally anonymous."

Jack bit back a curse to have his suspicions confirmed. After he'd reined in his irrational anger, he'd realized that Talia probably wouldn't have contacted him if she hadn't been scared. It wasn't exactly her style to call him just to shoot the shit.

"And it freaked you out." He couldn't blame her. Some women might like the idea of having a secret admirer, but not Talia. Not after spending too many years constantly watched by the sick fuck who controlled her.

"It wasn't just that they were anonymously sent," she said. "I wouldn't have gone to the police for that. I'm paranoid, but not that paranoid. But they were gardenias."

Jack cocked an eyebrow. He didn't know anything about flowers. "Not following."

"David sent me gardenias for the first time two weeks

Jami Alden

after we met. He sent a fresh batch to my house every week until Nate tried to kill me."

Jesus fuck. "The necklace and now the flowers. That can't be a coincidence."

Talia slipped on her gloves and strode across the room to work on the big bag. "Yeah, try convincing the police. When I went to talk to them this morning, they said it's probably someone who knows me from the restaurant, trying to gear up the courage to ask me out." Her fist made a loud *thwack* as it hit the bag. "And they said even if there's malicious intent, there's nothing they can do until someone actually tries to hurt me. Not every girl gets a stalker who sends her flowers and jewelry, right?"

He went to work on the bag next to Talia's. Jack knew firsthand how bad the police could be at protecting women and children. Sure, flowers and jewelry might seem like pretty benign offerings, but there was no predicting when a harmless crush could turn violent.

"And then they asked me if there was anyone who might want to cause me harm. I was like, where do I start?" *Thwack.* "With the dozen or so government muckety-mucks who got fired when those videos were leaked?" *Thwack.* "Or what about their families that fell apart after the scandal hit? Or maybe the families of the girls who were killed while I stood by and did nothing?" *Thwack.* She landed a series of jabs in quick succession, then paused, breathing hard as she bent over with her hands on her knees. "I'm not even saying I wouldn't deserve it if someone tried to come after me. It's just... there's been nothing for two years. Why now?"

Jack shook his head, his mouth tightening as he saw a look of self-loathing cross her face. He hated that she was still eaten up with it, that even though she'd moved on with her life, a big part of her still believed she deserved everything that had happened to her now.

"You were as much a victim as any of those girls," he said, his jaw clenching as she shook her head in mute response. He wished he could make her forgive herself, but he knew a few words of reassurance from him weren't going to erase it.

He couldn't fix her, but he could do his damnedest to fix what was happening. All he could do was try to look at the situation objectively and see what they could come up with. And take whatever measures he could to help keep her safe.

"Who else knew about the gardenias?" he asked. She'd never mentioned it, and he'd never seen any flowers around the club.

"No one but David. And Rosario, sort of, but she'd never do something like this."

Someone was definitely trying to fuck with her, no doubt about it. His first instinct was to scoop her up and tuck her away someplace safe where he could watch over her 24-7 and make sure no one got within a hundred feet of her. But he knew that wasn't an option, mostly because there was no way she'd go for it. And even if she would, Jack couldn't just drop everything at work and leave Danny and the rest of the guys holding the bag.

"Come on." He led her into one of the empty studios where Gus taught his group classes. "We're going to brush up on your self-defense moves."

Talia grabbed a towel and wiped her face. "I train almost every day—"

"Yeah, not like this. It's one thing to know how to

fight, but you need a refresher on how to take a guy down if someone comes after you."

"I'll start carrying my Taser again."

"You won't always be able to get to it." Without warning, he swept her feet out and came down on top of her, pinning her hips with his as he pressed her hands into the floor.

"Hey." She squirmed underneath him. "I don't like this." She thrashed harder.

He held her there. "See, like this, you feel totally helpless, right?"

"Yes."

He could hear the undercurrent of real fear in her voice, knew she was starting to freak out at the sensation of being pinned down.

"First thing, you have to stay calm. You can't panic."

"Get off me!" The muscles of her arms bulged as she strained against his hold.

He could feel her hot puffs of breath against his skin. "Do you see how easy it is for me to hold you down?"

"Because you're a fucking monster!" She bucked again, her breath coming in harsh pants.

"Any guy, even one a lot smaller than me, is probably going to have more upper-body strength than you do. Come on, Talia, think. You can't panic in this situation."

"How can I not panic when you're pinning me to the floor?" she asked, her voice breaking a little.

He felt a pinch in his chest but he wouldn't let up. He couldn't. He leaned in closer. "If you're this scared with *me*, what's going to happen if someone's really trying to hurt you? Take a deep breath. I know you know what to do because I taught you myself."

He could see the moment the fear drained from her eyes, replaced with determination.

In a split second her head snapped up. Jack barely jerked back in time to avoid her head smashing into the bridge of his nose.

As it was, her forehead bumped the tip hard enough to bring tears to his eyes. When he jerked back and reflexively released her, she flipped to her stomach and squirmed out from under him, aiming kicks at his groin as she scrambled to her feet.

Jack let out a grunt as she landed a blow a little too close to the target. He winced, then looked up to see her smiling in triumph.

Her cheeks were flushed, her hair looked like it had been in a tornado, and her breasts were heaving up and down underneath the tight tank top.

She looked fucking gorgeous.

"Okay, let's try something else."

Jack put her through a series of holds she had to think and fight her way out of, and soon she was cackling as Jack took a hit on the inner thigh.

"Not so tough, now, are you, big boy?"

They worked through the moves, Talia wanting to go through them over and over. But now that she wasn't scared, Jack had another problem. Part of the reason she was getting away so easily was because he couldn't focus with her sleek body pressed so tightly against him. And the scent of her...holy Christ. He wanted to bottle it up and rub it all over himself.

It was torture, but he couldn't stop. He'd take any excuse to touch her, even if it meant getting beat up by a girl who clocked in at half his body weight.

He warned himself to pay attention before he ended up with a broken nose or a smashed testicle. Minutes later he was flat on his back, Talia's elbow cocked menacingly over his face. She sat straddling his hips like he was a mountain she'd conquered.

His hands went instinctively to her hips and he got a flash of her wearing nothing but her golden skin and a smile as she climbed on top of him. His cock, which he'd managed to keep at half-mast through sheer will and gritted teeth, surged fully, almost painfully to life.

His fingers sank into the soft curve of her hip as he struggled to resist the urge to grind himself against her. Told himself to push her off while there was a chance she might not notice.

"Are you..." Her eyes were wide in disbelief, her lips parted.

Too late.

She scrambled off him and backed clear to the other end of the studio.

"Sorry," he muttered as he got slowly to his feet. He felt the heat rise in his face and hoped maybe that would mean some of the blood would leave his dick. No dice. He was still tenting out the front of his shorts, and Talia was staring with what he wished was awe but was probably closer to disgust. "I can't exactly control it." He picked up a bottle of water. Maybe it would cool him off.

Yeah, maybe if you pour it on your dick.

She blinked, her cheeks going red as she pulled her gaze up to his face. "I know, I mean, not exactly a virgin here. I know how those things work. Friction and all," she said with a nervous laugh. "I know it's not because you're, like, attracted to me."

He froze, the bottle halfway to his lips. "What exactly do you mean by that?" He could have kicked his own ass as the words were coming out of his mouth. He so did not need to head down this conversational path with her.

Her already-rosy face turned the color of a beet. She yanked her hoodie over the tank top that fit her like a second skin. "Come on, Jack, I don't need to spell it out for you. You've made it pretty clear I don't exactly do it for you."

He took a slug of water, telling himself it was a good thing she was so oblivious—meant he was doing a good job at keeping his attraction on the down low. He wanted her to feel safe with him, and that wouldn't happen if he was panting after her with his tongue out.

But, Jesus, could she really be that ignorant? Against his better judgment, he took a step closer. "You can't be that clueless."

Her thick eyelashes fluttered and she shot him a nervous look. "What do you mean?"

Another step. He was close enough to see a bead of sweat trickle down the side of her neck. He was going down a dangerous road—for both of them. But it was like something inside him had snapped and he could no longer keep up the front of the distant protector. He was tired of keeping himself away from her.

"Do you really think I go hard as a spike for every woman I happen to rub up against?"

"Of...of course not," Talia sputtered. She took a few steps back, her retreat halted by the wall. She glanced down at the front of his shorts like she couldn't help herself. Her face was so red now Jack fully expected her head to burst into flames.

It was hard to reconcile this blushing, sputtering woman with the gorgeous woman who had greeted him over two years ago on his first evening at Club One. He hadn't been immune to her calculated beauty and seductive manner then, but he found this—the real Talia—so much more appealing it was a wonder he'd managed to keep his distance for so long.

"It's just," Talia continued, her eyes now glued to his face, "you made it clear, that time—"

Jack closed the distance between them and propped one hand against the wall beside her head. "What time?" he asked, his voice barely above a whisper even though he had a bad feeling he knew exactly where she was going.

Talia squeezed her eyes shut like she was trying to hold back tears. Her hands clenched into tight fists at her sides. "That time, in the first safe house. I told you I would... we could—" She let out a shaky breath. Her eyes opened, dark, accusing. Shiny with tears. "You looked at me like I was something you'd scraped off your shoe."

The hurt in her voice hit him like a kick in the gut. At the time, he'd been so angry, so offended, that she would lump him in with the other assholes who had hurt her. And she'd looked so fucking relieved when he'd denied her advances with a curt "no" that it hadn't occurred to him that his rejection had stung, much less festered inside her for the past two years.

The anger rose again, at himself, for inadvertently hurting her. At her, for actually believing for one second she disgusted him, for thinking so little of herself she'd put her life in his hands anyway.

And with the anger came the lust, the need, swelling like a wave inside that had finally broken through the containment wall that could no longer hold it at bay. In the space of a breath, he was pressed against her. His erection throbbed between them, squeezed against her stomach as her breath caught in her chest.

"Don't kid yourself for a fucking second that I don't feel anything for you."

Her lips parted in shock, but before she could get a word out, he covered them with his own. She made a high, startled sound in the back of her throat.

Pleasure, red, blinding, exploded through him at the first taste. Sweet, spicy, better than all his fevered imaginings. Her lips soft and giving against him, her tongue delicious and moist as he sucked it into his mouth.

One hand cradled her cheek while the other slid up her rib cage, around her back, fitting her to him until he could feel her soft breasts with their hard nipples burrowed into his chest. He rocked his hips, felt himself grow even harder at the delicious friction as he rubbed his cock against her stomach.

Some small voice of reason made him grasp for control, reminded him that if he was ever so lucky to finally get inside Talia Vega's gorgeous body, he did not—no matter how bad his body was raging—want the first time to be on the floor of a boxing gym with him sweaty and dirty and smelling like a goat.

Not to mention, as he pulled his mouth from hers, Talia herself was looking not so much swept away by lust as absolutely shell-shocked.

Shit.

Still, he wasn't going to let her go until they had some things straight. "That's what's been going on for me for a long time now, and in case it isn't obvious now, what

I feel sure as shit isn't disgust. The reason I turned you down that time was because I didn't want you to fuck me because you thought you owed me."

Her gaze flicked up nervously at his harsh tone.

"If I'm ever with you, Talia," he said, his voice low, his mouth hovering so close to hers he could feel the heat of her nervous breath, "it will be because you want me so bad you feel like you're going to die if you don't have me."

Her dark eyes flashed with anger. "You want me to beg? You want to humiliate me?"

Jack's resignation sank in his gut like a cannonball. "I don't want to do anything to hurt you, Talia. All I want," he said, struggling to keep the frustration from his voice, "is for you to want me the way I want you."

———— ⁓ ————

Talia could barely hear through the roaring in her head. She stared at Jack, dumbstruck. She held her hand up to lips that throbbed and tingled from the pressure of his kiss.

His own lips were swollen and moist, his cheekbones slashed with color, a hot glint in his icy-blue eyes as he stared down at her. So close she could feel him, the steely hard muscles of his chest against her, and lower, the heat and length of his erection. Hard as a club and throbbing against her stomach.

All I want is for you to want me the way I want you.

"I can't. I can't. I have to go." She ducked from his arms. He didn't try to stop her as she rushed from the studio on shaky legs. She felt poleaxed, panicked, like the world had suddenly flipped its axis and she didn't know which way was up.

She left in such a daze she was halfway into her drive home before she could start to parse through what had happened. And to mentally kick her own ass for reacting the way she had.

Jack wanted her.

He wanted *her.*

The question was, what did she want to do about it?

Her knee-jerk reaction was to reject it. She wasn't ready to be with a man. Her few failed attempts at dating proved it. No matter how nice the guy was, every time things got to a certain point physically, she closed up.

After a few tries, she resigned herself to the reality that even if she could get over what Nate had done to her, get over the idea of letting someone see the scars he'd left when he'd cut her up, she didn't think she could handle the feel of another man pawing her skin, shoving himself inside her, grunting and sweating on top of her while she moaned and writhed and faked it.

I want you to want me like I want you.

Jack wouldn't want her to fake it, she thought with an undeniable thrill deep in her belly. A thrill that was immediately chased away by cold, hard reality. If she didn't fake it, what could she do? It wasn't like she knew any other way.

It wasn't like she was capable of anything else.

But as she took the freeway exit close to her house, she found herself licking her lips, trying to capture the taste of him on her lips. Savoring the memory of the hungry way he kissed her, the way his tongue slid against hers. The heat of his hands, sliding down her body, clutching her so close, like he was dying for the feel of her.

The memory of his touch sure as hell didn't elicit revulsion, that was for sure.

In fact, the warm glow burgeoning between her legs might even bear a passing resemblance to desire.

Maybe, she thought as she focused on that warm glow, maybe she wouldn't have to fake it.

Not faking it wasn't the same as matching Jack's desire. And he wouldn't tolerate anything less.

The thought sent a shiver of mingled fear and—yes, she was pretty sure—desire rippling through her.

But could she really do this? Offer herself up to him and let go of all the baggage, get over everything and give Jack what he wanted?

What she was starting to think she wanted herself.

Was she crazy to entertain the possibility? Jack knew all of her secrets. With him, there would be nowhere to hide. Yet, knowing everything he knew about her, he still wanted her.

The thought sent an undeniable thrill bubbling through her.

She churned over it as she clicked open her car door and pulled into her garage. Maybe, she thought as she retrieved her gym bag and purse from her trunk, the problem was herself. Rosario was always trying to tell her that—that she dwelled too much on the past and what she considered her own part in what happened to her to let herself get over it.

Wasn't she just thinking the other day how good it had felt when Jack had held her, even before she realized what was under the surface? How much she wanted to be normal enough to be attracted to a guy and brave enough to go after what she wanted?

Still, part of her quailed at the idea of going up against Jack and all his fierceness straight out of the gate.

His words echoed through her brain, building in strength and volume. *I want you to want me like I want you.*

There would be no practice round, no dipping her toes in to see if she was really up for it. To quote one of her favorite movies, with Jack it was do or do not. There would be no try.

But, she acknowledged as she disarmed the alarm, unlocked the door, and walked into her kitchen, if she was going to ever try, it could never be with anyone but Jack.

The first man in nearly a decade to make her want for something more. The only man she could ever trust with her body.

She stripped off her clothes and got in the shower, and as she soaped and rinsed, her resolve grew. Whoever was out to scare her could send all the creepy gifts they wanted. She was not going to let herself be burdened by the past. She was not going to continue to let the memories of David Maxwell drag her back to that place where she could do nothing but exist, her life stagnant, colorless.

Jack's kiss, the realization of what had been simmering underneath, scared the hell out of her; there was no denying that. But it made her realize how much of herself she'd been holding in check, even as she worked to open herself up and connect with the people who were part of her new life.

"You be back by midnight, you hear me?" Gene's mother's demand, issued in Estonian, echoed through the house's dim interior. Though they'd immigrated when he was four, she insisted on speaking it in the house.

His shoulders knotted as he realized he hadn't made it past her unnoticed. He didn't answer and kept heading for the door, regretting it when he heard the chair scrape across linoleum followed by her muffled footsteps on the carpeted floor.

"Gene!" she snapped, rounding the corner to the entryway. Though barely fifty, his mother looked seventy, her small body wiry and shrunken as though the years of bitterness had consumed her from the inside out. She stopped short when she saw him, curling her lip like she smelled something. "What the hell do you think you are wearing?" she asked as she took in his heavy, military-style boots, black pants, and black T-shirt, topped with a black canvas jacket.

"I have to go, Mama," he said, and tried to slip out the door, but she jumped in front of him. He tried to draw back but she grabbed his cheek between her thumb and her forefinger and squeezed.

"You think some girl is going to want a loser like you, dressed up like some *kakker*?" She looked him up and down again. "But no clothes can change you." She stood up on her tiptoes and pulled at his cheek.

Though every cell in his body rebelled, he had no choice but to bend his head closer. "You are loser, like your father. You and him, both losers who ruined my life."

He forced himself not to pull away, to beat back the urge to wrap his hands around her neck and squeeze until her eyes popped out. He wanted to slam her head through the window and scream that he was no loser, that he was capable of things she couldn't even imagine.

But he took a deep breath and swallowed back the nausea. "You're right, Mama. You're always right."

Her harsh frown melted into a smile. "Good boy," she said, patting his cheek. "Even though you're a loser, I love you. Nobody will ever love you like Mama."

"I know," he said tightly.

"Now tell me you love me and give me a kiss."

He closed his eyes and bent his head, forced himself to rest his shaking hands gently on her shoulders as he pressed his mouth to her cheek. Somehow he managed not to vomit as the stench of cigarettes, boiled cabbage, and sour wine invaded his nostrils.

Control. That was the key to his success. He had to control himself now and learn to control himself with the women. Only then would he be ready for her.

For Talia.

As he escaped his mother's clutching hands and headed out the front door, a wave of anticipation shot through him like an electrical current. It curled in his stomach and pulsed through his veins, chasing away the revulsion his mother's touch had caused.

He slid into the car and slipped on a pair of leather gloves. He pulled the plastic case from his pocket, unable to keep from grinning at the thought of Talia's reaction to his gift.

Chapter 6

Talia spent the rest of the afternoon anxiously checking her phone, but after a curt text that said only, *Call if something else happens,* Jack maintained complete radio silence. At first she was confused. She'd been out of the game for a while, but after a guy made a move like that, much less a declaration of that magnitude, wasn't some kind of phone call in order?

By the time she left for work, confusion had morphed firmly into annoyance. What the hell? Two years and he'd barely kept in touch, given no indication there was anything there.

He'd managed to keep it totally on the down low, from her of all people.

She shook her head, muttering to herself as she wiped down the bar and readied the glassware for the night. She might not be looking for herself, but she had what she considered a more highly evolved sense of when someone was lusting after someone else.

Either Jack was a master at masking that kind of thing, or the last two years had wreaked total havoc on her intuition.

In any case, it was wholly unfair of him to drop a bomb

like that, to kiss her like that—like he was desperate for the taste of her and only her—and then leave her hanging without so much as a call or a text.

Talia snatched up a corkscrew and wrenched the corks from several bottles of wine.

"Is everything okay?" Susie watched her from the entrance of the main dining room.

"Yeah, why?" A cork came free of a bottle of cab with a satisfying pop.

"If you're not careful, you're going to crack the neck off that bottle."

Talia loosened her grip and carefully set the bottle down on the back bar. "I've got a lot on my mind."

Susie approached the bar, lines of concern creasing her usually smooth forehead. "Is this about the necklace? Did they find out who sent it?"

The mention of it immediately sent Talia's stomach plummeting, reminding her that she had much bigger things to worry about than Jack's unexpected advances.

"Not yet," she said, grim. "And to make it worse, I got some flowers last night."

Susie cocked a perfectly waxed blond brow. "How do flowers make it worse?"

"It was a gardenia plant—the same kind of flowers he used to give me." No need to clarify who *he* was since Susie knew all about her past with David Maxwell.

Susie winced. "Let me guess—no idea who they're from."

Talia shook her head. "It has to be someone close to him. The only other person who knew he gave me gardenias was Rosario."

Susie gave a little shudder. "You called the police, right?"

"For all the good it did. As of now, anonymously giving jewelry and flowers isn't a crime."

Susie rolled her eyes. "Right. But they'll get right on it once you have a knife in your chest—" She clapped her hand over her mouth as she realized what she'd said. "Oh, God, that wasn't funny—"

Talia gave a little laugh and held up her hand. "No offense taken. Anyway, you're right. Until someone actually threatens me or tries to hurt me, there's nothing they can do about it."

"Well, you should tell Jack, if you haven't already. He seems to jump at the chance to come to your rescue."

Talia wasn't sure if she was being paranoid or if there was a snide undertone in Susie's voice. Either way, the mention of Jack brought a rush of heat to her face.

"Yeah," she mumbled, and ducked down beneath the bar under the guise of retrieving glasses, praying Susie hadn't noticed her blush.

But as she straightened, she found Susie studying her as if she were a bug under a microscope. "Something happened." It wasn't a question.

Talia's cheeks flamed higher. "No, nothing, I mean, not really—"

"Spill it," Susie said.

Talia pressed her lips together, debating whether to tell Susie the truth. Susie had made no secret of her interest in Jack, and Talia didn't want to hurt her feelings. But the tangled mess of confused desire was too much for her to keep contained.

"Jack kissed me," Talia blurted. At Susie's urging, Talia quickly filled her in on how Jack had practically mauled her at the gym. How he'd kissed her with heart-pounding desperation before telling her how much he wanted her. Wanted her to want him back. How Jack's kiss had sent electricity surging through every pore. "I haven't felt anything like that since high school," Talia said, amazement in her voice.

Susie leaned back. "Why do you look so surprised?"

"I guess I'm surprised I liked it so much. And I had no idea he was even attracted to me—"

"Then you're the only one," Susie said. "The other night? In my office? There was so much heat coming off you I was afraid my office was going to spontaneously combust."

Talia shrugged. "Even so, probably nothing is going to come of it, not after I ran out of there like a freak, and he hasn't even called me, just a text telling me to let him know if I get any more creepy gifts."

Susie smiled knowingly. "You'll hear from him before the night is through. In fact, I wouldn't be surprised if he just happens to show up at your place later, just to make sure you're safe. Maybe he'll even tuck you into bed, tell you a naughty bedtime story—"

Talia slapped at her with her rag and Susie skittered away with a laugh.

The place began to fill, and soon Talia was kept hopping. She was grateful for the distraction the crowd provided. It meant that she could only check her phone every fifteen minutes or so to see if, following Susie's predictions, Jack had been in touch, and it kept her from watching the door the entire night, hoping he'd show up in person.

A group of business types bellied up for happy hour. Later a pack of women came in, laughing and chattering as they ordered bottle after bottle of wine. From snippets of conversation, Talia deduced they were a group of moms ready to tie one on and let their hair down away from their children.

Talia didn't care who they were, as long as they tipped well and didn't argue when she took their car keys shortly before last call. She watched as the last woman fell into a cab. The bar was now silent except for an alternative rock song playing softly over the stereo system.

Reality began to creep in, and with it thoughts of Jack, the kiss, and the unsettling "gifts" she'd received in the past week.

Talia buttoned up the bar and went back to the office to retrieve her purse. Susie was at the desk, stylish, heavy-framed glasses perched on her nose as she stared at the computer screen.

"Good night tonight?" She looked up as Talia came in.

"Excellent night," Talia replied. "We cleared over five hundred in tips at the bar alone."

"Thank God," Susie said. "I've been trying to streamline costs—changing our liquor vendor like you suggested has helped, but we're still running thin."

Talia nodded sympathetically. The restaurant business was merciless in the best of cases and got hit doubly hard when the economy took a dump. The fact that Suzette's had survived the past few years was a home run. "I'll look over the bar numbers again tomorrow and see if there's any other places to cut."

Susie thanked her. "You heading out?"

Talia nodded. "If that's okay with you. I haven't sat down since five-thirty. I think I'm about to collapse." She collected her coat and her purse from the hook on the wall.

She started out the back door to her car and gave a startled cry as a heavy hand fell on her shoulder. She whirled and found herself nose to chest with Peter, one of the sous-chefs. He was six foot three and easily three hundred pounds and looked like he should be lining up on a football field instead of stirring risotto at the stove.

He held up his hands, a look of embarrassed apology on his dark face. "Sorry, Talia, I didn't mean to scare you."

"No, it's fine. I'm just a little jumpier than usual. See you tomorrow." She started for her car, but Peter stayed in step with her as they reached her little Honda. "Is there something you wanted to talk to me about?" she asked as she fished out her keys. In the six months that she'd worked at Suzette's, she'd had a few friendly conversations with Peter, but he didn't usually seek her out.

"Susie told us some weirdo is sending you stuff," he said. "We agreed we're gonna take turns making sure you get home safe."

The gesture was so kind and so unexpected that Talia felt the sting of tears in her eyes. "Oh, that's so nice, but not necessary—"

He held up one massive hand. "We don't have security in the parking lot and you live by yourself."

"I appreciate a walk to the car, but following me home is too much to ask."

"Between all of us, no one has to go more than once a week, and you're only five minutes away. It'll make us feel better if we know you're home safe."

Talia searched his face, looking for an angle. But all she saw in his dark, kind eyes was sincere concern. She felt a prick of shame that she was so scarred that her gut instinct was to question his motives.

"Can't always depend on the law to help us out," Peter continued, "so it's important we look after each other."

Talia nodded, an upwell of emotion making her throat so tight she could barely push a heartfelt "thank you" past her lips. Suddenly she was blinking back tears.

She got into her car and pulled out of the parking space and waited till she saw Peter's headlights behind her. As she pulled out of the parking lot, there was a burgeoning warmth in her chest.

From the glow of headlights behind her. From the knowledge that after so many years of feeling so alone and hating herself for allowing David Maxwell to use her, she'd found a new life with people who found her worth caring about.

It was no longer just her and Rosie and Jack, her mysterious, reluctant hero whose motives for helping her were not so mysterious any longer.

She shied away from the thought as she pulled into her driveway, as though Jack might somehow hear it and be offended. His words rang in her head. *I didn't want you to fuck me because you felt like you owed me.*

It wasn't fair to Jack to lump him in with the amoral lowlifes she'd dealt with most of her life. Jack had proven that over and over again in the past two years. There was no doubt what kind of a man he was.

A man who wants me, she thought with a pulse of excitement as she pulled into her garage.

She grabbed her phone from the center console and reassured herself that, no, she hadn't missed a call or a text or a—she waited a minute for her mail to load—no e-mail either.

Nothing but a text from Rosie saying she was back in

her dorm room and didn't want to disturb her sleeping roommate.

She slung her purse and coat over her shoulder and climbed out of the car. Once she was safely inside, she took a quick look around. She opened the front door and let out the breath she didn't realize she was holding when she found no mysterious flowers, no envelopes, nothing. She waved at Peter and flicked the porch lights on and off to show she was in safe, and he flashed his lights in turn.

With her newly appointed posse of guardian angels, she wouldn't need Jack around.

It was weird, but even her irritation with Jack felt kind of...good. When was the last time she'd gotten in a snit over a guy not calling? When had she actually felt genuinely attracted and interested enough to care?

For years all she wanted was for the man in her life to leave her alone. And now here she was, channel surfing on her couch while sparing the occasional glare at her still-silent phone.

In spite of everything that had happened this week, it all felt so refreshingly...normal.

She gave a little smile and entertained the morbid thought that maybe a seemingly benign stalker wasn't a bad thing if it had gotten Jack to finally show his hand and make a move.

But what if he hadn't called because he regretted it? Worse, what if he changed his mind or hadn't meant it in the first place?

There was something to be said for being numb to the whole man-woman craziness, she thought as her brain futilely churned. She stood from the couch and paced to the kitchen to pour herself a glass of wine. Maybe the alcohol would calm her down enough to sleep.

On the way back to the couch, the blanket she'd wrapped around herself to ward off the chill snagged on the buckle of her purse strap and sent it and its contents skidding across the linoleum. Talia swore, set her wineglass on the table, and bent to gather her wallet, sunglasses, lipstick, and other miscellaneous items that littered the floor.

As she reached for a small tube of hand cream, she noticed a square red envelope next to the refrigerator. She picked it up and felt something flat and hard inside. She tipped it, and a disk slid into her hand, silver, shiny, unremarkable.

Except for the fact that Talia was damn sure she hadn't put it in her purse.

Her hand shook with dread as she turned the disk over. There was a typed label stuck to the front. Her stomach bottomed out as she read, *To Talia. Hope you enjoy this walk down memory lane. Wish I could be there to watch with you.*

Watch. A video of some kind. Even as her brain screamed at her that she was guaranteed not to like what she was about to see, her hands were pressing buttons on the TV and loading the disk into the player as though on autopilot.

The scream filled her living room and turned her knees to water. Talia sank to the floor, frozen, her eyes locked helplessly on the screen.

On herself. Naked. Bound.

On Nate Brewster, naked, hulking, his almost grotesquely muscular body covered in tattoos, a wickedly sharp blade in his hand.

The hand arced down and she watched as the blade sliced into the skin of her back. The scar in her back burned, the pain as real to her now as it had been in that basement. Terror washed over her, pulled her under, and she was back there, naked, helpless.

She huddled on the floor for long minutes after the recording ended, her body racked with shudders so fierce they bordered on seizures.

Somehow she managed to crawl to her phone. Her hands were shaking so badly it took her five tries to dial. Finally there was a ring on the other side.

Normal. Hysterical laughter burst from her chest as she held the phone to her ear. Had she really thought for one second her life could be normal?

As she waited for Jack to answer, she curled into herself, her heart shriveling at the certainty she'd never get away from her past, never get away from what happened. It would always be there, lurking, waiting to suck her under all over again.

Chapter 7

The party at the Four Seasons in Palo Alto was in full swing, the crowd so loud Jack wouldn't have known anyone was calling if not for the violent buzzing in his pocket. He pulled the phone out and felt a tightening in his gut when he saw Talia's number.

His stomach tightened with fear. While he wished she was calling to chew him out about the way he'd mauled her at the gym today, his gut was screaming that something had happened.

He thumbed the button, praying he was about to get an ass-chewing as he practiced his apology.

"Talia?" he said when he was greeted with nothing but silence.

The choked breath sent his stomach down to his knees. Crap. Something else had happened. "Talia, what's going on?"

"C-can you please come over?"

The raw fear in her voice made his blood run cold. "What happened?"

Another shaky breath. "I . . . It's me, Jack. It was in my purse—" Whatever she said devolved into sobs, and Jack could only make out every third or so word.

Jack did a quick check on the Blankenthorn's position and moved to a quieter corner of the ballroom. "Talia, slow down. What was in your purse?"

He heard gulping sounds as she tried to stifle the sobs. "Please, just come over."

His heart thudded to a stop as the connection was broken. He tried to call back but Talia wouldn't pick up.

Cold sweat filmed his body underneath the suit and dress shirt that had been required wardrobe for tonight's assignment. He dialed Talia again, still no answer. He looked up and saw Diana Blankenthorn frowning pointedly at the phone in his hand and quietly swore. He knew what he was about to do might cost him his job and Gemini Securities an important client, but he didn't care.

Both Alex Novascelic and Ben Moreno, senior security specialists like Jack, were covering the party. The Blankenthorns would be well protected.

But Talia was alone. Alone and terrified.

The knowledge propelled him out of the ballroom, ignoring Alex's questioning frown as Jack brushed by him.

"Gotta go," Jack said curtly.

"Danny's not going to like this," Alex called.

"I'll deal with Danny," Jack snapped over his shoulder. "You tell Moreno to cover the south entrance."

Jack rushed to his car and within a few minutes was hauling ass up the freeway. He called Talia to let her know he was on his way. Still no answer. His adrenaline spiked and he forced himself not to dwell on all the reasons why she might not be picking up the phone.

Striving for some semblance of calm, he called the sheriff's department and got a promise they'd send someone over to check on her. He disconnected, doubting a black-and-white would make it there before he did.

He looked at the clock. After midnight, an obnoxious hour for a call, but Jack knew from long experience working with Danny—first in the Green Berets as a member of his team and then after getting hired on with Gemini—that Danny liked to receive pertinent information as soon as it came in. There would be hell to pay if he found out he'd been kept in the dark.

Then again, there would be hell to pay any way Jack cut it, but there was no sense in delaying the inevitable.

Jack braced himself as he used the voice activation to make the call. Danny's reaction to the news Jack had switched up the security detail was met with predictable enthusiasm.

"Are you fucking kidding me? You're bailing on one of our most important clients for Talia Vega?"

Jack hadn't mentioned Talia by name; he'd told Danny only that he'd had to leave the Blankenthorns in Moreno's care to deal with a personal emergency. "How did—"

"Oh for Christ's sake," Danny said wearily, "you forget how well I know you and your goddamn damsels in distress. What else could it—"

Danny cut out and Jack could hear a feminine voice murmuring in the background, one that no doubt belonged to Caroline Taggart, Danny's wife. "Nothing, baby, go back to sleep." Danny's voice was muffled with an undercurrent of tenderness Jack wouldn't have believed Danny capable of had he not heard it himself.

"Nice work, asshole," Danny snapped at Jack. "You woke up my wife with this shit too."

"Tell Caroline I apologize," Jack said, striving to

keep his own anger under wraps. "I didn't feel I had a choice—"

"Yeah, whatever," Danny interrupted. "Just have your ass up and ready to focus on the job first thing tomorrow morning or I swear to fucking God…"

It took Jack a few seconds to realize he'd been hung up on. *Asshole*, he thought, but without any real heat. Danny had a unique, some would say harsh manner when it came to dealing with everyone but his wife, but Jack had never known a more loyal friend.

It made it stick that much harder in his craw, knowing he was letting down a friend who had had his back too many times to count in the last few years.

But Jack couldn't live with himself if he let down Talia.

The drive to Talia's little bungalow seemed to stretch to infinity but in reality took only about fifteen minutes. It felt like hours since she'd called in a panic, but when Jack checked his watch, he saw that it was just shy of twenty minutes since she'd called. His gut churned as he pulled up to the house. No cops in sight.

The lights were blazing in the living room, but he couldn't see any movement inside. He rang the bell. When several seconds passed with no response, he started pounding, then called Talia's name.

A light switched on next door and he heard an angry voice yelling, "Keep it down, or I'll call the police!"

"Go ahead," Jack yelled back. "If we're lucky, maybe they'll actually show up!"

He turned back to Talia's door and caught a blur of movement through the small beveled windows to the side of the door.

"Jack?"

His knees turned watery with relief. "Yeah, it's me. Open up."

There was the *thunk* of the dead bolt being thrown and then the door opened. "What the hell are you thinking not answering—" His harangue about his ignored calls stopped midsyllable when he caught sight of her face.

Leached of color, her lips bloodless, her pupils dilated, she looked lucky to be breathing, much less standing on her feet. He stepped through the door, then closed and locked it behind him. A shudder ran through her and she swayed on her feet.

He reached out to steady her, felt her muscles rippling under his hands. "What happened, honey?" he asked softly. "Why didn't you answer when I called?"

"I dropped my phone on the stairs," she said. "I was afraid to come back down."

She was getting a dazed, far-off look in her eyes. Her hands were ice cold as they clutched his, and he feared she was going into shock. He yanked off his coat and threw it over her shoulders and gathered her close, rubbing his hands up and down her arms and back to try to get some warmth into her.

She sagged against him and he bit back a curse as he wrapped his arm around her to support her weight. He wanted to know what the hell had put her in this state. Christ, the last time he'd seen her in such bad shape she'd been bleeding from a stab wound and multiple lacerations. But he couldn't see any physical injury. Nonetheless, she was crashing, all systems shutting down.

He hustled her into the kitchen and gave a satisfied grunt when he found an inch of coffee left over in the pot. He quickly heated it in the microwave and dumped in a couple tablespoons of sugar and held it out for her. "Drink."

When she didn't respond, he took her hand in his, wrapped it around the mug, and brought it to her lips. She began to drink, slowly at first, then with more enthusiasm. By the time the mug was empty, her lips had some of their dark rose color back and she didn't look so much like a corpse.

Jack inched his chair closer to hers until their knees were almost touching. "You want to tell me what sent you so far over the edge?"

She set the mug on the table. He watched, confused, as she bent and retrieved something from the floor. She handed him the slip of paper. *To Talia. Hope you enjoy this walk down memory lane. Wish I could be there to watch with you.*

Jack suddenly felt like spiders were crawling up his back. Without a word, Talia pushed to her feet and walked to the front room. For the first time Jack noted that the TV was on, the screen a vivid blue as the set waited to receive a signal. "What did he want you to watch?" He was sure he didn't want to know the answer to the question.

Talia picked up the remote from the floor and pushed a button. "This."

No! Noo! Jack's blood curdled at the first scream. His eyes locked on the screen. He wanted to look away, but his vision tunneled. Talia's living room disappeared and it was like he was in that dungeon room with her.

"Holy mother of God," he whispered, blood roaring in his ears as he saw Nate Brewster's naked form, rippling with muscle and covered with tattoos, enter the frame.

And Talia, so small, her dark eyes wide with terror as

she lay in a naked heap on the floor, so heavily drugged she could barely move even as Nate pressed the glowing end of a cigarette against the tender skin of her breast.

But she could scream, loud, anguished, the sound of it ripping down Jack's spine. Another scream joined Talia's off camera—that would be Megan Flynn, trapped in the basement by that psycho Brewster.

Jack's stomach cramped and he barely swallowed back a surge of vomit as he watched Nate's arm come down on the screen, the blade of the hunting knife flashing as it made a diagonal slice across the skin of Talia's back.

He turned from the screen and took two lurching steps toward Talia and grabbed the remote. He pressed at the buttons with shaking fingers.

The TV went silent as he pulled her into his arms and collapsed with her onto the couch. He was shaking and so was she.

He buried his head in the crook of her neck and squeezed his eyes shut, but the images were seared into his brain. Jesus. He'd been there for the aftermath, had been the one to wrap his coat around her naked body, had felt her blood soak his hands as he'd held his shirt over the stab wound in her abdomen until the paramedics arrived.

It had been bad, but he'd seen worse. Christ, he'd been a soldier for over a decade. He'd seen and suffered plenty of bullet wounds and shrapnel and had built up a tough skin when it came to witnessing violence.

But seeing Talia, witnessing her attack as it happened... it sent him reeling, spinning out into a black hole of memories he had no desire to go exploring.

Goddamn you, stop hurting her! You stop hurting her or I'll fucking kill you!

The sound of his father's palm hitting his mother's face echoed across the room. He threw himself at the old man, landed a haymaker to the side of his head that sent his father staggering back. "Get out of here," he yelled at his mother and his sister, Lizzy, who was crying in the corner. Lizzy sprinted for the front door and didn't look back, but his mother heaved to her feet and screamed at him.

"Jack, stop!"

Jack turned to protest. "Mom—"

"Don't you dare raise your hand to me, boy!" His father's fist caught him full in the face, knocking him flat.

"You better apologize to your father." He looked up into his mother's bruised face, her eyes filled with fear as she watched his father.

The memory curdled his stomach and Jack forced it away, focusing on the woman in his arms.

"It's going to be okay," he whispered, as much to himself as to her. "I'm here. I'm not leaving. I won't let anything happen to you." He pulled Talia closer, his arms so tight she squeaked, but still he couldn't let her go.

Unlike the others, he could still save her.

Chapter 8

I have no idea how someone got ahold of the recording," Talia explained to Officer Martinez, who had responded shortly after Jack had shown up. She sat at her small kitchen table nursing another cup of coffee Jack had forced on her, while he stood directly behind her.

Though he'd released her long enough to let the officer in, he hadn't moved more than six inches from her side. And while the first frame of that recording had eliminated any desire she might have had about seeing where that kiss from Jack might lead, his warm, solid presence was the only thing keeping her from splintering into about a million pieces.

"I assume it was entered as evidence after"—Talia swallowed heavily—"after I was attacked, but David Maxwell had enough contacts in the police force for him or anyone in his organization to get ahold of it."

"Even if it originated with someone in Maxwell's organization," Jack said wearily, "all it takes is a click of a button to send it across the world. Any whacko could have pulled it off the Internet. Who knows how many copies there are of that thing."

The recording hadn't surfaced in the two years since

the attack, and Talia had assumed it was in the bowels of the Seattle PD evidence locker. She should have known better. "But what about the note? Doesn't that prove it's someone who knows me?"

"No offense, Miss Vega," Officer Martinez said, "but even though you've kept a relatively low profile, the press coverage that case garnered gave you a fair bit of notoriety. I'm sure there are lots of people who feel like they know you even if you don't know them. And you said it just appeared in your purse?"

Talia shivered as she felt icy fingers trail up her spine. It could be anyone. She'd thought it was bad before, when she was in hiding from David Maxwell and his cohorts, knowing that to show her face meant certain death. At least with David she knew the identity of her personal monster.

This was worse, the idea that someone was lurking, wanting to terrify her, maybe planning to harm her, like an evil shadow that darkened every corner of her life. "Yes. Someone slipped it in there sometime today, either when I was at the gym or at the restaurant. Those are the only times my purse was out of my sight."

Jack's hands came up to curve around her shoulders, and the tension in his fingers told her he was wondering the same thing. While they were sparring, while he was kissing her, at that very moment was some sick fuck slipping the DVD into her bag? Or was it later, while she was at the restaurant, alternately annoyed at Jack for not calling and mooning over him in fantasies about having something resembling a normal relationship with him?

Whenever, however it was done, it had served its purpose, terrifying her, bringing up all the pain and fear of the past. A vivid reminder of who she was, what she'd been, and why she would never, ever be able to let her guard down.

Why she was too broken to be with any man, even one as strong as Jack.

"I'll need to take the DVD with me," the officer said. "We'll check it for fingerprints and have our techs analyze it to see if they can pull any information from it."

"What kind of information?" Talia asked as the officer covered his hand in a latex glove and retrieved the disk from the player.

"Honestly, I'm not up on all the particulars, but I think they can figure out if it's a duplicate copy, if it was downloaded from a website, that kind of stuff."

"If it's different from the original, they'll be able to tell that too."

"Sounds like you know all about it," the cop said.

"I work in security," Jack said, and handed the cop his card. He said it casually, but the subtext was unmistakable. *I know what I'm doing just in case you don't, and I'll be all over your ass if you fuck this up.*

The cop studied the card and gave Jack a once-over. "Probably not a bad guy to keep around until this blows over," he said to Talia.

Talia forced herself up and managed to walk the cop to the door.

"I'm sure we'll have more questions," he said.

"I'll help any way that I can." *Anything to make this stop.*

She shut the door behind the officer and slid the dead bolt home, its metallic thud echoing through the room.

She turned to find Jack a few feet behind her, propping

himself on the back of the couch. His face was grim as he studied her.

How odd that only a few hours ago, she'd been stewing over the fact that he hadn't called her after that shocker of a kiss. Now he was here in her living room, apparently with no plans to go anywhere anytime soon.

What would have made her night hours before now had her as jumpy as a drop of water on a hot skillet. "You don't have to stay, you know. I'll be fine, with the lock on and the new alarm system." She walked back to the kitchen and busied herself loading the empty coffee mugs into the dishwasher. "I feel like such an asshole now, giving you and Ben such a hard time about upgrading." She'd never been much of a nervous babbler, but she couldn't seem to stop herself as Jack continued to study her without a word, his gaze so intense it was like a hand rushing over her body. "When you talk to him, you'll have to thank him for me because this definitely makes me feel better about staying alone—"

"In what universe do you think I'd ever leave you alone after that?"

Talia turned to face him as something that felt a lot like relief washed through her. No getting around it, she'd sleep a lot better knowing a big, strong, ex–Special Forces badass was in the house with her.

Okay, maybe not any Special Forces badass. Just Jack.

Yet the thought of him being under the roof of her small house after what had happened earlier today... "Really, I don't want you to put yourself out any more than you have," she said, wincing at the way she sounded like a broken record.

"Just stop," Jack said, holding up a silencing hand as

he crossed the small living room into the kitchen. "To be crystal clear, I'm not getting more than ten feet away from you until we catch the asshole who's doing this."

Part of her wanted to throw herself at his feet and thank him for, once again, taking care of her. Yet she still rankled at the idea that she needed to be saved, that once again she needed to depend on him, that she would have another obligation to add to the pile of unpaid debts she already owed. "What about work? You're here on assignment. How are you supposed to protect your clients if you're stuck trailing after me?"

"I'll figure out something."

"I don't know Danny that well, but there's no way this will go over well with him."

Jack shrugged and took off his suit jacket to drape it over a kitchen chair. "Let me worry about Danny. He might get pissed, but he'll understand. I can't let anything happen to you again. Jesus, seeing you like that..."

Talia saw it then, the crack in his no-nonsense armor, the trauma in his eyes that mirrored her own as he remembered the horrific images. He raked his hand through his hair, and as he did, she saw it was shaking.

He squeezed his eyes shut and when they opened again, they were once again cool, steady. Determined. "Nothing is more important to me than keeping you safe, got it? And if that means pissing off my friends or even losing work over it, tough shit."

She swallowed hard and blinked back the sting of tears. It was just stress, she told herself. Someone wanted to terrify her—and was succeeding—so why wouldn't she deserve a good cry?

But it was more than that, and she knew it. This was

all new for her, having someone want to look out for her, having someone tell her she was important to them. Having someone like Jack put everything in his life on hold just to help her didn't and would never make sense to her.

Are you forgetting what happened this morning? I think someone finally showed his true colors.

As though reading her mind, Jack said, "I don't want you to worry about what happened earlier today. It was completely inappropriate and unfair of me to do that to you."

"Unfair how?"

His dark brows knit as though he was surprised by the question. "After everything you've been through, for me to put you in that kind of position where you might feel obligated to—" He broke off, and Talia wasn't sure if it was a trick of the light, but he might actually be blushing.

"To fuck you out of some sense of gratitude or obligation?" she asked, her own face hot.

"Exactly," Jack ground out. "Especially since I know there's no way in hell you could ever return the sentiment."

After this morning, she wasn't so sure that was true. And it rankled that he thought she was so damaged, so broken that she could never recover enough to ever give a man another chance.

Yet, as the images from the DVD drifted back through her head, she had to admit that even if she hadn't regressed all the way back to the terror-filled weeks and months after the attack when she'd been forced into hiding, seeing herself like that was a serious step back in whatever healing she'd managed.

"There's been some stuff building and for a second, it slipped out of my control. But I don't want you to worry about it. I've got a handle on it, and nothing like that will happen again."

Some perverse part of her wanted to ask, exactly, how he planned to handle it. Take matters into his own hands, as it were?

Or find someone else to help take the edge off? He wouldn't have to look far.

A twist of jealousy she had no right to feel settled in her stomach at the thought.

But the fear-induced adrenaline rush was quickly wearing off, sapping her of energy and leaving her too tired to do any verbal sparring tonight. "I'm not worried," she said finally, and then covered her mouth to hide a jaw-cracking yawn. "You can sleep in the spare room. It's just a twin bed, so sorry if it's a little small."

"I'll be fine. You get some sleep."

Her eyes drooped and her lips pulled into a smile. "You know, with you here I think I actually might."

—⁓—

Jack wished he could say the same. He watched Talia's retreating back until she disappeared up the stairs. When he heard the door of her bedroom click closed, he breathed a sigh of relief. His face relaxed now that he didn't have to conceal everything he was feeling.

Rage at the sick fuck who would do this to her pulsed through him, the kind of anger that made him want to kick and punch and break a few bones. He paced Talia's house like a caged animal, tempted to put his fist through the TV screen that had displayed such horror.

Yeah, that would go over well. Wrecking Talia's home-entertainment equipment when she was already nervous about him turning into a lust-crazed beast.

If nothing else, he thought grimly, the horrific images of Talia's attack had momentarily chased away the lust that had been kicked into hyperdrive at the first taste of her.

Still, it took a gargantuan effort to resist the urge to walk up the stairs, open the door of her bedroom, join her on her big bed, and pull her into his arms and just hold her.

Because after the brutal reminder of her attack, he knew that's about all she'd be up for. And it was a sign of how far gone he was that he would settle for the feel of her warm and safe against him when what he really wanted...

Shit.

He stalked into the kitchen and rummaged through her cabinets. When he unearthed a bottle of rum, he felt like he'd won a prize. Not his first choice, but a couple ounces poured straight over some ice would do the job.

He wasn't about to get hammered, but he definitely needed something to take the edge off. He knew this state all too well and knew what he was capable of when he was in it. He reached for the TV remote, and as he powered it on, his stomach did a little flip as he half expected Talia's naked, bleeding body to flash back up on the screen.

Turning the volume low, he tuned it to the History Channel. He didn't give a rat's ass about the Civil War documentary on the screen, but his brain needed some distraction before it delved too deep into the dark place he worked overtime to avoid.

He was so used to being in control, calm and cool to the

point that his veins could have been full of ice instead of water. But situations like this, seeing a woman—especially one he cared about—being threatened. Seeing the helpless fear in her eyes as she looked desperately about for a protector and found none—it was guaranteed to send him reeling.

He drained the rum, wishing he could go for a refill but knowing he couldn't drink more than one and stay sharp. But one drink and the din of another World War II documentary wasn't enough to keep the darkness at bay. He stared at the TV, but all he could see was Talia, sobbing in pain, bleeding from the cuts Nate inflicted to tease and torture.

Then other women joined Talia. His mother with one of her countless split lips and black eyes. Warning signs that his father was in more than one of his usual rages if he couldn't control himself enough to deliver blows only to the places that wouldn't show.

His sister, Lizzy, and the stark look of betrayal in her eyes the first time his father's fist had connected with her ribs. Jack, fourteen, had tackled his father, fists flying while Lizzy fled to the bedroom. Though he was big and tall for his age, he was no match for his father, a six-foot-three behemoth fueled by thirty-year-old single malt and unadulterated rage.

It would take a few more years before Jack would be able to best him. A few more years for his father—with his mother's unwavering blessing—to kick Jack out. He would have been more than happy to leave the house of horrors if it hadn't meant leaving Lizzy behind to fend for herself.

Jack had helped as much as he could. But despite the

fact that Lizzy had gone off to college, then culinary school, and was now working her way through the ranks in a swanky restaurant in New York, it would never be enough.

A father who beat the crap out of you and a mother who stood by and took it? There was no undoing damage like that.

But that didn't stop Jack from trying to undo his, stepping in to save his "broken birds" as Danny called them. *No matter if the bird in question flat-out refused to be saved*, he thought, and shoved away another rush of bitter memories.

At least in Talia, he'd set his sights on someone who welcomed his interference. After the crap he'd gotten himself into in the past, there wasn't much more he could ask for.

Gene wished he could have seen her face when she watched the video. After he'd slipped it into her purse, he'd lingered in his car across the street from the restaurant's parking lot. He'd watched her leave accompanied by a big black man who must have been a line cook based on his wardrobe. The man escorted Talia to her car, then got into his.

Smart girl, taking precautions. That alone wouldn't have prevented him from trying to take a peek into her windows or even try to find a place to hide in her house so he could watch her reaction.

But Rosario had told him about the beefed-up security system Talia's friend had installed. If it had been a standard system with schematics available to download, it would have been a joke to crack—he was unraveling the secrets of the human genome in his PhD dissertation, for Christ's sake—but the nonstandard system gave him pause.

He would have to find another way to breach her fortress. He wasn't worried.

It was almost better this way, being able to imagine her shock, her horror. Build up the anticipation of seeing her face when *he* was the one standing over her with the knife. When *he* was the one cutting into her body.

When he succeeded where the Seattle Slasher had failed.

But not tonight. Tonight he would continue his studies.

Ten minutes after he watched Talia drive away, Gene was finding his way through the dark concrete tunnel. Though he had night-vision goggles in his bag, he didn't bother putting them on yet. He knew his way by heart. He'd been down this path dozens of times in the last few months since he'd found his lair. Since he'd realized his true calling, he realized he needed a dedicated, hidden location to hone his craft.

When he got to the door, he slipped on the goggles so he could see and open the padlock he'd installed. Heavy metal scraped against concrete as he shoved the door open.

He stepped in and closed the door behind him. His nose wrinkled at the odor that greeted him. The lack of plumbing was one of the few drawbacks to a nearly perfect location. Although, he mused, it would be a problem in any case, as it was impossible to use a toilet when you were locked in a pitch-black room and your hands and feet were bound.

He was glad he'd brought the bleach. Tonight he'd treat the floor before and after. He smiled at the sound of scuffling in the corner, the little whimper as she tried to get as far away from him as possible.

He quickly located her green-tinged form through his goggles. He pulled a blindfold out of his bag. Ignoring her cries of protest, he wrapped the scarf tightly around her eyes. Retreating to the door, he slipped off the goggles and clicked on the overhead light. He took a moment to admire her. According to the driver's license that had been tucked into the pocket of the jeans he'd cut off her, her name was Madison Delaney, but he liked to think of her as Number 4.

Number 4 had sustained more damage than the other three, which made sense since he'd had her here nearly a full week already. It had taken that long to get the fight out of her. Her bare legs were covered in bruises and scrapes from where she'd tried to hurl herself against the walls of the shed. Her arms, sticking out of the sleeves of the T-shirt that covered her top half, were similarly battered.

Now she didn't move except from the convulsive shivering. It was cold down here and the concrete floors and walls made it even colder. He could see her tension in the way her chin was tilted up, her head cocked to the side as she listened. For the first few days, she screamed incessantly whenever he came to visit, but she'd since learned that it didn't do any good.

In hell, no one can hear you scream.

He didn't say a word as he cleaned up the concrete floor, watched her nostrils quiver as the smell of the bleach hit her. Then he went to his bag and pulled out the wipes, the kind you'd use on a baby.

He crossed to where she lay in the corner, his hands shaking at the anticipation of touching her.

He cautioned himself not to let his excitement overwhelm him.

He needed to study.

He grasped her around the ankle, his penis thickening at the way she whimpered behind the gag and tried to jerk out of his hold. He let her try to yank away a few times, laughing a little at the futility of it all.

He plucked several wipes out of the box and pulled her closer across the cement floor. "You'll never get away," he whispered. "Not until I'm ready to let you go."

She froze, and he could feel her skin quivering under his hands as he slid the wipes over the skin of her calves, then up to her thigh. His breath quickened and sweat beaded under his clothes as he took a fresh wipe and went up, between her thighs.

Her legs clamped around his hand, and she whimpered as he thoroughly cleaned her. By the time he was satisfied she was clean, he was fully erect, straining against the fly of his pants.

He gathered the used wipes and zipped them into a plastic bag to be disposed of later. He resisted the urge to throw her to the floor and take her now. There was a methodology he had to follow.

He backed away, pulled his iPad out of his bag, and took a seat on the folding chair in the opposite corner. The girl didn't move for several moments, propped against the wall with her legs slightly splayed, back arched from having her arms bound behind her.

After nearly a minute, she decided it would be safe to move, and she slowly, carefully, as though she was trying to get away with it, curled her knees into her chest and hid her face against the wall.

He focused his attention on the iPad on his lap.

A few finger swipes and he had what he wanted. His heartbeat picked up as the footage started to roll. He licked his lips as Talia was thrown to the ground and her attacker hunkered over her to slice off her clothes.

He smiled a little as the Slasher touched the burning tip of a cigarette to the unblemished skin under Talia's left breast. Her cry of pain sent lust searing through him and he closed his hand over himself, stroking the hard flesh. Oh, to have been in that room, to be the one to mar that perfect flesh...

He snatched his hand away and shoved aside the lust. He could not get carried away. He had to learn to hold himself back, to analyze the footage with a more clinical, analytical eye.

That was his problem. He got distracted, lost in the moment, and didn't pay attention to the details. He put his hand on his thigh and dug his fingers into the muscle, using the pain to keep him focused.

He focused on the blade, glinting silver as it arced toward Talia's back, slicing a clean diagonal line across the smooth expanse. His hand fisted, and he could almost feel the weight of the handle in his own hand, feel the skin yield to its razor sharpness.

In the video Talia screamed, and he turned down the volume as the high, frantic sound threatened to snap his control. He watched as the Slasher made the second cut, on the opposite diagonal, forming a perfect X. That was where Gene always got messed up. Even if he didn't get overexcited from the first cut, from the cries of pain and the first crimson stripe welling up and spilling over, it was an awkward angle to cut with his right hand, right shoulder to left hip. Brewster had the advantage of being ambidextrous, so he was able to make the second cut as perfectly with his left as he'd made with his right.

Gene had to find a way to overcome his shortcomings.

There were, however, areas where he had an advantage over Brewster. For all the terror he instilled in Talia, Brewster hadn't been able to get it up and fuck her like a real man.

Gene would have no such failings. When he completed his mission, he would take Talia as she deserved.

He skipped over the part where the Slasher was beating the other woman. Gene had no interest in her. Then Talia, foolish girl, made the mistake of going after him, hurling herself at his back.

Nate Brewster reared his hulking body over her, and in that moment it was like Gene was living it himself, like he was one with the beast, his own hand arcing down to deliver what should have been a fatal blow.

Yet, despite the blood pooling around her too-still body, it hadn't been.

When the time came, Gene wouldn't make the same mistake.

The screen showed Brewster's naked, muscular body as he dragged the other woman out of view. Then there was a muffled crash and the screen went dark as the camera was knocked aside in the struggle.

He shut off the video app and slipped the iPad back into his bag. He forced himself to breathe deep and slow, calming himself, taking the edge off the rush that always overtook him when he watched the video.

A rush that was even keener tonight, knowing that Talia had seen it too, perhaps for the very first time.

His gaze locked on the girl, frozen and whimpering in the opposite corner. Licked his lips in anticipation of feeling her hips clutched in his hands, of feeling the heft of the knife as it pressed into her yielding flesh.

His penis throbbed at the thought of her body squeezing around him as she stiffened in terror and pain.

But he had to follow the rules.

First he laid out the blanket. Cheap, a wool blend, one of dozens he'd bought at Costco.

Then he stripped and put on his protective gear. Latex gloves. Cap pulled over his closely cropped hair.

And finally, at last, a condom rolled down over his erect penis. He slipped the knife out of his bag. Gene had researched what kind of knife Brewster had used on his victims. It had taken him months to find a close match on eBay.

Polished and sharpened to razor sharpness, it was without flaw. None of the mistakes in the past could be blamed on equipment. It was all operator error.

He pulled the girl to her feet and half dragged, half carried her to the blanket. She thrashed, her legs kicking wildly. But the struggles petered out in a few seconds, her energy quickly sapped after several days without food and little water. He cut the bonds holding her hands behind her back and quickly retied them in front of her body.

He pushed her onto her stomach and pinned her down by kneeling on the backs of her thighs. His knife cut through the stained T-shirt like butter, the ripping sound echoing through the closeness of the shed.

His hand slashed down to make the first cut.

Perfect.

Drawing a line from her left shoulder to the top of her right hip, the tip of his knife sliced through the thin layers of skin and fat, stopping just short of the muscle.

Number 4 screamed behind the gag and duct tape, trying to arch away against the unforgiving concrete of the floor.

The cut was so clean it didn't bleed for several seconds. First beading, then welling over until dark crimson spilled over the sides.

He traced his finger in the wetness, dragged his finger back and forth to spread the lovely color over her skin. "Beautiful," he murmured.

Number 4 sobbed.

He took a deep breath, forced his hands to steady as he prepared to make the crucial second cut. The one he had botched the three previous times. Each time he'd attempted it, it had been too jagged, too deep, or too shallow.

He dug his knees harder into the backs of her thighs, felt the muscles and tendons grind against her femur bones. Carefully, he positioned the knife at the top of her shoulder and drew it slowly, carefully diagonally across her back.

Perfect.

His breath caught in his chest and a surge of fresh lust pounded between his thighs as the magnitude of his achievement hit him.

Triumph pulsed through him and a wild laugh ripped from his chest as he flipped her onto her back.

Only one more mark to make.

He dug his knees into her thighs. She was sobbing behind

the blindfold, her desperate, animal sounds trapped behind the gag. He leaned in enough for her to feel the hard length of his penis against her stomach, letting her know exactly what was coming.

Right after he made the final cut.

The tip of the knife flashed silver against the pale skin underneath her breastbone. Almost delicate as it parted just the top layers of skin as he drew another smaller, perfect X to match the one carved into her back.

Unlike Talia, Number 4 wouldn't feel the full length of his blade sinking into her.

But she would feel something else.

He shoved her thighs wide and drove himself into her.

Chapter 9

So you understand this is serious, right? I'm not going off half-cocked again."

Talia could hear Jack's voice as she padded down the stairs.

He was wearing a short-sleeve T-shirt and gym shorts that exposed his powerfully muscled calves. His feet were bare, and his hair was sleep ruffled into short little spikes.

He looked powerful, rumpled, and right at home in her living room. She'd fully expected to spend a restless, nightmare-haunted night, but miraculously her sleep had been deep and dreamless. As though her subconscious knew that with Jack here, she was safe.

Don't get used to it, she scolded herself. *He's helping you out, and you owe him for that, but you can't let yourself depend too much on him or anyone else.*

"I'll extend a personal apology to Blankenthorn for dropping out as the lead, but I can't ignore what's going on here, Dan."

Her stomach clenched. He was talking to Danny Taggart, no doubt about dropping off the assignment that had brought him down here. She hoped Danny was in an understanding mood. She didn't want Jack losing his job over her.

He must have heard her on the stairs, because he turned in her direction. His ice-blue eyes flicked up and down her body in that disconcertingly thorough way of his. Even though she was covered head to toe in two layers of clothes—her more revealing workout gear hidden under a navy hoodie and matching knit pants—she felt suddenly exposed.

Jack gave her a silent nod, which she returned and left him to finish his conversation as she darted past him to the kitchen.

Jack had been up long enough to make and drink coffee. There was about half an inch of warm liquid in the bottom of the carafe. She tossed it and set about making a fresh pot.

She poured water into the coffeemaker, embarrassed at the way her hands shook as she spooned grounds into the filter. God, she hoped they caught whoever was messing with her soon. Being terrorized aside, she wouldn't last long with Jack in close proximity if all it took was a look from him to throw her completely off-kilter.

She heard Jack's heavy footsteps behind her as the machine started to bubble and hiss. "That was Danny, right?"

Jack nodded and reached past her to the cabinet behind her to retrieve a coffee mug. The act brought him within inches of her, close enough for her to catch his scent, all soap and shaving cream layered with the spice of his own skin. "I let him know I won't be available for any assignments until your situation is resolved."

She had to stifle the urge to bury her nose in the hollow of his throat.

He stepped back and she took a moment to pull herself together. Right. Her situation. That's what she needed to focus on, not how she was suddenly obsessed with how good Jack Brooks smelled first thing in the morning. "I can't pay your regular rates," she began, "but I can do something to offset the loss of income—"

The look Jack gave her was so frosty she was surprised the coffee didn't turn to ice crystals in the carafe. "We talked about this last night. Your safety is important to me. I don't want your fucking money."

Talia swallowed nervously. Though he tried to hide it, she could see by the way the muscle throbbed in his jaw that she'd really pissed him off. Still, she was tired of feeling like his charity case. "I know you work on contract, so if you're not working, you're not earning income. How are you supposed to pay your bills—"

"Talia," he interrupted, "you don't need to be concerned about my financial situation. I've got..." He paused and something flickered across his face.

"What?" she probed.

He was silent for several more seconds, as though trying to decide how to put it. "I've got a nice buffer saved up."

"Must be nice," Talia muttered, and went to retrieve some cream for her coffee. "But you have to understand why I don't like feeling obligated to you, financially or otherwise."

Jack set his mug down with a thud. "Why can't you get it through your head? You're not obligated for something I'm offering up without you even asking. Not everything in life is some kind of transaction."

"No one does anything out of the pure goodness of

their heart." *Not even you*, she thought silently. The memory of his mouth, hot and fierce on hers, flared to life. "People always want something in return."

His mouth tightened, and she knew he was thinking about that kiss. It was unfair, yet another cheap shot in the series she couldn't seem to keep from lobbing at Jack. Maybe if she brought it down to the only level she had known, she wouldn't experience that uncomfortable thrill every time she thought of it.

"Fine," he snapped. "You can pay me a per diem of twenty dollars if that eases your mind."

Talia rolled her eyes. "That doesn't even cover gas money—"

She snapped her mouth shut when Jack's eyes went from icy to molten hot in the space of a breath.

"Don't. Push. Me."

With his jaw clenched tight, the muscles bunching and knotting under his skin, Jack looked like he was on the verge of giving her a shake or . . . something else.

She was pretty sure he'd never hurt her, but she wasn't prepared to deal with whatever "something else" might be. Talia retreated.

Jack took his cup of coffee to the living room while Talia flipped open her laptop to check her e-mail. Reading the one legitimate message, from Rosie, and scrolling through spam took all of five minutes. She stole a glance at Jack, settled on the couch as he leafed through the paper. For all that he looked relaxed, there was, as always, an energy about him, an alertness, a readiness to jump into action at the slightest provocation.

Maybe she needed a nice professor or dentist in her life, not a former Special Forces warrior. Someone who didn't know her past. Someone who didn't radiate that kind of intensity.

She could feel it, almost like a buzz in the air. She doubted if he ever let his guard down completely, even when he slept.

Unbidden, an image of Jack came to her, his harsh features softened with sleep, his big body sprawled across a bed, the sheet in a tangle around his waist, leaving his broad, muscular chest bare. She'd never seen him shirtless. She wondered if his chest was hairy or smooth. She bet he had a six-pack...

"What?"

She jumped at the sound of Jack's voice. Oh, God, how long had he been frowning at her as she stared, slack-jawed, drool practically running down her chin? What was wrong with her? Last night she'd been terrorized by footage of her own attempted rape and murder, and now she was fantasizing about Jack's naked torso?

The DVD was the sum parts of all of her damage, all of the reasons she was too broken to be with someone right now. Maybe ever. She couldn't afford to let herself fantasize that it could be different.

And more importantly, Jack didn't deserve to be jerked around by anyone, especially not her.

She jumped up from her chair. "Did you eat yet?" She opened her refrigerator to survey the contents. "I eat a lot at the restaurant but I have enough here to do an omelet or cereal or something."

"I had some toast before you got up," he replied. "You don't need to worry about me. I'm not here to cramp your style, so just do whatever you would normally do and pretend I'm not here."

Right. Because it's so easy to ignore a drop-dead-gorgeous six-foot-four wall of muscle who had planted himself in her living room. "In that case, my usual routine is to go to Gus's for a couple hours."

"Sounds good." Jack stood from the couch and stretched, his arms so long they nearly touched the ceiling. Talia made herself a protein shake while Jack changed into workout gear, and within ten minutes they were heading out.

Normally she would have started with a cardio boxing class, but she didn't want to subject Jack to a roomful of women in leotards.

At least that's what she told herself. Really, it had nothing to do with not wanting to watch dozens of women ogle a prime specimen of man that Talia was incapable of enjoying herself. They focused on drills and sparring, and Talia noticed Jack was careful to keep his distance. No grappling holds or self-defense training today.

Despite the lingering tension between them and the lingering uneasiness from last night, the physical exertion as always calmed her down, bringing her stress level almost back to normal. And once they settled into a rhythm, trading off the focus pads and giving each other pointers on form, Talia realized it was actually fun working out with Jack. He was so much bigger, so much faster than anyone else she worked with, and she found herself enjoying the challenge.

Then there was the unexpected feeling of camaraderie as they put each other through their paces and good-naturedly razzed each other. She found herself smiling, even laughing, and Jack was too.

A warmth coursed through her that had nothing to do

with physical exertion. They were having fun, and for a few minutes they were able to forget the unfortunate events that had brought Jack back into her life and could just have a good time together.

Like buddies.

Maybe not exactly buddies, she thought, feeling her face heat as she caught Jack staring at her heaving chest about two seconds after he caught her admiring the hard muscles of his butt.

But the friendly dynamic all but disappeared when it came time to hit the showers. "Absolutely not. I'm not letting you go in there by yourself."

Talia glared up at him. There was a steam bath in that locker room with her name on it and she told Jack so. "What, are you afraid someone's going to come after me with a disposable razor? No way am I going to give up one of the few pleasures I still have in life because some asshole started sending me creepy gifts."

Jack leaned closer and Talia forced herself to stand firm. "That asshole could be here right now, just waiting for me to leave you alone."

Talia did a quick scan of the room. She recognized several women from her classes and a handful of men, regulars like her. No one who looked like they'd pose much of a threat.

"You could stand guard at the door—"

"There are other ways to get in there. There's no way." He paused and gave her a speculative look. "Unless you want me to go in there."

Though he'd done his best to put his attraction to her back under wraps, there was no missing the heat in his gaze. She swallowed hard, wondering if he was having the same thoughts of hot steam swirling around naked bodies, slick skin over rippling muscles. "Fine. I'll shower at home."

On the way back to her place, they made a quick detour to the Hyatt Executive Suites in Palo Alto to pick up Jack's stuff. Talia followed him up, her nose wrinkling at the stale air smell of the sterile room. "This is depressing," she muttered.

Jack shrugged as he emptied the dresser and closet and packed everything into a generic black wheelie bag. "It's not so bad. When I'm on assignment, I work a lot of nights, so it's not like I'm here a lot." He straightened up and surveyed the room. "But after one of these trips, I'm always happy to get back to my boat."

"You have a boat?" She didn't know why that surprised her.

His brows quirked in a puzzled frown. "No, I live on one," he said, his tone implying that she should have somehow known that. "I rent a houseboat out on Lake Union."

"I had no idea," she said. It hit home, once again, how little she really knew about him despite how big a part he'd played in her life.

He shook his head ruefully. "No, I guess you wouldn't," he said, studying her with a funny look on his face. "It's a nice place, with a second-floor deck that looks right out over the city. I'd like to show you sometime."

There was a sudden charge in the tiny efficiency suite as Talia imagined Jack taking her hand to lead her onto his houseboat, taking her up to the deck to enjoy a glass of wine and the view.

And then...

It was like a metal door slammed shut in her brain. As it always did when she tried to imagine what came after. She didn't want to relive it, the humiliation, the pain that went beyond the physical.

Of course, logically she knew it would be different with Jack, but since she couldn't remember what different might feel like, she wasn't even capable of fantasizing about it.

"I don't imagine I'll get back up to Seattle any time soon. Not with Margaret Grayson-Maxwell running around."

Jack's mouth tightened. "She doesn't have any power over you or Rosie. If you want to come back, I can make it work for you—"

Talia cut him off. "I appreciate the offer, but I think the wounds are still a little too fresh for me to go back." She turned and walked to the window that looked out over a side street. "Besides, with Rosie in school here, it's not like I have anything or anyone to go back to."

Jack was silent a few seconds. Finally he said, "No, I don't guess you do."

But when they got back to her house and she was standing under the hot spray of her own shower, she couldn't stop thinking about what it might be like to visit Jack on his houseboat, for no other reason than they wanted to see each other. No dark past, no memories of what she'd done and what had been done to her.

A lovely fantasy, she thought as she dressed, put on makeup, and dried her hair. Too bad it was about as likely to happen as Sarah Palin retreating to a quiet life out of the spotlight.

She trotted down the stairs, wondering how she was going to kill another two hours in close quarters with Jack before it was time to go to work. She whipped around the corner to the kitchen and, distracted, didn't see the wall of tanned skin and muscle until she was nose to chest with it.

Talk about a fantasy. She'd been speculating just a few hours ago what Jack might look like without his shirt. Now her mouth went dry as she was mere inches away from the reality, a reality that was leaps and bounds better than anything she could have imagined.

He was as muscular as she imagined, the muscles of his chest and abs chiseled from granite as they bunched and shifted. There was not an ounce of fat visible under a layer of tanned, tight skin.

And Jack was no waxed-up metrosexual either, what with his chest dusted with a light coat of dark hair that narrowed into a silky-looking stripe that bisected his belly and disappeared beneath the waistband of the pants that hung from his narrow hips. Her fingers tingled, itching to trace that happy trail to see if it was as soft as it looked, to feel that tanned, smooth skin.

He wasn't without flaw, though. Scars of varying size and shape scattered his torso. Up under his right shoulder was a pucker of flesh that looked like it might have been a bullet wound. Those perfect abs were marred by a neat white line about six inches long where it looked like he might have had surgery. The left side of his rib cage was peppered with pale spots, which, as she looked closer, were scars left by small divots in his skin.

"Those are from when an IED went off next to me. The shrapnel sprayed me all up and down my left side." He twisted so she could see the path the divots made up his side and the back of his shoulder, all the way up to his neck until they disappeared beneath his thick, dark hair.

As she looked down, the white flecks dipped beneath his waistband. "Tore up my leg pretty good. Looked like hamburger from my hip to right above my knee."

Her hand reached out, and before she could stop herself, her fingers were tracing the white flecks dotting his rib cage. As her fingers made contact, Jack flinched.

Talia jerked her hand away and choked out an apology. "They don't still hurt, do they?" she asked stupidly.

"No. Just look a little nasty."

On the contrary, she wanted to tell him, the scars actually made him even hotter, if that was possible, the evidence of the wounds he'd survived adding another layer of credibility to his air of toughness, his attitude that said he could take on the world and come out the victor.

Mortified at having been caught staring dumbly for the second time in one day, Talia had to pry her tongue from the roof of her mouth. "I see a lot worse every time I get naked in front of a mirror."

Heat flared in his eyes, letting her know in no uncertain terms that her scars wouldn't be a deterrent if he ever got her naked.

But the scars on the inside were the ones she feared she'd never overcome.

—⁓—

He couldn't get to her.

Gene's hands shook as they curled around the steering wheel. His car had been parked across the street for hours now. He'd followed her all day, starting at the boxing gym. He wasn't going to grab her in broad daylight—he wasn't that stupid—but he wanted to see her nonetheless.

And her fucking gorilla hadn't left her side. Even when she went to use the bathroom, he wouldn't allow her to go to the locker room but made her use the single uni-sex bathroom whose entrance he guarded like a Roman centurion.

Gene had been forced to take a break for several hours in the middle of the day to go to the lab where he was working on his research to support his dissertation. There were also papers to grade for the undergrad classes he taught.

And, of course, there were office hours with Rosario Vega, an appointment he wouldn't have missed if someone held a gun to his head. She was so young, so sweet, so...fresh.

The way she looked at him with stars in her eyes and gushed about how smart he was. He didn't kid himself that she was actually attracted to him. He'd seen her around with that loser she dated.

You are a loser. You are nothing.

Yes, she had the hots for a fucking leech who treated her like garbage. It was her only flaw, but he couldn't fault her. How could she not know better than to cheapen her-self after she was raised by that whore of a sister?

But the way she looked at him, with unadulterated admiration for his superior brain, it was like a breath of fresh air. She was even coming to appreciate his sense of humor. They were becoming not just teacher and student, but friends.

Which would make it that much easier to use Rosie to get to her sister.

And he would need all the help he could get.

Perhaps he had gone too far in sending her the DVD.

He'd expected her to be scared. But he hadn't foreseen the hiring of a full-time bodyguard, a huge brick wall of a man who accompanied her everywhere—the gym, work, and now home. Gene had been watching the house for hours and the gorilla showed no signs of leaving.

No matter how ready he was, he couldn't get to her tonight. The knowledge made him feel like a thousand spiders were crawling over his skin. The gorilla was smart, highly trained, and hypervigilant. There was no easy way past him.

Anything worth having was worth waiting for, he reminded himself.

In the meantime, he'd released Number 4 just this morning. The police should be aware of her soon, if they weren't already.

He wondered if the police would find her unconscious form before the drugs wore off like the other girls, or if she'd come to in the open space preserve where he'd dumped her. He'd given her a little extra—she was a fighter and he didn't want her waking up and alerting anyone until he was long gone.

He started the car and pulled away from the curb across from Talia's house. There was nothing more to be done with Talia tonight.

He thought of Number 4, struggling under him as blood ran down her back and sides. Felt the surge build up inside him as he envisioned the perfection of the cuts.

He couldn't have Talia, but he could have another.

He would take advantage of this opportunity to run through the process one last time. To fine-tune every step so everything went exactly the way he wanted.

Chapter 10

Though the situation wasn't exactly comfortable, by the morning of the third day, Jack and Talia had settled into something of a routine. Jack, always an early riser, was usually up at least an hour before Talia regardless of how late they stayed up after Talia got off work.

He spent the time catching up on e-mails and phone calls to Danny, who was also a crack-of-dawn riser. Even though Jack wasn't on so-called active duty right now, he could add some value in strategizing how to approach certain clients' unique needs.

This morning Danny wanted his opinion on the best way to ferret out a spy in a case of suspected industrial espionage at a local biotech company. Before he hung up, Danny said, "You're coming Saturday, right?"

Jack's mind drew a blank. He usually had no problem committing his schedule to memory, but lately his close proximity to Talia was scrambling his brain so much he was going to have to work harder to keep his shit together.

"Jesus, I know you're walking around with most of your blood in your dick, but don't tell me you forgot my father's engagement party?"

Right. Now he remembered. After years of living like

a monk as he searched the world for his missing wife, Joe Taggart and his sons had finally discovered that Anna Taggart had been dead for nearly two decades. Finally able to move on, Joe had found love again in the arms of a woman who had worked with Gemini to find her missing daughter.

Jack squeezed his eyes shut. "I don't think so, Danny. Talia works Saturdays and I can't leave her alone—"

"Bring her. Tell her to take the night off."

"I don't know if it's such a good idea—"

"Goddamn it, Jack, you're one of my best friends and you've known my dad for years. You're really going to let us down for some damaged goods who's never going to fuck you—"

"Don't you fucking talk about her like that," Jack shouted. If Danny had been in front of him, Jack would have had his hands around his throat. "I know we go way back, and you're worried about me getting pulled into another bad situation. But I care about Talia and I don't want to see her hurt, especially by my so-called friends."

He cringed at Danny's satisfied chuckle. Danny loved nothing better than to find a person's weak spot and give it a good poke. "Bring her Saturday. Let her prove to me she's worth the trouble. I promise I'll be nice."

"I swear to God if you so much as look at her sideways, I'll put your ass in a sling."

"You are such a goner."

Jack hung up, a lump of dread in his stomach as he realized his friend was probably right. He was a goner, and the last few days had only rammed the truth home.

Why the hell did he do this to himself? Why couldn't

he just find some nice, normal girl who didn't need saving? Or at least someone capable of overcoming her dysfunction enough to have a semi-normal relationship?

Although, Jack reflected, given his history, he didn't know if he'd recognize a normal relationship if it came up and bit him in the ass.

So yeah, here he was again, charging in like a superhero for a woman who wouldn't or couldn't give him what he wanted. And it was getting worse the more time he spent with her.

Yeah, his physical reaction to her after seeing her for the first time in nearly two years had hit him like a sucker punch. But the more time he spent with her, the more he realized he really liked being around her.

Even now, though it was bordering on torture to have to be so close to her and not lay a finger on her, he was anticipating the moment when she'd emerge from her room and walk down the stairs.

A door opened and closed upstairs and his heart gave an extra hard thud against his ribs. As he heard her footsteps on the stairs, he poured her a cup of coffee and added milk. She walked into the kitchen and accepted the cup with a smile.

"You're spoiling me," she said, and took a long drink. "I could really get used to having you around."

So could I, Jack thought with a funny twist in his chest. Take away the creep who was forcing Talia to relive her past trauma, and they were like any other couple. It was way too easy for him to imagine days like the last few—wake up to chat over a cup of coffee, go work out, run errands, work, followed by a good-natured squabble over whether to watch a documentary on the History Channel or another episode of *Top Chef* before heading off to bed—stretching endlessly into the future.

Okay, to be fair, if he had his way, he'd skip the TV and go straight to bed. With Talia. Where they could argue over who got to be on top before he had her until they were both too weak to move.

But yeah, that wasn't happening. "So far Cole has no leads on how the recording got leaked, so you're stuck with me for now."

Talia didn't say anything, but her full lips curved into a little smile that hit him square in the gut. The smile was gone in an instant and she once again turned serious. "It has to be someone from David's organization. No one else could possibly know about the necklace or the flowers. Someone who would have had access to Nate's computer files...." She shuddered a little.

Jack leaned one hip on the kitchen counter and watched her move about the kitchen preparing her customary preworkout smoothie. She grabbed a container of yogurt from the refrigerator and looked at him with a raised eyebrow. At his nod, she grabbed another and set about making smoothies for two.

Suddenly his brain flashed back to the afternoon, roughly two and a half years ago, when he'd showed up at Club One for his first day of work as the new head of security. The first time he'd ever laid eyes on Talia Vega. She'd been dressed in black, a dress that covered her from neck to knee yet did nothing to hide a siren's body that would have tempted the pope to sin.

She'd raked him up and down with her dark, heavily made-up eyes, her red, painted lips curled into a parody of a smile. "So you're the one they sent over to keep an eye on things? Let's hope your brain is bigger than your biceps."

If someone had told him then that he'd be standing in a kitchen with that same woman while she made him a smoothie, Jack would have thought it portended the coming of the apocalypse.

"That makes the most sense, but it will be tough. After Nate was killed, Maxwell nuked any and all records of anyone associated with him. It will be difficult to track everyone down. I'm trying to find the guy who hooked me up with the security company that got me the gig at Club One, to see if he knows what any of the rest of the crew are doing, but he's dropped off the map."

Talia filled two glasses with the yogurt and fruit-protein-powder concoction and handed him one. "How did you ever end up with that bunch of losers anyway? It's obvious you had connections—wasn't Danny's company established by then? If you were going to go into security, why sign on with a bunch of criminals?"

There were a lot of reasons, but the last thing he wanted to do was start unloading his tragic baggage on what had started out as not a terrible morning.

"I mean, I know how I ended up there," Talia continued, "because I was stupid enough to fall for Maxwell and think he was going to give me a shiny new life in the suburbs, but I would think that you'd be a hell of a lot smarter than me."

Jack's jaw tightened. At the time, smart had nothing to do with it. He hadn't given a shit about the work, himself, or much of anything else. However, he'd had the good sense to realize if he'd taken Danny up on his offer of a spot at Gemini Securities, he probably would have fucked it up in the state he was in. In which case he would have been out a job and, more importantly, minus a friend.

"It seemed like a good fit at the time," he said.

She looked at him, one slim dark eyebrow cocked in a look that was reminiscent of the Talia he'd met at the club, a look that said he was full of shit and wasn't fooling her for a second.

Realizing she wasn't getting any answers out of him today, she shrugged and finished her drink. "What about Margaret? All of this started when she got out."

Jack nodded. "You'd think she'd want to keep her nose clean. But—"

"She's a stone-cold bitch and I wouldn't put it past her," Talia interjected. "Do you know she used to send me brochures about the group home Rosie would go to if I lost custody? As if I needed to be reminded what was at stake if I tried to screw them over." She set her empty glass down, the glass rattling on the countertop, and looked at him. Her eyes dark and troubled. "What if she hurts Rosie? She knows that's the best way to get to me—"

Jack wanted to pull her into his arms and reassure her, but he settled for taking her hands in his. Her hands were cold. Jack brushed his thumbs over the backs of them. "Don't get ahead of yourself. So far, everything is targeted at you, and we don't even know if Margaret's behind the threats. But it's a good theory, which is why I'm having Toni take a look at Margaret's financial activity and see if we can connect her with anyone who might have been on David's payroll in the past."

Jack had assured her that Toni, Ethan's wife, and Gemini's resident computer whiz, would be able to follow any cybertrail Margaret might have left. "Did you find anything?" Talia asked.

"Not yet," Jack said, reluctantly dropping his hands before they found their way up her bare, silky forearms and up over her shoulders to drag her against him. "It's a lot of data to sift through, so it might take a while. In the meantime, I can ask someone at Gemini to keep an eye on her."

Talia looked up at him as though he were crazy. "I know that for whatever reason, you've picked up some sort of superhero complex where you're willing to drop everything to hang with me twenty-four-seven, but I doubt anyone else at Gemini is going to make do with a twenty-dollar-a-day stipend out of the pure goodness of his heart."

True, Jack knew. But he knew it would be easy enough for him to hire someone himself—maybe one of the newer guys they'd just hired who weren't as busy yet—and pay them on the side while he let Talia think they were willing to accept charity wages.

"And that being the case, there's no way in hell I can afford them and tuition too."

Jack could. In fact, he could afford to pay for round-the-clock security for Rosie, her undergraduate and graduate degree from Stanford if she wanted it, and still have plenty of money to retire in luxury tomorrow if he wanted to.

He'd barely touched a dime of the trust he'd inherited from his grandfather—not for himself, anyway. He didn't want to touch a penny from the mean old bastard who'd in turn created the mean bastard who had been Jack's father. But he hadn't hesitated to use it to help Talia, and others, over the years.

A fact he sensed she wouldn't appreciate if she knew. Just to test the waters, he said, "I get paid well, and I've saved up a fair chunk of my paychecks the past few years. I could—"

"No, absolutely not," Talia said, her cheeks flushed, mouth tight. "I can take care of us now, financially anyway. If it comes down to it, I'll pull Rosie out of school and use the money to pay for security, but right now I'm not going to mess up her life just because some asshole wants to mess with me."

With that, she strode past him and trotted upstairs, then trotted back down a few seconds later with her gym bag in tow. "You ready to go? I need to hit the grocery store before I go to the restaurant tonight."

Jack grabbed his own bag and followed her through the door that connected her kitchen to her garage. "Speaking of work," he said, "you need to ask Susie if you can take Saturday night off."

Talia froze, her hand halfway to her door. "I do? Why?"

"Because Joe Taggart's engagement party is that night, and I promised Danny I'd be there."

She shook her head. "I don't want to go to a party."

"Well, I need to be there, and since I'm not leaving you alone, unless we catch the asshole who sent you that stuff before Saturday, you're going too."

She shook her head again, the expression on her face making her almost look scared. "I don't think it's such a good idea."

Jack's temper flared. "Danny's one of my best friends, and I've known his family for over fifteen years. You can't take one night off?"

He saw her wince and immediately regretted his harsh tone. "I'm sorry—"

She held up her hand, cutting him off. "No, I'm sorry.

You're right. After everything you've done for me and Rosie, it shouldn't be a big deal for me to switch my work schedule around."

"Thanks," he said as they settled into the car. "But will you promise to try to look a little happier when we go?"

Her eyes flicked to him. "I promise." She was silent as he opened the garage door and backed her Honda out of the garage. "It's just—"

"What?" he asked when she cut herself off. He glanced over and saw that she was biting on her lower lip in a way that made him want to drag his tongue across the plump, pink surface.

She shook her head. "I don't think Danny likes me. And I'll feel weird, being there with you, knowing he doesn't want me there."

How to put this politely. "No offense, but Danny doesn't care if you're there as long as I'm there. And I made him promise he'd be nice."

Talia gave a soft chuckle. "I'll believe that when I see it." She was silent a few more blocks, then said softly, "I don't want to be an imposition to anyone."

Jack shook his head. "It won't be an imposition. In fact, you'll be doing me a favor, keeping the wives from trying to hook me up with every single friend they have."

"Glad I can be somewhat useful," she muttered. He half listened as she pulled out her phone and called Jennie, another one of the bartenders, to trade her Saturday shift for Jennie's regular Tuesday slot. "Okay, we're cool," she said as she hung up. "What am I supposed to wear?"

He shrugged. "Clothes?"

She let out a frustrated sigh. "Did Danny say like, casual, cocktail, black tie?"

"He didn't say anything about clothes. It's a barbecue in their backyard, so I doubt it's fancy. And it's California. It's like Seattle. No one dresses up."

"Yeah, but doesn't Danny's dad live in Atherton?"

"So?" He didn't see what the location had to do with it.

"Guys are so lame," Talia huffed. "I haven't hung around that many crazy wealthy people, and I'm sure you haven't either..."

Don't be so sure of that.

"But," she continued, unaware she was sitting next to someone who came from a fortune that totaled well into the nine digits, "from what I've seen, there will be women there carrying purses that cost more than my car."

"Wait, how did we get from purses to cars?"

"You know what I mean," she said.

He really didn't. Still, he tried to think back to when his parents used to host backyard pool parties when he was a kid. *Soirees* his mother used to call them, whatever the hell that meant. All he knew was that while fifty or so people were milling around the pool deck eating weird things off crackers and sipping drinks, his father would be on his best behavior. He'd put on a big show of being the loving family man, hugging his wife, bragging to anyone who would listen about how well Jack was doing in football and how Lizzy was taking advanced algebra as a seventh grader.

Of course, later, after the last guest had departed, his father, fueled by single malt, would go to town on all of them, racking up the list of the ways they'd all embarrassed him in front of his friends and colleagues.

Jack had learned early that the party was never over until one of them had a black eye or a cracked rib.

He shook off the ugly memories and tried to remember

what his mother and the other women had worn at those "casual" backyard get-togethers.

"How about a sundress or something?" Come to think of it, he wouldn't mind seeing Talia's legs on display.

Talia rolled her eyes. "You're useless. I'll ask Susie."

The rest of the day was business as usual, a rough workout followed by food and errands. They ran into Susie at Gus's gym, and Talia got her wardrobe consultation and called Rosie to go shopping with them the following afternoon.

Jack reminded Susie they would be at the restaurant a couple hours before they opened for dinner so he could install the upgrades to the security system. They still weren't sure if whoever had slipped the DVD into Talia's purse had done it at the restaurant, but Jack wasn't taking any chances.

If the sick fuck who was messing with her tried anything at Suzette's, he would catch it on video.

Jack was mounting a tiny surveillance camera in a light fixture outside the kitchen door when Talia came over, clutching her phone in her hand, her face pale.

"What?" he asked as he climbed off the stepladder.

"I just got a call from Detective Nolan of the Redwood City PD. He wants to talk to me about the DVD of my attack."

—⁂—

Jack's brows knit together at the bridge of his nose. "You're out of his jurisdiction."

Talia nodded and tried to swallow back the anxious knot that had settled at the base of her throat. "He thinks it may be relevant to a case he's working on. He wouldn't give me any more details than that, but he'll be here in fifteen minutes, so I guess we'll find out soon enough."

Talia left Jack to his work and went back to the bar, where she was using the extra time to do a thorough check of all the stock and make sure everything was set for Jennie to cover her shift on Saturday.

Her mind was spinning with questions. Her attacker was dead, shot three times, the last one a head shot, by Cole Williams. What could her near rape and murder at the hands of Nate Brewster have to do with anything? Distracted, she nearly cut off the tip of her index finger when she was prepping the lemons.

She was stacking the glasses behind the bar when she caught a shadow of movement in the corner of her eye. She turned around to see a tall man a couple years older than her with chiseled features and light brown hair cut in a short, no-nonsense style. He wore a dark suit that wasn't overly expensive but that fit his rangy, broad-shouldered frame nicely.

"Talia Vega?" he asked.

She nodded.

"I'm Detective Nolan." He flashed his badge and offered his hand to shake. He smiled slightly, showing white teeth and making his dark eyes crinkle at the corners. He was good-looking, Talia decided, though the touch of his calloused palm against hers didn't make her stomach do any back handsprings. "Thanks for taking the time to talk to me."

Talia shrugged as she released his hand. "Thanks for not making me come to you."

Jack, who must have had ESP because there was no

way he could have heard Detective Nolan come in, strode through the archway in the wall that divided the bar and the main dining room.

"You're the cop?" Jack said as he gave Detective Nolan an assessing stare.

"Detective Nolan," he replied, giving Jack an equally hard look. "You're a friend of Miss Vega's?"

"More like a human guard dog," Talia muttered, earning her another half smile from the detective.

"Jack Brooks." His eyes narrowed on the detective's smile as he strode forward and offered his hand. She could see the muscles shift and bunch as he gripped the detective's hand. "I take Talia's safety *very* seriously." *So don't fuck anything up.* He didn't have to say it out loud. The look in those ice-blue eyes said it all.

Detective Nolan didn't flinch. "Right. So let's get down to business." He slipped his hand from Jack's grip and did a quick scan of the bar and adjoining dining room. Though the restaurant wasn't opening for another hour, several employees were moving around doing prep work for dinner service. Nolan turned to Talia. "Is there someplace private we can talk?"

Talia nodded and led him back to Susie's office, not surprised when Jack followed.

Susie, whose blue eyes widened at first sight of the handsome cop, was more than willing to give up her office for the meeting. "And feel free to stay for dinner on me, uh, on the house," she said with a blush. Despite the macabre circumstances, Talia couldn't stifle a grin. In the months she'd worked here, she'd seen her friend flirt with dozens of men, but she'd never seen her so flustered.

Nolan, for his part, looked like he'd been hit on the

head with a bat as he said, "Sure. That would be nice." His infatuated gaze followed Susie as she rose from her desk.

As she rounded the desk, Susie knocked into the corner because she was watching Nolan instead of where she was going. She flushed and a giggle more suited to a thirteen-year-old burst from her mouth. "So, I'll just leave you to it."

She left, closing the door behind her. Nolan stared at it for several beats before shaking his head as though to clear it. He turned back to Talia, his dark eyes still looking a little dazed. Talia wasn't surprised. Susie had that effect on people. What did surprise her, though, was her friend's equally intense response.

"So you said you think the DVD I received could be related to a case you're working on?" Talia prodded.

The last of the haze cleared from Nolan's expression. His face grave, he darted a quick look at Jack.

"He stays," Talia said before Jack could even respond. "He knows about everything that's happened. He was there when..." She cleared her throat around the tightness that choked off her words. "He pulled me out of that hole. He saved my life."

She didn't see Jack move closer, but she felt him come up behind her. Not close enough to touch, but close enough for her to feel his warmth, his solid presence at her back. The feel of him was enough to ease her tension a degree. Though it rankled her to feel so dependent on him, she knew that no matter what Nolan was about to tell her, with Jack at her side she'd somehow get through it.

"Recently there have been attacks on several women. So far they've all occurred in Redwood City and Menlo Park," he said, referring to the two towns immediately north of Palo Alto. "The victims are kidnapped, held in an unknown location for several days, and then they are repeatedly sexually assaulted. He then drugs them and dumps them, unconscious."

Acid burned in Talia's stomach. "I've been following the story on the news. I have a younger sister at Stanford. I told her to be careful."

"What does this have to do with Talia?" Jack asked, his voice tight.

Nolan's mouth pulled tight. "Do you have any idea who would have sent you that DVD?"

Talia shook her head. "Our best guess is that it's someone from Seattle, someone connected to David Maxwell or perhaps his wife, but that leaves dozens of possibilities. But I don't understand how there could be any connection to the attacks here."

Nolan folded his arms over his chest and leaned back against the door. He lowered his eyes to the floor as though he were mulling something over. Finally he gave a heavy sigh and looked at them from under arched brows. "Look, what I'm about to tell you is highly confidential, details we're purposely keeping out of the media. If it gets out that I gave this information to anyone outside the investigation, my ass will be in a sling. Got it?"

"We'll keep it strictly confidential," Jack said.

Talia nodded vigorously in agreement, though she had a sick feeling in her stomach that the details Nolan was going to reveal weren't going to make her feel any better.

"Our perp doesn't just rape the girls. He mutilates them too."

"Mutilates how?" Talia choked out through lips gone bone-dry.

He slipped the folder he was carrying out from under

his arm and moved to place it on the desk. But he didn't open it. "Burns them with cigarettes, cuts them. Mostly on the back, but sometimes on the stomach and breasts too."

Talia swallowed back the bile rising in her throat.

"We found the latest victim two days ago. She'd been dumped in a clearing in Foothills Park. Like the first three victims, she was heavily drugged. Unfortunately, unlike the other victims, she hasn't regained consciousness yet. Doctors are afraid the overdose may have caused permanent brain damage.

"One of the first officers on the scene was Martinez, who you may remember?"

Talia nodded. "He came the night I found the DVD. He's the one who brought it in."

"When he found the victim, he noticed the cigarette burns and said the placement of the cuts looked very familiar."

Talia could feel Jack tense behind her, and she instinctively took a step back, needing his warmth to counteract the chill that coursed through her, making her skin prickle with goose bumps and her fingers tremble.

Nolan reached for the folder, then hesitated. "These are pretty graphic."

Talia nodded. "Is it worse than what I experienced myself?"

Nolan flipped open the folder, revealing the first photo. It was a close-up of the victim's back. Two diagonal slashes that went from the top of the shoulder to the opposite hip, meeting in the middle in a perfect X.

The matching scars on Talia's back burned under her shirt.

Nolan flipped the picture over, revealing the one underneath. The victim was on her back now, her face invisible, as the picture was from the neck down. Her breasts were bare, the pale skin mottled with bruises. And on the right one, a few inches below the nipple, was a circular mark, angry and red, surrounded by black.

"Is that a cigarette burn?"

Jack's voice sounded like it was coming from the bottom of a barrel. Talia's vision tunneled, focused on another mark. This one was in the center of her torso, right underneath her breastbone.

The exact same spot where Nate's knife had plunged into Talia's body. Her hand went to the spot on her own body, and as she stood in Susie's tiny office, it was like she could feel the cold sting of the blade as it penetrated skin and muscle.

Her knees turned to water and she would have crumpled had it not been for the strong forearm that caught her around the waist.

"That's enough." She heard Jack's voice over the roar in her head as he guided her carefully to the chair behind the desk.

Talia hung her head between her knees until the buzzing faded. She sat up and looked at Jack, who had gone as pale as she felt. "It's like he's using it as a blueprint," she whispered.

Nolan nodded. "At first, we didn't realize it was a pattern. In each of the previous victims there was only one long, clean cut, and the one that drew from the right shoulder was shorter, more ragged. And this fourth victim was the only one to be cut under the sternum."

"But he didn't stab her," Jack said. "He just marked her. I wonder what that's about."

"We have no idea," Nolan said grimly. "So far, we can't get much information from the victims. All they remember is a stick in the neck—he injects them with something, GHB or Rohypnol—and then he keeps them, blindfolded and gagged. Usually for two to three days, but this latest victim was missing just shy of a week."

"Why?" Talia asked, futilely she knew. "Why would he try to imitate what Nate did to me?"

Nolan didn't answer. There was nothing to say.

He left, with a promise to keep them apprised of any leads, and she and Jack promised to let him know directly about any other incidents or harassment she experienced. She heard the door close behind him and looked up, catching Jack's stare.

His blue eyes were dark and troubled under his wrinkled brow, staring at her without really seeing.

Anger, helpless and bitter, rose in her chest. She knew exactly what he was thinking and she hated it. Hated that whoever was doing this had the power to rip her world out from under her at his whim. Hated that she had once been weak and stupid enough to put herself in a position where she'd end up in that hole.

Hated that no matter what happened between them, part of Jack would never stop seeing her as she'd been in that moment when he pulled her bleeding and naked from Nate's torture chamber.

"Stop looking at me like that!" she snarled, heaving herself out of the chair.

Jack's head snapped back. "Like what?"

"Like I'm some victim. Like I'm pitiful!"

"I don't think you're pitiful—"

"You think I'm weak, and stupid, and that I need you

to take care of me." All of which was true, but she hated having him see it. Angry tears burned her eyes.

His jaw clenched tight; his face was as hard as granite. "I feel a lot of things for you, Talia, but pity isn't one of them."

She stormed past him, out to the bar. The restaurant still hadn't opened for dinner service yet, but Detective Nolan was huddled with Susie at the end of the bar, sipping a bottle of microbrew while she cradled a glass of chardonnay. Like he didn't have a goddamn care in the world. Like he hadn't just come in with a wrecking ball and dealt the deathblow to her already crumbling sense of safety and security.

Somehow she made it through the rest of the night. Jack urged her to take the night off, but she snapped that since she was already giving up her most lucrative shift of the week for his stupid party, she couldn't let a little thing like a serial rapist keep her from working tonight.

With the bar rapidly filling up, it was easy to distract herself from Jack's grim stare and the thought that her tormenter could be at Suzette's and she would have no idea.

Or he could be somewhere with another faceless victim, keeping her blindfolded, helpless, as he tortured her.

She cast a nervous glance around the bar. Given the two choices, she prayed the monster was here.

Chapter 11

*T*he smell of blood was everywhere. Dark and meaty, metallic, noticeable even here, through the closed front door of the little bungalow he'd helped Gina rent. He didn't want to go in, but his hand reached out, twisting the doorknob against his will.

The late afternoon sun poured through the open shades, casting long shadows across the worn carpet of the living room. A breeze blew through the screen door, carrying the scent of apple blossoms from the tree out front.

A large form was slumped in the corner. A man, dressed in a T-shirt and shorts, half of his face blown away.

His heart pounded in his chest as he walked down the hall to the bedrooms. He pushed open the door on the right. There was another body here on the floor. But smaller, so much smaller than the one in the front room. The boy was on his stomach, his sturdy legs sticking out from the legs of his shorts, bare feet tipped with round little toes.

He looked like he'd collapsed into a nap where he was playing, as he'd done so many times over a puzzle or a pile of LEGOs.

Except the crimson stain on his shirt and the match-

ing one under him on the rug made it clear Toby wasn't taking a nap.

"Nooooooo!!!" But his cry was muffled and strange, his lips rubbery like they couldn't form the denial. Why? Why this sweet boy who loved to run in the grass and ride his bike?

He moved down the hallway, the sense of dread growing until it threatened to consume him. He knew what he would find, but he had to see for himself. See the horror he hadn't been able to prevent no matter how hard he tried.

It felt like he was walking in quicksand, but finally he made it to the end of the hall. Last door on the left. He knew where the master bedroom was even though he'd never been inside, no matter what Troy had thought.

The door was open, and Gina was there. Lying on her back, her blond hair spread out like a halo. Her sprawled legs were bare, their long lines revealed by the shorts at midthigh. Her eyes were open, as was her mouth, her face frozen forever in a look of pain and shock, as though even at the end she couldn't believe Troy had come back and pumped four shots straight into her chest.

One he'd saved for Toby. The last for himself.

"Oh, God." He crumpled to his knees at the foot of the bed, laid his hand on her cold foot as though he could somehow bring her comfort.

He'd failed. Goddamn it, he'd failed again.

"Jack."

He looked up, shock pouring through him. "Gina?"

But it wasn't Gina. It was Talia. She was wearing a white shirt and the blood was gone. She was sitting up, her dark eyes open. Accusing.

"You can't save me, Jack. You can't save any of us."

As he watched, a tiny pinprick of red formed on the front of her shirt. She shuddered and gasped as though in pain, and the stain grew until it was soaking her hands. Desperate, he grabbed at sheets, pillows, anything to stop the flow of red gushing from her body, soaking his hands and arms.

"You can't, Jack. You can't save me."

"NO!" he shouted. "I won't let him hurt you. I won't let him hurt you this time."

"Jack! Jack! JACK!"

He jolted awake, shaking and sweating like a racehorse. He was on his knees, hovered over the bed. He heard a rustling sound.

"Jack! Wake the hell up." He winced and jerked back as a small fist connected with the side of his face.

He reached up and snapped on the lamp and realized he had Talia pinned to the bed and he had a pillow pressed against her stomach.

—⁓—

The first screams had jerked Talia from sleep. She'd lain in bed for several seconds, frozen with fear. Was Jack being attacked? She grabbed her Taser from the nightstand and crept down the hall. If there was an intruder, Jack would want her to get the hell out, but she couldn't just hide like a coward if there was something she could do to help.

The incoherent cries got louder as she went down the stairs, and she quickly realized they weren't noises made in the heat of combat but those of someone in the throes of a nightmare. She flicked on the hall light, and when she opened Jack's door, she saw that he was thrashing around, groaning.

"Jack?" she called. He turned toward her but didn't wake up. She came closer, put her hand on his shoulder, and gave him a little shake. "Jack, wake up."

Without warning, he reached out and grabbed her, and the next thing she knew, she was pinned under two hundred and twenty pounds of muscle clad only in a pair of boxer shorts. She knew Jack, awake, would cut off his own hand before he hurt her, but in the state he was in now she wasn't taking any chances.

She struggled, yelling his name as she landed whatever blows she could on his arms and back and tried to buck him off of her. But he was too big, too strong.

She watched as he grabbed a pillow. Oh, God, was he going to kill her in his sleep? Was he having some god-awful PTSD flashback like Owen on *Grey's Anatomy*?

But instead of covering her face with the pillow, he shoved it against her abdomen, groaning and muttering something that sounded like her name and "no, won't let you."

She yelled his name, louder this time, and his eyes flickered. "Wake up!" she yelled, emphasizing her point with a punch.

His body jerked, and he froze for a second, trying to get his bearings. Still not letting her up, he reached out and flicked on the bedside lamp. His eyes were open, but they still looked foggy, confused, as though he wasn't quite sure where he was.

"Jack? Are you all right? Can you let me up?"

He didn't answer but threw the pillow across the room and without so much as a word yanked her tank top up her stomach. He would have ripped it off her if she hadn't grabbed the hem with both hands.

Panic surged through her. God, please not this, not Jack.

It took her a moment to realize Jack wasn't trying rip her clothes off. Instead, he had his hand on her stomach, his index finger tracing the scar under her sternum as he whispered, "No blood. You're okay. There's no blood."

Talia stopped struggling and covered Jack's big hand with her own. "Of course there's no blood," she said softly. "I'm okay now."

His gaze snapped to her face, and she recognized the moment he became fully aware of what was happening. His eyes widened and he scrambled back. "Jesus, I'm sorry. I didn't hurt you? I didn't mean to hurt you."

He was awake but strung tight as a wire, his muscles twitching under tawny skin that glistened with a layer of sweat. He swung his legs over the side of the bed and rested his head in his hands.

Talia pushed herself up to sit next to him and laid a tentative hand on his shoulder. "I'm okay. You didn't hurt me."

"Bet I fucking scared the shit out of you, though. Jesus, I'm sorry—"

"You startled me, that's for sure." Her hand moved unconsciously up and down his back, trying to soothe him. "But I know how it is. I know how bad the dreams can get. I don't think I got a peaceful night's sleep for the first year after I was attacked."

"I haven't had one this bad in a while," he said. "You were bleeding, so much blood, and you kept telling me I couldn't save you. And she—" He snapped his mouth closed. "You were dying."

Her heart twisted at the sound of his voice, like the words were being ripped from his chest.

He turned to her, his eyes blazing in the shadows cast by the small lamp. "I know you don't want me to think of you that way—"

She shook her head and her hand stilled on his back. "I was upset. I shouldn't have taken it out on you—"

"But I can't help it," he continued as though she hadn't spoken. "I failed, and you almost died. And I don't want to remember but it fucking haunts me. What if I can't save you next time?"

She wanted to say there wouldn't be a next time, but after what Detective Nolan had revealed tonight, Talia knew she'd have to be a fool to believe that. So she sat silently, stroking the sweat-slick skin of Jack's back until his heart slowed enough that it didn't feel like it was going to jump into her hand and his breathing slowed to something approaching normal.

It was a subtle shift, but Talia could feel it the second the last dregs of the nightmare slipped away. Jack turned to her, his gaze raking her up and down, taking in her thin tank top that left her arms, shoulders, and a wide expanse of her chest bare. Glowing with heat so intense she felt it sizzle on her bare skin.

The air in the guest room was charged with electricity. She snatched her hand from his back as though it burned her, suddenly intensely aware that he was wearing nothing but boxers. His muscles coiled with tension, his fingers curling into fists as though it took a physical effort not to touch her.

A battle he lost. Talia's mouth went dry as he reached up with one big hand, slowly, carefully, as though she were a wild animal he didn't want to scare. The brush of his calloused fingers against her cheek sent a wicked shiver down her spine. She sat there, frozen, as his thumb traced across her bottom lip.

"What I wouldn't do for you..." he whispered, his eyes dark and stormy. He slid his hand into her hair and leaned close enough for her to feel the heat of his breath across her cheek.

Blood roared in her ears, and her heart pounded against her ribs as her lips tingled in anticipation.

To her shock, he dropped his hand and leaned back. "You better go, because I'm about two seconds away from doing something I know you don't want me to do."

Talia was motionless for several seconds, her fingers clutching the edge of the mattress as every muscle in her body coiled tight. What exactly would he do? What if she did want it?

The images flashed in her brain, naked skin against skin, tangled limbs, mouths and hands and fingers exploring.

The jolt of heat that shot through her was so powerful, beyond anything she'd ever experienced, stunning in its intensity.

Terrifying.

She leaped from the bed and bolted from the room, not stopping until she was up the stairs and safely behind the locked door of her bedroom.

And spent the rest of her sleepless night cursing herself for being such a coward.

—␣␣␣—

God, what a goatfuck, Jack thought the next morning as he pounded away at the heavy bag at Gus's gym, trying his damnedest not to stare at Talia with his tongue hanging out while a trainer ran her through speed drills.

She'd bolted from his room like a terrified rabbit, so fast she practically left skid marks on the hardwood floor.

Really, what had he expected? He'd as good as told her he was about to throw her across the bed. He hit the bag hard enough to feel the jolt all the way up to his shoulder. Like she was going to turn to him, throw herself into his arms, and beg him to do all of the things he'd been dying to do to her from the second he'd walked into Suzette's two weeks ago?

Only in his dreams. And he'd had several of them last night after she left. Of her, naked, over him, under him, clutching him to her as he sank into her wet heat. Dreams so vivid that when he woke up, he swore he could taste her mouth on his, smell the sweet musk of her need.

Except when he opened his eyes, it wasn't her naked skin brushing his but a cotton sheet, and the hand wrapped around his cock was his own, stroking himself to a depressing climax just to ease some of the tension building inside him.

He hit the bag again and dropped to the mat for a series of push-ups, sit-ups, then several minutes of high-speed jump roping. Anything to take the edge off, to stave off the edgy, restless feeling that had him aching with frustrated need, walking around in skin that was two sizes too small.

He knew the signs, knew himself well enough to recognize he was nearing the breaking point. In the past, when he got like this over anything—a woman, a mission—if he didn't get a handle on it, quick, an explosion would be imminent.

But there was nothing he could do to quench the raging need he had for Talia. God, he was so focused on protecting her, who would have ever thought he'd have to worry about protecting her from himself?

He couldn't have her, and he couldn't find any relief elsewhere. Not only was it impossible for him to leave her side long enough, the idea of using another woman as a substitute for the one he really wanted was even more depressing than the idea of jacking off alone for the next decade.

He had to make do with punishing workout sessions and his own right hand and hope that he could keep the wolves at bay.

They worked out for nearly two hours, Talia keeping her distance while Jack got himself to the point where the blood was too busy rushing to the muscles he'd worked to near exhaustion to pool in his groin.

They went back to her place to clean up and she met him in the kitchen, a tight smile pasted on her freshly scrubbed face, her eyes fixed firmly on his face in a way that said she was trying not to remember how close to him she'd been in his near-naked state less than twenty-four hours ago.

She didn't have a lick of makeup on and was dressed in a long-sleeved navy shirt with a blue and gray scarf around her neck and close-fitting jeans, yet one look at her undid any progress made from the workout and the cold shower that followed.

"We should get going," she said, trying to keep any trace of tension out of her voice. "I told Rosie we'd pick her up in fifteen minutes to go to the shopping center."

As if the day could get worse, now he had to go sit

in a froufrou department store, imagining Talia getting undressed and dressed over and over again while she looked for the perfect outfit for the upcoming engagement party.

Jack made a mental note to give Danny a punch in the nuts for forcing the issue.

—⁓—

Talia could practically see the waves of tension emanating from Jack as they drove over to Stanford to meet up with Rosie. The last thing she was in the mood for was shopping. She was exhausted. After she'd left—no, fled—the guest room, she'd spent the night tossing and turning in her bed, feeling like the world's biggest coward even as she told herself she wasn't even close to being able to give Jack what he wanted.

He wanted her to want him. She didn't even know what that meant. Other than a few passionate make-out sessions with boys from her high school days—and those she attributed more to her own hormonally charged body than any great attraction to the boys in question—Talia couldn't remember ever feeling anything approaching what she'd seen in Jack's eyes last night.

Need. Lust. So hot and all-consuming it drove him to the very edge of control.

So intense it called up something in her, strong enough it had its own gravitational pull. As if, regardless of the demons of her past, her body couldn't help but respond to him, even if it was only a mere echo of what Jack was feeling.

But even that mere echo was enough to send a rush

of heat through her. She shifted in the passenger seat, felt a tingle low in her belly as she remembered the hot silk of his skin under her finger. And now, his huge, solid presence in the car, the scent of him filling her brain in a heady rush, was enough to kick up her heart rate by a couple dozen beats per minute.

Still, she feared it wasn't enough. There had been a time when sex was fine, even fun. Back at the very beginning of her "relationship" with David, she'd had no complaints. She'd been starry-eyed, stupidly in love with the man. Or at least the idea of him.

David had proven himself a rather selfish lover, but Talia had put up with it because for her, the sex wasn't the big deal in the relationship. For her, it was all about the fact that David loved her, cherished her, and for once she finally had someone in her life who would take care of and protect her instead of her always trying to take care of everyone else. For a brief time, at the very beginning of their affair, she had finally felt safe.

Right. She'd been about as safe as a rabbit in a cobra's cage. By the time she realized that, it was too late. And sex with David went from tolerable to revolting in the blink of an eye. What she'd once given willingly was taken from her on a regular basis, and he made sure she knew exactly what would happen to her and Rosario if she ever tried to leave him. Worse, she had to pretend to like it. Pretend that letting him use her body whenever and however he wanted wasn't consuming her soul from the inside out.

She swallowed back a wave of nausea as the memory obliterated any spark of arousal Jack had elicited.

And that was the crux of her problem right there, she thought gloomily as she studied Jack's grim profile. She was afraid that whatever chemistry she felt with Jack, whatever answering lust he conjured up in her, it wouldn't be enough to keep the demons at bay. What if in the heat of the moment, the familiar revulsion of a man's hands on her resurfaced? What if, God forbid, she panicked?

What if he looked at her and remembered what she'd been? Remembered what she'd let herself become?

That was the greatest fear. The deepest, darkest stone she kept secret in her heart. That no matter how much he wanted her, Jack would always see her as David Maxwell's woman.

His mistress.

His whore.

When has Jack ever given any sign he sees you like that? Talia recognized that voice. It was the same stupid voice her then-twenty-two-year-old self had listened to when it told her David Maxwell was the answer to all of her romantic dreams and was going to love her and give her the life she always wanted.

She shoved it aside. So what if Jack never brought up David's name? The reminders were everywhere. They were the reason he was even in her life.

Lust only went so far.

But look at all he's done for you—is doing for you, that little stupid voice piped up. *Would a guy like Jack go to all this trouble if he didn't actually care for you? If all he wanted was to get in your pants?*

God, she wanted to cling to that idea and run with it. If she could trust that, she could take the risk. She could stop being such a coward.

But that would take a leap of faith she wasn't capable of. Not anymore. She needed to squelch whatever stirrings

Jack might cause and keep her distance. Any other course was too dangerous.

She pulled herself out of her reverie and realized Jack had turned onto Campus Drive. He moved into the right lane. "No, take a left up here."

"Her dorm is that way."

"We're not meeting her at her dorm," she replied. "We're meeting her at the coffeehouse. She had a meeting there with her physics TA."

Jack's only reply was grunt, a sound that sent a shooting pain through her head, intensifying the headache that had been building. A result not only of her sleepless night, but also of the stress of spending the morning with a smile pasted on her face as she exhausted every small-talk topic on the planet in an effort to engage him in conversation and defuse the tension between them.

All she'd gotten were grunts. It was his damn fault she was tied up in knots, and he couldn't even trouble himself to be courteous.

She was officially done trying.

Jack did a quick lane change, almost taking out a biker in the process, and made a left toward the center of campus. He parked in the pay lot behind the student union. When Talia took out her wallet and headed for the pay station, Jack cut her off without a word and slid in his ATM card. Apparently chivalry wasn't dead, even in the face of his sour mood.

They walked into the coffeehouse and it took Talia's eyes a few moments to adjust to the dim interior. The tables were crowded with students and a handful of older professors. Some were quietly poring over books or working on laptops. Others were deep in conversation, and there were even a couple of groups crowded around pitchers of beer, getting the weekend started early on a Thursday afternoon.

Talia looked at them all with a mingling of jealousy and wonder. Did these kids—most of them the products of some of the most privileged families in the world—have any idea how lucky they were?

"God, I used to love afternoons like that," Jack said, an unfamiliar tone of nostalgia in his voice. "Finish up classes early, take an afternoon to goof off with my buddies."

Though Talia could understand the appeal, her usually subdued contrarian streak decided to rear its head. "I wouldn't know. We were too poor for me to do more than a semester of community college."

"You could still go."

"Right. After I pay for Rosie and the rest of what I owe you, I should be able to afford it sometime in the middle of this century. I'll have to use a walker to accept my diploma."

Jack opened his mouth but Talia cut him off when she spotted Rosie across the room. "There's Rosie," she said, and started toward the table Rosie was sharing with a young man with dark hair.

Talia stopped beside the table and Rosie looked up with a smile. "Hey, Talia, we're just finishing up." She turned to the man who was sitting across from her. He was staring up at Talia. Behind his wire-rimmed glasses, his eyes were pale green, studying her with such curiosity Talia felt a bit like a bug under a microscope. "Eugene, this is my sister, Talia. Talia, this is Eugene Kuusik, my physics TA."

"Nice to meet you." Talia held out her hand, and there were several awkward seconds as Eugene just stared, unmoving. Talia was about to pull her hand away, wondering if she'd somehow offended him, when he seemed to jerk awake.

"I'm sorry," he said with a sheepish smile as he held out his hand. "It's stunning, how much like your sister you look." His grip was surprisingly strong, and as she looked closer, she saw that while she'd initially categorized him as thin, the arms sticking out of the short sleeves of his T-shirt were corded with muscle.

He wasn't massively built like Jack—few were—but he was lean and fit, in a compact, sinewy sort of way.

"I'll take that as a compliment," Talia replied, although she found his comment a little strange. Sure, she and Rosie resembled each other enough—no one was ever shocked to find out they were siblings—but with the differences in features, height, and build, they'd never be mistaken for twins.

"Oh, you absolutely should," Eugene said, his face breaking into an almost sweet smile. He shot a quick look at Rosie, whose cheeks were flushed.

"I'm Jack," Jack's gruff voice broke in, and the offer of his hand forced Eugene to drop Talia's. "So you're her physics tutor?"

"Her TA, actually, for Physics Forty-Three class. In my spare time I'm working on my PhD in biophysics."

"Jack was a physics major at West Point," Rosie chimed in.

"Small potatoes compared to a PhD candidate," Jack said, for the first time today sounding almost pleasant.

"And that's why you're a bodyguard instead of a PhD," Talia said peevishly.

"Are you really a bodyguard?" Eugene asked, sounding almost impressed.

"I'm a security specialist," Jack said, shooting Talia a glare.

"That sounds a lot cooler than physics geek," Eugene said with a chuckle.

"Talia's been getting some strange gifts," Rosie said, leaning forward as though she was about to disclose a juicy secret. "We think she has a stalker."

Eugene grimaced sympathetically. "That sounds scary."

"It's totally freaky," Rosie said. "It started with just a necklace and some flowers, but then—"

Talia glanced at Jack, who was shaking his head at a totally oblivious Rosie.

"Rosario," he snapped, causing Rosie to look up with a startled, slightly hurt look. "We're trying to keep the details on the down low—no offense, Eugene."

Eugene nodded with a look of concern. "Of course, I understand."

"Sorry, I didn't realize," Rosie said, then gave Eugene a pleading look. "You won't tell anyone, will you?"

Eugene gave Rosie a gentle smile and patted her hand. "Of course not. And who would I tell anyway? The only people I know are geeks like me." He closed his laptop and slid it into his bag. "It was nice meeting you," he said to Talia and Jack as he rose. "If you'll excuse me, I have to get ready for my next class. Rosario, I'll see you tomorrow in study section."

Talia slid into the chair Eugene vacated.

"I thought we were leaving too," Jack snapped.

Talia glared up at him. A headache throbbed in her

temples. "I need to brace myself before we hit the mall." She flashed Jack a smile that was more a baring of teeth. "Get me a coffee?"

"Sure." Jack practically spat out the word and started to turn and walk away.

"I want a half caf light foam nonfat latte with one pump vanilla syrup and make sure it's extra hot. Got all that?"

"Got it."

"You guys are doing it, aren't you?"

Talia was glad she didn't have her coffee yet because Rosie's question would have made her spew it all over the table. "What on earth are you talking about? Of course not. Why would you say that?"

Rosie sat back in her chair, arms folded, regarding her with a knowing look that made her look thirty-five instead of eighteen. "You're totally acting like people who hooked up but then got in a fight and neither of you wants to apologize." She cocked her head. "But now that you say it, I think the problem is that you haven't done it yet."

Talia felt the color flood to her cheeks and she looked frantically over her shoulder to make sure Jack wasn't anywhere close. "That's ridiculous and you know it. Even if he wanted to, and I thought I wanted to...I can't...we can't...after everything that happened—"

Rosie leaned forward and covered Talia's hands with her own where they rested on the table. "You have to get over it."

Talia jerked back. "It's not that easy. You have no idea—" She tried to tug her hands away but Rosie held them in a surprisingly strong grip.

"I have a pretty good idea," Rosie said quietly, and in

that one sentence every trace of the happy-go-lucky coed disappeared. "You didn't tell me everything, but I think I figured most of it out. You have to know Jack would never hurt you that way, not in a million years."

"Of course I do. Jack's not the problem."

"Then I don't understand," Rosie said.

And Talia never wanted her to. "Let's not talk about my nonexistent love life, okay?"

"It's only nonexistent because you want it to be," Rosie said, undeterred. "I swear, the way Jack looks at you, he'd be on you in a nanosecond if you gave him just a little encouragement."

"Nanosecond? Is that what you're learning from your cute physics TA?" Talia struggled to keep her tone light despite the pounding in her skull.

Rosie wrinkled her nose as her lips pulled up at the corners. "You think Eugene is cute?"

Thank God Rosie took the bait. "Yeah, in a quieter, studious kind of way. He seems to be in to you."

Rosie shook her head. "I can see what you're saying. He's nice enough and I don't mind hanging out with him. But he's a grad student, so he's kind of boring and... old," she finished with another disdainful nose wrinkle. "Besides, I just ended things with Kevin."

Though Talia had been overjoyed at the news of their breakup, her hackles rose at the thought of Rosario wasting another second mooning over that grade-A d-bag, and she told Rosie as much.

"Hey, I know you never liked him but that doesn't mean I didn't care about him—" Rosie's sullen protest was interrupted as Jack practically dropped the paper beverage cup on the table.

Talia rolled her eyes and took a sip, her lip curling at the bitter taste of black coffee without a hint of milk or sugar to curb the edge.

Her gaze darted from Rosie's pout to Jack's look of smug satisfaction as he watched her take another sip of the coffee.

It was going to be a long afternoon.

Chapter 12

Hours later, Gene was still shaking from his encounter with Talia Vega. He'd been completely caught off guard when she'd walked into the coffeehouse. Rosario had said nothing about meeting her sister at the end of their session.

It was heaven and hell wrapped up in one miraculous, awful encounter. She'd stunned him. Of course he'd been aware of her beauty, watching her, tracking her as he had. But he'd never been up close enough to see the smooth grain of her skin. Nearly flawless even without the heavy makeup she'd worn in older pictures he'd seen.

Never been close enough to appreciate the subtle shifts in her expression, the way her eyes lit up with pride when she smiled at her sister and darkened in irritation when she spoke to the gorilla.

Well, maybe not a complete gorilla, Gene thought—that is, if the story about Jack studying physics at West Point was true. Like Jack said, a bachelor's was nothing compared to the kind of work Gene was doing, but it indicated that the man was not a lumbering brainless meathead who could be easily dismissed.

Oh, and Talia had touched him. Even now he rubbed

his fingers together, savoring the memory of her small, smooth-skinned hand in his, the fine bones that would be so easy to crush in his grip.

God, it had been so difficult to maintain his facade of calm. He'd nearly blown it at the very beginning, the way he'd frozen at the first sight of her as his mind swirled and roared with thoughts of all that he had in store for her.

Thoughts that made him grateful he was seated and the small table could hide his body's response until he got himself under control. For a few moments he'd been so tempted to grab her, take her, right then and there.

But he would have failed. And he'd come too far, worked too hard to prepare himself, to let a loss of control ruin everything.

Then an edge of panic had set in. Could she possibly know? Would she look into his eyes and sense the monster barely leashed inside him?

But then she'd smiled, offered her hand. As clueless as a lamb going to slaughter.

A wave of calm had settled over him and he'd pulled himself back under control. Listened, hiding a smile as Rosario carelessly talked about the gifts Talia had received from her stalker.

What would she do if she knew that he was the one who had sent the recording of her attack? That he'd watched it dozens of times, studied it until he'd memorized every cry of pain.

But his delight had faded as he registered what Rosario was saying. *Gifts*, she'd said. Not *gift*.

A necklace, flowers, to remind Talia of her past.

Her house getting broken into.

Things Gene had had no part in.

Someone else is trying to get to her.

The realization had filled him with such fury, his vision had momentarily blurred. He'd pulled it together enough to excuse himself, but he barely remembered the across-campus walk to his office.

Someone else is trying to get to her. Making sure she never forgets the sins of her past.

He wouldn't stand for it. Talia Vega was his, dammit. His to take, his to destroy.

—⁓—

Talia studied her reflection in the mirror and lifted a finger to wipe away a fleck of mascara that had fallen on her cheekbone. She looked critically at her makeup. Was it too heavy for what was essentially a fancy barbecue?

Deciding her full lips were too prominent painted that shade of pink, she snatched up a tissue and wiped them clean.

Then reapplied it as she realized that without the lipstick, her face looked washed out against the vibrant teal green of her dress.

She stepped back, her stomach in knots as she took in her entire reflection. Rosario—and Susie after she'd insisted Talia model it for her at the restaurant the night before—had assured her that it was perfect. Dressy without looking like she was trying too hard. Pretty and feminine without being froufrou. Appropriate without looking frumpy.

Sexy without being too revealing.

It was that last part Talia was having trouble with. Ending a couple inches above the knee, the dress's skirt was hardly a micromini, but it was still shorter than anything Talia had worn in over two years.

Objectively she had to admit that Rosie and Susie were right when they said the dress looked amazing on a frame that, though leaner than it once had been, still sported decent curves. First there was the color, a rich jade green that was both eye-catching and elegant, contrasting beautifully with her dark hair and caramel-hued skin.

The sleeveless top draped gently over her breasts, hinting at but not clinging to the fullness. It fastened with a single button at her nape, leaving a keyhole opening in the back. That normally would have been a no-go—no way was she taking those scars out on parade.

But thanks to a knit camisole layer underneath and the way the fabric draped, the scars stayed hidden, the dress giving only the illusion of being revealing. A beautifully beaded sash cinched her in at the waist, keeping the flowy style from looking too boxy on her frame.

The above-knee skirt combined with the nude pumps made her legs look about two miles long, and she couldn't help but admire the lean muscles of her calves and thighs, developed over long hours in the gym doing squats and kicks.

She had the legs of an athlete now.

The legs of a survivor.

"You about ready? We're kind of pushing the bounds of fashionably late."

She jumped at the sound of Jack's muffled voice and the light rap of his knuckles against her bedroom door. She looked at the clock. Sure enough, she had lingered as long as she could. It was time to stop dithering and nitpicking over her appearance and open the door already.

Ease up. It's not like this is a real date. You're just tagging along. It doesn't even matter what you look like. Just try not to embarrass yourself or him.

Time to man up, she told herself. She stuffed her lipstick, her ID, a credit card, and some cash into a small purse and took a deep, bracing breath as she opened the door. "I'm ready," she lied.

Jack was leaning against the hallway wall. "Jesus, took you long enough." As he turned, she could see the irritated expression on his face. "It's a damn barbecue, not the royal wed—" His eyes fully locked on her and he froze midsentence.

The nervous knot in her stomach took on an edge of panic. "What's wrong?" Oh, God, was the dress too short, too tight, too revealing? Did she look like a slut and not even know it? "Is it the dress? I can change. I shouldn't have bothered... I have black pants and a nice sweater—"

"Don't you fucking dare change," Jack nearly yelled. He closed his eyes and held up a hand. "Shit, I'm sorry. I didn't mean..." He paused and cleared his throat. "It's just... you... uh..."

If Talia didn't know him better, she'd have thought he was actually flustered.

"You look gorgeous," he finally said. "Really, amazingly beautiful." Jack shook his head as though trying to get his bearings. "I always knew you were beautiful, but Jesus."

"Oh" was all Talia could manage as she rocked back on her high heels, her legs suddenly unsteady under the force of his admiration. She'd been complimented for her looks a lot in her life, mostly with words like *sexy*, *smokin'*, or the perennial *hot*.

She'd taken them in stride, validation that her looks had the currency necessary to navigate her chosen path.

But none had ever had the impact of Jack's. More than the words, it was the tone of his voice. Sincere, almost reverent. And the look on his face, like she was some wondrous creature he couldn't quite believe was real.

For the first time since he'd had his nightmare, she felt the tension between them ease, the air between them no less charged but with a different kind of energy.

One that felt more like anticipation than frustration.

It was too much. "I can still clean up pretty well," Talia quipped. "You don't look bad yourself."

An understatement if there ever was one. His clothes couldn't have been more simple—boring even. Hell, if a guy had walked into Club One in a plain white button-down shirt, dark khaki trousers, and a navy sport coat, she would have made him pay double to get into the VIP room.

But custom tailored to Jack's massive frame, the conservative clothes somehow made him stand out even more. Like he was trying to hide a body that was ready for action at any time behind a veneer of casual business wear and failing miserably.

The jacket emphasized the broad line of his shoulders; the white shirt contrasted against skin browned from hours spent training outside. His shirttails tucked into his pants emphasized his trim waist and lean, narrow hips; the cut of the pants hinted at the powerful muscles of his legs.

Too big, too tough, too rugged to be a model. But to Talia he was infinitely more appealing.

He moved so she could precede him down the stairs.

Even though she reminded herself for the millionth time this wasn't a real date, it was hard not to feel that way as Jack helped her into her coat and held open her car door for her.

They rode in companionable silence as Jack drove. Though Danny's father's house couldn't have been more than five miles away, as Jack turned off the main road and started winding his way through the neighborhood, the contrast between her cute, tidy neighborhood and this one was startling.

Streets were thickly lined with oaks to obscure the views of the houses from the road. Well-kept single-level ranchers abruptly gave way to multimillion-dollar mansions whose rooftops were visible above massive privacy walls.

Jack turned a corner onto a street already lined with cars.

"Here's the house," Jack said as he pulled up alongside a comparatively modest but beautifully refurbished rancher that sat back from the road behind a sprawling lawn. "I can drop you off here so you don't have to walk in those," he said, glancing down at her pumps with their three-and-a-half-inch heels.

"I'm fine walking," she said. She hadn't worn heels in years and had barely made it down her own front steps, but she'd walk till her feet bled before she'd walk into that party alone.

Jack had to drive more than halfway down the block before he finally found space for his car.

Talia climbed out and walked with Jack down the street, using her heels as an excuse to walk as slowly as possible. "How many people do you think are here?"

she asked, unable to keep the nervous tightness from her voice.

"Not too big. Maybe a hundred, hundred fifty," Jack said.

Talia decided to find herself a spot in the corner and keep to herself.

"There's no reason to be nervous," Jack said. He paused and caught her hand in his. "Joe Taggart is a great guy. These are nice people."

"I'm not nervous."

"Your hands are freezing." His fingers tightened on hers and he leaned close. His eyes flicked to her mouth, and for a second she thought he was about to kiss her.

The thought did nothing to calm her nerves, but it provided a hell of a distraction.

Her eyelids started to drift closed, but instead of his lips on hers, she felt the soft brush of his fingers on her neck. "And your pulse is going about a hundred miles an hour."

She swallowed hard, willing moisture back into her mouth that had gone desert dry. "Maybe a little nervous. I'm not so good at talking to new people."

Jack looked down at her, a slightly confused smile on his face. "You're a bartender. You talk to new people all the time."

"It's different." She pulled her hand from his and started walking again. "I just have to be polite, serve them a drink. Even with the regulars, it's sort of anonymous." It was the same when she'd worked at Club One; the line between customer and service provider created an invisible barrier that kept her from having to worry about whether anyone she met actually liked her.

"You're with me. Don't worry about it."

Somehow that didn't do anything to ease her nervousness. She was all dressed up, walking in on his arm. Just like a real date.

Just like Jack wanted.

But because something inside her balked at taking the next step, she couldn't help but feel like an imposter.

As she walked in and took in the elaborate setup of the party, it became very clear her idea of a backyard barbecue and Joe Taggart's were not the same. The two fully stocked and staffed bars were on either end of the expansive lawn. A massive grill was manned by a chef, complete with the hat, and buffet tables were set up on the far side of the pool. White lights were strung from the trees and the wooden awning that covered half of the flagstone patio. Heat lamps were placed strategically throughout the grounds, throwing off enough warmth to make her coat unnecessary.

Talia did a quick survey of the guests, glad as she did so that she'd taken Susie's and Rosie's advice on her wardrobe choice. Though she wasn't wearing the most expensive outfit—she recognized designs that must have set the wearers back thousands of dollars—her dress wouldn't exactly be dismissed as a pile of rags.

"Jack! Glad you could make it!"

Talia followed Jack in the direction of the voice and they ended up in a cluster of people standing a few feet away from one of the two bars set up on opposite ends of the yard. Jack returned the smile of a tall older man. He held out his hand, only to be pulled into a rough, backslapping hug.

"Talia, this is Joe," Jack said, motioning her forward.

Talia shook hands and smiled at the man who, with his light eyes, ruggedly handsome features, and body that was still broad and fit despite his age, was obviously father to Danny Taggart and his brothers, Ethan and Derek.

Joe offered her a warm, admiring smile and said, "About time Jack brought someone around for me to meet."

It was on the tip of her tongue to blurt out that he had the wrong idea, but at the last second, she felt the warning pressure of Jack's hand on her back as he said, "She hasn't figured out she's slumming it yet, so I'd appreciate it if you put in a good word for me, sir."

Talia snapped her mouth shut, feeling a blush creep up her cheeks at the way Jack's thumb brushed against a patch of skin left bare by her dress.

Jack gave the woman next to Joe a quick buss on the cheek and offered his congratulations. Must be the fiancée, Talia thought, and had her suspicions verified in the next second when he introduced them. "Talia, this is Marcy Kramer, Joe's fiancée."

Marcy was a thin, pretty blonde who might have looked like your generic social X-ray had it not been for the genuine warmth in her blue eyes and the adoration that filled them as she looked at her soon-to-be husband. "So lovely to meet you, Talia. Jack's told us a lot about you over the years."

Talia felt her smile freeze in place. Was Marcy just spouting the usual social niceties, or had Jack actually talked about her to his friends and family?

And what, she thought as her stomach churned, exactly had he told them?

"May I get you something to drink?" a server asked.

"Vodka on the rocks with a splash of tonic," she said, ignoring the way Jack's eyebrows shot up as he ordered his own club soda. She knew what he was thinking—in the entire time he'd known her, she'd barely touched alcohol. Never during their work at Club One, and since then, he'd seen her indulge in only the occasional glass of wine after work.

But as she met Danny Taggart's coolly assessing stare, she knew she was going to need all the help she could get, alcoholic or otherwise.

"Nice to see you, Talia," Danny said with a nod. Talia nodded back and gratefully accepted her drink from the server. "You've met my wife, Caroline, and the rest of this ragtag crew at one time or another."

Talia smiled and said hello to Danny's wife. Even in the late stages of pregnancy, Caroline Taggart somehow managed to look elegant in a dark red dress that gorgeously showcased her pregnancy-enhanced curves and contrasted with the thick, dark brown hair that fell nearly to her waist.

Talia also recognized Ethan Taggart, as tall and handsome as his brother with his dark blue eyes and gold-shot brown hair. Next to him was his wife, Toni, looking like Snow White meets alterna-chick with her pale skin, red lips, and almost black hair. She was tall and slender despite the fact the baby she cradled wasn't more than six weeks old.

Jack greeted the men with the handshake half hug that guys did, kissed the women, and, in a move that made Talia's heart jump for no good reason, nuzzled the baby's head. "How's little Joey tonight?" Jack said, his face creased in a grin like Talia had never seen before.

"Oh, he's all right," Toni said with a little smile.

"He's already increased his body weight by twenty percent," Ethan said, unable to keep the paternal pride out of his voice.

"Considering he was almost ten pounds when he was born, that's saying something," Jack said, impressed.

"Ugh, don't remind me," Caroline groaned. "You Taggarts with your monster babies—"

She was cut off by a crash and a childish howl.

"Speaking of monsters," Danny muttered, and darted off. Caroline followed, the elegance Talia had so admired obliterated as she hurriedly waddled after him.

"Anna just pulled over the ice sculpture," a breathless feminine voice broke in.

Talia turned and recognized Alyssa Miles Taggart, followed by her husband, Derek.

"Oh my God, is she okay?" Talia asked, nightmare scenarios of crushed skulls and broken limbs racing through her head.

"She's fine," Derek said, shaking his dark head, "but the caterer is ready to roast her up and serve her with barbecue sauce."

Marcy hid a laugh behind her hand. "We heard the crash—Danny and Caroline are on their way. I'll go smooth things over with Betsey."

As Marcy rushed off, Joe removed his wire-rimmed glasses and rubbed his tired eyes. "I swear to God, that girl is going to be the end of Danny. You boys gave me a run for your money but I'd take a dozen of you boys over one girl."

Ethan and Derek laughed and exchanged knowing looks. Talia had been shocked when she'd first met them and Jack informed her they were twins. Though they were both tall, almost as tall as Jack's six foot four, and heavily built—having arms roughly the circumference of her waist must run in the gene pool—the similarities stopped there.

While Ethan's dark hair was streaked with gold, Derek's hair was a dark, coffee-colored shade. Where Ethan's blue eyes were bright with humor, and his smile flashed easily, Derek's expression was guarded, his dark eyes revealing nothing about his emotions.

Except when he was looking at his wife. Then his whole face changed, his eyes softening with a warmth that seemed to come from the center of his soul.

Alyssa was oblivious as she launched herself at Talia with a hug that was as enthusiastic as it was genuine. "Talia, it's so great to see you," she said, her slender arms winding around Talia's back. "I've been traveling so much lately I haven't been able to get to Suzette's to catch up with you and Susie."

Talia returned her hug, touched by the sincere warmth of Alyssa's greeting. She was pleasantly surprised to find that, other than Danny's reserved greeting, the rest of the group was welcoming.

Talia found herself fascinated as she watched Jack. His laugh was loud and easy, his smile broad. He looked more relaxed and happy than she'd ever seen him.

He'd always struck her as a loner, keeping to himself, but she saw now that he was part of this group. His line about Joe Taggart being like a father to him wasn't spouted just to guilt her into coming to the party.

There was genuine love and affection between Jack and Joe, his sons, and their wives. It made Talia wonder about Jack's real family, which, now that she thought about it, she'd never heard him mention. And she'd never asked.

Watching him laugh and joke good-naturedly with his friends, she was struck again by how little she knew about Jack, what he did with his real life when he wasn't busy trying to save hers.

Chapter 13

Soon their small group dispersed to mingle. Jack introduced her to Marcy's daughter, Kara, a tall, stunning blonde who looked to be in her early twenties. "You look great, kiddo," Jack said, and gave her a brotherly hug.

Kara turned to Talia and offered her hand. "Nice to meet you," she said distractedly. Though she smiled, Talia noted a slight downcast pull to her mouth as she looked at something—or someone—past Talia's shoulder.

Talia looked and saw Ben Moreno, handsome as sin, teeth flashing whitely against his dark skin as he chatted up a brunette whose dress left no detail of her surgically enhanced curves to the imagination.

She felt a surge of sympathy as she turned back to Kara. Nothing but trouble could come from pining after a player like Moreno.

Kara's face morphed into a hard smile. "Let me introduce you to some people," she said, taking Talia by the arm and leading them into the crowd, away from Ben and his latest conquest.

Talia smiled and made small talk as Kara introduced her and Jack to what felt like dozens of guests. Everyone was friendly enough, but Talia couldn't get past the feeling that they were looking at her, assessing. Judging.

Jack must have read her tension. He curled his hand around her arm and bent his head close. "You okay?"

His warm breath tickled her ear, sending a tingle of awareness through her. "I'm fine," she said, her mouth gone suddenly dry. "I just need to excuse myself for a minute."

Following Kara's directions, she hurried to the restroom. On the way back, she made a detour at the bar to grab another cocktail. But instead of going back to Jack's side, she lingered on the edge of the crowd, watching.

"Having fun?"

Talia turned, automatically returning Alyssa's warm smile. "It's great."

Alyssa nodded. "Sometimes these things get overwhelming, though. So many people. I start to get maxed out after a while."

"I can relate," Talia said. She took a sip of her drink and moved next to Alyssa.

Alyssa waved off an offer of a shrimp skewer from a passing server. "I heard through Derek about the trouble you've been having. Are you any closer to catching whoever is harassing you?"

Talia shook her head. "It has to be someone who knows about my relationship with David," she said, pitching her voice low so the other guests milling around them wouldn't hear. Alyssa nodded in understanding. She knew enough about Talia's sordid past not to need clarification. "If I had to guess, I'd say it's someone close to Margaret—David's widow—if not Margaret herself. But so far she's clean, and it's not like I didn't ruin a lot of lives and careers when I helped Krista Slater take him down."

Alyssa wrinkled her nose and looked so adorable it would have been annoying if Talia didn't like her so much. "That sucks, to say the least. I know exactly how that feels, always looking over your shoulder, never knowing who to trust. Well, except for Jack, of course," Alyssa said, a sly glint in her green eyes. "Just like I had Derek."

"I think that was a little different."

"You know that's how Derek and I met, right? My uncle hired him as my bodyguard—actually more like my watchdog."

Talia's fingernails dug into the wooden armrests. Right now, being here with but not really with Jack, getting a glimpse into his inner circle of close friends that he never would have offered up if it hadn't been absolutely necessary, Talia didn't want to be reminded of the vast differences between Alyssa's relationship with her once bodyguard and her own relationship with Jack. "I'm not his client," Talia said, trying to keep her tone light. "I'm his charity case."

Alyssa cocked an eyebrow, a knowing look in her green eyes. "Jack's got a generous streak a mile wide, but he doesn't drop everything to play hero for just anyone."

Talia stiffened. "I'm nothing special, believe me."

Alyssa leaned toward her, her expression grave. Talia flinched but didn't jerk away when Alyssa covered her hand. "I know exactly where you're coming from. Before I got my act together, I felt exactly the same way. I made big mistakes in the past and I knew exactly what people thought about me—it was all over the news. But that didn't stop Derek from loving me. And that won't stop Jack—"

She broke off as Derek appeared at her side and she took the drink he offered.

Talia gave a silent prayer of thanks for the interruption.

She liked Alyssa and knew her intentions were the best, but she didn't really want to get in a big discussion about her mistakes, and her damage was way worse than anything Alyssa had ever gotten herself mixed up in.

A couple of tabloid scandals were nothing compared to having a long-term affair with a man she knew was a criminal. They couldn't hold a candle to helping to put a man on death row.

Still, as she watched Derek hover around his wife, it was hard not to feel a pinch of something that felt a little like envy.

Derek leaned in for a kiss hello, but it quickly turned hot enough that Talia had to turn away, her face burning.

And her heart—and other parts of her—aching.

She didn't have faith she could have something with Jack that even approached what Alyssa and Derek clearly shared, but dammit, didn't she deserve a taste?

She spotted Jack walking toward one of the buffet tables as Danny waved him over, and her stomach gave a funny little flip at the sight of his tall, strong body moving through the crowd.

Hadn't she suffered enough for her sins?

She started after him.

—⁓—

Jack surveyed the wreckage of the ice sculpture while the catering staff rushed around, picking up glasses and trying to keep about a thousand custom-printed cocktail napkins from fluttering away in the wind that had suddenly kicked up.

Off to the side, Danny and Caroline were issuing a stern lecture about being careful and the dangers of running near massive blocks of ice carved into the shape of a swan to almost three-year-old Anna. Tonight the little heartbreaker was in a white and pink dress with a ruffled skirt. A matching pink bow was threaded through her dark curls, and her gray eyes that matched her dad's were huge and spilling over with tears at her dad's scolding.

"It was a assident, Daddy," she said, her little chest heaving with sobs. "I d-didn't mean to mess up the ice."

"Nevertheless," Caroline said, "we told you when we got here that you were not allowed near the ice swan. That means no cake tonight."

To her credit, Anna didn't scream or yell. Little shoulder's stiff, bottom lip pouted out, she sniffled, her chest heaving in silent sobs.

It was heartbreaking.

It was also, apparently, very effective. Though Danny did his best to keep his expression stern, Jack saw the second he cracked. "Aw, sweetie, you can't have cake, but I bet Grandpa still has some of that rainbow sherbet in the freezer from last time."

The tears dried up as though a switch had been flipped, and a bright, glowing smile replaced the pout. "Okay! C'mon, Mom, wet's go get ice cweam."

Caroline glared over her shoulder as Anna tugged her away. "You are such a p-u-s-s-y," she said, spelling it for Anna's benefit.

"Damn, and you think I'm too much of a sucker for a pretty face," Jack said.

"She's got me right where she wants me, all right," Danny said with a rueful shake of his head, "but at least she's mine." When Jack ignored the pointed comment, Danny shrugged out of his jacket and pointed his chin at the ice swan, which was on its side on the flagstones. "Help me get that thing out of the way."

Jack shrugged off his own jacket and followed Danny's lead. "Where do you want to take it?" Jack waited as Danny did a quick consult with one of the caterers.

"Kitchen." Danny scored several cloth napkins from a server and handed some to Jack.

The swan was mostly intact, though the spindly neck had snapped. Jack wrapped his hands in napkins to block some of the cold. He righted the thing and squatted on one side as Danny took position on the other. Grunting, he and Danny stood with the sculpture, which had to weigh at least one hundred fifty pounds, balanced between them.

The crowd that had gathered parted as they made their way slowly and carefully toward the door.

"Speaking of girls who aren't yours, do you have any leads about who's bugging Talia?" Danny said, his voice straining a little under the weight of the ice.

At the mention of her name, Jack did a quick scan of the crowd. He didn't see the bright greenish blue of the dress or the honey glow of her skin, and figured she must still be helping Alyssa. Probably for the best, considering he was going to have to concentrate to maneuver the block of ice through the house and Talia in that dress was hell on his equilibrium.

"Not really," Jack said, swearing a little as one of the napkins wrapping his hand slipped and the side of his right palm went flush with the ice. He blocked the discomfort, carefully stepping through the sliding glass door that led into the Taggarts' living room as he waited for the numbness to set in. "We know it has to be someone connected to David Maxwell—everything goes back to him."

"Except that fucked-up DVD."

"Yeah, but since David's connection to Nate Brewster was what got Talia on Nate's radar in the first place, it's still connected." But Danny had a point. Up until the DVD, the tokens, or whatever you wanted to call them, weren't related to the violence. Like the giver had suddenly snapped, losing patience for the light torment and going straight for the jugular.

Still, escalation wasn't unusual when you were dealing with predators. Jack knew too well a man could go from giving a woman flowers to stabbing her in the heart in the blink of an eye.

"The obvious one to look at is Margaret Grayson," Jack continued, referring to David Maxwell's widow, released from prison after serving only eighteen months because she agreed to give up all of the details of her husband's illegal activities, which spanned the globe. "Cole's been checking up on her but she's keeping a low profile, hiding out at the family estate on Bainbridge Island."

"Doesn't mean she didn't hire muscle to harass Talia."

Jack paused as a guest squeezed past them in the hallway that led to the kitchen.

"True, but so far we haven't been able to find any links," he said as they finally backed through the door of the kitchen and sidled up to the sink.

"On three," Danny said, and started the count. On three they lifted the bird over the lip of the sink and lowered it carefully into the stainless-steel basin.

Danny grabbed a bottle of beer from the fridge and offered one to Jack. Jack shook his head. "Until we find this fuck, I'm on the clock twenty-four-seven."

Danny just rolled his eyes and took a long pull on his bottle.

"Thanks for letting us use Toni, by the way. I know she doesn't have much time, with the baby and all, but with her digging around in Margaret's dealings, if there's something to be found, she'll find it."

Danny tilted his beer at Jack. "It's not generosity. I need you to figure this shit out so you can get back to work. The Blankenthorns are covered, but I've had five calls from clients in the Seattle area that I've had to turn down."

Jack felt a surge of guilt. "You know I don't want to let you down. But what would you do? What if it was Caroline?"

Danny cocked a dark eyebrow and folded his massive arms across his chest. "Caroline's my wife. I love her more than anything. But as far as I can tell, you and Talia aren't even bumping uglies so—"

Jack was on him in a second, the collar of Danny's shirt twisted in his fist as he shoved him up against the stainless-steel refrigerator. "Don't fucking talk that way about her."

Danny's mouth tilted into a half smile. "Nice to see you got that temper of yours under control."

Jack felt a vein pulse in his forehead and forced himself to release his grip on Danny's shirt as he stepped back. As he returned to awareness, he realized several of the servers had frozen, eyes wide as they wondered if the two men were going to throw down.

Danny rolled his shoulders and smoothed his shirt-front. "You want to go, we'll go, just not at my dad's engagement party."

Embarrassment heated Jack's face as the full magnitude of what he'd been about to do hit him. Shit, he'd been about to start a brawl with his best friend at a party celebrating Joe's engagement.

"And I shouldn't have talked like that," Danny conceded, "but you're not some dumb fuck just out of basic anymore. You can't throw everything away on some woman who doesn't even appreciate you. Look at what happened with Gina—"

Jack closed his eyes, trying to block out the memories. "She's not Gina. It's nothing like that."

Danny was silent for a few seconds. "Maybe not. All I know is I remember how you were then, and I remember what happened after, and I don't want to see you fucking yourself all up again for another one of your broken birds."

Jack flexed his hand. He didn't want to argue with Danny about how what he was doing for Talia had nothing to do with his mother or with Gina, or how he wasn't using her to fix anything that had gone wrong in his past.

It was about Talia herself, and keeping her safe and whole so she could have the life she'd worked so hard to build.

Even if all indications showed she didn't have any interest in that life including him. "There's more to it than the gifts. A cop came to see us the other night." His gaze darted around the kitchen. The catering staff was bustling around, loading trays up with food and exchanging broken martini glasses—from the swan fiasco, no doubt—for undamaged ones. "Let's go someplace a little more quiet."

Danny nodded and led Jack into the living room. Through the sliding glass doors on one wall, they could look out and see the party in action, but no one would hear their conversation. "The cops find something? Why didn't you tell me?"

"It wasn't specifically about Talia's case, and they told us this in confidence, so you have to keep it to yourself."

Danny nodded. "No problem."

"Seriously, you can't even tell Caroline, or Derek and Ethan. If any of this leaks out, it could fuck up their investigation."

"I'm a vault. Now spill it."

"Have you heard about the rapes that have happened in the last few months?"

Danny grimaced. "You mean the dude who kidnaps the women and keeps them for a while before dumping them? Yeah, and that's the reason none of the wives go anywhere alone after five p.m. until they catch the fucker."

"He doesn't just kidnap and rape them. He cuts them too." He closed his eyes and fought back a shudder at the memory of the pictures Nolan had showed him. And hot on its heels, the memory of Talia, helpless, her blood covering her and him as he desperately tried to stop the flow. "He slices up their backs, not enough to kill them but enough to scar them up pretty bad. At first they didn't notice the pattern, but when they took the DVD from Talia, they realized it's a perfect match. Whoever is doing those girls, he's using Talia's wounds as his blueprint."

Danny grimaced and went to the full bar tucked in the corner of the living room. Without a word, he poured two fingers of scotch and took a long drink. "You sure you don't want some of this? To take the edge off?" he asked as he topped off his glass.

Jack shook his head.

"Do they think the rapist is the one targeting Talia?"

Jack shrugged. "They know about as much as we do, which isn't much, but we'd be stupid not to assume it. Though kidnap and rape is a little out of bounds for a thug for hire."

Danny waved him off. "Not necessarily. A lot of these guys get into it because they get off on hurting people. He wouldn't be the first to do some things on the side for the pure pleasure of it."

Jack swallowed back a wave of nausea and took a seat on the edge of the wood-framed sofa. "The pictures of the women... We've been to some bad places, Danny, and seen some bad shit."

"The worst."

"And I still can't wrap my head around the idea of someone actually getting off on doing that kind of thing to someone who can't even fight back."

Danny's big paw settled heavily on his shoulder. "And God knows Anna drives me batshit on a daily basis, but I can't imagine how a father could point a gun at his own kid and pull the trigger. But we knew one of those too." He gave Jack's shoulder a squeeze. "There are a lot of fucked-up people on the planet. I just don't want to see you taken down."

Jack didn't either, but he'd let himself get taken down before he let some psycho get near Talia. "But do you get it now, why I have to see this through?"

Danny lowered himself into the armchair across from Jack. "And after that? What happens then?"

Jack didn't really want to think too far ahead. Didn't want to think about the fact that once they caught the sick fuck who was tormenting Talia, he'd have no excuse to live in her back pocket.

He could continue checking up on her without her knowing, but ever since she'd pointed out how his unsolicited upgrade of her security system bore similarities to the cameras David Maxwell had used to monitor every move she made in Club One, his under-the-radar surveillance of her—no matter that it was well intended—had left a bad taste in his mouth.

There was a lot he wanted from Talia, but he wasn't going to take anything she wasn't willing to share.

—⁓—

Talia sat with Toni and Caroline and Alyssa at one of the dining tables set up on the lawn. Toni, who was feeding little baby Joey under a wrap, had sent Ethan to get her a plate while Derek did the same for Alyssa.

Talia half listened as they expounded over little Joey's seemingly endless appetite.

"I swear to God I thought my nipples were going to fall off in the first two weeks," Toni said matter-of-factly.

Caroline had her hands full keeping little Anna in line. Talia offered to keep an eye on her so she could get dinner but Caroline demurred. "Being this pregnant is like having lap band surgery. I ate, like, two shrimp and a couple of those cheese puff things and I feel like I ate half a cow. I'll let everything settle while I wait for Danny."

Talia was too anxious to eat, her brain buzzing with curiosity after the snippet of conversation she'd overheard between Jack and Danny in the kitchen. She'd ended up there after getting turned around on her way back outside to join the party.

She'd been about to make her presence known when she heard Danny say something about getting Jack back to work in Seattle.

She listened quietly to hear Jack's reply, her stomach sinking when he didn't make any protest about heading back up north once her tormentor was caught.

Which was completely expected. So why did she feel so disappointed about the idea of Jack leaving, especially when she'd done absolutely nothing—other than attract the attention of another psychopath—to encourage him to stay?

Then Danny said something about her and Jack "bumping uglies."

Disgusted and embarrassed, she took that as her cue to leave when Jack slammed Danny up against the refrigerator. Unsure of whether to interfere, she'd ducked behind the pantry door and waited to see what happened.

The intense, cryptic conversation that followed raised about a thousand new questions about Jack.

She looked past Toni's shoulder but didn't see any sign of him.

"Sorry, Talia," Caroline said, reaching out to snag Anna before she made a beeline for the cake table. "I know we're probably totally boring you with all of the baby talk."

"I'm not bored. Just looking for Jack. And if I ever have a baby, I know who to come to with my questions."

Caroline grinned. "Weddings, pregnancy, and babies. Three things guaranteed to cause diarrhea of the mouth in any woman who's experienced them."

Talia's answering smile faltered a little as she felt a little pinch somewhere in the region of her heart. Once upon a time, she'd dreamed about all of those things. Her parents' horrible relationship—with her father's drinking, screaming, and the occasional knocking around before he finally left for good—didn't sour her on the idea of falling in love and getting married someday.

And then when Talia was eight, Rosie had come along, a souvenir, Talia was reasonably sure, from the affair Talia's mother had had with the neighbor's husband. Mama had called her a mistake, but from the very beginning, Rosie, with her pink mouth that was too full for her face, giant doe eyes, and cheeks made for kissing, had become the center of Talia's world.

When she grew up, she told herself, she'd have a baby just like Rosie, but she'd do it right. She'd be different from her mother, she knew. Smarter. She'd pick a good man, someone worthy of her love and devotion. Someone who would adore her and their kids and provide a good life for them instead of drinking away most of his paycheck. Someone who didn't screw around on his wife and deny that the growing bump under his mistress's shirt was his responsibility.

After a couple of false starts with guys from the neighborhood who turned out to be losers, Talia resolved to stay single as long as it took to meet someone good. Then Mama died, and it became even more important for Talia to find someone who could help support them and be a good parental figure when she got custody of Rosie, who had been stuck in a foster home.

Then she'd met David Maxwell and thought all her dreams had come true. He'd gotten Rosie back for her, but at what cost? Her involvement with David had not only nearly gotten her killed, but it had also crushed whatever was left of her dreams of a happy future. Husband, babies. Love.

It had been so long since she'd even entertained the possibility of it, she'd decided that path was closed to her. But here, today, surrounded by so much marital joy and pregnant women everywhere she looked, she couldn't help but wonder what it would be like to have everything that they had.

How it would feel to carry a baby in her body, to cuddle it close as she fed it. To smile down into that sweet face capped with dark curls and startlingly light blue eyes.

"You okay?"

Talia jumped in her seat at the sound of Jack's voice. He stood to the left of her seat, looking down at her face with a look of concern in his eyes. Startlingly light blue eyes.

The baby she'd been envisioning was Jack's.

She swallowed hard and felt her face burn at the realization. "I'm fine," she said, wincing at the nervous pitch in her voice.

"If you say so. But I've asked you twice if you wanted me to get you a plate."

"Sorry, I was just"—*fantasizing about what it might be like to have your baby*—"wondering how Jennie's handling things at the restaurant."

Jack gave her a suspicious look but then shrugged and repeated his offer to get her a plate.

"I'll take a look for myself," she said, and got up.

As he motioned her to precede him through the crowd, her mind teemed with questions about his past, the mysterious Gina, and the other so-called broken birds. But she wasn't exactly sure of the best approach, especially when it meant copping to eavesdropping on him and Danny.

About ten yards away from the barbecue line, her heel caught in a crack in the flagstone. Talia's leg faltered and she felt the stomach-sinking, humiliating certainty that she was about to fall, hard, in front of all these people.

Strong hands grabbed her before she hit the pavement, lifting her back to her feet, keeping his arm around her to steady her.

"It's okay. I've got you," Jack murmured, and warmth like nothing she'd ever felt rushed through her.

"Thank you," she said, smiling up at him in gratitude and something else she didn't quite know what to call—it had been so long since she'd felt anything close to it. All she knew was that she didn't want this moment to end, Jack's strong arm around her, his blue eyes crinkling at the corners as he smiled back down at her.

He kept his hand on the small of her back as he guided her up to the buffet, and Talia pushed away all the questions swirling in her head. Now was not the time to delve into the secrets of Jack's past, to wonder about the women who came before and who might come after.

Though she'd stopped believing in fairy tales a long time ago, right now Talia was going to revel in the feeling of having Jack beside her and indulge in the fantasy that he would always be there to catch her when she fell.

Chapter 14

Jack could feel Talia's stare on the drive home, but every time he glanced over to catch it, she quickly averted her gaze out the window. It only served to heighten the frustration he'd worked overtime to hide throughout the night.

Other than his aborted scuffle with Danny, the night had been pleasant enough. Or it would have been if Jack had actually just been going to a party with Talia as his actual date, instead of living in some bizarro side world where the only reason she was with him was because he needed to keep her safe from the creep who was out to get her.

Usually he liked hanging out with his friends, liked seeing them—especially Danny—get taken down a peg by the gorgeous women who had them totally whipped. Liked watching little Anna run her daddy ragged and the panicked look Ethan got on his face every time baby Joey so much as squealed.

But tonight it had been torture. As he'd watched Talia move throughout the night, coming out of her shell with the others, talking and cracking sly jokes until even Danny was laughing, it had occurred to Jack that she could fit right into this crowd.

They could be a couple just like the others, sharing knowing glances and touches under the table that they thought no one else noticed.

Jack had never realized how much he wanted that until tonight, when every loving gesture was a sharp poke in the chest. Taunting him, reminding him of what he couldn't have, at least not with Talia.

And every flash of her beautiful smile, the sound of her laugh, every glimpse of her legs under that flirty dress hammering home the fact that Danny, Derek, and Ethan would go home, settle into bed, and wrap themselves around the loves of their lives.

And Jack would go back to Talia's house, watch her retreat up the stairs to her solitary bed, hard as a spike, every cell in his body aching for her, the bitter taste of futility on his tongue.

Shit. Danny was right. Jack was a fucking sap, a sucker who was once again throwing everything aside as he threw himself at a woman who, although she might care for him, would never be capable of giving him what he wanted from her. What he needed.

Ironic, considering as he left the party tonight, Danny had pulled him aside and said in a low voice, "Maybe you're on to something with this one."

He was on to another dead end, Jack thought grimly. But it wasn't like he had any other choice. Contrary to what Talia might think, he would never in a million years cut and run just because he wasn't going to get a payback.

It wasn't her fault Jack wanted more. It wasn't her fault that every time he saw her smile, heard her laugh, or caught her clean, soapy scent in the air, he had to fight the urge to yank her to him and never let go.

And most of all—the one thing he wished she'd realize—it wasn't her fault she'd fallen for David Maxwell's good looks, charm, and cash. And it wasn't her fault Nate Brewster had tortured her down in that cellar.

That one was all on Jack. He was prepared to spend the rest of his days at her side, protecting her from monsters if that's what it took. All while keeping his hands very much to himself.

But it was one thing to accept that, Jack thought as he pulled into the garage and turned off the ignition, and another to live the reality. The spirit was willing, but the flesh was weak, as they said. Or in his case, the flesh was in blue-ball hell.

He went into the house first and had her wait in the garage while he did a quick sweep of the house and disarmed the alarm. At his all-clear, she came in and immediately kicked off her shoes.

"Oh, that's better," she said as she wiggled her toes on the linoleum and did a couple of calf raises. "I can't believe I used to wear shoes like that for hours on end." She yawned and stretched her arms to the ceiling.

Jack couldn't manage more than a grunt in reply because he was transfixed on the way her skirt slid up her thigh, exposing a couple more inches of smooth, honey-colored skin. He forced his eyes upward. "I'm going to watch some TV."

He flopped onto the couch and pretended to be engrossed in a show about the Battle of the Bulge, which was nearly impossible when Talia settled onto the cushion next to him and curled her legs under her. Even more impossible when Talia gave a little sigh and said, "I actually had fun tonight, Jack. Thanks for taking me."

"It's not like I had a choice," Jack said, his gaze never leaving the TV screen. He was afraid if he looked at her with her smoky dark eyes and exposed skin of her shoulders and legs, he'd lose it.

"Well, thanks anyway," she said, sounding a little irritated. She swung her legs onto the floor and stalked to the kitchen. He heard the sound of glass rattling and ice clinking.

He looked up to see her, hip propped in the doorway, sipping on a clear drink that could have been seltzer but he suspected was a cocktail. It was at least her third of the night. "What's with the booze?"

She took another small sip and curled her lip. "I need to do something to dull the edges around here."

Jack's gaze swung back to the TV but he could still feel her gaze on him. That probing, curious stare she'd been giving him from the time he'd returned from his little chat with Danny.

He snapped his eyes up to meet hers, and this time she didn't try to pretend she hadn't been looking.

"What?" he snapped. "You've been giving me looks all night. Is there something you want from me? Because if not, I could use a break." He knew he was being a dick, but this night—this week—had been utter hell on his equilibrium, and any fuse he had was wearing mighty short.

Her gaze didn't falter and she continued to stare at him over the rim of her glass. "Who's Gina?" she asked, and took another sip of her drink.

Shit. She must have overheard him and Danny earlier. "She's someone I used to know." He grabbed the remote and hit the up arrow on the volume.

Talia walked over, took the remote, and clicked off the power, and then sat down next to him. "It sounds like it was more than that, Jack. And since Danny seemed to think I bear some similarities—what did he call us? Broken birds? I feel like I deserve to know."

Jack scrubbed his face with his hand. The memories were nearly a decade old, so dark and ugly and not anything he wanted to revisit.

"Come on, Jack," Talia said, her tone gentler. "You know the deepest and the dirtiest about me, and I know next to nothing about you." She let out a little laugh. "You saved my life, you saved Rosie's life, and I didn't even know you lived on a houseboat until two days ago!"

"You seemed fine not asking questions before."

"You weren't living in my house before. My memories are vague, Jack, but I think this is what people who care about each other do. Ask questions, share stories from their past, and get to know each other."

"So you care about me now?"

He focused on the delicate lines of her throat as she swallowed. "Of course I care about you, Jack." She reached out a hand but stopped short of touching him.

He stifled a harsh laugh. Great. She cared for him. She could twist him in knots with a look and she "cared for him."

"I just..." She trailed off. "I want to know about you, Jack. To be honest, I've never understood why you stepped up to help me the way you did. Maybe if you tell me, I'll get it."

"I helped you because you needed it, and you weren't going to help yourself." Just like Gina, and look where that got her. "Okay, fine. Gina was married to one of the guys on the team with Danny and me. I knew he was beating the crap out of her. One night I gave him a taste of his own medicine and ended up spending a night in jail. I would have been brought up on assault charges if Danny hadn't had my back."

"Did you love her?" Talia asked.

Jack had to think about that. There was a time when he would have said yes. "I loved the idea of her. She was pretty, blond, blue eyes, wholesome, you know?"

"Sounds adorable," Talia said, unable to keep the edge from her voice. "Funny, you don't strike me as a homewrecker."

"Nothing ever happened," Jack said, sounding offended. "I'd never make a move on a married woman. But I couldn't live with myself if I didn't try to help her. She and Johnny got married right out of high school. She was a kindergarten teacher. When I first met them, they seemed kind of perfect, you know? And even though I had zero interest in settling down, I thought how nice it would be to be married to a pretty girl who'd stuck by my side through everything, waiting for me back home after a grueling mission. Then they had a kid and he was so damn cute..." Jack swallowed convulsively at the thought of little Toby. "He had this mop of brown hair and big blue eyes like his mom."

"Had?" Talia whispered.

Jack ignored that for a moment. Now that he'd started, he needed to get it out, to make her understand why couldn't leave her alone, even when she would have pushed him away. "It was about a year and a half after Toby was born, we'd been deployed to Central America for six weeks. We'd been back for about a month before I saw them together and I just knew."

"That he was hitting her? She didn't tell you?"

Jack shook his head. "She didn't need to. I knew the look in her eyes, the way she carried herself around him." He turned to face Talia, looked her straight in the eye. "It's the same look I saw on my mom's face until I left home for good when I was eighteen."

Talia reached out and covered his hand with hers. Out of sympathy, he knew, but he'd take what he could get. "I'm sorry, Jack."

"At first Gina tried to pretend it wasn't happening. Then she tried to get him into counseling, thinking it would get better."

Talia's fingers curled into his palm. "It never gets better," she said bitterly.

"Then when I found out he went after Toby, I lost my patience and went after him. He broke my nose, and I fractured his wrist. Bad enough he had to stay behind on our next deployment." He leaned his head back against the couch, staring sightlessly up at the ceiling as he thought of the horror that had followed.

"I had some money saved up—my grandfather left me some when he died—and I set Gina up with a new place to live and some money in a bank account. Somehow Johnny found out. I don't know if she told him or what. But three days after we left, Johnny walked into his house and shot himself, but not before he took out Gina and Toby too."

"Oh, God," Talia breathed beside him.

"He shot her in the head, and then he walked up to Toby and just shot him in the chest. In the pictures I saw, it looked like he was napping." He closed his eyes but he couldn't keep the gruesome slideshow from playing in his head. "I still have nightmares, but instead of the pictures it's like I'm there, walking through the house and finding their bodies."

Beside him, Talia was silent, but he could feel the trembling of her hands and hear the occasional sniffle.

"I was dreaming about them, you know, the other night when you heard me screaming. At least it started out that way, but then in the dream Gina turned into you." He couldn't suppress the shudder at the image from the dream that ran through his head.

"Did something happen...after? What Danny said made it sound—"

Jack cut her off. "It's hard to say if there was direct cause and effect. I was fucked up, that's for sure. We were at the end of our tour and Danny, Moreno, Novascelic— they all decided it was time to get while the going was good."

"But you didn't."

Jack shook his head. "I couldn't. I didn't know what to do with myself. Danny wanted to start Gemini Securities and wanted me to join with the other guys, but I couldn't get my head back into normal life. I needed to get away; I needed action. I needed...I don't know, to feel useful or something because I'd fucked up everything so badly." His mouth pulled into a rueful smile. "I couldn't save Gina or Toby, but I could still fight for our side. And then that all went to shit too. I only lasted one more mission before I was sent home."

"Were you wounded? Was that how you got the scars?"

"I was wounded but this time it was just a shoulder wound." He gestured to the spot under his shirt where the skin was puckered from the bullet. "But I got sent home because I beat the shit out of my commanding officer. I was lucky I didn't get court-martialed."

He felt her tense next to him and waited for her to scoot away. He should have never told her any of this. You tell a woman like Talia—hell, any woman—too many stories about beating the crap out of people and they start to get nervous. And he couldn't blame her. Even though he would cut off his right arm before he'd lay a hand on her, given her background, it was only natural that she'd worry about him turning physical on her.

"You had to have a good reason," she said, the certainty in her voice surprising him. More shocking, instead of scooting away, she shifted a couple inches closer, close enough for her bare thigh to brush against his.

"I thought I did at the time," he replied, interlacing his fingers with hers, the simple touch sending warmth up his arm and through his body. Maybe holding confessional with Talia was a good thing if it meant she'd get close of her own accord.

"We were in Afghanistan, north of Kandahar. Out in the desert in the middle of nowhere. We were supposed to deliver medical supplies to a village about ten miles to the west. About ten minutes outside the wire, we got word that we were being ordered to change course and check out a suspected drug lab. The officer in charge had sent another ranger unit out about a few days before to find it, but he'd fucked up the coordinates and sent the team to the wrong place. Now he was looking to save face and use us to do it."

He closed his eyes and it was like he was back there, the ever-present dust sucking every bit of moisture from his throat as the sun beat them down with its relentless heat. "I told them it was impossible, that the only route was through a narrow valley that would leave us completely vulnerable if the Taliban troops spotted our location." His mouth twisted bitterly.

"Our convoy was spotted by a goat herder. We tried to pick up the pace, but trying to get over land there— you have no idea. And the valley got so narrow there were spots where the sides of the vehicles were scraping by. The next thing you know, there was this huge explosion and it was like the whole side of the mountain came down on top of us. Boulders as big as a bus raining down, RPGs hailing down on us. We were pinned down for over four hours. By the time air support arrived, I managed to pull only two other guys out with me."

"You saved them?"

"Yeah," Jack said tightly. "But one is minus a leg and the other has the mental faculties of an eight-year-old. And all because someone wanted us to cover his ass. So when the asshole came to see us in the hospital, I just... I just fucking lost it." He shook his head.

"He deserved it," Talia said, "just like Johnny did."

Jack shook his head. "It's one thing to give someone what's coming to them. It's another to totally lose control. I don't want to be that guy, Talia. The guy who goes into the blind rage and doesn't realize the damage he's doing until it's all over. I don't want to be like my father." The words slipped out before he realized what he was saying. He let out a low curse. "Anyway, I was lucky I was able to get a general discharge."

"You're not like your father, Jack," Talia said. Of course she'd pick up on that. "People like your father, like

Johnny, like David, they don't try to save the broken birds. They crush them under their heels."

"So far my track record in saving isn't so great."

The grief, the defeat in Jack's voice was so profound it squeezed Talia's heart like a fist. "You saved me."

"Barely," Jack said.

"Although," Talia continued as though she hadn't heard him, "I think I'd prefer the term *wounded bird* instead of *broken*."

Jack turned to her, shadows from the dim light of the table lamp playing over his chiseled features. "Why's that?"

"*Wounded* implies you can heal. *Broken* sounds more permanently damaged."

His eyes locked on hers.

"For a long time, I was convinced I was broken." She dropped her gaze to their interlaced fingers. Focused on the warmth of his touch, the steady sound of his breathing, the warm scent of his skin.

On him.

So loyal. So brave. So gentle, in spite of his propensity to kick ass and take names.

And did she mention hot?

And he wanted *her*. The thought sent a sizzle of heat straight to her core. Shocking her with its intensity.

Maybe she should start trusting someone else's opinion instead of her own. Maybe she really wasn't so broken after all. Only one way to find out for sure.

"Kiss me," she whispered, and reached out to cup his cheek in her hand.

"Be careful, Talia. The way I am right now, I can't guarantee I'll be able to stop at just a kiss."

She paused a moment to absorb what that implied. A

small voice urged her to retreat. That was the broken bird talking, and Talia was not broken. Tonight, with Jack, she wanted to fly. She reached up, stroked his cheek, her thumb tingling as it rasped against the dark stubble darkening his jaw. "I want you to kiss me, Jack. And I'm not afraid of what happens after."

He went completely still, so still he might have been carved out of granite. Then his breath hitched in his chest and he whispered, "Are you sure?"

Talia didn't answer, just leaned forward to close the last few inches separating their mouths. His lips were firm and warm, and they parted at the first touch of hers. Just that slight contact sent a jolt of heat through her. The first time he'd kissed her, she'd been caught off guard, so shocked and panicked she'd barely been able to register how he felt, how he tasted.

Now the light touch of his lips against hers made her crave more. Hot shivers coursed over her skin and she pressed closer, threading her fingers through his hair, opening her mouth to get a better taste. Her tongue flicked tentatively across his lips and he opened on a groan, and suddenly she found herself pushed back against the cushions of the couch, his mouth devouring hers with hot, wet kisses.

They were necking like teenagers on the couch and she'd never been more turned on in her life. It felt so good, so right, it almost made her giddy.

She ran her hands up his back, shoving the heavy fabric of his jacket out of the way. With an impatient grunt, he yanked it off, contorting his body so his mouth never left hers. She stroked him through his shirt, the fabric thin enough to let her feel the heat of his skin, the muscles coiling and tensing under her touch.

So much strength. So much power. And he would focus every ounce of it to keep her safe.

The whisper of desire turned into a roar.

She needed more, needed him closer. She wanted to feel his bare skin under her hands and tugged his shirt from his waistband and slid her hands up underneath.

She swallowed his groan at the first touch of her hand on his smooth, hot skin. His hand slid from the curve of her hip, explored the dip of her waist, and slid higher to cup the fullness of her breast.

The contact jolted through her. Even through the layers of her dress and bra, she felt his touch like a brand. Her nipple beaded hard against the brush of his thumb.

It sent a bolt of heat straight to her core, making her ache and throb. Her hands froze on Jack's back and she gave a startled little cry against his lips.

He jerked his hand away and sat up.

Talia blinked in confusion. Had she done something wrong? Accidentally kneed him without realizing it?

"Shit, I'm sorry," he said, running a hand through his hair as he sat back against the couch. "I didn't mean— Forget what I said. I don't want to do anything you don't want me to do."

In that moment, Talia realized Jack had mistaken her reaction for fear. A smile spread across her face. She moved over to Jack's lap, loving the startled, hopeful look on his face as she positioned herself facing him, her knees on the outside of his hips as she settled her weight on him and took his hand in hers.

"You didn't do anything I didn't want, Jack." Slowly, deliberately, she raised his hand to her mouth and kissed the center of his palm. She watched the slashes of color on his cheekbones darken as she placed the hand over her breast and arched into his touch. His lips parted on a gasp, and she could feel his erection surge underneath her, hard as a club and pulsing against the curve of her ass.

She took his face in her hands and kissed him hungrily, sucking his tongue into her mouth to tangle with hers.

"To be honest," she whispered in between more of those slow, wet, mind-blowing kisses, "I don't think there's anything you could do tonight that I would say no to."

A shudder rocked through him. "You're absolutely sure? I don't want to push you—"

"You're not pushing me, Jack. I want you." She opened her knees wider and her dress pushed higher up on her thighs. She rocked her hips until she was riding against the hard ridge of his cock. She moaned as she rubbed against him, the silk of her panties creating a delicious friction against her overheated flesh. Surely he could feel it, the heat, the wetness, even through the heavy fabric of his pants.

But just in case he couldn't, she whispered again, "I want you, Jack. So much. More than I ever thought it was possible for me to want a man."

He took her mouth again and rocked his hips against her, letting her feel the full strength and hardness of him underneath her.

She started to unbutton his shirt but got only a few buttons down before she was distracted by the tug of his hands at the button at her nape, then the tease of cool air on her back and chest as the sleeves were tugged down her arms. She pulled her hands from the sleeves and the dress pooled around her waist. A rush of apprehension coursed through her. This was as close to naked as she'd been with another person since that night. She forced the fear back. She wouldn't allow the past to leave its ugly fingerprints on what she was feeling right here, right now, laying herself bare to Jack's strong hands.

She looked up to see his gaze locked on her face, not on her breasts, covered by the beige cups of her bra. Studying her, careful, wary as he took her one step closer to full surrender.

She couldn't deny him anything. She reached behind her and unhooked the bra, leaving breasts completely bare to his stroking hands.

Her mouth sought his, licking, sucking, leaning into his touch as she tried to tell him without words how much she wanted him, needed him. How desperate she was for his touch, how she'd needed him, needed this, all along and hadn't even realized it.

His mouth slid from hers, down her neck, and he bent his head to capture a nipple in his mouth. She moaned at the first tug of his lips, the flick of his tongue, the scrape of his teeth. Heat pulsed between her legs, so intense it was almost painful.

She threaded her fingers through his dark hair and held him close, pushing for deeper contact as he sucked at first one, then the other breast.

Her nipples were tight points, dark red and glistening in the dim light.

"You are so fucking beautiful," he murmured against her. "You make me insane." He sucked at her left nipple again, then released it, pressing soft, hot kisses to the inner curve of her breast and underneath.

Until his tongue was there, tracing the small, round

pucker of flesh left from where Nate Brewster had burned her with a cigarette.

Talia stiffened, cold fear threatening to chase away the heat of desire. But she felt Jack's mouth, so gentle, kissing and licking at the scar like he would erase it and all the pain that came with it.

"Beautiful," he whispered again. She looked down and had to blink back tears at the look on his face.

Almost reverent. As though she really was the most exquisite woman on the planet and he was the luckiest man in the world to be with her.

She'd never felt more beautiful, more adored. She was going to grab on to that feeling and hang on tight for however long she could make it last.

Jack bent his head and kissed his way back up her neck. He closed his teeth over her earlobe. His voice was a deep rumble in her ear, and she felt the vibrations in the tips of her breasts and the ache between her legs.

"I want to make you feel good. I want to take you to bed."

Chapter 15

Y es."

The single word sent a jolt of lust straight through Jack. The blood pounded in his groin, and his cock, already rock hard as it rubbed against the curves of her incredible ass, felt like it grew about another inch.

He kissed her again, the taste of her sending a rush of electricity through his already-overloaded system. He knew he had to be careful, knew he had to go slow, but, Jesus, after wanting her for so long, to finally touch her, kiss her...

And oh, Christ, he thought as she sucked his tongue into her mouth, felt her fingers slide inside the front of his shirt to touch his chest, to have her kiss and touch him too...

It was like getting the most awesome, most coveted Christmas present in the world, and he knew that if he tried to open it with too much enthusiasm, it would shatter into a million pieces.

So even as his body demanded relief from the frustration that had dogged him for what felt like decades, Jack rode the brakes hard.

He sucked and nipped at her lips, rubbed her tongue

with his, the taste of her, sweet and hot and tasting faintly of the lime she'd had in her drink, hitting his brain with a rush more powerful than any drug. He cupped her breast, the silky skin, the hard point of it nuzzling into his palm, threatening to send him into the stratosphere.

But nothing, nothing got him hotter than the little sounds she was making in the back of her throat. Helpless moans and sighs, the little gasps when he rolled her nipple between his fingers that told him exactly how much she liked it.

How much she wanted his hands and lips and tongue on her.

How much she wanted *him*.

Part of him didn't really believe Talia would ever be able to get past the damage, the guilt, the pain to be able to give herself to him without at least a dusting of obligation.

But the moans into his mouth, the arching into his touch, and—sweet Jesus—the way her hips were rocking against him didn't feel like obligation.

It felt like everything he'd kept pent up inside him echoing back on him. Lust. Need. Desire. And something else, a little too powerful and scary to put a name on just yet.

He slid his hands up her smooth thighs and cupped her ass, filling his hands with the firm curves. He felt her hands between them, and then his shirt was spread open. He pressed her harder against him so he could feel the heat of her as she rubbed herself against the mammoth bulge in his pants.

Her nipples brushed against his chest and they both gasped at the contact. She pressed closer, chest to chest, belly to belly, and the feel of her skin against his was so good Jack felt like the top of his head was going to pop off.

He needed her naked, to feel every inch of her skin against his.

Cupping her hips, he pushed off from the couch as she wrapped her legs and arms around him. Never taking his mouth from hers, he carried her down the hall to the downstairs bedroom and laid her gently across the double bed. He shoved his shirt the rest of the way off his shoulders and reached for her dress.

He curled his hands in the fabric bunched around her waist, his gaze seeking hers as he started to tug it down. "Okay?" he whispered.

Her eyes were hidden in the shadows, and though her pulse was thrumming against the delicate skin of her throat, there was no apprehension, no hesitation in her voice when she answered. "Okay."

Jack pulled the flimsy green fabric over her hips, down the sleekly muscled legs. He let it fall to the floor and took a few seconds to just look at her.

What he saw made his breath hitch in his chest and every nerve in his body tighten in response. Wearing only a pair of panties that were somehow sexier for their plain cotton simplicity, she was all silky caramel skin over tight muscle and soft curves. Full breasts, their tips dark and tight, seemed to beg for his lips and tongue. Her stomach was a smooth, flat plane, lush hips flaring out from a waist he could fit his hands around.

He curled his hands around her ankles, needing to touch, to feel, to prove to himself she was actually here, letting him see her, letting him touch her in a way that she hadn't let any man touch her in a very long time.

Christ, as if he didn't feel enough pressure to make it good for her . . . He slid his hands up her legs, wondering if she could feel the slight tremble in his fingers. He hadn't been this nervous since the first time he'd talked Mary Blake into sneaking off to his parents' pool house in the tenth grade.

But the nerves fled, chased away by heat as Talia pulled him over her, her legs bent, knees parted so he could settle his hips exactly where he wanted them.

He took her mouth as his hand slid down, pausing to savor a breast before it continued down the smooth line of her stomach. He felt the muscles jump under his hand, tensing as his fingers teased the waistband of her underwear.

"If I'd known I was getting lucky tonight, I would have worn something other than granny panties," she said, a breathless quiver in her voice.

Jack felt a smile tug at his lips and then bent to kiss a sweet patch of skin under her ear. "I like them. Reminds me of high school when I was trying to convince the good girls to be bad with me."

Her hand tangled in his hair and stroked down his neck. "I was never a good girl. You should know that by now, Jack."

He kissed her again, hard, trying to make her feel in that one touch how amazing he knew she was. How much he wanted her, admired her.

Loved her.

Oh shit.

"You're a lot better than most and you don't even know it," he muttered against her lips. His hand slid a couple of inches inside her waistband. He heard her shaky breath. "I want to touch you." His fingers slid a little farther, enough for him to feel soft hair and the top of the slit hidden beneath.

She caught his wrist in her hand, and for one horrible second he was afraid she was going to pull his hand away.

Just the thought was enough to make him burst into tears.

Instead, in a move that made him feel like his dick was going to rip through his zipper, she pushed his hand down, down that last inch.

He parted her with his fingers, groaning as he felt her, hot and slippery wet with need. Any doubts he had about how much she wanted this—wanted him—disappeared as he circled her clit, dipped his fingers in her tight core, and felt her clench around him.

He was so hard he hurt, desperate to sink inside her. But he could feel the slight quiver in her lips as he kissed her, knew if he went at her like the beast inside him was demanding, he risked calling up the old demons she'd finally managed to beat back enough to be with him.

But Jack knew all about demons. Knew they didn't like to stay quiet for long, and one false move would bring them screaming back to the forefront. He shoved his own need aside and focused every cell in his body on her. On what she wanted, what she liked.

What would make her come so hard she'd forget all about the demons that haunted her dreams.

He kissed his way down her body as his fingers rubbed and stroked, every moan, every hitch in her breath sending a sizzle of triumph through him.

His lips traced the waistband of her panties and she let out a cry of protest as he slipped his hand free. "Why are you stopping?" she said, and he smiled at the note of irritation in her voice.

He hooked his thumbs in the waistband and slid

them off with one swift tug. Before she could react, he hooked her left knee over his shoulder and pressed a kiss to the top of her mound. "Trust me, this is only going to get better." He licked his lips in anticipation. She was as gorgeous here as she was everywhere else.

———∿———

Oh my God, was he...The thought dissolved as Jack parted her with his thumbs and bent to take her with his mouth. Talia arched up from the bed, a high, startled cry ripping from her throat as pleasure like nothing she'd ever felt jolted through her. She'd been stunned already at the pleasure she felt at Jack's touch. Shocked at how wet and ready he'd made her, how her body thrilled at the feel of his hands on her skin, his lips and tongue on her breasts. When his hands slid inside her panties, when he'd pressed his thick, powerful finger inside her, she'd never known anything could feel so good.

But, God, this, the feel of his tongue circling her clit, his lips sucking at her.

She felt a tiny ripple of embarrassment. He wasn't really enjoying this, was he? She'd never met a man who did....

"You don't have to if you don't want to—" she started, but her words stuck on another gasp as he slid one thick, long finger inside of her.

"Are you kidding?" He lifted his head but replaced his tongue with his thumb, circling, stroking, making it almost impossible for her to concentrate on what he was saying. "I've been dying to taste you like this forever." His eyes were molten blue flames. "I crave you like a drug and I don't want to miss a single inch of you."

Any lingering reserve dissolved as he pressed his mouth to her again, his unmistakable groan of pleasure vibrating through her. He took her lovingly, hungrily with his lips and tongue, feasting on her like she was the most delicious thing he'd ever tasted.

She could feel something building, churning inside her, pulling every sinew tight as her pleasure focused on Jack's mouth against her core.

It was like teetering on the edge of a cliff, looking out into the abyss. What would happen if she let herself fall?

Another finger slid in to join the first, stroking and thrusting. Her body clenched and shuddered around him as though trying to pull him deeper. She'd never felt like this before, powerless to control the thrust of her hips, the high cries ripping from her throat. Oh, God, it was so good, it almost hurt, her whole body reaching, yearning...

"Jack!"

The tight knot burst, shattering her into a million glittering pieces as time seemed to stop at the monumental force of her orgasm. In what could have been seconds or hours, or hell, even days, Talia came back to herself and felt the pieces start to settle back together.

Yet everything was a bit off, not quite the same as she'd been before. But as Jack pressed a kiss to the still quivering muscle of her inner thigh, Talia somehow felt more right in herself than she ever had before.

—⁓—

Satisfaction surged through Jack as he felt the lingering pulses of Talia's orgasm shimmer though her body. He'd always tried to be a considerate lover, but the stakes riding on Talia's pleasure were higher than anything he'd ever faced.

But hearing her sharp cries, feeling the tug of her fingers in his hair and the tight clench of her muscles around his fingers as she came...

The thought of burying his cock in that tight, clenching heat...his cock throbbed behind his fly. He was so hard he hurt, desperate to shove himself inside her and pound his way to satisfaction.

He kissed his way up her body and tried to keep himself under control. Even though Talia had liked having him go down on her, it didn't mean she was ready for him to drop trou and have at her like a caveman.

He took her mouth and settled between her legs. He could feel her hot and wet against the muscles of his abs, could see the blurry look of satisfaction in her eyes.

He had done that. Wiped away the fear and hesitation and replaced it with something dark and sultry. Kissed that plump mouth until it was swollen and red.

"You're looking very pleased with yourself," she said. Her fingers threaded through his hair and he leaned into her touch.

"Do I deserve to?" He bent and tasted the sly smile on her lips. It felt so damn good to be with her like this, teasing and kissing. He didn't know what was going to happen next, and he wanted to draw this out as long as he could.

"Considering I had an orgasm for the first time in nearly a decade, I'd say yeah, you've earned your swagger tonight."

Jack jerked back a little. "You're exaggerating, right?"

"Oh, God, I can't believe I just admitted that." Talia dropped her gaze and looked like she wanted to retreat, but there was nowhere to go with Jack's arms framing her head on the pillow and his weight pressing her into the mattress.

There was no way. Despite her past, once you broke through the wall, Talia was a passionate, responsive, sexual creature. Tonight had finally proven that without a doubt. He didn't kid himself this was only about him. "But I know you loved..." He stopped himself. He didn't want to utter the fucker's name, didn't want him to pollute what they had here.

She smiled up at him, a little sad. "He never took the time to make me feel like this. No one did."

Her eyes were suspiciously shiny and Jack felt an answering tightness. He had about a million things to say swirling around in his head but he couldn't get any of them past the lump clogging his throat.

Instead he cupped her cheek and bent his head and kissed her, trying to tell her without words how much he cared about her, that she was worthy of kindness and consideration and, goddamn it, pleasure and didn't have to settle for assholes and losers who didn't care about anything but their own selfish desires.

But his own selfish needs quickly roared to the surface. His kiss turned hungry, demanding, even as he warned himself to back off. Yet when he tried to pull back, slow it down, Talia wouldn't have it. She sucked and nipped at his tongue and wound her legs around his hips. She slid her hands down his back and slipped her fingers into the waistband of his pants, under the top of his boxers to curl them into the tight muscles of his ass.

She moved her hands to his hips. "Lift up," she whispered, and he held his breath as her hands came around to the front of his waist and her fingers landed on the tab front closure. The muscles of his arms quaked as he held himself over her, perfectly still as though any sudden movement might send her fleeing from the room. He could hear the pounding of his heart, the panting of his breath as she flicked his pants open at the waist. She dragged the zipper down, and even through his boxers he almost came at the first brush of her fingers against his cock.

She caught her lip in her teeth as she shoved his pants down his hips and he rolled to the side, squirming to kick his legs free. Then he was on his back, his erection tenting out the front of his boxers so outrageously it would have been funny if he weren't so hard he felt like he was going to burst through his skin.

Talia lay on her side next to him, dark waves falling across her cheek. So beautiful it almost hurt to look at her as she slowly leaned over to kiss him. He gasped into her mouth at the first brush of her hand against his stomach. The hand slid lower to brush against the waistband of his boxers. Then lower still, and she curled her fingers around him and stroked him through the fabric of his underwear. He let out a low groan against her mouth, then swore as her hand slipped under the waistband to take him into her hand.

Silky and warm against his hot flesh, it was all he could do to keep himself from coming in her hand. But she seemed into it, too, her breath coming faster as she gripped him in her fist and stroked him from root to tip. Her thumb swept over the head, spreading the droplet of precome that had pearled at the tip, and Jack felt his balls tighten against his body. Talia was making those hot little sounds in the back of her throat again, and as she pumped him again, he knew he'd reached the end of his rope.

Breathing like he'd run a marathon, he ripped his mouth away and wrapped his fingers around her wrist to hold it still.

"What's wrong?" she said, and even through the roar of blood in his head, he could hear the thread of anxiety. "Nothing," he gasped, "not one goddamn thing except for the fact that if you don't stop touching me like that, I'm going to come in your hand."

Her cheeks darkened with a blush, and he took a second to marvel at the fact that this woman who had once led men around by the sheer force of her sex appeal was so easily embarrassed by crude language. He could spend the rest of his life working out all of her contradictions.

"Look," he said through gritted teeth, fighting the urge to pump against her hand still wrapped around him, "I could settle for a hand job tonight and be totally satisfied." Okay, that was a huge exaggeration. "I know this is a lot for you and I don't want to push you into anything you're not ready for."

A smile spread across her face, its glow sending a warmth that had nothing to do with lust rushing through him. She tugged her hand from his grip and released him with a last, teasing stroke and brought her hand up to cup his cheek as she pressed him back against the pillow.

She leaned over him, and he felt that smiling mouth against his lips as she whispered, "That's my Jack, noble to the bitter end."

He parted his lips with little urging and sucked her tongue inside. He pulled her against him until they were breast to chest, her legs brushing against his as she hooked one knee over his hip.

"I'm all in, Jack, and I'm as ready as I'll ever be."

To prove her point, she took his hand in hers, guided it between her legs.

Take it easy, take it slow, Jack chanted silently as he rolled her to her back and took himself in his hand. He pressed the head of his cock against her hot, moist core, pushed inside. Oh, Christ, he was barely inside her and he was about to lose it. Nothing had ever felt this good, ever. She was hotter, wetter, tighter, every sensation turned up to eleven as he eased himself in a millimeter at a time.

Then, like a hammer blow, it hit him why it felt so ridiculously good.

He pulled out with a curse and flung himself onto his back.

"What?" Talia asked, breathless.

"I don't have a condom," he groaned.

"Oh," Talia said with a little laugh. "It's okay." She nuzzled his neck and nipped at his earlobe. "I'm on the pill," she whispered.

He could be inside her, nothing between them? For a second Jack thought the top of his head was going to blow off. He held himself still, digging deep for self-control as he struggled not to drive himself full length inside of her.

"I'm...I'm clean too," she said, the embarrassment evident even in her whisper. She squirmed underneath him and he bit back a groan at the feel of her wet flesh sliding against him. "I can see why that might worry you, but I was with only David for a long time, and of course no one since."

It was hard to form the words with the blood roaring in his ears. "God, of course I'm not worried," he said. "And for the record, I had everything done on my last physical and I'm good and—"

He broke off as he pushed the head of his cock against her, felt her tightness close around him as he pushed inside. "God, I've never done it without a condom. It feels..." He trailed off, unable to find the words. He bent his head, kissed her, pushed in a little farther. So hot. So tight. Like a wet, silky fist closing around him as he worked himself in inch by torturous inch.

Talia sucked Jack's tongue into her mouth, whimpering as he rocked his hips in careful, shallow thrusts. He was huge, hot, squeezing inside her tightness until pleasure danced on the edge of pain.

She started to stiffen as old, ugly memories threatened to rear their heads. Rough hands holding her down, harsh breathing in her ear as the heavy weight pinned her to the mattress.

"Talia," Jack breathed in her ear. "You feel so good, so perfect."

The memories fled as she opened her eyes on Jack's face. His eyes were squeezed tight, his face a mask of pleasured agony. "Jack."

His eyes opened at the sound of his name. Glittering hot, it felt like an electric current arced between them.

"Jack," she whispered again, reaching up to thread her fingers through his hair and pull his mouth down to hers.

His skin was hot under her hands, his coarse chest hair rasping against her nipples in a way that sent jolts of pleasure coursing through her. Jack's huge, strong body settling over her and oh, God, driving hard and deep inside of her.

Heat sizzled through every cell as he kissed her lips, sucked her neck, whispered how good she felt, even better than he'd imagined.

Talia wanted to tell him that before tonight, she wouldn't have even been able to imagine feeling anything like the pleasure he was giving her. Never would have known it was possible to have her entire world center on the feel of his thick hardness inside of her, cramming her full but making her crave more.

She moaned and felt the familiar tightening, heard his answering groan as her body squeezed and pulsed around him. He slid his hand between them and found her clit with his thumb. Rearing back on his knees, he circled and stroked in rhythm with his thrusts. Talia gripped the hard muscles of his ass in her hands urging him harder, faster...

She came with a sharp cry, flying apart once again as pleasure burst between her legs and rippled through every nerve ending. Jack rode her through it, his pace slow and steady until the last pulse shimmered away.

She looked up to see him poised above her, muscles tight, veins bulging through his skin with the force of his restraint. She dug her nails into his ass and slid her knees up either side of his rib cage. "Your turn," she said with a smile.

He flashed her a quick, almost pained smile in return and started to move in quick jarring thrusts that made her appreciate just how much he'd been holding himself back. He threw his head back and she felt him twitching and jerking inside her, bathing her with heat as he shuddered in release.

He collapsed and rolled to the side, hauling her against him until they were glued breast to chest, so close a light particle couldn't get between them. "You okay?" he whispered.

Was she okay? She was better than okay. With his one hand sliding up and down her back and the other combing through her hair, she felt warmer, safer, better than she had in years. Maybe ever.

And that was even before she factored in the languid relaxation that came from two back-to-back orgasms.

As far as she was concerned, she could spend the rest of her life in this bed with him and be perfectly happy.

Jack seemed to agree, and within a few breaths he'd drifted off to sleep. Talia lay there, her ear pressed to his chest, listening to the steady beat of his heart. He was the most amazing person she'd ever known, and tonight he'd proven himself to be the most patient, gentle, satisfying lover a woman could ever ask for.

She'd fought to keep him out of her life, certain she didn't need him, convinced he could only make her miserable as he served as a living reminder of everything she'd struggled to leave behind.

But the past had come back to haunt her, and once again he proved to be the only one she could count on to get her out of the muck. The only one she wanted to count on.

He would go back to Seattle when this was over, she reminded herself. He'd made no promises, made no claims to his emotions other than that he wanted her.

He *wanted* her. Nothing more and nothing less than

the few that had come before, except he was a lot less selfish about it.

He wanted her, and tonight she'd realized she wanted him right back. The discovery should have made her happy, should have brought her comfort and reassured her that contrary to her fears, she really was capable of feeling desire, of having amazing sex with this amazing man.

And it would have, had she not had another terrifying realization.

She was in love with Jack Brooks.

Admitting it to herself, even in her head, was so terrifying it propelled her up and out of the bed. She grabbed blindly and snatched up the first article of clothing she could find—Jack's shirt. She wrapped it around herself and darted from the room, down the hall and up the stairs to her own room. She closed and locked the door behind her before climbing onto the bed.

She curled up against the headboard, calling herself a hundred kinds of idiot as pure, icy panic made her heart pound and her stomach churn. She didn't even realize she was crying until she saw the drops hit her bare knees and reached up to feel where the wetness was coming from.

Even as some rational part of her brain tried to remind her that this was Jack she was talking about, not a monster in disguise like David Maxwell, it couldn't drown out the steady lament of "I can't, I can't, I can't."

She was so stupid, thinking sex was the biggest stumbling block. Good for her, she could have orgasms.

But she couldn't allow herself to be vulnerable again. Couldn't go back to that place where her entire world revolved around a man who might turn on her at any moment. Couldn't let herself be under someone's thumb, dependent on a man for her happiness and security.

She'd worked too hard to put her life back together, and she couldn't afford to risk it on an emotion that had nearly destroyed her in the past.

She couldn't trust anyone—not even Jack—with her heart.

Chapter 16

By the time Jack reached out a hand to stop her, Talia was already out the door and halfway down the hall.

Shit. Goddamn it.

He should have known it was too good to be true. It was too much to hope that tonight's breakthrough would be the beginning of something—finally—between the two of them.

Not that he expected her to just flip a switch, sleep with him and be good to go with happily-ever-after, but was it too much to ask her not to go sprinting from the room before the sheets even got cold?

Screw it. From the second he'd realized he had it bad for Talia Vega, he'd known there was no hope. So it should be no problem to just go back to normal.

And hey, at least he had the added bonus of relieving the unrelenting sexual frustration that had dogged him for the past week straight. Although, given his body's swift and eager recovery from an orgasm that had nearly made him black out, he had a bad feeling this was going to be one of those one tastes that only makes you crave more.

Fuck.

And they were no closer to catching the shithead who

was tormenting her, so he was stuck here for the foreseeable future.

But really, what happens when you do find the guy? You really going to just tuck your tail in between your legs and run back to Seattle without a fight?

Everything in him rebelled at the thought of simply packing up and heading back to Seattle. Alone.

Jesus, when had he turned into such a pussy? He'd never shied away from a fight in his life.

Yeah, but taking down a couple Taliban soldiers is nothing compared to dealing with the damage Talia's already suffered.

But he had to try, he thought, swinging his feet over the side of the bed and pulling on his boxers before he was even conscious of moving. He didn't know exactly what he was going to do as he climbed the stairs, only that he couldn't leave it like this.

Tonight Talia had been able to overcome her demons enough to turn to him. She felt it, too, this thing between them. She might not be ready to admit it was love, but she couldn't say it was nothing. And Jack wasn't going to let her run away from it, especially when it could turn out to be the best thing that ever happened to both of them.

He raised his hand to knock. When she didn't answer, he tried the doorknob and found it locked. "Talia, come on, let me in."

"Go away."

"Dammit," Jack said, unable to keep the irritation from his voice, "you can't just run off like nothing happened."

"It doesn't have to mean anything, Jack. It doesn't have to be important."

"It's important to me," he said with another thump on

the door. "Really fucking important." He waited several more seconds. "Come on, Talia, please open the door."

There was no movement. He contemplated the consequences of picking the lock. Just as he'd decided he could live with them, he heard her footsteps and the spring of the lock popping on the doorknob.

His irritation evaporated at the sight of her tear-streaked face and swollen, trembling mouth. With his shirt swallowing her up and hanging down past her knees, she looked small and so fragile a stiff wind could sweep her away. "I'm sorry, Jack," she said in a tight whisper. "I can't do this. I thought I could do this..."

Jack pulled her into his arms, ignoring her stiffness and the way she held her arms up between them. He should have seen this coming. Talia had been shut down physically for so long, it made sense that the first time she finally let someone in—literally and figuratively—she would freak out.

He just had to keep proving to her that no matter what happened, she was safe with him.

"It's going to be okay, Talia," he said, stroking her hair. "We'll take things slow."

"You don't understand," she said, shoving at his chest. "I can't do this again. I can't let anyone in. I can't let anyone hurt me."

"I'm not going to hurt you," Jack said, holding her tighter when she tried to pull away.

"I know that," Talia whispered against his chest. "Logically, I know that, but there's something wrong with me. Something I can't fix. Tonight, for a minute there, I thought we could fix it, but it only made me realize how broken I really am."

Jack grabbed her by the shoulders and held her away enough that he could look in her face. "You are not broken."

She pulled away from him. "How can you say that when you know exactly what I've done, what I am?" She turned away from him, and he saw her arms moving but didn't realize she was unbuttoning her shirt until she slid it off her shoulders and down her waist. "Isn't this proof enough?"

The scars were white, puckered lines against the honey gold of her skin. Even now, the sight of them was enough to make fury boil in Jack's blood. He wished, as he had a thousand times, that he'd been the one to kill Nate Brewster for the damage he'd done to her body. That he'd been the one to kill David Maxwell for the damage he'd done to her soul, making her feel cheap and used. Exploiting her love for her sister to manipulate her into doing things that continued to eat at her conscience until she felt unworthy of love and happiness.

Broken.

"And that sick piece of shit, whoever he is," she said, almost to herself, "it's like he wants to remind me exactly who I am and what happened." Her breath caught in a sob that made his chest squeeze. "Like I don't remember every goddamn day when the ugliness is carved in my skin."

Jack stepped closer and reached out to stop her when she would have pulled the shirt back up to cover her back. Slowly, as carefully as if she were a wild animal he wanted to touch, he traced his fingers down the length of one scar. "When I see you, I don't see broken, and I sure as hell don't see ugly," he said, his voice rough.

"Don't," she whispered, but she didn't pull away when he landed a kiss on the smooth skin of her shoulder. His lips parted and he sank to his knees as he ran his lips and tongue across her back, along the length of one scar.

He could feel her tremble, hear her breath speeding up as he slid his hands around her waist and kissed his way across to her right hip and followed the other scar back up to her shoulder. He pulled her back against him and slid his arms around her waist.

He nuzzled his face in her neck and whispered, "When I look at your scars, when I remember what you went through, it reminds me how brave you are, how loyal. How much you love your sister that you'd do anything to protect her." He straightened to his full height and pulled the shirt back over her shoulders.

Talia let out a little sob and turned in his arms. "I'm just afraid—all I know is that caring about someone makes me weak, makes me stupid," she sobbed against his chest. "The last time I was with someone, he ended up controlling everything. I'm afraid of letting myself be that way again, even with you."

Jack leaned down until his forehead touched hers. "You aren't stupid, and you aren't weak. And I don't want to control you. Protect you, yes." He shoved aside the little tickle of guilt that she might not see the distinction if she ever discovered that he'd "invested" in Susie's restaurant and that he'd been secretly keeping tabs on her for the past two years.

"I just want to be with you, Talia, that's all. I'm not going to push you into anything you're not ready for," he said, sounding like a broken record. "But it could be good between us. Really fucking good."

She shifted against him, and he could feel his skin

heat, his muscles tighten at the feel of her bare breasts against his chest. "Try to let go and we'll see what happens. Just be with me."

—⁂—

Talia didn't answer, her breath stuck in her throat at the feel of his hot breath on her neck, the growing hardness of him against her stomach. She wasn't sure she could let go, wasn't sure she knew how. *Just be with me.*

It couldn't be that easy, especially with someone like Jack, with the strength and the will to run roughshod over her if she wasn't careful. But when had he ever pushed her into doing anything she didn't want to do?

When had he ever gone behind her back and manipulated her into a corner until she had no other choice than to do what he demanded?

Just be with me.

A simple request, calling up the answering yearnings in her heart and her body that had been buried for so long under the black muck of her past. She'd had a taste of paradise tonight before the demons reared their ugly heads.

She wanted it again. She didn't want to let the demons win. What she felt for Jack had to be stronger. And as she looked up into Jack's face, his blue eyes full of emotions she was still too scared to name, she realized that if she was with Jack, she wouldn't be fighting alone anymore.

Still, she felt as if she were sailing over the edge of a cliff as she wound her arms around his neck. "I'm scared," she said softly.

"Me too," he breathed against her lips right before they came down on hers. And then there was nothing but heat and need curling low in her belly as his tongue slid against hers and he pulled her hips against his.

He backed up until the backs of his knees hit her bed. She reached down and shoved his boxers down his hips. He sat down on the edge of the mattress and pulled her down to straddle his lap. The thick head of his cock brushed the inside of her thigh and she felt a rush of heat and wetness between her legs.

Already her body was throbbing in anticipation and she marveled at this new craving to touch and be touched, this need to take his body inside hers. She reached between them and wrapped her hand around him, loving the way his breath hitched as he bucked his hips. He was as big and powerful here as he was everywhere else, and if she hadn't already known how good he would feel in her, she might have been intimidated.

"Please," he groaned as he ran his hands restlessly over her body. "I need you so much."

He pulsed in her hand and she guided him to her core, rubbed him against her slick heat until they were both panting and shaking, their kisses almost frantic now.

Finally, when neither of them could take more teasing, she drew up on her knees and sank down, taking him all the way inside with a low sigh. He touched her everywhere, his hands on her back, sliding down to her hips as his lips nipped and sucked at hers. Skin on naked skin, sweat slicked and flushed with need.

He bent his head and took her nipple between his lips, sending a shock of pleasure straight to her core. Her orgasm hit her then, with such speed and force it ripped a startled cry from her chest.

Jack wasn't far behind. Afterward, he pulled her down

next to him, covered them up with the quilt, and wrapped his arms around her tight, like now that he had her where he wanted her, he was never going to let her go.

And for the first time in her life, Talia couldn't find a single reason why she'd want to escape.

—⁓—

The alarm shrieked them awake at four in the morning. Talia shot straight up in bed and had a moment of confusion when she found herself totally naked. When she would have swung her legs over the side of the bed, strong arms pulled her back.

Still muddled with sleep, she started to fight, thrashing and punching.

"Talia, stop!"

Jack's voice penetrated the panic and calmed her down a degree. "What's going on?" she asked in a shaky whisper. In the dark she could barely see the outline of Jack's broad shoulders leaning over her. "That's the alarm," she said stupidly.

"I know," Jack whispered, and reached over to turn on the bedside lamp. "And I want you to stay up here while I check it out."

Jack was a badass, but if someone was still here, she didn't want him taking them on alone and unarmed. "The police will be here soon," she protested. "Let's just wait."

Jack was already out of the bed and pulling on his discarded boxer shorts. "No way. If the fucker is anywhere near here, I'm going to take him down."

She didn't like it, but she could tell from the hard set to his features there would be no arguing with him.

"Do you still have your Taser?"

Talia grabbed it from her bedside table and handed it to him. It was eerie, how his entire demeanor changed in an instant. Wearing nothing but his underwear and armed only with a small Taser gun, he should have looked silly. But somehow it was like an invisible cloak had dropped down over him.

Gone was the tender lover who waited patiently, even uncertainly for her to accept him. Now Jack was a warrior, tough, dangerous, afraid of nothing and capable of taking on the world.

Still, concern made her stomach tight as she locked the door behind him. Jack was tough, but what if someone was still down there with a gun or a knife...

She pulled on a sweatshirt and a pair of yoga pants and waited for what felt like hours but was probably only a couple minutes for Jack to knock and give her the all-clear. When she opened the door, she saw that he'd gotten dressed, too, in a T-shirt and jeans, a pair of black running shoes on his feet. They had a few damp blades of grass clinging to the top. He must have gone outside.

"No sign of him?"

Jack shook his head, his mouth pulled into a tight line. "Whoever it was lobbed a brick through the window over the kitchen sink."

"The one that faces my neighbor's house?" she asked as she slipped on a pair of flip-flops and followed him downstairs.

Glass crunched on the linoleum as she walked across the room to assess the damage. The lower panel of the window was gone, only a few shards hanging from the frame. There was a pile of glass in the sink, scattered across the counter and on the floor. Carefully, she leaned over the sink to peer through the window. Jack had turned on the outside lights, illuminating the narrow strip of land that separated her kitchen wall from the neighbor's fence. Roughly six feet high and lined by a row of tall myrtles on the other side, it completely blocked her from seeing into the neighbor's lawn.

"If he threw it from behind the fence like I think he did, there's no way we'll have him on tape," Jack said grimly, as though reading her mind.

Talia shook her head, frustration boiling up to chase away the fear. "This is getting ridiculous. He goes from sending me the DVD to throwing a stupid brick through my window? Seriously, is he going to do anything or just torture us for the rest of my life?"

"It wasn't just a brick," Jack said, and motioned to the kitchen counter. It was only then she noticed the envelope sitting there. "I didn't want to open it until the cops got here."

As if on cue, there was a loud knock on her front door, and Jack went to answer. She heard the low murmur of voices, and Jack came back to the kitchen with Officer Roberts in tow.

He nodded in greeting. "Sorry to be out here again."

"Me too," said Talia.

She gave him a quick sequence of events and then indicated the envelope on the counter. She watched, her heart in her throat as Officer Roberts pulled on a pair of latex gloves and used a knife to slice it open.

She couldn't help remembering what she'd found the last time she'd been left one of her creep's "tokens" and braced herself for the worst. Jack came up beside her and threaded his fingers through hers. She clung for dear life as Roberts slid a photo out of the paper sleeve.

Talia's knees went watery as a cold that had nothing to do with the breeze coming through the broken window chilled her to her core.

"You know this girl?" Roberts asked as he held up the photo so she could get a better look.

"That's my sister, Rosario. She was here the first time you came. She's a freshman at Stanford." The words seemed to come from very far away.

"Look at the time stamp," Jack said, pointing to the yellow digits in the bottom left corner. "It was taken earlier today."

Talia scrambled for her phone and dialed Rosario's number. Her call went straight to voice mail. "She's not answering," she cried. "Why isn't she answering?!"

Jack closed his hands over her shoulders. "Don't panic. She called and checked in at eleven like always, right?"

Talia knocked his hands off. "Don't tell me not to panic! It's been hours since then. She could be anywhere. This could be a warning— Oh my God, maybe this is that sick fuck's way of telling us he took her."

She grabbed her purse and ran for the kitchen door, vaguely heard Jack say something about finishing up with him once they knew Rosario was safe.

"Okay if I look around?" Roberts called as she was stepping through the door that led from the kitchen to the garage.

"Knock yourself out," Talia called. She was already buckled into the passenger seat and redialing Rosario's number when Jack climbed in beside her.

"Still no answer," she said, her throat tight.

"They don't have a landline?"

She bit her lip to stop its shaking and shook her head. "She and Dana decided it didn't make sense since they both had cells."

As Jack pulled out of the driveway and headed down the street, she scrolled through her contacts to see if by some chance she'd taken down Dana's contact number, but no dice.

"You have her phone in your GPS locator system, right?" Jack reminded her. "Why don't you check and I'll try to get the campus police over to check her room."

Talia logged onto the tracking site, though she half suspected that Jack's suggestion was more to distract her than anything else. It would be easy enough for someone to disable the signal if he knew what he was doing.

Still, as she half listened to Jack's conversation with the Stanford campus police, she pulled up the device's tracking, cursing as it loaded at a snail's pace. Mingled guilt and fear threatened to choke her at the thought of how she'd let Rosie's earlier call go straight to voice mail.

Because she's been too busy fooling around with Jack to answer her phone. "If anything happens to her... because we left her alone..." She buried her face in her hands, replaying the moment when her phone had rung. Talia had looked at the display, seen it was Rosie calling at her usual time, and had rolled back over to bury herself in Jack's embrace. What if she had answered? Would she have heard something in her voice, a trace of fear that wouldn't have come through on the voice mail she'd left? "I won't be able to handle it if something happens to her because of me."

"I'm sure everything will be okay," Jack said, reaching over to rest his hand on her thigh.

For the first time, the warmth of his hand didn't bring her any comfort.

She looked down at her display and saw that the GPS tracking site had finally loaded. She felt a small measure of relief when she saw the dot that represented Rosie's phone showed up at her dorm's address. Still, if someone grabbed her, what was the likelihood that he'd let her take her phone with her?

They reached the parking lot of Rosario's dorm just as the police were pulling up. Talia waited impatiently for the kid who was sleeping on the lobby couch to rouse himself and let them in.

He eyed the cops nervously, and as Talia got closer, she understood why—the kid smelled like he'd spent the night at the bottom of a keg.

"Hey, you're not s'posed to go up without signing in—"

Talia ignored him and bounded up the stairs to the second floor, Jack hot on her heels. "Rosie," she called, pounding on the door. There was a muffled thump and some shuffling and finally the door opened.

Dana, Rosie's roommate, squinted through the narrow opening. "Talia? What's up?"

"Is Rosie here?"

Dana's eyes widened with surprise at the sight of Jack flanked by two cops behind her. "No—I came back after midnight and she wasn't here. Is she in some kind of trouble?"

Talia's heart went into overdrive as she pushed past Dana into the room. Sure enough, there was Rosie's phone on the desk. When Talia tried to turn it on, she saw the battery was drained. She started to hyperventilate. "Jack"—she couldn't keep the panic from her voice—"we have to find her. Promise me we'll find her."

"Her backpack isn't here," Dana said cautiously. "Let me check my phone. Maybe she left me a message."

Talia barely kept it together as a thousand nightmarish scenarios burned through her brain.

"Yeah, she texted me around eleven-thirty," Dana said, and held out the phone. " 'Heading over to Kevin's will probably stay over see you in the morning.' "

Talia's panic dialed back several degrees, but she knew it wouldn't disappear entirely until she saw Rosie with her own eyes. "You could have told us that before," Talia snapped.

"Sorry," Dana snapped back. "It's not like I get Rosie's crazy sister and the cops pounding on my door every Saturday night—Sunday morning," she corrected herself.

Talia winced. "I'm sorry, Dana. It's just, I don't know if Rosie told you anything about what's been going on with me—"

"Does this have something to do with your stalker?" Dana asked. There was no mistaking the slightly titillated note in her voice. "Has he been watching Rosie? Do you think he's been spying on us?" Her eyes flitted around the dorm room as though looking for a hidden camera on the bookshelves.

Talia knew better than to put anything past anyone, but since the picture of Rosie had been taken outside of the library, she took that as a hopeful sign that no one had invaded Rosie's personal space.

Yet.

Jack gave a small shake of his head, as though Talia

didn't already know not to give any more information than necessary. "It's probably nothing," Talia said as she headed for the door. "But I just need to make sure Rosie's okay. And if anything out of the ordinary happens, don't be shy about calling me."

"Or us," one of the cops quickly interjected.

Before she left, she made sure she had Dana's contact info for future reference and looked up Kevin's phone and address in the campus directory. He lived off campus in an apartment complex that flanked the campus's north side.

She buzzed his apartment repeatedly on the intercom system. It took a full minute before he finally answered. "What the fuck?"

"Is Rosie there?"

"Who the fuck wants to know?"

"It's her sister, Talia."

There was muffled conversation; then Rosie's voice came on over the intercom. "Talia, what are you doing here?"

Talia's knees went watery with relief, and if Jack hadn't caught her around the waist, she might have sunk down onto the pavement.

"We'll let you in on the details in a little bit," Jack said, "but right now your sister really wants to see you."

All the energy seemed to drain out of her. She turned her face into Jack's chest, absorbing his warmth as she took a deep, bracing inhale of his spicy scent. She could hear voices whispering and footsteps across the courtyard as they approached the gate.

"Shit, you didn't say she'd brought the cops," Kevin said, stopping short of the gate.

"Talia, what happened?" Rosie said as she shoved open the gate, the clang of metal on metal echoing through the courtyard.

Talia didn't say anything, just grabbed Rosie in her arms and breathed a deep sigh of relief. She stepped back, reaching up to stroke her sister's hair as she did a quick once-over to make sure she was okay. Her nose wrinkled at the hickey on her sister's neck, and as she looked closer, she saw Rosie was wearing a worn T-shirt bearing Kevin's fraternity letters, too big to belong to her sister.

She bit back a snide comment. As much as she was disappointed by the fact that at some point over the last two days Rosie had gotten back together with Kevin, she'd take finding Rosie in her unworthy boyfriend's bed any day over any of the horrific scenarios that had played in her head.

"Jesus, you didn't tell me she brought the cops with her," Kevin repeated. "What the hell?"

"You have something to hide?" Jack asked in a menacing voice.

Kevin lifted his chin and flipped him off like the arrogant snot nose that he was. "You'll never know without a warrant."

"Jeez, Kevin, do you have to be such a dick? Talia wouldn't come here without a good reason." She turned back to Talia. "What happened?"

Talia quickly brought her up to speed on the picture that accompanied the brick crashing through the window.

Rosie's hand went to her throat. "I didn't see anything. But I've had a weird feeling lately, like someone was watching me."

"Why didn't you say anything?"

Kevin interrupted before Rosie could answer. "God, you are so much more of a pain in the ass than you're worth."

Rosie whirled on him. "And you are so much more of a dick than I even gave you credit for. Someone is, like, stalking me. Don't you even care? God, I'm such an idiot. I can't believe I let you talk me into giving you another chance."

She started stalking toward the parking lot, ignoring Kevin saying, "Rosie, wait, I'm sorry."

"Asshole," Rosie muttered under her breath. "He only gives me the time of day when I ignore him. So are you going to catch this guy or not?" Rosie said, and it took Talia a couple seconds to realize she was addressing the cops.

"We called them to go to your dorm room when I couldn't reach you on your phone," she said, the anger and frustration at not being able to reach her once again flaring to the surface now that she knew Rosie was safe. "Why the hell was it dead? Why didn't you have it with you, for God's sake?"

"It's not like I knew some creep was watching me—"

"You said yourself you felt like someone was watching you. Why didn't you say anything?"

"Because I didn't want to freak you out any more than you already are! And I seriously thought it was just your paranoia rubbing off on me."

Guilt knifed Talia's stomach. She'd tried so hard over the years to keep her fear from affecting Rosie's ability to live a normal life. But that was nothing compared to the truth, that once again, despite all of her efforts to protect her, Rosario wasn't safe from the evil person determined to make sure Talia never forgot her past.

She was startled from her thoughts as a series of squawks burst from the radios strapped to the cops' belts. "Looks like you've got everything under control here?"

Talia nodded.

"Be sure to call us if you have any problems," they said to Rosie, "even if you think you're just being paranoid."

Rosie nodded and they bid them good night.

But Rosie wouldn't be calling them, because until they found the creep responsible, she wouldn't get a chance to feel paranoid. "You have to go to a safe house," Talia said without preamble. "Tonight, if Jack can arrange it that fast?"

She turned to Jack, who nodded. "Let me make a call."

"No way! No way am I going into hiding again."

Talia grabbed her sister by the arms. "It won't be for long. Just until we figure out who is behind this." Although given the complete lack of clues, there was no telling how long Rosie's exile might last.

"I have midterms coming up this week! If I don't take them, I'll have to do the whole quarter over—"

"I could give a shit about paying for an extra quarter of school if it means keeping you safe."

"You promised," she said, her voice breaking in a sob. "And you promised too!" she said, pointing an accusing finger at Jack. "You said it was over when David Maxwell died. You promised me we would never have to hide again. You promised our lives would be normal!"

"Rosie, stop," Talia yelled as Rosie stormed across the parking lot.

She took off after her as did Jack, who caught up with

her first. "Okay, if you don't want to do the safe house, you come stay at Talia's. I can keep an eye on you both."

Rosie stomped her foot in a move more suited to a three-year-old than an eighteen-year-old. "But I have midterms next week."

"All of your exams are in the daytime, right? Should be no problem for us to go with you."

Talia felt a spurt of irritation that Jack was laying this out as a choice without consulting her. "I don't think—"

"What about study groups and extra office hours? Do you know how screwed I'll be on my physics exam if I don't make Gene's office hours?"

Jack rolled his eyes. "Whatever I can't help you with, you can have Gene come to the house or the restaurant if need be—I'll buy him dinner. As for the study groups, schedule them when we can go with you, or Skype in."

"Do I get any say in this?" Talia asked.

They both ignored her. "This is so lame. I don't see why I can't just stay at the dorm if I promise to be careful and never go out alone—"

"It's either this or the safe house."

"You can't make me," Rosie muttered, again channeling her inner three-year-old.

Jack folded his arms across his chest and glowered down at Rosie. "You want to test me on that? I'm not the cops. I'm not worried about your civil liberties. You can try to charge me with kidnapping later. I don't give a shit. The only thing I care about is keeping you"—his gaze floated over Rosie's head to lock on Talia—"and your sister safe from this asshole."

"Fine," Rosie said sullenly, and slung her backpack

over her shoulder. "And I guess this means I don't get to go on the dorm camping trip next weekend."

"Not unless Talia can get off work so we can go with you."

Whereas part of her wanted to call him a jerk for using his size and his attitude to intimidate her sister, Talia had to admit it was kind of hot, the way Jack took charge and wouldn't take no for an answer.

But it didn't stop her from getting in his face as he took off for their car. "I think I should make the decision about whether Rosie goes to the safe house. If this guy is after me, won't she be safer if she's not under the same roof?"

Jack glanced at her and his face looked suddenly weary. "And what then? If Rosie's in the safe house, you'll want me there, keeping an eye on her, and that means I'll have to get one of the other guys to keep an eye on you."

Talia's nose wrinkled at the thought.

"Unless you want to go into hiding with her," Jack said.

Everything inside her rebelled at the thought. "I'm not going to let some asshole take away my life again," she said fiercely.

"Exactly," Jack said. "And you shouldn't let him. And you shouldn't let him take Rosie's either."

"I just want her to be safe," Talia said, and didn't resist when Jack pulled her into his arms.

"I know. And she will be. I'll make sure of it. I'll take care of both of you."

The statement should have made her want to flee for the foothills in the distance. But instead the idea that Jack was here, ready and willing to protect them, to take care of them, wrapped around her like a warm fleecy sweater that she never wanted to take off.

"Umm, will we be able to come back in the morning to get my stuff?"

Rosie's voice had her jumping from Jack's arms, and the night air did nothing to cool the embarrassed heat that rushed to her face.

They drove home in silence. Jack moved his stuff out of the guest room to make room for Rosario and taped a plastic garbage bag over the hole in the kitchen window and double-checked the alarm.

As Rosario got herself a glass of water from the kitchen sink, Jack settled onto the couch and pulled out his laptop.

"You're not going to sleep?" Talia asked uncertainly.

"I'm going to take a look at the camera feeds," Jack said, barely sparing her a glance over the top of his laptop. "See if we managed to get a look at this guy. I'll be okay on the couch."

"Oh," Talia said lamely as she returned Rosie's sleepy hug. "So . . . I guess . . . see you in the morning."

"Good night."

Talia climbed the stairs, trying to ignore the hollow feeling in her stomach. Stupid really, with everything going on, to dwell on the fact that Jack had bid her good night with barely a second glance. But as she climbed into bed—alone—all she could think was, so that's it? After all of his I want yous and I need yous, he finally got what he was after and now he could move on like nothing had happened?

She wasn't sure how long she'd been asleep when she awoke to the sound of her door clicking open and the heavy creak of footsteps. Anticipation sizzled in her blood as the covers were lifted back and a heavy weight settled on the mattress beside her.

Jack pulled Talia against him. "I hope this is okay, but I couldn't stay away," he said huskily.

His hand slid up the back of her tank top, and she felt the hard ridge of his erection against her stomach. Her mouth found his, her lips parted as she breathed him in. In the dark, every sense was heightened; every sound, every touch seemed amplified. Jack quickly stripped off their clothes, the rustle of fabric sending hot need shooting to her core.

Then he was there, between her legs, sliding inside her as his mouth came down over hers to muffle their cries. Talia wrapped her arms and legs around him, taking him deep, holding him as close as she possibly could.

Despite the drama of the fear-soaked night, right here, right now, everything was finally right with her world.

Chapter 17

Y ou know you guys aren't fooling anyone, right?"
Rosario said.

Jack looked up quizzically as he picked up the strategically rumpled comforter from the couch. "What do you
mean?" he asked as he folded the comforter and placed it
on the end of the couch.

"I know you guys are totally doing it," Rosario said.

Jack heard a clatter in the kitchen and something
sounding like Talia choking.

"What?" Talia came out of the kitchen, blotting at
the front of her T-shirt with a towel. Her cheeks were
flushed.

Rosario was gathering up her books as though nothing
was amiss. "It's stupid, making Jack sneak down at the
crack of dawn and pretend to sleep on the couch."

"I'm not . . . we're not . . ." She looked helplessly at Jack,
but he was enjoying her discomfort too much to come to
her rescue.

The first morning after Rosie came to stay with them,
Talia had poked him awake before the sun came up and
sent him back down to the couch.

"She's eighteen," Jack had grumbled as he pulled on

his jeans. "We found her at her boyfriend's, for Christ's sake—"

"God, don't even remind me," Talia had groaned. "I'm trying to set a good example for her, and I'm not comfortable brazenly sharing a room with you like it's no big deal."

Irritated but too tired to argue, Jack had crept down the stairs like a sixteen-year-old trying to avoid his girlfriend's father and curled his too-big frame onto the too-small couch.

And it had been the same for the last three nights, waiting for Rosie to go settle in her room after they got back from the restaurant and then giving her a good hour, sometimes two, to actually turn out the lights and go to sleep. While he liked Rosie and enjoyed her company, he was looking forward to the day when their living arrangements could go back to normal.

A day that was still no closer to arriving. As expected, the footage from the security cameras didn't give any clue to the identity of the stalker, and the next-door neighbor hadn't seen or heard a thing until Talia's alarm went off.

So every night for the past three, Jack would creep upstairs like a thief in the night and slide into bed next to a usually sleeping Talia.

And okay, that next part didn't suck, the way she turned to him in the dark, her soft hands sliding over his skin and pulling him close. In the past three nights, Jack had explored every patch of skin on her body, discovered all the secret places that would make her shiver.

Kissing, licking, touching her until she had to clap her hand over her mouth or bite his shoulder to muffle her moans. Driving them both crazy until he felt as if he would spontaneously combust if he didn't have her again.

Clearly the subterfuge wasn't working, he thought as he met Rosie's all-too-knowing look.

"Give me a break," Rosie said as she shoved her laptop into her bag. "I came out the other night to get a drink of water and Jack wasn't on the couch. And, Jack, you might want to shave, because Talia has whisker burn all over her neck."

Talia snatched her hand to her neck and went to examine herself in the hall mirror. Jack's hand automatically went to his chin and he felt the wiry rasp of his beard coming in. He couldn't stop the involuntary smile from spreading across his face. He hadn't noticed the whisker burn on her neck because he'd been too concerned about the other places that were getting a little chafed from his attention.

Places like her smooth inner thigh and the inside curves of her breasts. Places he'd tried to soothe last night by massaging them with cream from Talia's medicine cabinet. He felt a heavy rush between his legs at the memory. And like every morning for the past three, he wondered how the hell he was going to make it through the day.

"Get that smirk off your face," Talia snapped.

"And even without that, it's totally obvious the way you guys are together," Rosie said. "You're always smiling and touching each other when you think no one's looking. And no offense, Talia, but you're in a really good mood for someone who has a stalker."

"I...we...," Talia sputtered, but she couldn't seem to get the words out.

Rosie went over and gave her sister a little hug. "Stop freaking out. I'm not upset about it." She cocked an eyebrow and shot Jack an arch look. "No offense, but I'm surprised it took you this long to make a move."

Jack slid his arms around Talia's shoulders and pressed a kiss to the top of her head. She stiffened but didn't pull away. "Your sister has some pretty elaborate defensive countermeasures in place."

"You didn't need to hide it," Rosie said with a pointed look to her sister. "It's good you found someone to make you happy, Talia. It's not like I'm going to be bummed you guys are together."

Together.

The word rocketed through him and he unconsciously tightened his arm around her.

"You are together, right? This isn't just some casual hookup?"

He could feel Talia stiffening up again beside him. He looked down and met her tense, anxious look. They hadn't talked about any of this, and knowing how skittish Talia was about everything, he'd been reluctant to push it.

He hadn't planned on declaring his intentions in front of her younger sister. "Trust me," he said finally, "the way I feel about Talia is anything but casual."

He could feel the tremble in her lips as he bent to kiss her. "If you feel differently, it's probably best to tell me now," he said fiercely, his breath catching as he waited for Talia's answer.

"I don't think it's possible to be casual with you, Jack," she said with a soft smile that made it impossible for him not to kiss her again. The tightness in his chest loosened at the warmth of her response. It was no grand declaration, but it was a baby step in the right direction. Maybe for once his relationship wasn't doomed to failure after all.

"Ugh, get a room, you guys," Rosario said, her grin overshadowing the mock disgust in her voice. Then the smile disappeared as she raised a finger of warning at Jack, her expression grave. "But just so you know, you break her heart, I'll kick your ass."

Jack wasn't sure it was Talia's heart they should be worried about.

—⚍—

Once she got over her embarrassment, Talia embraced the novelty of being part of a real, out-in-public couple. It had been so long, she'd forgotten how good it felt to walk down the street holding someone's hand, to have a man casually put his arm around her and tuck her close to his side.

Not just any man.

Jack.

Going back, way back, to the day they had met, it was hard not to marvel at the idea that they were walking hand in hand across the Stanford campus, enjoying the spring sunshine and each other's company as though they didn't have a care in the world.

Of course, the only reason they were on campus today was to escort Rosie to her world civilization exam because they were still no closer to finding out who was harassing her, but at the moment she chose not to dwell on it. Jack was by her side, keeping them safe. With him around, she didn't need to worry about constantly looking over her shoulder.

Jack did the job for her, constantly on alert, his gaze never ceasing its relentless sweep of their surroundings. Knowing Jack, Talia would lay money that he could give a detailed description of every person who had passed within ten feet of them.

They walked Rosario to her exam room, stopping along the way for coffee and snacks to sustain them through the wait. The room was crowded full of students whose faces bore the proof of late-night cram sessions. Jack did a quick check of the room and, satisfied there were no easy access points other than the main door, pulled up a couple chairs for them to sit in.

Talia took out a book and sipped at her coffee while Jack flipped open his laptop. After several minutes of working in silence, she heard Jack mutter, "Son of a bitch," under his breath.

"What?" Talia snapped to attention. "Did you find something?"

"Maybe," Jack said. "We've been going through Margaret's finances and Toni just pulled a whole batch of accounts we didn't know about before."

He motioned her over and Talia scooted her chair close enough to see the screen. It was all a blur of numbers and codes she couldn't make sense of.

"Jesus, they have money hidden everywhere," Jack said. "The Caymans, Belize, Panama, for Christ's sake. Most of it hasn't been touched, but in the past several weeks there have been several transfers from this account," he said, indicating with his finger a string of transactions that showed nearly a hundred thousand dollars moving out of the account in the space of a week.

"Any way to figure out where it's going?"

"Not yet." Jack sighed. "But don't worry. The money always leads somewhere. If Margaret is somehow connected, we'll figure out who she's working with soon enough."

Talia nodded and tried to take comfort, have faith that all of this would eventually lead them to the bad guys.

And Jack would no longer have a reason to be by her side 24-7.

"What happens then?" she blurted out before she could stop herself.

Jack's fingers froze on the keyboard and his ice-blue gaze locked on hers, steady and unwavering.

He didn't pretend not to know what she was talking about. "I guess you'll have to decide what you want from me once you don't need me around to protect you anymore."

Talia swallowed hard. No, she wouldn't need him around to keep her safe, but she was afraid she already needed him in her life on a much deeper, fundamental level. "What about you, Jack? What do you want?"

He flipped his computer closed and placed it on the floor next to him. He covered her hands where they were twisted together in her lap, a little half smile pulling at his lips. "I want the same thing I've always wanted. For you to want me the way I want you."

Heat flooded her cheeks and she dropped her gaze at the intensity of his stare. "I think we've already established that," she said, her face and body getting hotter by the second as her mind flashed on all of the ways she'd shown Jack in the past few days that her passion for him matched his for her.

"I'm not just talking about sex, Talia."

She looked up at the sudden note of intensity in his

voice. It was matched by the look in his eyes, burning icy hot with desire and conviction and something else she wasn't quite ready to put a name on even though she was pretty sure it was mirrored in her own gaze.

"I want everything."

—⁓—

I want everything.

Jack's words echoed through her brain later that night as she struggled to keep pace with the uncharacteristically heavy Tuesday night crowd at Suzette's.

Everything. What did that even mean?

She hadn't had a chance to explore that bombshell since shortly after Jack made the declaration, the door opened and Rosie and her classmates came spilling out, alternately exclaiming that they kicked the exam's ass or groaning that the exam had kicked theirs.

From there they'd followed Rosie to the coffeehouse for a study group and then it was time to head to the restaurant for work, with no real chance to dissect that comment and have any kind of meaningful discussion about their relationship going forward.

Relationship. Commitment. Giving someone a say in her life. For the first time in two years the idea of opening herself up, giving part of herself over and trusting it in someone's care, didn't send her into a panic.

Because it was Jack, she thought as she put sugar and mint into a cocktail shaker and muddled them together for a customer's mojito. She snuck a glance at him. He'd taken up his usual post at one end of the bar, his gaze constantly sweeping the crowd.

It no longer made her uncomfortable to have him here, watching her every move and those of everyone around here.

Now it made her feel safe, cared for.

She handed over the mojito with a smile and gave Jack a quick signal that she needed to go to the storage room to restock. He gave her a curt nod and started to follow.

"You have to stay with her," she said, indicating Rosie, who was sitting at a table in a far corner with Gene the physics TA, who had generously agreed to meet Rosie at the restaurant tonight for a last-minute cram session before her physics final tomorrow.

Jack's mouth pulled into a grim line, and the man waiting next to him took one look at his harsh expression and took a startled step back. It wasn't like anything was likely to happen, but Talia made the trip to the storage room in record time, knowing Jack would sweat every second he didn't have her in view.

As she rounded the corner back to the bar, she saw Susie and Jack in what was obviously a tense discussion.

"Seriously, you need to tone it down a notch," Susie was saying.

"I don't know what you're talking about," Jack said impatiently as he looked over Susie's head so he could keep Rosie in sight.

"I've had several customers ask me about you this week, wondering if there's a problem."

Talia's stomach sank and the bottle of vodka gained about twenty pounds in her hand. The knot in her stomach grew worse as her gaze snagged on Susie, the irritation and exasperation unmistakable. Pitching her voice low, Susie said, "It's one thing for him to hang out like another customer, but standing at the end of the bar like you're waiting for someone to make a move—"

"Which is exactly what I'm doing—" Jack snapped.

"Well, thanks to you, people are scared to go to the bathroom," she said, indicating the hallway behind him.

"Sorry," Talia said. "He needs to see me and Rosie too."

"Right, and she and her study partner are taking up a table that could be used for paying customers."

Talia bit the insides of her cheeks. It wasn't Susie's fault that any of this was happening. "Do you want us to go? I would hate for the business to be affected because of me."

Susie and Jack exchanged a long look that Talia couldn't decipher but made her uneasy just the same. Then Susie took a slightly panicked look at the crowd growing at the bar. "God, no, not tonight anyway," she said, and sent Jack another sharp look. "But seriously, Jack, you look like you're about to kick the crap out of someone if they make one wrong move."

—⁓—

Susie wasn't far off in her assessment. Something was up tonight, something he couldn't put his finger on. But from the moment they'd left the house earlier this evening and headed to the restaurant, Jack couldn't shake the tight, tingly feeling between his shoulders.

Call it intuition, a sixth sense, whatever you want, but shit was about to go down. It was just a question of when and how. He was on high alert, trying to keep tabs on everyone in the restaurant and bar. But it was nearly impossible with a crowd this size and the dim lighting and constant movement.

He itched to get Talia out of there but knew there was no way she'd go for it. No way would she leave Susie in a lurch short-staffed on what turned out to be a busier-than-usual night. Plus, it was only eight-thirty and she was already on track to double her usual amount of tips, and she'd made a big production this morning about paying him another installment on what she thought she owed him.

If she had any clue the amount of money he had waiting for him to tap, she'd see what a ridiculous drop in the bucket the two hundred dollars she'd given him was. But ever since Saturday night—ever since they'd slept together—she'd been making an even bigger deal about paying him back. Making it clear that the sex was in no way, shape, or form to be seen as payback for anything he'd done for her.

It was kind of silly, considering if Jack had his way, eventually they'd make their relationship more permanent in the what's-mine-is-yours-and-what's-yours-is-mine category. But for now, he'd indulge in her need to reassure him that any favors she granted, sexual or otherwise, were 100 percent freely given.

He scanned the crowd again and felt someone jostle his side. He looked down and met the startled face of an older woman in her late fifties.

"I'm sorry, I just wanted to get to the ladies' room," she said, backing up a step.

Susie's admonishment in his mind, he did his best to soften his expression. "Of course, I'm sorry," he said, stepping aside and gesturing with his arm for her to continue.

His focus went back to the bar. The customers seated on the tall stools along the bar and those sitting at the small tables didn't appear to pose a viable threat. Mostly couples in their late thirties, a couple of small groups, and a few tables full of women on a girls' night out. And Rosie, of course, tucked into a corner with physics genius Gene going over her lecture notes for her exam tomorrow.

He rocked back on his heels and kept his hands folded in front of him, struggling against the urge to twitch. He hated this, this every-nerve-on-alert, skin-too-small-for-his body feeling. More than that, he hated the impotence that came with dealing with an enemy he hadn't yet identified.

Jack was a man of action, always had been. Identify the target and go after it. But this asshole—this coward—who had targeted Talia just kept lobbing his little bombs and scurrying back to his hole. Eventually he would fuck up and they'd get a bead on him, but Jack was slowly going crazy from the wait.

It gave him the best excuse in the world to stay close to her, but that wasn't enough of a perk for him to tolerate any threat to the woman he loved. He took a deep breath and flexed his fingers. They'd get the guy eventually—failure wasn't an option. For now he had to dig deep, stay vigilant, and be ready to spring when the opportunity arose.

He watched as Talia walked over to Rosie and Gene's table and saw her mouth move. She turned back toward the bar and was heading in his direction when he heard the blast. Everyone jumped and screamed at the muffled boom that came from the parking lot adjacent to the restaurant.

The chaos was instantaneous as people jumped from tables and ran to see what was happening. "Call 911!"

Jack yelled as he pushed through the crowd to the window that overlooked the parking lot. Through the glass, he could hear the din of dozens of car alarms going off, and there in the center was the cause.

A small sedan—maybe a Honda or a Toyota, it was hard to tell with the flames coming out of the windows—had been hit with an explosion large enough to blow out the windows and set the car on fire.

This was it. The shit that he'd known was going to go down. He turned to find her, and in that second, the restaurant's fire alarm went off. He yelled Talia's name, barely able to hear himself over the din. Desperate to escape a drenching from the sprinklers spraying down from the ceiling, dozens of customers surged for the front door.

Working against the tide of customers, Jack looked desperately through the crowd and saw that Rosario's table was empty. He spotted her by the door, Gene at her side as he tried to protect her from the jostling crowd and move her to the door. Jack gave her a quick wave and turned back toward the direction of the bar.

Talia had disappeared.

—◦◦◦—

Talia followed Susie's lead and tried to caution people to slow down and be patient as they moved to the front door. She tried to signal several people to the exit in the back, and finally a large enough chunk broke off in that direction to ease some of the congestion moving toward the front.

She hung at the back of the throng, ushering people forward to make sure they made it out safely. She did a quick check behind her for Jack, but he must have still been stuck near the front because she didn't see him.

There was a little flutter of panic at the thought of going outside the restaurant without him. It was silly, though. There were dozens of people around and she just had to make her way to the front of the building to find him.

He grabbed her from behind and stuck the knife in her side so quickly she barely had time to take a breath. She could feel the icy point cutting through her blouse, hitting her hard enough in the ribs to feel the sharp tip but not enough to break the skin.

A voice, deep and gravelly, growled into her ear. "Don't make a fucking move or I'll gut you like a fish."

In that moment, the restaurant disappeared and she was back there in Nate's basement. Bound, naked, helpless to defend herself as he sliced the blade through her skin. Her breath seized in her chest and her heart seemed to stop beating as she went down the well, to a place even fear couldn't reach as she waited for the deathblow to come.

But she felt herself being shoved forward, and reality came back in a sickening, vertigo-inducing rush.

"Be nice now, and it won't be too bad. No one wants you dead. Yet."

Fight. You know how to fight.

The whispering voice grew to a shout as they got closer to the exit, and she knew with every cell in her body that she had to escape before he got them out that door. She shoved the fear away and focused on her training, first from Jack, then from Gus.

Bracing herself, she pretended to stumble and fell to

her knees. She heard the guy curse as his grip weakened for a split second. Flipping onto her back, she swung her leg in a high arc and landed her boot against his forearm.

He cursed and lunged at her, and Talia sprang to her feet, knowing she wouldn't have a prayer if he managed to pin her down. Screaming over the still-shrieking alarm, she ducked to avoid his grasp and brought the heel of her fist up hard under his nose.

She heard the satisfying crunch of bone and his bellow of rage. As he staggered back, she caught him with a solid kick to his chest. He reached out and grabbed her foot, twisting until she felt sure her ankle was going to crack. She lashed out with her other foot, managing a blow to the inside of his thigh as she fell back on her butt.

He winced and sucked in a breath, his grip shifting just enough for her to slip out of her boot. "You goddamn bitch," he bellowed, his face a mask of rage, blood streaming from his nose to drench his chin and drip down his shirtfront.

Her brain automatically took in details of his appearance. He was big—not as big as Jack, but bigger than her and powerfully built under his dark T-shirt and cargo pants. His hair was light brown, clipped close to his head. His misshapen nose dripped blood down his thin mouth and blunt chin. He still had the knife in his hand, held loosely, almost casually. But his dark, deep-set eyes tracked her every move, like a cobra waiting to strike if she made a break for the exit behind him.

He took a step toward her and she feinted forward as though she were going to make a run for the door. But at the last second she hurled herself into the door of the ladies' room on her left. The door swung in and she had the fleeting thought that maybe she'd be able to escape out the window or lock herself inside or at the very least find something to use as a weapon to fend him off until someone heard her screaming.

But her progress was halted as the door hit something and opened only a few inches and refused to budge. She heard a muffled cry as she tried to squeeze herself through the narrow space, then screamed in pain as a fist tangled in her hair and pulled her back into the hallway.

She flailed with her elbows, not caring if she got cut now as long as she could get away. Suddenly, there was an inhuman roar over the din of the alarm. A heavy impact, and it felt like half of her scalp was ripped away as her assailant lost his grip on her hair.

She rolled to her feet, and through the sprinkler shower, she saw Jack bring his hand down on the thug's forearm hard enough to send the knife clattering to the ground. The man turned and sprinted for the exit, bursting through it hard enough to send the heavy door bouncing against the brick outside.

Ignoring her shouts, Jack charged after him. Talia followed and made it outside in time to see Jack take the guy down in a flying tackle. They landed in a heap with a sickening crunch against the pavement.

To her shock, her attacker sprang to his feet, assumed a fighting stance, and hit Jack with two swift blows to the face. Jack countered with a kick aimed at the guy's chest that he managed to spin away from at the last minute.

It quickly became clear that the guy had some training, maybe even the same level of training as Jack. His moves were swift and well calculated, and like Jack he seemed to be able to anticipate Jack's moves a split second before he made them.

He'd been toying with her, she realized, or maybe he didn't want her badly hurt in her efforts to fight him off.

"No way—you stay and fight, you goddamn coward," she heard Jack yell when the guy made another attempt to flee. Jack slammed him hard against the brick siding, hard enough for any normal man to be down for the count.

She winced as another blow landed on Jack's face. Jack grunted in pain but didn't loosen his grip on the guy's shoulders. His knee came up, landing a brutal blow against the man's stomach. Then another and another until the man was sagging, Jack's hands on his shoulders the only thing holding him up.

He slid to his knees and she saw his hand snake out at the same time he surged back to his feet.

"Jack, look out!" she screamed as he struck out with the broken bottle. Jack didn't need her warning. He saw the bottle coming and jumped out of the way as the jagged edge whipped past his stomach.

Still, Talia hurled herself at the man's back, rage at the way he'd tormented her fueling her as she wrapped her forearm around his throat. He grabbed at her, his fingers digging into her skin hard enough to leave bruises, but she didn't care. Riding his back, she squeezed with all her might, determined to take him down.

She could hear the sirens approaching and Jack shouting. Then she saw nothing but stars as she was slammed hard into the brick wall. All the air left her body in a stunned whoosh and her arms went slack as noodles.

She sat on her butt, struggling to breathe, and saw Jack charge the man, the look on his face one of such unholy rage she would have been terrified had it been anyone but Jack.

The man was skilled, but he was nothing against the full force of Jack's fury. Jack body-slammed him into the brick wall, then swung him around by his arm, twisted his wrist up his back, and ran him face-first into a Dumpster.

Talia heard a sickening crunch and a scream of pain over the sound of approaching sirens. The guy gagged and sank to his knees, but Jack was relentless. His fist met the guy's chin with enough force to knock him backward. Jack gave him a kick to the ribs and pinned him down with a knee to his torso. He drew back his arm, his elbow aimed at the guy's head.

Talia shook off the last dregs of dizziness as she realized if she didn't stop him, Jack was going to kill this guy.

Chapter 18

J ack, stop!" Talia cried, but he didn't seem to hear. "Stop!" she yelled again, louder, and this time her voice was joined by several others.

The cops, she realized as she propelled herself forward and grabbed Jack's cocked arm.

His head whipped around, the rage in his expression so fierce that for a split second she was afraid he would hit her without thinking. His eyes quickly softened in recognition but his face remained in grim angry lines. "Let me do this, Talia."

Talia wrapped her arms around his torso and tried to tug him away, but it was like trying to move a concrete wall. "As much as I'm enjoying watching you kick his ass, I don't want to see you get arrested for manslaughter."

"It would be worth it."

"Not to me," she said fiercely.

The cops were surrounding them now, shouting for them to get on the ground, hands behind their heads. She knew if they didn't move soon, they'd break out the batons and Tasers, never mind that she and Jack were the real victims. She moved her mouth closer to his ear and pitched her voice low, forcing him to listen. "And if you kill him or put him in a coma, we'll never find out how he knew about the jewelry and the flowers. We'll never know why he's targeting me."

Jack let her pull him off the guy and stayed low, placing his hands behind his head as Talia did the same. One of the cops, gun drawn, approached with his cuffs out while another checked on the other guy who was on his back, groaning as he struggled to prop himself on his elbows.

"Wait, Jack didn't do anything," Talia protested as the cop clipped a metal cuff around Jack's wrist.

"It's okay, Talia," Jack said. "We'll get it straightened out."

But Talia wasn't having it. No way could she stand by and let Jack get arrested for coming to her rescue. Again. She rose to her feet and stepped toward Jack. "No, that guy attacked me," she said, struggling as another cop grabbed her from behind. "He held me at knifepoint and threatened me. I think he's the one who— Ow!" she cried out in pain as her arm was wrenched up her back.

"Hey, ease up!" a male voice called from behind her.

Talia craned her neck, relieved when she saw Detective Nolan jogging down the alley, flashing his badge.

Susie followed. "I called him right after I called 911," she said, looking a little shell-shocked. "I thought he might be able to help."

Talia had never thought she'd be particularly happy to see a police detective, but tonight she was damn glad Susie had him on speed dial, especially when a quick discussion with the other officers had them taking the cuffs off both her and Jack.

She rushed to Jack, wincing when she saw his split lip

and his rapidly swelling eye. "Are you okay?" she asked at the same time he did.

"I'm fine," she said, and let him fold her into his arms. She tried but couldn't hide a little gasp of pain when his hand pressed against her back.

He held her by her shoulders and pushed her back. "He fucking hurt you." Angry white lines bracketed his mouth, and she could see the muscles tighten under his shirt. She saw his glare shift to her attacker, who was cuffed, swaying on his feet as he blearily responded to the cops' questions. "I'm okay; it's just a bruise," she said, and slid her hands up his chest and around his neck. "I'm okay," she repeated, and pulled him close, needing to feel his solid warmth against her. He let out a shaky sigh and wrapped his arms around her, careful to avoid the sore spot on her back. "You got to me in time."

She could feel his heart thudding in his chest and he let out a shaky sigh. His big hand cupped her cheek and he took her mouth in a rough kiss. Talia kissed him back, hard, not caring about the crowd that had gathered and was closing in to get a closer look at the ruckus.

A throat cleared somewhere behind her and she reluctantly pulled her mouth from Jack's but didn't move from his embrace. She turned to see Detective Nolan. "You think this is the guy who's been harassing you?"

"He didn't say as much"—her brain flashed back to that moment in the hall when the guy had said something—"but he did tell me no one wanted me dead yet. Do you think he's the one who—"

Nolan silenced her with a quick shake of his head. "I'll be looking for a possible connection," he said.

Oh, God, was he the same person who kidnapped and

raped the other women? Is that what he'd planned for her? A shudder racked her at the thought. *No one wants you dead. Yet.* Those other women weren't dead, but she was sure there had been moments when they'd wished they were.

Nolan started to ask her something, but she was distracted by a high, frantic voice calling her name.

Relief flooded through her as she saw Rosie following Eugene as he made a path through the crowd for her. Rosie's hair and clothes were as drenched as everyone else's from the sprinklers. When she reached Talia, she grabbed her in a fierce hug that made her aware of every bruise her attacker had left on her body. But Talia didn't care about the pain. She didn't care about anything except the fact that Rosie was safe, she was safe, and now that they'd caught this guy, they would stay that way.

"Oh my God, are you okay? Someone said they saw him grab you, but we were trapped in the crowd."

"That's him?" Eugene said, nodding in the direction of her attacker, who was sitting, cuffed, on the back of an ambulance. An EMT was shining a light in his eyes. Talia couldn't hear, but it looked like the cop next to him was attempting to ask some questions.

The man's mouth moved, but it was clear from the glazed look on his face and the erratic movements of his head he was pretty out of it.

"You really worked him over," Eugene said to Jack, a note of admiration in his voice.

"He got off easy," Jack growled. His arms tightened around Talia. "He deserves a lot worse after what he's done."

Rosie scooted off to go gawk at the firemen who'd

arrived while Talia and Jack gave their statements to the police on the scene. She watched as Nolan went over to question her attacker, anxious to find out what he learned.

After several minutes, her attacker was loaded into the ambulance. She could feel Jack shifting impatiently as Nolan pulled a phone out of his pocket and made a call before coming back over to talk to them.

"They're locking him up, right? Fucker better not be back out tonight or I'll—"

Nolan held up a hand for silence. "He's in custody, but the EMTs think he needs to go in for some scans. You rang his bell pretty hard."

"Any idea who he is?" Jack asked.

"He didn't have ID on him but he says his name is Joe Smith."

"That's a load of shit," Jack said.

"You're probably right, but he did say something else that was kind of interesting. He's pretty out of it, but he kept saying, 'She just wanted her scared. I wasn't going to really hurt her. She just wants her scared.' Any idea what that means?"

Jacks fingers flexed against her arm. "The old bitch sent a goon after you."

Nolan cocked a questioning eyebrow.

"Margaret Grayson-Maxwell," Talia said.

Nolan nodded as understanding dawned. "You think she hired him."

"It's the most obvious answer."

Talia thought of the man, his evident skill at fighting. "He fits the mold of all of David's—Maxwell's," she clarified for Nolan's benefit, "goons that he used to hire. All jacked-up former-military muscle."

Jack nodded. "He had training of some kind, spec ops, Special Forces. It wasn't easy for me to get the drop on him."

"If he's ex-military, he'll be in AFIS," Nolan said. He pulled out his phone again and made sure "Joe Smith's" prints were run ASAP so they could get a possible ID.

"I can't believe she would go to all that trouble just to torture me," Talia said with another shudder. "The necklace, the flowers, the DVD." She broke off as the memory of the video mingled with the images from the photos Nolan had showed them of the rape victims. "And those women—was he doing that on the side to feed some sickness?" Her mind could barely grasp the possibility.

"He had access to the recordings from Margaret," Jack said. "I'll call Cole and find out if there are any cases that are similar up north—"

"Let me worry about that," Nolan said, and leaned closer. "Right now I need you two to keep the possible connection to yourselves until we have something that solidly links him to the attacks."

Jack nodded. "You let me know as soon as you know who he is and if he gets out on bail."

Nolan nodded. "I can't imagine they'd be able to arraign him before tomorrow, so I think you're good for tonight at least." He said something about finding Susie and headed back to the restaurant.

Talia started to follow. Now that the adrenaline had faded, she felt like she was about to collapse, and all she wanted to do was collect her stuff and go home. She drew back, startled when she almost ran smack into Eugene. "You're still here," she said.

He shrugged. "I offered to give Rosario a ride home but she wanted to wait for you."

"Thanks for looking out for her. Where is she?"

He pointed his thumb in the direction of the restaurant. "She went in to see if she could help clean up."

Talia's stomach sank as she thought of the mess the sprinklers had left, but nothing could have prepared her for the carnage that awaited them inside.

The floor was covered by half an inch of water, and as she passed the kitchen, she saw stoves and countertops littered with pots and pans of waterlogged, ruined food. As she walked down the corridor to the bar and restaurant area, she saw that not only was everything soaked, but also most of the tables had been upended, glass and tableware smashed as the crowd had charged the exit to escape the spray.

Susie was in the dining room, frantically mopping at the floor. Rosario was walking through the dining room, bending occasionally to retrieve something from the floor. It took Talia a few seconds to realize she was picking up the unbroken plates and glasses she found.

So far there were only four glasses, and the stack of plates was pitifully thin.

"You need to let it dry out a bit," Nolan was saying. "Right now you're just moving the water around."

"If you're not going to help, then at least shut up!" Susie snapped.

"Susie, I'm so sorry—" Talia started, then snapped her mouth shut at Susie's glare.

"Don't," Susie said, her thin shoulders knotted under her damp blouse. "Please don't. I know this wasn't in any way intentional, but right now, I'm looking at hundreds of thousands of dollars in damage that can be traced directly back to your personal issues."

Talia started toward her. "Let me have the mop. I can at least help clean up. And I'll handle everything with the insurance company—"

"If they'll even cover it, since they'll try to claim the sprinklers went off accidentally."

"I'll figure out how to pay the difference," she said, but a knot settled in her stomach at the knowledge there was no way on earth she'd be able to come up with the kind of money required to get the restaurant ready to reopen. She could take out a loan, get another job during the day maybe . . .

"It's not just the restaurant. People were injured! Did you know that when you crashed into the bathroom, you knocked over a seventy-year-old woman with the door so hard she fell and probably broke her hip?"

"I'm sorry," Talia said, the words squeezing past the guilty lump in her throat. "I never meant for anyone else to be at risk—"

"Please, just go," Susie said, her body drooping with weariness as she leaned on the mop handle for support.

Talia started moving around the dining room, righting chairs and upended tables, gathering the scattered silverware. "I can help. I'll stay all night if you need me—"

Susie shook her head and looked at Talia, her expression grave. When she spoke, her mouth trembled around the words. "You're not just my employee; you're my friend, okay? And I'm afraid if you stay even one minute longer, I'm not going to be able to keep myself from saying things that I can't take back. So right now, I really need you to go."

Talia swallowed around the lump in her throat and nodded. She walked back to Susie's office, swiping at the tears that were trying to leak out. She retrieved her purse and jacket, both of which were drenched. From across the small space, she could see Susie's computer screen flickering crazily, no doubt shorting out from all the water.

God, how much was it going to cost to replace all of the computer systems that handled the ordering and inventory? She was going to spend the next fifty years trying to pay Susie back.

"I hope you're ready to break out the checkbook."

Talia winced as Susie's furious voice carried down the hall. She gathered up her things and started back out to the dining room.

"Of course I'll take care of it," Jack said. Talia's stomach clenched at the thought of Jack taking this on too. This was her fault, and she would be handling this. "You don't have to worry about anything—"

"This is going to require a hell of a lot more than a fifty-thousand-dollar investment in the place," Susie continued. "That would barely cover the deductible on my policy."

"You know I'm good for it," Jack said, looking over his shoulder as though he was worried about being overheard. "You'll have however much you need and some extra on top. Maybe now you can get the patio seating area you wanted to do."

"Patio area?" As far as Talia knew, she'd never heard Susie mention wanting to expand the seating outside.

Jack turned, and a look of surprise and something else flickered across his face when he saw her. "Susie mentioned it at some point," he said, shooting Susie a hard look. "I figured as long as she'll have to renovate, she might as well look into expanding."

Something pricked at the back of her mind. This was the second time Jack and Susie had exchanged odd looks tonight. There was something out of place here, something she couldn't quite put her finger on.

"And, Jack, you're not paying for any of this. This is my problem, and I'll figure out a way to handle it."

Susie cocked her brow and shot Jack a knowing look. "Wait, why are you looking at each other like that? What's going on?"

"Nothing," Jack said flatly.

Talia stared at him hard, trying to penetrate his carefully neutral expression. But the emotional and physical trauma of the night were taking their toll, leaving her too exhausted to wrap her brain around whatever subtext was happening here. "Fine, let's go," she said. "I'll call you tomorrow?" she asked Susie hesitantly, and was gratified when Susie gave her a curt nod.

He led her out to the car, followed by Rosario and Eugene. "Thanks for hanging out tonight," Rosario said, and gave Eugene a quick hug that he awkwardly returned.

He pulled away and gave the rest of them a little wave and started for his car. "No problem. Good luck on the final tomorrow, Rosie."

As they drove home, Jack got a call. "Hey, Nolan."

Talia's ears perked, but Jack's side of the conversation was maddeningly uninformative.

"The guy who attacked you is Greg Sutherland, former Marine Force Recon," Jack said in a darkly satisfied tone. "And that old harpy was behind it, just like we suspected."

"Margaret was paying him," Talia said.

Jack nodded. Talia could see his grim smile in the lights of the passing cars. "She hung up on him when he called her from the hospital, and he rolled over on her right away. He used to work for her and David, and she contacted him right after she got out of prison to come after you."

"God, what a psycho," Rosie said from the backseat.

Jack nodded. "She had him track you here, gave him all the information about the jewelry and the flowers."

"Did she give him the DVD too?" Talia couldn't suppress another shudder.

"He says he doesn't know anything about it, or the rapes either, but Nolan thinks it's bullshit. It's one thing to admit to harassment and assault. Aggravated rape puts you into another category entirely."

If that's what he'd had planned for her...what if Jack hadn't gotten to her in time? She started to shake and couldn't seem to stop.

Jack reached over and covered her hand. "He claims he wasn't going to hurt you, that Margaret promised him a big payout if he could get you and hold you for a few days."

"Right," Talia said. "I'm sure he would totally change his MO." Helpless, hysterical laughter erupted from her chest. "He likes to rape and cut other girls, but he'd be nice to me."

Jack and Rosario didn't say anything, and by the time they pulled into the driveway, Talia had pulled herself back under control.

Once they got inside, Rosie reminded them that her physics final was the next morning and she'd need a ride to campus by seven-thirty.

"You better get to bed, then," Talia said as she looked at the clock. It was already close to eleven.

Rosie nodded. "And now that they've caught what's his name, it's safe for me to stay on campus after my test?"

Every instinct rebelled against the idea of letting Rosie go back out on her own. But Talia knew it wasn't fair to keep her sister confined just because Talia couldn't shake off the lingering fear. She gave Rosie a reluctant nod.

"And," Rosie said in that wheedling tone she used to use when she was trying to convince Talia to give her a piece of cake before dinner, "I think it's probably safe for me to go on the trip to Yosemite this weekend, right?"

Talia shook her head. "I'm not comfortable with you going away. This guy could get out on bail and try to hurt you."

"How would he even know where I am? And do you really think he would follow me to a tent cabin in the middle of Yosemite if he knows the police are keeping tabs on him?" She turned imploring eyes to Jack. "Come on, help me convince her. You'll know if he gets bailed out. You're going to keep track of him, right?"

"I'll make sure he doesn't get within a mile of either one of you," Jack said.

"See, it will be just fine," Rosie said, turning back to Talia with a bright, hopeful smile.

There was no way she could let her go, even for the weekend. She opened her mouth to deny Rosie's plea. But then her mind flashed back on that night over two years ago, when Talia had loaded a bewildered Rosie onto a private plane flown by strangers. With the barest of explanations, Talia had sent Rosie into hiding for months, erasing every bit of normalcy from her life.

"When can I come back home?" Rosie had asked, her eyes huge and full of tears.

Tonight her eyes weren't teary, but they had that same pleading look, that same hint of desperation to have life go back to the way she knew it.

"Okay," Talia said. "But," she added as Rosie started to jump around the kitchen in excitement. "You call me or text me every few hours."

"What about the middle of the night?"

Talia rolled her eyes. "Last call at eleven."

"What if my cell doesn't work?"

"Find a pay phone and call me."

"Fine," Rosie said, exasperated, but grabbed Talia in an enthusiastic hug. "I'll be totally fine. You'll see." She grabbed her bag and started for her room, her cell phone already in hand to start spreading the good news.

Talia listened to her excitedly call Dana, knowing she wouldn't get a good night's sleep until Rosie came back, maybe not even then.

Jack pulled her into his arms and she turned into his chest with a sigh. She closed her eyes, absorbing his warmth as he pressed a kiss to the top of her head. "I'll keep tabs on Sutherland," he said. "She'll be fine, just like that time this winter when she went up to Tahoe. Now how about we go upstairs and kiss each other's owies?"

As he led her upstairs to the bedroom, she got the feeling she had back in the restaurant that something wasn't right. He closed the bedroom door, pressed her up against it, and tilted her chin up to meet his kiss.

But even the heat surging through her blood couldn't distract her as the last several seconds of their conversation played through her mind. Then it hit her.

She pulled her mouth from his. "How did you know about that?"

His eyes were slightly dazed, his lips parted. "What?"

"Rosie's trip to Tahoe. I never told you about that." Then Rosie's voice flashed in her mind. *Jack and I talk sometimes.* Inwardly she scolded herself for her moment of doubt. "Never mind. I forget that you and Rosie have kept in touch."

Why do you have to go looking for trouble? The last thing Jack deserves is your suspicion.

"Did she tell you that I texted her every three hours until she threatened to throw her phone in the lake?"

Jack didn't smile at her joke. Instead, as she watched, something—guilt?—flashed in Jack's eyes before it disappeared behind that carefully blank expression he liked to assume when he didn't want to give anything away.

When he wanted to hide something.

She felt that unwelcome, all-too-familiar tightening in her stomach. "Rosie didn't tell you about the trip, did she?"

She could see the truth in his face even before he opened his mouth.

"Have you been spying on us?" She felt like her chest was being slowly squeezed by a vise.

"I wouldn't call it spying—"

She shoved against his shoulders and launched herself away from the door. "What would you call it?"

"I was looking out for you, checking in to make sure you were safe."

"You followed me—"

"It was usually Ben or Alex since I was out of town so much," he broke in as though that would make it better.

"Fine, so you followed me, had me followed. Whatever. You kept tabs on me without me knowing it, and I'd call that spying."

—∽—

Jack knew the second Talia had looked at him sideways back in the restaurant that he was in deep shit. He'd done his best to shut Susie down on the topic of his past and future payoffs for the restaurant before Talia clued in, and he thought he'd dodged a bullet.

Then, in an incredibly boneheaded move born of an adrenaline high and the fierce need to get her naked and under him so he could prove in the most elemental way that she was safe and unharmed, he'd slipped up and revealed his knowledge of something he had no business knowing about.

She was glaring daggers at him, her arms wrapped protectively around her waist, her mouth tight with anger.

What the fuck was wrong with him? He was a former fucking Green Beret, not some bumbling idiot. Maybe, he thought in a sudden flash of self-awareness, he'd let it slip on purpose. As though his subconscious knew that if they were to really move forward past tonight, once the danger surrounding her was eliminated, they needed to get everything out on the table.

No past, no baggage, no lies between them.

Or maybe he was just a fucking idiot too focused on getting into the pants of the woman he loved to keep hold of his tongue.

Either way, she was about one hundred degrees past furious, and he knew it was only going to get worse before it had a chance to get better.

"I didn't do it to hurt you," he said, sounding lame to his own ears. "I just needed to see for myself that you were okay."

A humorless laugh tore from her throat. "You couldn't pick up a goddamn phone?" She held her hand to her ear and mimed making a call. " 'Hi, Talia, it's Jack. I'm just calling to see how you're doing.' Like this cloak-and-dagger bullshit is so much easier?"

"I didn't think you'd want to talk to me," Jack bit out, hating how needy and weak he sounded, like some insecure fifteen-year-old afraid to ask a girl to prom. "After everything that happened to you, I figured you'd just want to forget."

"You figured right," she snapped. "All I wanted was to forget everything and get on with my life. And then Margaret had to send that creep after me, and you came busting in, making sure that I would never, ever escape it." She let out a wrenching sob, and the sound was like a knife to Jack's chest.

"I never, ever wanted you hurt. Everything I've done, it's been to help you get on with your life, just like you said."

"All I ever wanted was to get over that feeling of being hounded, of knowing that almost every detail of my life was scrutinized. And all those times I got the prickle on the back of my neck and kicked myself for being paranoid, it was probably you watching me," she said, pointing an accusing finger. "It was you making me feel that way."

"I'm sorry," he said. It had no more effect now than the first time he'd said it, but there was nothing else to say. She scrubbed angrily at her face and narrowed her gaze. "Before, back at the restaurant, Susie said the damage was going to cost more than a fifty-thousand-dollar investment, and you said, 'I know.' What was going on there?"

Jack chose his words carefully, not wanting to lie outright. He was already in the hole. He didn't want to dig any deeper. "It was obvious the water damage is going to cost a lot more than that to repair."

Talia shook her head. "And the expansion plans? How do you know about that?"

When he hesitated, she came up and slammed her palm against his chest. "Tell me the truth!"

Resignation formed a hard knot in his stomach, and along with it a sharp stab of grief. He was losing her. The last few days had been paradise, offering the first glimmers of hope for a real future together. Now she was slipping away like water through his fingers and there was nothing he could do to stop it.

That it was his own damn fault only made the pain that much keener.

"When you first moved here and were looking for a job, Alyssa connected me with Susie. I agreed to make an investment in Suzette's if she would agree to hire you and keep you on for at least a year."

———ᴡᴡ———

Talia's knees went weak at Jack's admission. The closest place to sit was the bed, but she couldn't bear to touch it. The bed where Jack had shown her more pleasure in the last four days than she'd known in her lifetime. Where she'd finally felt like the scars of the past had healed enough to let her look forward to a future that was big and bright and full of Jack. The man she'd fallen in love with.

The man who'd been lying to her all along.

She stumbled over to the chair in the corner, slapping Jack's hand away when he reached out to steady her. "I don't need your help," she snarled. She sank down and buried her face in her hands. "You had to pay her to hire me. God, you must think I'm so useless," she half laughed, half sobbed.

"I wanted to help you and Rosie get on your feet. I knew you'd never take money from me, so I wanted to make sure you had an income. And Rosie's school is expensive—" He broke off midsentence.

Another lightbulb flared to life in her brain. "Please don't tell me the scholarship is fake."

Jack shifted on his feet, and the sinking sensation in Talia's stomach became so acute she was afraid she was going to fall through the floor. "It's not fake," Jack said. "But the Spectra Foundation that sponsors it was started by me five years ago. And the scholarship was established last fall. So far Rosie is the only recipient."

Talia's head swam. The scholarship was worth twenty thousand a year and covered over half of Rosie's tuition as long as she kept her GPA above 3.0. She knew he was well paid working for Gemini Securities, but how could he possibly afford that, plus the fifty thousand on top? She shook her head to clear it. "You have a foundation?"

Jack nodded. "I use it to fund projects and shelters that help women and children who are being abused."

"Your broken birds," Talia breathed. "I'm just another one of your broken birds."

That was how he really saw her. A poor, pathetic creature

too weak to pick up the pieces of her life. Deserving of his charity. His pity. He said he'd admired her strength but all along he hadn't believed she could change, that she could be strong.

She could barely breathe through the sharp ache stabbing her chest.

She could see the muscles of his jaw working, and there was an uncharacteristic pleading look in his eyes. "You are so much more than that to me. You have to know that. I—"

"How much?" Talia interrupted. At his puzzled look, she clarified, "Exactly how much are you worth?"

"I don't think—"

"Oh, come on," Talia said, rising from the chair as she felt a little devil come to life inside of her. "If I'm going to be kept by another rich man, I should know exactly how much I'm working with."

His nostrils flared in anger and his mouth flattened in a tight line. "Roughly a hundred million, give or take a few million in either direction depending on what the market is doing."

Talia pasted on a seductive smile and sauntered over to him. He was still as a statue as she ran a finger down his granite-hard chest. "Wow, that much," she said, and there was nothing fake about the amazement in her voice. "That's more than David ever had." She flashed him a saucy look from under her lashes even as her stomach churned at the thought. "Looks like I've managed to trade up."

God, she was ridiculous. Susie's face flashed in her mind, and she cringed, thinking about how she'd actually thought Susie was her friend. All the confidences and conversations they'd shared, and all the while her "friend" had essentially been paid to endure Talia's presence in her life.

All this time priding herself on pulling herself up by her bootstraps and making a new life for herself, only to find out she was at the mercy of yet another wealthy man pulling the strings on her life.

A little voice tried to remind her that Jack was nothing like David, that he would never use his money to hurt her. But the betrayal was too fresh, too raw, for her to pay the voice any heed.

"Don't," Jack said, catching her hand in a tight grip. "It's not like that and you know it. I never thought of you that way. You need money, I have it, and I want to spend it to help you."

She batted her eyelids and licked her lips, the mock siren. "But of course you have to want something in return." She reached out with her free hand and cupped the bulge between his legs. Angry or not, he rose up immediately against her hand, thick and hard and ready for whatever kind of repayment plan she offered. "Ah, there you go." She rubbed up and down the length of his shaft.

Hot color flushed his cheeks. From arousal or embarrassment at his immediate, involuntary response, she didn't know, and she didn't care. She couldn't see past her own anger, the seething hurt and all the old ugly things she thought she'd gotten past rising back up in a rotten tangle. Making her want to lash out, to hurt him, to show him that no matter what he said or did, he was no better than any other man. No better than the dirtbags who had made her feel cheap and used and broken.

"That's an awful lot of money you've spent on us already. It's going to take me a while to work it off."

"Stop it," he said tightly, grabbing at her hand as it gave his dick another firm squeeze. "I know you're angry—"

Talia ignored him and pulled her hands from his. Before he could stop her, she sank to her knees and reached for the button on his pants. "Maybe a little blow job to start. I'm out of practice but that has to be worth at least a hundred bucks, right? Maybe later I'll let you do something really special—"

"Stop it!" Jack roared, grabbing her by the shoulders and lifting her to her feet. He gave her a little shake. "Don't do this. Don't do this to us."

The devastation on his face sent the devil running, leaving nothing but a bleak emptiness inside her.

"Please don't do this to us," Jack said, the pleading in his eyes almost enough to make her crumble. She'd never seen him like this, never known it was possible to make him look like this. Never imagined she would be the one to bring him here.

"Please, Talia, everything I've done, it's because I wanted you to be happy. I just wanted to take care of you—"

Anger flared back to life and she shoved his hands off her shoulders. "I don't want to be taken care of! Why can't you understand that? I had that before and look where it got me!"

"I'm not like David!" Jack shouted in a voice so loud it made her ears ring. A vein pulsed in his neck. "I would never hurt a goddamn hair on your head." His finger stabbed the air as he loomed over her. "I would lay down my fucking life for you, so don't you dare equate me with him."

Rather than intimidate her, his flare of temper only fueled her own. She liked this, she realized, in a sick, twisted way. Before she'd always been too dependent, too powerless to do anything other than meekly take what was doled out to her. "You messed with my life behind my back. You made decisions for me and Rosie you had no right to."

"I never made decisions for you," he protested. "I just set things up to move in a direction I thought you wanted."

It was like talking to a brick wall. "Don't you see that it was important for me to do that on my own? That after everything that happened it would be important to me to stand on my own feet, for me and Rosie?"

The anger seemed to drain out of him. His arms dropped to his sides, his palms facing out as though to say, *I give up.* "You didn't have anyone. I just wanted to be there for you."

The regret in his voice was unmistakable, but it wasn't enough. "Then you should have tried to be my friend. Not my secret benefactor."

"I can still be your friend, Talia—and more. Give us another chance."

She shook her head. Even though part of her wanted to fling herself into his arms and never let go, she knew there would always be part of her that would feel weak. Useless. Foolish at her misplaced faith in herself. "I can't."

He stepped toward her and she kept her eyes glued to the hardwood floor. His big booted feet came into view. His scent hit her, deep and rich and calling to someplace deep inside her even as she steeled herself to push him away. She could feel his warm breath ruffling her hair.

"Please. Please be with me."

His boots blurred as the tears welled, and she swallowed past the thick knot in her throat and once again shook her head.

"I love you," he said, the words sounding ripped from his chest. "I love you," he said again, softer this time.

She felt like she was being eaten alive from the inside out, his words ripping through her so painfully she was surprised there wasn't blood pouring from the hole in her chest. "You went behind my back and had me followed. I can't trust you."

"I promise I'll never do anything like that again. I'll show you that you can trust me. We can get past this, Talia. I'll do whatever it takes."

Part of her wanted to so badly it was like a beast howling inside. How, it wondered, could she be so stupid to push this man away? This man who had never done anything to hurt her and everything to help her.

This man who loved her and, God help her, who she loved back.

But love wasn't enough, a lesson she'd learned too many times in the past. It wasn't enough to overcome the black hole of betrayal that had formed in her gut, spinning and sucking her in. Gathering force as it pulled in all the pain of her past and too many examples of why she could never place her faith in anyone other than herself.

"Actually," she said, the words rasping her throat like sandpaper, "all you've shown me is that I can never really trust anyone."

Chapter 19

"Sutherland made bail." Nolan didn't try to hide the anger in his voice.

"That was quick." Jack grimaced as he glanced at the clock on the nightstand that flanked the king-sized hotel bed where he'd crashed last night. It was just after 11:00 a.m. Less than fourteen hours had passed since Sutherland had been picked up.

And less than twelve had passed since Jack had his heart ripped from his chest and ground into the floor. The twelve-hundred-thread-count sheets were like sandpaper across his skin, mocking him with their softness.

"They could only book him for assault and stalking. So he got to go straight from his comfy hospital bed to the courthouse, without even a second spent in jail," Nolan replied.

"You still think he's the serial rapist?" Jack sat up and swung his feet over the side of the bed, wincing as the sliver of light peeking through the curtains seared through his eyeballs and bored into his brain.

"He's my best lead so far, but I have no grounds to arrest him yet. There was nothing on him or in his rental car to link him, and for whatever reason we're having a hell of a time getting a warrant pushed through to search his hotel room."

Jack forced himself to the mini coffeemaker and managed to get it going with hands that shook a little from last night's excesses.

"And with him so eager to roll over on Margaret Grayson-Maxwell, the judge was happy enough to get him out of their hair for a few days."

Jack punched the power button. "Where did you say he was staying?"

"I didn't. Stay away from him, Jack. You did enough damage last night that he'd have a case if he wanted to bring assault charges against you. Don't make trouble for yourself."

Like hell. Jack wasn't afraid of trouble, especially after last night. What the hell did he care if he went to jail for pounding the fucker's face in? It wasn't like he had anything going for him anyway.

Jack said good-bye to Nolan and nipped his pity party in the bud. Jesus, the only thing worse than a guy with a broken heart was a guy who laid around wallowing and moaning about his broken heart.

And he'd done enough of that last night, after Talia had torn him to shreds. He'd told her he loved her and she'd kicked his ass out. He'd tried to protest, tried to convince her that she should keep him around just in case.

Even he had to admit that he'd been thinking less of her safety and more about the fact that if he just stayed close, he'd be able to wear her down. Hell, even seduce her back into his arms and into bed. Show her with words and body how much he fucking worshipped the ground she walked on.

How much he loved her.

Talia wasn't about to let him play into her fears, and she sure as hell wasn't going to fall for his all but nonexistent charm. With her tormentor in jail, she'd pointed out, she couldn't be much safer.

"I'll be fine without you," she'd said, cutting him to the quick, as it was clear she wasn't just talking about last night. "I don't need you."

Part of him wanted to sink to his knees, bury his face in her stomach, and beg for another chance.

But he'd been kicked around enough, cast off by other women he was convinced needed him—first his mother, then Gina. He didn't have a ton of pride left when it came to moments like this, but he had enough to gather his things and get the hell out.

Though he never spent excessively and took pride in living a lifestyle that didn't so much as hint at his massive trust fund, last night he'd perversely decided to say fuck it.

Talia was going to fault him for being wealthy, when he would have happily spent every last cent on her if it would make her life better? Well, screw it. He was going to live large and for once take advantage of what his money could afford for his own goddamn self.

Instead of heading back to the efficiency complex that had been good enough on every other business trip here, last night he'd driven across town to the Four Seasons.

Booked a suite. He proceeded to annihilate the minibar and then called down to room service to bring him up a bottle of bourbon whose price had been marked up about a thousand percent.

No matter how hard he tried, he couldn't drink her

image away. The look of absolute betrayal, the fury when she realized he'd been keeping tabs on her.

The humiliation when he admitted he'd bribed Susie to hire her. He knew it would do no good to tell her that since Talia had started, Susie had told him on several occasions what an awesome job she'd been doing, that sometimes she felt like she should pay him for sending such a great person his way. It wouldn't take the pain away, so he'd kept his yap shut.

Jesus, all he'd wanted to do was make her happy, and he'd managed to fuck even that up. By the time he made it halfway through the bottle, he felt like everyone and everything in the world was mocking him and his attempts to get Talia to fall for him. Even the luxuries of the five-star hotel seemed to taunt him.

She should be here with him, sinking her bare feet into the plush carpet. Soaking in the Jacuzzi tub big enough to take a swim in.

Rolling around on that giant bed.

He'd wanted to treat her like a queen. Wake up every morning and tell her that he loved her. Give her everything she ever wanted because he wanted to make her happy, not because he expected anything back. Show her that everything he gave her was given freely, with no strings or obligations attached.

He poured himself a cup of coffee and muddled his way over to the window. He threw back the curtains and let the bright sunlight penetrate his skull. Hoping the pain would distract him from the empty, hollowed-out feeling. Hoping it would drown out the voice in his head that mocked him for being a stupid idiot.

What made him believe this thing with Talia could

end up differently, when nothing had ever worked out before?

He sucked down the contents of the minipot and pulled up his phone. Jack knew Talia would freak out if the news of Sutherland's release caught her off guard. He quickly texted both Talia and Rosario that Sutherland was going to be released on bail soon. And while he didn't think the guy would be stupid enough to try anything, especially when the woman bankrolling him was lawyering up and refuting every one of his claims against her, it would be a good idea for them to be careful.

Not that Sutherland would get close to them even if he wanted to. Jack would see to that. After a shower and breakfast of room service, Jack made short work of finding out where Sutherland was staying. Amazing what a good relationship with the local cab companies and a couple of twenties could get you.

He let out a mirthless laugh when the cabdriver told him he'd dropped Sutherland off at the same hotel Jack had been staying in up until last week. Jesus Christ, the guy had been right under his nose and he hadn't known a thing.

A quick diversion in the form of activating the emergency exit alarm was able to distract the desk clerk from his post long enough for Jack to duck behind the counter, call up Sutherland's room info, and make himself a card key.

Blocking all thoughts of Talia, he walked across the hall and called the elevator. He cautioned himself not to let his temper get away from him, but before his visit was over, Sutherland would have no doubt what would happen to him if he or Megabitch Grayson-Maxwell ever tried to fuck with Talia again.

—᙮᙮—

He slipped from the stairway and was headed for the first camera on the floor when the elevator's ding nearly sent him to the ceiling. Heart beating a million miles an hour, Gene ducked back behind the door, but not before he got a good look at the familiar broad back and hard profile of Jack Brooks. He watched, barely breathing, as Jack stepped off the elevator and headed toward Sutherland's room.

Fury surged inside him. Sutherland was his prey. He'd stuck himself in the middle of Gene's plan and tried to harm Talia.

The bloodlust had risen up the night before when she'd been attacked. It had screamed at him to take revenge on the man who messed with his claim. He'd kept his control by a thread, knowing that if he lost it at the restaurant and killed Talia's would-be attacker right then and there, he'd never get to Talia.

He'd never complete his mission.

Now that last thread threatened to snap. He would kill Sutherland, and he would kill Brooks too, for keeping him from Talia this long.

He watched as Jack used a card key to gain entry, heard Sutherland shout in surprise as Jack shoved the door open. Gene eased the door to the stairwell open and crept along the wall, keeping himself out of the camera's view. Fortunately the hotel's security system was far from sophisticated, and with a few slices of his knife, the camera was out of commission.

He systematically took out the rest of the cameras on the floor. As he got closer to Sutherland's room, he heard shouting. As he reached up to knock, there was a loud thump of a body hitting the door hard enough to shake the hinges.

His hand froze. *What do you think you're doing?* For once he didn't try to shove his mother's voice from his head. What was he doing, taking on these two men, bigger than him and obviously trained fighters to boot?

They might have brawn, but he had the far superior brain—or at least he should. The high emotions and lack of sleep the night before were clearly affecting his processing. No, Jack had added another layer of perfection to his plan, and Gene nearly hadn't seen it.

Clutching his small duffel bag in one hand, his knife safely tucked up his sleeve, Gene retreated back to the stairwell to wait.

He didn't have long to wait. In less than ten minutes, Jack reemerged. Nearly delirious from anticipation and the lack of sleep, Gene had to stifle a laugh. For someone who was supposedly a security expert, Jack was totally oblivious to the fact that he was being watched as he walked down the hall and called the elevator.

Gene waited a few minutes after he disappeared behind the elevator doors. When the hallway remained deserted, he made his move.

He walked swiftly down the hallway to Sutherland's room. With all of the security cameras out, he didn't worry about his presence being detected. He gave Sutherland's door three swift raps.

As he hoped, Sutherland assumed it was Jack again. He flung the door open. "What the fuck do you want now?" he demanded.

Gene knew from watching Sutherland this morning

that the other man was in bad shape from the fight the night before, and now Jack had roughed him up even more. Good thing, since under normal circumstances, it would have been hard for Gene to overpower this man.

Today, though, it took only the split second from the time Sutherland flung open the door to when he realized the person outside wasn't Jack for Gene to make his move.

Lunging forward, Gene caught Sutherland by surprise as he shoved him back into the room and simultaneously kicked the door shut. Sutherland tried to fight but Gene landed a blow to his already bruised ribs. Sutherland doubled over, wheezing in pain.

He started to straighten up. "What the he—"

His words broke off on a gasp of pain and shock as Gene sank his knife deep into Sutherland's abdomen. Right below the sternum so he wasn't hampered by any bone. The blade sank to the hilt with a meaty, tearing sound. Sutherland's eyes bugged out and he made a choking sound as he tried to push Gene away with hands that had gone weak.

"This is what happens when you mess with what's mine," Gene said with a savage twist of the knife. There was a roaring in his ears as power, rich and intoxicating, flooded his senses. It was like what he felt with the girls but better.

This was what it felt like to be a god. To exercise the power of life and death. To see the light in his enemy's eyes fade to nothing as his blood poured over his hand.

Sutherland's eyes rolled back in his head and he gave a final gasp. Gene jerked the blade free and Sutherland collapsed to the floor. Gene leaned over and touched shaking fingers to Sutherland's neck, but his own pulse was beating so powerfully it was impossible to be sure if he was dead.

He had to be sure.

He planted his knee in Sutherland's chest. Panting, sweat running down his face, he grabbed a handful of Sutherland's hair and pulled his head to the side. The hunting knife sliced through his throat like butter. Blood pulsed out of the cut to pool around Sutherland's head.

Gene surged to his feet, swaying a little bit as the mad rush of the kill started to fade, leaving behind a satiation unlike anything he'd ever known. It was better than any orgasm he'd ever had in his life. And though he'd had concerns about killing Sutherland first—he'd wanted to stay pure, for Talia to be his first—now, as his entire body pulsed with satisfaction, he knew he'd made the right decision.

He took a deep breath, put thoughts of Talia aside for the moment, and retrieved his duffel from where he'd dropped it by the door. He unzipped it and removed several items. An earring. A bracelet. A toe ring.

Little things he hadn't disposed of in the biowaste disposal bin back near the lab. All this time he'd doubted the wisdom of keeping them, knowing the smartest move was to get rid of any shred of evidence that might connect him to his victims. But something had compelled him to cling to these small souvenirs.

Now he knew their purpose. These would help Detective Nolan flesh out his theory that Talia's stalker for hire had been playing his own sick game on the side. Gene wrapped them carefully in a silk square and tucked them into Sutherland's toiletry kit, so the police would be sure to think these were special mementos Sutherland wanted to keep close.

And in case there was any room for doubt, Gene had

one last item in his bag. The knife was identical to the one he's used to kill Sutherland. But unlike that knife, it bore the traces of all the women who had come before.

He withdrew the knife from the bag carefully, and although he always wore gloves handling it and had cleaned the handle after each use, he wiped it down one more time just in case.

He placed the handle carefully in Sutherland's hand and wrapped his dead fingers around it, pressing tight to make sure the prints made an impression. He pressed Sutherland's finger and thumb onto the blade for good measure. He slid the knife back into its leather sleeve and hid it in a side pocket of Sutherland's suitcase, where the police would eventually find it. The prints, combined with the blood of the victims, would be the nail in Nolan's case against the dead man.

Once he finished, he stripped off his bloodstained clothes and stored them in a plastic garbage bag. He would need to do a thorough scrubbing once he got home, but for now he changed into a fresh T-shirt, jeans, and another dark, hooded sweatshirt.

Then it was out the door and back the way he came, slipping out the back exit to avoid the lobby as he made sure he stayed out of view of the security camera.

His car was parked a couple blocks away. He tossed his duffel bag into the trunk and slid behind the wheel, still buzzing with a high that beat out that of any drug. As he started the car, the reality of what he had done hit him once again.

He had killed someone! Eugene, the physics nerd who everyone overlooked, who faded into the background.

I didn't realize you were still here. His hands shook

and his blood heated as he remembered Talia's words from the night before. She hadn't realized he was even still there, lurking in the shadows, taking in every word and watching every move.

She was so stupid, like all the rest of them, to underestimate him. He planned to make an unforgettable impression on her the next time he was with her.

The beast inside him demanded he go soon, now even. To ride this high to the final climax and bring Talia to her inevitable end. But no. He needed to be patient. He needed to sleep and restore himself, refine his plan so he could carry it off without incident. He needed to make sure everything would be perfect.

He needed to stop by campus to get rid of the bloody clothes, but it was only barely noon. There would be too many people to potentially catch him dumping the bag in the hazardous-waste bin. He needed to wait until dark.

Which was fine, because he was so tired from the sleepless night and subsequent adrenaline surge and crash he knew he was likely to fall asleep if he didn't go directly home. As it was, when his phone chirped to indicate an incoming text message, he nearly drove into a parked car. It was from Rosie, telling him she'd finished up the exam.

Good for her. It was the last physics exam she'd ever take.

By the time he got to his house, he was practically sleepwalking, his mind in a fog as he retrieved the duffel bag from his trunk and staggered through the front door.

His mother wasn't home, thank God. Gene hurled himself up the stairs to his room, stopping only to take a piss before he collapsed onto his unmade bed. He closed his eyes, a smile pulling his mouth as he fell asleep to visions of Talia, naked, begging for her life as an ocean of blood surged up to consume her.

—⁓—

"Are you sure you're okay with me going?" Rosie asked for the dozenth time in the last hour. Talia was treating her to pizza at Applewood in Menlo Park, a restaurant a few miles from campus that served some of the best pizza in the area. Talia knew Rosie was champing at the bit to go out and celebrate the end of midterms, but thankfully she had enough sympathy for Talia's recent triple whammy—being assaulted, losing her job, and breaking up with Jack—to throw her sister a bone and keep her company for a few hours.

"I could stay and keep you company. Or wait, I know, you can come with us up to Yosemite and go camping."

Okay, so she was pitiful, but not that pitiful. Talia shook her head and managed a small, reassuring smile for Rosie. "That's just what you need is your fun-sucker sister tagging along, being a total downer. Besides, I don't have a sleeping bag or any other camping equipment."

Rosie rolled her eyes. "We're not leaving until tomorrow morning. Target's open late enough to buy stuff. It's not like you have to go to work or, uh…" Realizing her mistake, Rosie cut herself off. "Sorry, didn't mean to rub salt in it," she said, and took another bite of her pepperoni pizza.

"It's okay," Talia said tightly. She picked up, then put down her barely nibbled slice of pizza, her stomach churning as she contemplated the black hole of the next few days. Had it really only been last night that she'd thrown Jack out of her house? It felt like a century ago. And the only contact he'd made was to text her late this morning to let her know Sutherland had made bail and that she should be careful.

The idea that he was out made her uneasy, and a big part of her wanted to beg Jack to come rushing back to her side. He'd probably do it too, even after the things she'd said and the way she'd treated him. The thought didn't bring her any satisfaction.

Regardless of the way he'd gone behind her back, Jack was a good person, and he didn't deserve to be used or to have her take advantage of his feelings for her.

As for herself, she'd done enough leaning on Jack, intentionally or not, and now it was past time for her to stand on her own two feet. Sutherland was injured, and with the police keeping close tabs on him, he would have to be an idiot to come after her again. Not to mention it sounded like Margaret had cut off the gravy train.

Still, the DVD and the utter brutality of the attacks on the other women nagged at her, calling up a fear she couldn't shake off. Those weren't the actions of a rational mind. Police surveillance might not be enough to deter him from acting on that kind of sickness.

Talia shook off the paranoia as she had been all day. Now that she knew who she was up against, she could take the necessary precautions to keep herself safe. And hopefully the police would come up with the necessary evidence to shut him down for good. "I need to stick around and try to find another job. Figure out how I'm going to pay Susie back for all the damage."

"I don't see why you don't let Jack do it."

The mention of his name sent another stab of pain

through her chest, and she found herself swallowing back tears for the umpteenth time that day. Her eyes were already swollen to twice their size, puffy and tender from all the crying she'd done last night and into the morning. She knew if she started crying again now, she'd never stop. "Rosie, you know why."

Rosie shook her head and tossed down her pizza on her plate and looked at Talia with a faintly disgusted look on her face. "No, I don't. You have this amazing guy who is totally in to you, has done so much for you—so much for us—and you dump him because he covered a few bills for us?"

The reminder brought the anger surging back to the forefront. Talia seized on it, hoping it would chase away the anguish that had threatened to swallow her from the moment she'd woken up alone for the first time in five days. "He didn't just cover bills, Rosie. He spied on me and had me followed—"

"Because he cares about you and was worried."

"It's still not okay! And to top it off, he had to bribe Susie to hire me."

"Oh, poor you," Rosie said, and threw down her napkin. "Do you know how many women would kill to have a guy like Jack love them so much he'd pay fifty grand to get them a job?"

The mention of love brought Jack's confession crashing back. *I love you.* It clutched at her heart and made her indignation falter. Still, she couldn't let it go. Not now, not ever. "Do you realize how big of a loser that makes me feel like?"

Rosie folded her arms across her chest, glaring at Talia in a way that said she had little sympathy for Talia's side.

"Jack never saw you as a loser and you know it. If what he did makes you feel bad, that's your problem." Without another word, she grabbed her purse and stalked to the door.

Rosie's words hit her like a punch. She always knew Rosie idolized Jack, but to have her take his side when she was hurting like this and needed someone to lean on was like a physical blow. She pulled herself together and paid the bill, and walked outside to find Rosie waiting.

They drove back to campus in deafening silence. Talia pulled up in front of Rosie's dorm and before Rosie got out of the car, she leaned over and hugged her so hard her ribs ached. "I love you, Tal, and I'm sorry that I yelled at you," Rosie said. "But I hate seeing you throwing away something so great over a stupid thing like pride."

Talia sniffed back tears and hugged her back. "I love you too," she said, and pulled away, wiping the tears streaming down her cheeks. "You have fun this weekend, and be careful, okay?"

"I'll call you or text you when I get on the road," Rosie said, and got out of the car. Before she closed the door, she leaned down and poked her head back in. "You sure you'll be okay?"

I'll be fine. Unable to force the words through the knot in her throat, Talia merely nodded. She drove home, the emptiness of the little house closing in on her. The long night, the weekend, the rest of her life yawned in front of her in an endless black hole.

She'd never felt more alone.

Chapter 20

It took Nolan until after 5:00 p.m. to finally secure a warrant to search Greg Sutherland's hotel room. He called in four other officers to meet him at the scene and sped over, seething over the fact that the judge's delay most likely fucked his whole case.

By now, whatever evidence might have existed had no doubt been disposed of. His only hope was that Sutherland was careless and had left something behind, something compelling enough to make an arrest.

He entered the lobby, trailed by two uniformed officers, and flashed his badge at the wary desk clerk. "I need to gain access to one of your guest rooms." Nolan presented the warrant for his inspection.

After reading for a few moments, the clerk nodded and typed something into his computer. "He's in room four twenty-three, on the fourth floor. I'll have someone from housekeeping accompany you with a master key in case Mr. Sutherland has stepped out."

Nolan shifted his weight impatiently, and after several endless minutes, a Latina in her late fifties, dressed in a gray polyester uniform, appeared.

"This is Elvia," the clerk said. "Detective Nolan, Elvia will be happy to escort you to Mr. Sutherland's room."

Elvia kept her eyes glued to her white orthopedics for the duration of the short elevator ride. Sutherland's room was at the end of the hall. Nolan rapped sharply on the door. "Sutherland, this is Detective Nolan from the Redwood City Police Department. We need to ask you a few questions."

When there was no response, Sutherland knocked again, then nodded for Elvia to unlock the door.

There was a beep and a muffled click and Nolan opened the door.

The smell hit him like a physical force, and he knew someone was dead before he even saw the body.

"Shit," he whispered, as one look at the battered face verified that the body belonged to Sutherland. Nolan was no coroner, but based on the smell, the blood soaked into the carpet, and the fact that rigor had set in, Sutherland had been dead for at least four hours. Nolan checked his watch. It was 6:00 p.m. Sutherland had been released on bail shortly after eleven. For Sutherland to be in this condition, he had to have been killed shortly after he was released this morning.

"Shit," Nolan said again, his jaw clenching as he remembered his phone call to Jack Brooks earlier that morning. He nodded at one of the uniforms. "Call homicide."

He stepped out into the hall and took out his phone, questioning the wisdom of what he was about to do. He dialed, his spine tensing when Jack Brooks answered on the second ring.

"What's going on, Nolan?"

Technically, what Nolan was doing could get him in deep shit. But Sutherland had been a piece of shit for hire, and if he was the one who raped those girls, this was a better death than he'd deserved. If Jack was the one who took him out, he deserved a chance to get his shit lined up before the heat really came down on him. "You tell me. I'm at Sutherland's hotel and was just about to execute a search warrant on his room."

"You find anything?"

Nolan tried, but it was impossible to read anything in Brooks's tone. Did he know damn well what Nolan had found and was doing a good job of hiding it, or was he really clueless? "I found Sutherland, dead, and it was definitely a homicide." He deliberately didn't say how.

The silence stretched several seconds. "I didn't do it," Jack said finally. "You have my word."

Nolan wanted to believe him. "Unfortunately, it won't be me you have to convince if it turns up you were anywhere near here today. You'll be dealing with Palo Alto Homicide."

Jack's laugh was sharp and mirthless as it crackled over the line. "If the hotel surveillance system is working, it'll show that I was there about twenty minutes after you called me this morning."

Nolan's stomach sank. "Goddamn it, Jack, I told you to stay away from him."

"I didn't kill him," Jack said. "If I did, I wouldn't be stupid enough to let the surveillance cameras catch me paying him a visit."

Nolan ran his hand through his hair, frustrated. "Whether you did or not, best not leave town any time soon. And get yourself hooked up with a good lawyer.

A lot of witnesses saw you beat the shit out of him and threaten him the other night. I'm not going to point them in your direction, but if they see you on any recording, you can be damn sure they'll be coming after you."

—⁓—

Jack's call came at around 7:30, shortly after she got home after dropping Rosario off. The sight of his number on the caller display so soon after Rosario had raked her over the coals was enough to make her eyes burn with tears.

No way could she handle talking to him now, she thought as she let the call go into voice mail. He followed immediately with a text. *Please pick up. Really need to talk to you. Don't want to say this over VM.*

The phone rang seconds later and she selected the ANSWER button with a finger that shook as she wondered what he needed to say that was so important, especially after he'd already texted with the news Sutherland had been released on bail earlier in the day.

Please don't tell me you love me again. Please don't beg me for another chance. Because right now I'm so worn down, I don't think I have the strength to push you away.

But to her relief—at least that's what she kept trying to tell herself—he said none of those things.

"Sutherland is dead." He barely gave her a chance to say hello before he dropped the bomb.

Horrible as it was, the first thing she felt was relief. "How?"

"He was murdered. Nolan found him in his hotel room earlier this evening."

She took a few moments to digest the information.

At her continued silence, Jack asked, "Aren't you going to ask me if I did it?"

She weighed his words carefully and thought about what she knew about Jack. Killing someone during an act of war in the army? Jack would have no hesitation to do whatever was necessary to complete his mission.

But she never would have pegged him as a deliberate, cold-blooded killer. Then again, she never would have pegged him as a liar who would sneak behind her back and spy on her either.

Yet her initial instinct on this was unwavering. "Do I think you have it in you to kill someone with your bare hands if they threaten someone you care about? Yes. But premeditated murder? That requires a level of coldheartedness I don't think you're capable of."

He let out a chuckle that sent a shiver of warmth all the way to her toes. "Well, at least you don't think I'm completely evil."

Tears stung the backs of her eyes. Jack was the furthest thing from evil on the planet. *Do you know how many women would kill to have a guy like Jack love them so much he'd pay fifty grand to get them a job?* She felt herself weakening and knew she had to get off the phone quickly before she did something stupid. Like beg him to come over, take her to bed, and help her lose the turmoil of the last few days in mindless sexual pleasure. "If that's it, then—"

"Wait," Jack interrupted. "I don't know many details— the cops are keeping it pretty quiet, and out of respect for Nolan, I'm resisting the urge to enlist Toni's help in hacking into the police network. But the most obvious answer is that Margaret sent another flunky out to do him in before he could dig her in any deeper."

Talia scoffed. The crazy old bitch had to know the police would look at her. "She'd have to be stupid to try anything with me. She'd be the first one the police would look at—"

"Or desperate," Jack said quietly. "This could mean the difference between her going back to prison and for how long. And if she gets someone who can make it look like an accident, no one would ever know."

A shiver ran through her, and she automatically went to the front door to double-check the alarm and the dead bolt.

"I'm doing whatever work on my end that I can, trying to run through Margaret's contacts for any possible leads, but you need to be careful."

She ran her fingers over the brushed nickel surface of the lock. "I'm always careful."

"I want someone on you," he said. "I know you don't want to see my face anywhere near you."

More like she was dying for one last glimpse . . .

"But I can get Moreno and Novascelic to take shifts for the next few days, just until this gets cleared up—"

"No." She cut him off before he could finish. "I don't want to be followed. I don't want to be watched anymore."

"I know you're mad at me about what happened, but don't put yourself at risk just because you're pissed."

"Don't try to make me sound stupid," she snapped. "Look, this is all speculation. You have no idea if this is true. For all we know, it was someone he pissed off or owed money to. Or, hell, if he was the psycho rapist, maybe one of his victims tracked him down and had the revenge she deserved."

"I seriously doubt it was any of those things," Jack said, the irritation in his voice palpable.

"Please, Jack, you tracked me for the past two years without telling me. Who knows what kind of paranoid conspiracy theories you can come up with just to wheedle yourself back into my life?"

She was lashing out unfairly, she knew, but she couldn't stop herself. That tight, panicky feeling was taking hold again, that feeling she'd been trying to escape. The one she thought had disappeared oh so briefly with Sutherland's arrest and subsequent admission that he'd been harassing her at Margaret's behest.

"Fuck me for trying to help you then," he said, but the bitterness couldn't totally conceal the hurt in his voice.

It sent an answering pinch to her own chest. "If it will make you feel better, I'll think about going away for a couple of days. Rosie's out of town, and it's not like I have job to go to," she said, unable to resist delivering one last jab.

Predictably, Jack tried to convince her to go to one of the safe houses Gemini Securities had scattered around Northern California.

"No way. Unless they have one overlooking a vineyard or somewhere on the coast, no dice. If I'm lying low, I'm doing it in style." Which was utter horseshit given the current state of her bank account and its future prospects, but she wasn't about to confine herself to an ugly, nondescript house in an ugly, nondescript neighborhood.

"Fine," Jack bit out. "But wherever you go—"

"I know. I'll take public transportation and pay cash. I'll even use one of the old fake IDs you gave me."

"And let me know where you're headed and when you get there."

"Wouldn't it be more of a challenge if I made you find out yourself?"

He didn't take the bait, but she could practically hear his blood coming to a boil.

"Fine," she relented. "I'll let you know if I can figure something out."

—◆◆◆—

"What have you done?"

His mother's screech jerked Gene from a sound sleep. He sat up, disoriented, his mother's slap bringing him to full wakefulness.

"What have you done?" she repeated.

He looked around his room, dazed. What time was it? He had no idea how long he'd been sleeping. The clock by his bed said 7:15. But it was impossible to tell if it was morning or evening.

"What day is it?"

"It's Friday, you idiot. What the hell is wrong with you?"

His heart thudded in panic. Friday morning! Shit! He'd slept for over twenty hours. He'd missed the window to drop off the bloody clothes for the hazardous-waste pickup. He leaped out of bed, scrambling for his clothes, ignoring his mother as he muttered to himself in English and Estonian. "Stupid, *loll*, how could you be such an idiot?"

Oh, Christ, he remembered, this was the morning that Rosario was leaving on that goddamn camping trip.

He staggered to the bathroom to splash water on his face, hoping to jump-start his brain. What time was she leaving? Had she mentioned it in the text she'd sent yesterday right before he collapsed into sleep? Oh, God, where was his phone?

He went back into his room and started flinging things around as he looked for his phone. Maybe it was in the car.

"Where do you think you are going?" His mother's fingers dug like claws into his back and her voice in his ear nearly pierced his eardrum.

"I need to get to campus," he shouted back. He shoved her away, and for a moment, his look of shock must have matched her own. Never in his twenty-three years had he laid a hand on her.

She recovered quickly, her face twisting in a mask of rage. Her hand lashed out, the blow to his cheek hitting him with enough force to send his head whipping around. "You will go nowhere until you explain where you have been and what you are doing! First you stay out all night, ignore calls, then come home and pass out like you are drugged."

"I was working at the lab. And I'm not taking drugs, I swear," he said, and he wanted to tear out his own throat at how pitiful he sounded trying to defend himself.

Ignoring his protests, she said, "And then I look through your bag, and this I find!" She was shaking something in his face that looked like a bundle of clothing. He felt the blood drain out of his face as he realized it was his sweatshirt and jeans, the ones that were covered with Sutherland's blood. The clothes he'd left wrapped in a plastic bag, stuffed in his duffel bag and locked securely in his trunk until they could be disposed of.

His mother had gone snooping around and found them. "What is this, covered with blood? Is yours?"

Cold sweat broke out on his skin, and he felt himself start to shake. "It's...it's not mine," he stuttered, his mind totally blank in the face of her anger, unable to come up with a single plausible explanation for the bloody garments.

"What have you done, Eugene?" She stared at him hard, and he knew the instant she saw the guilt in his eyes. "You have done bad, I know it! I always know you are bad seed. I'm going to call police, have you locked up like you deserve."

You fucking coward! the beast screamed at him. As his mother turned to leave the room, it was as though he were propelled forward by an unseen force. Moving without conscious thought. But suddenly, he was screaming, "No," and his hands were around her neck and he was shoving her up against the wall outside his bedroom. Her eyes were bulging, her tongue sticking out like a pink slug between her lips. Her head made a hollow, melonlike sound when he slammed it up against the wall.

His lips pulled into a savage smile and he did it again. She was trying to scream, but nothing but ugly choking sounds emerged. Her fingers clawed at his wrists, leaving raw, red grooves behind, and she kicked at his legs, her blows growing more feeble.

As he felt the fragile column of her neck give to his grip, felt the crunch as her windpipe gave beneath the pressure of his thumbs, he felt the power roar through him once again, sending him high up into the stratosphere where he was ruler of the universe. Where no one could touch him, especially not her.

It was as though he'd flown outside of his body to look down on himself. He was delighted at the sight of his muscles cording in his arms as he squeezed. All that power. She thought he was nothing, was capable of nothing.

He was strong. She was weak. She might have given him life but he was going to end hers.

Her struggles ceased, and as he came back to himself, he saw she was unresponsive, her eyes open and sightless, the whites dotted by bursts of red. He let her go and watched her crumple to the ground.

He stood over his dead mother, breathing hard and shaking as he waited for a wave of grief to settle over him. She was his mother, after all, the woman whose approval he'd spent his entire life trying to gain. The only woman who could make him shake in dread of a single angry word.

But when the pain would have set in, the beast inside him countered, replaying a mental montage of all the hurt and humiliation she'd showered on him his entire life. Insulting him, telling him he was worthless, that he was nothing, would never be anything. Would never get a girl to look twice at him much less love him because he was capable of nothing.

He was capable of more than she'd ever known, but it had taken her own death to make the old witch realize it.

Good riddance.

Gene wanted to bask in his triumph a little longer, but he knew he didn't have time to spare. His mouth pulled in disgust as he looked at the body—no longer his mother, now a foul heap of rotting flesh and bone. He had no time to deal with it properly right now.

Grabbing her by the feet, he hauled her down to the

garage and wrapped her in a couple dark green heavy-duty garbage bags, his eyes darting around for a likely place to stash her. His eyes lit on the white freezer chest in the corner.

Perfect.

An hour later, he was pulling into the parking lot behind Rosie's dorm. According to her text, she was leaving at nine, which gave him forty-five minutes before she left. It would be easy enough to catch her coming from the dining room or on the many trips she'd no doubt make to pack the car.

He'd chosen to park in a spot near the back entrance, close to the Dumpsters that would help obstruct the view of his car. Thankfully, at this hour of the morning during exam week, there weren't too many people up and around. His plan wasn't without risk, but since he'd missed the window of darkness thanks to his twenty-plus-hour nap, this was the best he could do.

Besides, he thought with a smile, after the events of the last twenty-four hours, he was quite sure he was capable of anything.

It didn't take long for him to spot her, chatting with a girl he recognized as her roommate Dana as they walked through the courtyard that separated the dining room from the dorm. He called her name, almost laughing to himself as Rosario waved to him, said something to her roommate, and started toward him with a trusting smile.

Her roommate gave him a look that said he barely registered. If anyone ever thought to ask who Rosie was last seen with, even if Dana remembered his name or that he'd been Rosie's physics TA, he'd bet on his life she'd never be able to give a good description of his bland, unremark-able features.

For once, that was just fine.

After he was finished with Rosario and her sister, it would make it that much easier for him to disappear and make sure no one would ever find him.

"Hey, Gene, what's up?" Rosario smiled at him. Her hair was in a ponytail, her face scrubbed clean, and she wore a sweatshirt over her T-shirt and shorts in deference to the chill of the late spring morning. "I didn't see you at the midterm yesterday."

"Sorry about that—I had some last-minute things I needed to take care of at the lab. But I have some news about your exam that I wanted to share."

Her eyes lit up, and he had a moment of doubt. Maybe he should let her go on her trip after all. Let her go away and leave her out of what he had planned.

But before he could complete the thought, her phone rang. "Oh, can you hold on? It's Kevin. I've been trying to reach him for two days and I really need to take this."

Gene nodded and tried to hide his disgust. She may have a sweetness to her, but she was just as stupid and deserving of punishment as the rest. And when he imag-ined the look of horror on Talia's face when she realized that her sister would suffer her fate alongside her . . .

Nate Brewster may have killed more women, but he'd never instilled the kind of terror Gene was going to rain down on Nate's final victim.

He listened to Rosario plead with her asshole boy-friend to accompany her on a camping trip, ignoring the little pang in his chest at the thought that no one, ever, had wanted his company so much.

He shoved it away. This was no time for self-pity. He alone would have the pleasure of Rosario's company for the weekend whether she liked it or not.

Finally Rosario hung up and she met his stare with a wobbly smile. He had no sympathy for her hurt but he pasted on a look of concern. "You two have another fight?"

She shrugged. "I hope you have good news about my test," she said with a little sniff. "I could use some after that."

He looked around as though concerned about being overheard, even though there was no one around. "Let's go somewhere a little more out of the way. I'm not supposed to let any students know before the results are official, but I knew you'd be anxious."

He motioned her to follow him around the back of the building. "I have your exam in my car," he lied as they rounded the corner. "I think you'll be pleased."

"Oh thank God," she sighed as he popped the trunk. "After I turned it in, I was sure I totally failed."

He reached into his backpack and palmed a syringe full of Rohypnol as he simultaneously pulled out a blue exam book. He handed it to her and her eyes lit up at the score written across the top.

"Oh my God, I got a ninety-eight?" she exclaimed. Then she looked a little closer. "Wait, Eugene, this isn't my test. This is from—"

The needle sank into her carotid and he depressed the plunger before she could finish. She gave a squeak of surprise and looked at him in shock, which quickly went blurry as the drug went rapidly to work.

"Whannareyoo dooin'?" she slurred weakly, pushing

at his hands as he tipped her back into the trunk. She barely put up a fight as he pulled her phone from her hand and slammed the trunk shut.

—m—

Talia spent most of Friday moping around, too depressed even to work out.

So depressed, part of her wondered if she shouldn't have taken Rosie up on her offer to join her on her camping trip to Yosemite. Rosie had texted her at ten-thirty to let her know they were on the road, and again three hours later to let her know they'd arrived.

Even so, Talia had called a few times, thinking that hearing her sister's voice might help comfort her. Her calls went straight to voice mail, and Talia forced herself to give it up for the day. Even if she wasn't the victim of spotty cell phone coverage, it was likely Rosario didn't want to get stuck on the phone with her anxious, heartbroken sister when she wanted to enjoy time with her friends.

Though it stung, Talia couldn't exactly blame her. Still, Jack's call last night after she'd dropped Rosie off was unsettling on multiple levels. First there was Jack's voice. Even over the phone, it had the power to reach down to her very core, touching her like a caress even as the sound of it ripped her to shreds.

God, she missed him.

Then, of course, there was the news he'd shared about Sutherland's death. And though he hadn't spelled it out, despite his denial and her belief in it, it didn't take a rocket scientist to figure out that the police were going to take a serious look at Jack for the murder. She resisted the urge to call Jack and check in.

Instead she kept an anxious eye on the local news, which was abuzz with the story of the violent hotel murder in an otherwise quiet part of town. So far there had been no stories about anyone being arrested for the murder.

She spent some time on the Internet looking for a likely retreat for the weekend, which only added to her depression. The only places with any appeal were way out of her price range, and the only places she could afford were either campgrounds or crappy motels. Neither of which would provide her any security if anyone came after her.

And that was assuming Jack was correct in his theory that (a) Margaret Grayson-Maxwell had sent someone after Sutherland in the first place and (b) she would have that person come gunning for Talia too.

So far nothing had happened, which seemed to support Talia's decision to shut herself in her house all day and night, nursing her wounds, wallowing in her loneliness and generally feeling sorry for herself.

Saturday she woke up late, determined to kick yesterday's depression aside, or at least beat it into submission with a brutal workout at Gus's gym. After a quick text exchange with Rosie in which her sister gushed (as much as one could in a text) about how beautiful the view was from Yosemite Falls, Talia gathered her stuff and headed out.

As she climbed out of her car and walked through the front door, she got that strange little tickle on the back of her neck, that tightness between her shoulders like someone was watching her.

She whipped her head around and did a quick scan

of the parking lot and the street that paralleled the front. There were two guys getting out of a car, talking as they approached the entrance, and a handful of women Talia recognized from some of Gus's classes. Other than giving her a nod or a quick smile in acknowledgment, no one was paying her any particular attention.

Talia was about to step inside when she heard a voice calling her name. She turned to see Susie, rushing across the parking lot as she waved. "I was hoping that was you I saw pulling in ahead of me."

Talia gave herself a mental eye roll at her own overreaction at being tracked by her friend. No, wait, she thought with a wave of bitter sadness. Susie wasn't her friend. The only reason Susie had ever given her the time of day was because Jack had paid her to.

Even so, as Susie jogged up to the entrance, her blond ponytail bobbing with every step, Talia couldn't help returning her timid but sincere smile. Whether it was a lie or not, Susie had treated her well. Even if her friendship wasn't genuine, Talia had to give her credit for being a good person, and she felt pretty bad for her part in Susie's restaurant getting trashed.

There was an awkward moment of silence; then they both started speaking.

"I'm sorry for—" Susie started.

"I'm so sorry about—" Talia said at the same time. She stopped. "You go first." She opened the door so they could go inside.

"Okay," Susie said with a smile. "I'm sorry I was such a bitch the other night," she said as they walked toward the locker rooms.

"Are you kidding?" Talia asked as Susie held the locker

room door open for her. "I'm sorry the psycho who came after me ended up trashing the restaurant." She stashed her bag in a locker and waited while Susie did the same.

Susie looked at her, her blue eyes wide with concern. "I can't believe he was murdered."

Talia nodded. "Does Nolan know if they're any closer to finding out who did it?"

Susie looked uncomfortable for a moment, then shook her head.

Talia got it. They were still looking at Jack as the main suspect. They were just waiting to get the evidence together to make an arrest. Talia looked at her watch. "We better get to class or we won't get a good spot."

"The good news," Susie said with a falsely bright smile as they started for the studio for the cardio kickboxing class, "at least I guess you can call it good news, is that they found some things in his room to link him to the rapes. Philip can't give me the details yet, but he's pretty certain Sutherland was the one behind the attacks. Thank God they were able to catch him before..."

Her voice trailed off.

"Before he could take me," Talia finished for her.

"I shouldn't have brought it up," Susie said, reaching out to pat her shoulder as they paused in front of the studio.

Talia gave her head a rueful shake. "It's not like I haven't had the same thought a thousand times in the last few days."

Another woman sidled by them and Talia could hear the heavy bass of the music, signaling the start of class. "Wait for me after," Susie said as they entered the studio. "There's more stuff I need to talk to you about."

Talia had a good idea what some of that stuff was, and she wasn't exactly eager to get into it. But for the next hour, she was able to shove it aside and lose herself in the loud, thumping music, the kicks, the punches, and the pleasure of putting her body through a strenuous workout.

Afterward she went with Susie to refill her water bottle before she had her one-on-one session with Gus.

"So I'm hoping to have the restaurant ready to reopen by July," Susie said.

"Wow, that's fast," Talia replied. Jack must be throwing some serious coin at the problem to get it done so quickly. "I'll contribute as much as I can—"

Susie waved her comment away. "I don't want any money from you."

Right, Talia thought bitterly, because Jack, massive foundation and all, can fund the entire thing ten times over.

"What I want," Susie said, her falsely casual tone setting off warning bells, "is for you to promise you'll come back to work."

"I can't." It was out of the question.

"Please?" Susie said, bringing her hands together in a pleading position. "I need you."

Talia snorted. "More like you need Jack's money. Don't worry. Jack's not going to give you the shaft just because you don't take me back on." She started to push past Susie.

Susie caught her by the forearm. "So I guess you know the truth, then?"

"That he had to bribe you to give me a job? Yeah."

"I wouldn't exactly call it a bribe," Susie protested, "more like an investment to help me grow the business."

"He gave you fifty thousand dollars to hire me," Talia said, and jerked her arm from Susie's grasp. "I'd call that a bribe."

"Fine," Susie said, and rolled her eyes. "But he did it as an investment, one that's about to pay off. In part because of you."

Talia felt a tiny burst of pride, one that was immediately squelched by the vivid memory of sloshing through the two inches of water on the restaurant's floors. "Right, it was about to pay off until Suzette's was flooded by the sprinkler system."

"God, will you just give yourself a break?" Susie snapped, throwing her arms up in exasperation. "Whatever motivated me to hire you doesn't change the fact that you're damn good at your job. In the past eight months, you've saved me over fifteen thousand in overhead."

"All of which can now go to repairs—"

"So what? With the new layout and expansions I get to make, we'll make the money back in a year. And it's not just the money." She leaned close. "This thing with Philip, I really think it's something special," she said in a low voice, as though she would somehow jinx it if she admitted it out loud.

"He seems like a really great guy, and it never hurts to have a cop on your side." Talia tried to keep the bitterness out of her voice, but there was nothing worse than hearing about someone else's happy love life when your own heart was in a million pieces.

"That's part of the problem, though. Between the two of us, we work such bad hours it's almost impossible to make time to see each other," Susie said. "If we're going to have a chance, I'm going to need help managing the remodel and running the place once it's open again. And you are the only person I would trust to do the job as well as I can."

"Really?" Talia said, taken aback.

"Well, maybe not quite as well as I can," Susie said with a wink, "but close enough that I'd feel comfortable going out on an occasional date without freaking out that stuff wasn't getting done."

Part of her wanted to brush Susie's words off as blowing smoke, but Talia knew that if Susie was dead serious about one thing in her life, it was her business. "I'm flattered," she said. "But I'm just not sure . . . Jack and I aren't together—"

"Because of the investment?" Susie asked. "He just wanted to help you—"

"Going behind my back is not the way to help me," Talia snapped. God, why was everyone so quick to defend him? "Just because it was done with good intentions doesn't make it right." When Susie would have replied, she held up a silencing hand. "It was the money and other things too, nothing I want to get into right now. Let's just say it will be hard for me to be around him, and if he's involved—"

Susie nodded. "I totally understand. Jack's what we call a silent partner, and you'd never have to interact with him. Unless you wanted to, of course."

Talia closed her eyes against the sting of tears. Hell yes she wanted it, wanted him. That's what made it so dangerous.

"You don't have to answer me now," Susie said. "I'll give you a call in a couple days and we can talk more about it."

"Okay." Talia nodded and started for the gym.

"Wait," Susie said, and, ignoring the sweat from their workouts, grabbed her in a fierce hug. "No matter how we started out, you need to know that I truly consider you my friend. Whether you come back to work or not, if you need anything—shoulder to cry on over a couple glasses of wine—you let me know."

Talia nodded and left Susie with a little wave. Though she was still bruised over the subterfuge, she knew Susie meant what she said.

If nothing else, Jack had bought her a friend.

Chapter 21

Jack waited a solid thirty minutes for Talia to show up. He spent most of the time calling himself a hundred kinds of idiot. He should be digging into Margaret Grayson-Maxwell's financial records to find additional ties to Sutherland and see if she'd made any payments to other past associates of David's in the past few days.

He should be trying to find Sutherland's killer before the cops showed up to haul him away.

Instead he was lurking in his car across the street from Talia's house, going over his manufactured excuse to check up on her so it would ring true when he gave it. Finally she was there, and even the glimpse of her through the window of her car was enough to ratchet his heartbeat up a few more notches. She pulled into her driveway, and as the garage door started to go up, he knew he needed to make his move.

He wanted—no, needed—to see her in person as though his life depended on it. And he knew once she got behind the locked door, there was no guarantee she'd let him in.

Of course, he could easily pick the lock and override the alarm system if she'd even bothered to change the access codes. But he figured breaking into the house when she didn't want him there wouldn't win him any points.

He got out of the car and sprinted across the street, ducking into the garage just as the door started to slam shut. He took some small satisfaction in the fact that even though Sutherland was out of the picture, she was still following the regular safety protocols, entering through the garage and not getting out of the car until the door was shut.

However, Jack had just proven to himself how easy that was to bypass providing you moved fast enough. He made a mental note to address the deficiency.

Talia got out of the car, and as she went to the trunk to retrieve her bag, he called her name.

She gasped and jumped about a foot but recovered quickly, landing in a fighting stance as she looked around the dim garage. He knew the second she saw him because her expression morphed immediately from fear to a ferocious glare. "You asshole! How long have you been hiding out in here?" She popped the trunk, got her bag out, and slammed it shut.

"Actually I was waiting across the street for you to come home. I slipped in the garage before the door closed."

"Some foolproof security you set me up with," she sniffed. She punched in the alarm code, opened the door, and walked inside, and he followed about three inches behind. She must have showered at the gym, because she was dressed in jeans and a T-shirt and she smelled so good it was all he could do not to grab her close and bury his face in her neck.

He could see her hesitate, and he knew she was thinking about trying to slam the door in his face. She must have realized the futility, because she continued into the kitchen and let him in without a fight.

"Nothing is foolproof, which is why you have to be extra careful," he said, his eyes tracking her around the kitchen. As he watched her slim, toned form moving underneath the layers of clothing, his hands itched to touch her.

He curled his fingers into fists, afraid that any moment his control would snap and he would reach out and grab her. "How was your workout?"

Her eyes narrowed into dark slits. "Did you follow me to—" Before she got the question out, she looked down at the gym bag she still held in her right hand. "Oh, duh."

"I would have known without the bag. I've been keeping track of you through the GPS in your phone."

Her jaw dropped. "Seriously? You're still spying on me behind my back?"

"How is it behind your back if you knew I was tracking you and Rosie?"

"That was before."

Jack took a step closer, unable to stop himself. "I know you're pissed, and I understand why. But that doesn't mean I've stopped caring. Until we find out who killed Sutherland and why, I want to keep tabs on you, simple as that."

"And then what?"

"I'll go back to Seattle and you'll never hear another word from me," he said, the words burning his throat like acid. He took another step closer. "If that's what you want."

Her throat bobbed and he could see the tears in her eyes, and for a split second he saw the hurt that matched his own through the crack in her indignation. Dammit, if he could just push past the wall she'd put up and get her to move past her anger and give him another chance.

But she recovered swiftly, her stony expression back in place. "Why are you here? Did you find something out?"

Jack shifted uncomfortably. "I came to pick up a couple things. I left a T-shirt and a couple pairs of socks in the laundry the night I left."

Her face suddenly flooded with color. "The socks are in the dryer," she said, indicating with her thumb the direction of the hall closet where the washer and dryer were stacked. "And, uh, I think the T-shirt is in my bedroom."

She disappeared upstairs and came back seconds later, the gray T-shirt with ARMY emblazoned across the chest balled up in her right fist. "Here." She tossed it to him, and as the cloth unfurled, he caught the unmistakable scent of her skin clinging to it.

Jack's mouth pulled up at the corners. She'd fished his shirt out of the laundry and had been sleeping in it. She wasn't nearly so closed up as she pretended to be. He brought it to his nose and took another deep inhale. "Thanks."

Her cheeks darkened to crimson, her dark eyes snapping with heat. "You came all the way over for a pair of running socks and a ratty T-shirt?"

"It's my favorite," he said simply.

Though her bravado was dimmed by her embarrassed flush, her cocked eyebrow said she wasn't buying it.

"And I wanted to see you," he said simply. Screw it. She already knew exactly how he felt, so why bother trying to play it cool in anyway? "See for myself you're okay."

———×———

Oh, God, she was dying inside, splintering apart and so far from okay it was a joke. "I'm fine," she said tightly. "So now that you've seen that, you can go."

Instead he took a step closer, the T-shirt dangling from his hand. He was so close now she could smell him, soap and spice and musky man skin. He was so warm she could feel the heat radiating off him, feel his need rolling off him in waves.

"I've missed you so much," he said.

She saw him raise his hand and even as she knew it would be disaster to let him touch her, she stood, frozen, unable to force herself away. The light brush of his fingers jolted her straight to her core, sending a wave of heat rushing through her. "Don't." Even as she said the word, she was leaning into him, into his touch like a cat craving a stroking hand.

"Please, give me another chance," he said.

She squeezed her eyes shut so she wouldn't have to see the pain in his eyes, the yearning that matched her own. She felt his breath on her cheek, and even as she called herself an idiot and told herself to stop, to shut him down and get him out of here before she lost control, she tilted her mouth to his. Parted her lips on a moan to let his tongue rub against hers.

His hand splayed against her back, pulling her close until they were practically glued together as Talia rapidly spun out of control. She kissed him hungrily, savagely, as her hands tore at his clothes with a will of their own.

She could feel him, straining against the front of his jeans. She reached between them and rubbed him up and down. While the other night she'd done the same move in an effort to cheapen what they'd had, tonight she was desperate to feel him, hot and hard in her hands. She tugged clumsily at the button at the top and jerked the zipper.

"Easy," he breathed, "don't—" His words choked off in a surprised hiss as she shoved his jeans and boxers off his hips and closed her fingers around him. "I want you. I want you so much," he groaned.

She had no idea where this would lead, no idea if she had it in her to forgive him. Right now she was only certain of one thing. "I want this," she said, stroking him, pausing to swirl her thumb around the sensitive head. He pulsed and jerked in her hand, and she felt a rush of answering heat between her legs. "I want you inside of me."

Jack didn't waste any time. Taking his mouth from hers just long enough to pull her shirt over her head, he unhooked her bra and brought them both to the floor. He peeled her jeans and underwear off her legs, hooked her knees over his elbows, and settled himself between her legs.

He reached down and she quivered in anticipation of the first deep thrust.

But instead of squeezing inside, he circled the head of his cock around her clit, rubbing, stroking, bathing himself in her wetness until she couldn't take it anymore. "Stop teasing me and fuck me already," she moaned, too turned on, too desperate to be embarrassed by her own bluntness.

Jack obliged her with a sound that was half moan and half laugh, and she felt her body stretch to accommodate him as he entered her in one sleek thrust. She threaded her hands in his hair and pulled his mouth to hers, tasting his moans as he took her with deep, pounding strokes. Within seconds she was coming, squeezing and pulsing around him as her body shook with pleasure.

He was right there with her, his face pulled into a savage mask as he came, spurting deep inside her. He collapsed on top of her, bracing his weight with his elbows on either side of her head. "I love you," he breathed. "I love you so much, Talia."

As Talia came back down to earth, shame at her own weakness settled over her. And with it came the panic. God, one touch and she'd lost all control. She'd thought David Maxwell had controlled her with fear. But fear had nothing on what she felt for Jack.

With Jack, she wouldn't be vulnerable.

She'd be powerless. "Let me up," she said, shoving at his shoulders.

"Talia, please," he said, not budging.

Panic chased away the lingering tendrils of pleasure. "Let me up, I can't breathe. Let me up."

He rolled away and she scrambled for her clothes, aware that she was being irrational, that there was a better way to deal but unable to snap herself out of it.

"What are you so afraid of?" Jack demanded as he yanked his pants up his legs.

You. Me. Everything about us.

Before she could answer, a firm knock sounded at the door. She did a quick check to make sure all of her clothes were in place and went to see who it was. On her doorstep was a man in his fifties, medium height with a thick shock of salt-and-pepper hair. He wore a dark sport coat over a button-down shirt and jeans.

"Can I help you?" she called through the door.

"I'm Detective Carolla, Palo Alto PD," he replied, and held his badge up to the peephole so she could see. "I'm looking for Jack Brooks. We have reason to believe he's here."

Talia's blood ran cold. "Hurry, I'll stall them while you go out the back," she breathed.

Jack shook his head. "Let them in. The sooner we clear up this nonsense, the better."

"I'll tell them you were with me all day. I'll say—"

"No, you won't. I won't let you lie for me," Jack said tightly. "Whatever they ask, you tell them the truth. You worry about yourself."

Before she could protest, Jack opened the door, then held his hands out to the side to show he was unarmed. "I'm right here, Detective." He didn't resist as the detective cuffed him and placed him under arrest for the murder of Greg Sutherland.

———※———

Talia watched in shock as Jack was escorted out to the waiting police car. "Call Danny," Jack called over his shoulder. "He'll know who to send."

She ran back into the house, grabbed her phone, and dialed Danny as she ran for her car.

"Jack's been arrested," she said when Danny picked up.

"For Sutherland?" Danny asked.

When Talia confirmed, Danny let out a low curse. "Shit. Jack seems to have a knack for getting himself into sticky situations, doesn't he?"

Because of her. Even though Danny didn't say it, she

knew he was thinking it. "I never meant to cause him any trouble," she said as she turned to follow the police car.

"No one is saying you did. It just worked out that way," Danny deadpanned.

"Can you help him or not?" she snapped.

"Absolutely. I'll give my attorney a call and have him meet Jack at the police station. Don't worry. We'll have him out on bail in no time."

It was small consolation. It was the weekend, so it was likely Jack was going to spend at least a couple nights in jail. Worse, if they didn't realize soon they had the wrong man, they might actually go as far as putting Jack on trial.

She couldn't stand the idea of him going through all that because of her. And the worst part, she thought as she pulled up in front of the police station, was that unless she somehow stumbled across the real killer on her own, there was absolutely nothing she could do right now to help him.

Still, she went into the building, hoping to at least offer moral support. Predictably she wasn't allowed to see him. But the police were interested in talking to her about the events leading up to Sutherland's attack on her as well as the murder.

She answered every question as truthfully as she could, though she chose her words carefully.

"You've been involved with Mr. Brooks for how long?"

"Do you mean involved, romantically?"

"Have you been involved otherwise?"

She shifted uncomfortably in her seat. "I've known Jack for a little over two years. I first met him when we worked together at a nightclub in Seattle. He...helped me and my sister out of an unfortunate situation."

"That would be your involvement with...who was

it..." He scanned down the page on the table in front of him. "Ah, yes. David Maxwell?"

"Yes," Talia said. "I assume you've read the reports about David's criminal activity?"

The detective nodded.

"I was aware of some of his illegal businesses, but I was afraid if I told anyone or tried to get out of the relationship, he'd hurt me and my sister. Jack helped get my sister to a safe house and protected us both until David was killed two years ago."

"And he was protecting you again after Sutherland began harassing you as directed by Maxwell's widow."

"That's correct."

"Several people we spoke to the night Sutherland was arrested were pretty certain your relationship with Brooks went beyond professional."

"That's true," Talia said. "I guess you can say we've been friendly for the past two years, but recently we've become romantically involved." God, it sounded so tepid put that way, relaying nothing of the depths of the passion that had her tearing at his clothes and falling to the floor in the middle of the afternoon.

"Are you in love with him?" he asked her, point-blank.

"Yes." No use denying the truth.

"Do you believe he loves you?"

"He's said as much."

The detective sifted through the pile of papers. "Brooks has a bit of a history of violent physical altercations. Are you aware of that?"

"I know Jack's not the type to back down from a fight."

"At least one of these incidents involved another woman, a wife of one of his teammates?"

"Her name was Gina. Her husband was beating the crap out of her and her son."

"Says here Jack nearly sent him to the hospital. Sounds pretty similar to what he did to Sutherland."

"Who was trying to kidnap me at knifepoint," Talia snapped.

"He's very protective of the people he cares about. Doesn't it seem likely to you he'd be capable of killing Sutherland in revenge for what he did to you?" he asked, leveling her with a hard stare.

Talia met his stare and held it, not giving an inch. "I've known a lot of bad people, Detective. Some of them cold-blooded killers. There's a big difference between beating the hell out of a man in the heat of the moment and committing premeditated murder."

"We have him on videotape entering Sutherland's hotel the day of his murder."

Talia felt her stomach drop at the revelation. It ultimately proved nothing, but it was damning enough to make the charges stick for now. "I know he didn't do it," Talia said. "Jack wanted to nail Margaret for coming after me. He's not stupid. He knows that would be almost impossible without Sutherland's testimony against her."

"Were you with him the day Sutherland was killed?"

Talia licked her lips, the lie poised on the tip of her tongue. It would be so easy to give Jack an alibi, to say she'd waited in the car at the hotel for him to return, that there was no blood or any other evidence of his murder. But Jack's admonishment echoed in her head. She could lie all she wanted, but if Jack didn't give the same story she did, she'd only get them both into worse trouble.

"No," she said quietly. "After Sutherland was arrested, after we got back home, Jack and I got into a fight."

"About what?"

"I don't think that's relevant."

"Why don't you let me judge that."

Talia wasn't about to tell Detective Carolla about the covert surveillance, aware it might make Jack look obsessive and possibly unstable. "Relationship stuff," she said with an exasperated toss of her hair. "You know, where is this going, what happens now. I got angry that Jack was planning to move back to Seattle and I asked him to leave."

"When did you next see him?"

"Today. We spoke on the phone a few times in the past couple of days, and today he came by my house to try to patch things up. That's when you came in." Well, not exactly, she remembered with an inappropriate burst of warmth. First there was a lot of stripping of clothes and rolling around on the floor.

Detective Carolla started to rise from the plastic chair across from her. "He didn't do it," she said again. "You're wasting your time when you should be looking for the person responsible."

Detective Carolla gave her a patronizing look. "And who might that be?"

Talia told him Jack's theory about Margaret hiring someone else to silence Sutherland, and her own theory about one of the alleged rape victims getting her revenge. Detective Carolla left her with a promise to look at every angle.

Talia left the interrogation room feeling worn down from the intense questioning, shaken both from Jack's arrest and what had taken place in her house just a few short hours ago. She walked to the waiting area, surprised to see Danny there.

"Hey." He looked up with an expression that was surprisingly friendly, given his past behavior. "You're still here."

"They wanted to ask me some questions." Danny hit her with a sharp look, and she said, "I was careful. And I didn't want to leave until I know what's happening. Have you seen him?"

Danny shook his head. "The only person they let in is the attorney I hired for him. He's in with Jack right now."

Talia took a seat on the chair across from him. "Is he any good?"

"The best," Danny said with a grin. "He better be for five hundred an hour."

Talia's stomach churned as she mentally added legal fees to the tally of thousands Jack had already spent on her. "Can he get him released tonight?"

Danny's mouth pulled in a grim line. "Earliest they can arraign him is Monday morning."

Crap. As she feared, Jack was going to have to spend at least two nights in jail. Or even more if they refused to set bail. "They'll set bail, right?" she asked, knowing Danny had no more control over it than she did but needing the reassurance.

"It's always tricky with murder. If they think he's a flight risk..." He shook his head. "I think chances are good that he'll be out Monday." He chuckled. "At least no matter how high they set bail, the poor sucker will be able to pay it."

Talia didn't think there was anything remotely funny

about it. "I feel so awful that he's going through any of this," she said, to herself as much as to Danny.

"Just give him a hummer in the parking lot as soon as he's released and he'll forget all about it," Danny said, chuckling at Talia's no-doubt-disgusted look. His expression grew serious. "Jack loves you, and any man worth his stripes would go through this and a hell of a lot worse for the woman he loved. Hell, I took a bullet for Caroline once and I'd do it again in a heartbeat to keep her safe."

Talia grimaced. "God, I hope it never goes that far. Even Jack has his limits."

"You'd be surprised." Danny's phone rang and his face lit up with a bright smile that shocked Talia with its pure sweetness. "Speaking of the love of my life..." He held the phone to his ear. "Hey, sweets, what's up?"

She watched as all the blood drained from Danny's face and he shot up from the chair. "How much? When did it start? No, call the ambulance and I'll meet you there. Don't worry about Anna." He pinned Talia with gray eyes gone dark with worry. "I'm here with Talia. She can watch Anna."

Talia nodded fiercely. Whatever Caroline was saying it was enough to make one of the toughest men she'd ever known look like he was about to break apart with fear.

Danny hung up and hurried outside, moving so fast Talia had to jog to keep up with him. "Caroline started bleeding and she has really bad abdominal pain," he explained.

"When is she due?" Talia asked as she followed Danny to his car.

"Not for another eight weeks. So the baby should be fine, but she's losing a lot of blood."

Talia shuddered. "I'll meet you at the hospital and watch Anna as long as you need."

She followed Danny to Stanford's emergency room, polishing up her race car skills as she struggled to keep up. Caroline was already there, her skin alarmingly pale against her dark hair.

Anna, usually a ball of nonstop energy, stood quietly at her mother's side, sucking her thumb and clutching her mother's hand.

Talia watched as Danny squatted down to his daughter's level and had a quiet conversation. Fortunately there were only minimal tears as Jack handed her off to Talia. He gave her his house key and told her to make herself at home. "You're a champ," he said, and gave her a quick, fierce hug.

"It's no problem," Talia assured him. "And after today, I could use the distraction."

She took Anna back to Danny and Caroline's house, and after about a hundred assurances from Talia that her mommy and the baby brother in her tummy were going to be just fine, Anna settled in with a pile of dolls and demanded Talia play family. For the next several hours, Talia was too busy racing around after an almost-three-year-old to dwell too much on Jack's unpleasant accommodations for the weekend.

Finally, around 8:00 p.m. they were both starting to yawn, so she dug out a pair of jammies for Anna and settled into the rocker for stories. Her phone buzzed just as she was starting to read a story about a Siamese cat who thought he was a Chihuahua.

It was a text from Rosie. *Pigging out on weenies and s'mores by the fire. I'll call when I get back tmrw.*

"Athat?" Anna asked.

"That's a note from my sister. Her name is Rosie."

"She your big sister?"

"No, she's my little sister. I'm the big sister."

Anna sat up straight and put her thumb to her chest. "I going be a big sister!"

"You sure are!"

The little girl looked around the room as though searching for something. "Why your wosie not here?"

Talia sighed. "Rosie is on a camping trip with her friends." At Anna's befuddled look, Talia clarified, "You know, like when you sleep in a tent?" At the little girl's nod, she continued. "She's in a place with big beautiful mountains and tall trees. I bet she's having a really good time right now."

Chapter 22

Rosie had no idea how much time had passed from the time Eugene had shot her up with something and shoved her into the trunk. That had been Friday morning. When she'd come to, she'd found herself in a room so dark she thought she'd been blindfolded. Her hands were bound behind her back and all of her clothes except her underpants and what felt like an oversized T-shirt had been removed and she shivered in the relentlessly cold, damp air.

How long had it been? It was impossible to tell for certain, but she thought it had to be at least a day. Talia thought she was in Yosemite. Did she start to worry when Rosie didn't touch base? Maybe she was already looking, with Jack's help.

The thought was a bright spot of hope in the otherwise dark, terrifying reality. She prayed, another in an endless string of pleas to the heavens, that her sister would find her before...

She shuddered as visions of what she feared Eugene's plans were crept through her consciousness. Though he hadn't admitted as much, Rosie had read enough about the serial rapist who terrorized the area for the last several weeks to know that this was part of his MO.

He drugged me, and when I woke up, I was in a cold room with concrete walls and floor.

It was cold comfort that he still hadn't raped her. So far the only contact was some groping of her breasts and crotch, on top of her clothes, no skin-to-skin contact. She knew he kept his victims for days, sometimes up to a week, before he cut them, raped them, and left them drugged and unconscious.

But from the moment she'd come to and suspected who Eugene was, she felt an all-consuming dread that she most likely wasn't going to be allowed to live.

He kept me so tightly blindfolded, I never saw his face. All of the victims said the same thing.

Rosie couldn't make the same claim. Eugene had done nothing to hide his identity from her, not when he took her from the parking lot and not in the few times he'd come to visit her.

Though she prayed Talia, Jack, and the rest of the world were looking for her, she knew it would be impossible for them to find this level of hell. She had to find a way out.

Her head throbbed with dehydration and hunger. Eugene had given her only small sips of water and no food for as long as she'd been here.

She heard the door scraping open and instinctively shrank back, crying out as the movement sent a shock of pain through her shoulders. The sudden illumination of the overhead light switching on sent a stab of pain through her head and she blinked back tears as her eyes started to adjust.

"Miss me?" Eugene said. The sound of his voice made her skin prickle with revulsion. As her vision cleared, she stared up at him, at the bland features and dark eyes she'd once thought of as kind. How could she not have seen what was really underneath? Even Talia, so quick to see the devil in anyone, had bought his harmless, nice-guy facade.

Her gaze snagged on the water bottle in his hand. Dripping with condensation. Her dust-dry tongue crept out to lick her cracked lips.

"Thirsty?"

She nodded, wishing she had it in her to play it tough, play it cool, but she was cold, tired, thirsty, and scared, and it was everything she could do not to crumble into a ball and sob for her sister.

"You can have it, the whole thing." He came closer, waving the bottle tauntingly. "But I need you to do something first."

A horrified shudder racked her body and she prepared herself for the worst. *Just close your eyes and take yourself to another place.*

But he didn't shove her back and rip off her underwear, didn't grab her hair and drag her face to his crotch.

"I know what you're thinking and it's not time for that yet." Instead he took out a phone—her phone, she realized quickly, and held it up. "I just want to take your picture. Will you smile for the camera?"

Rosie did as he told her.

"Good girl," he said, and she felt bile rise in her throat as he bent down to kiss her on the cheek. He cracked the bottle and held it to her lips. She gulped it down, shivering as some spilled down her chin to soak the front of the T-shirt.

As he withdrew the bottle, she looked behind his shoulder and saw that the door was cracked open, no more than a few inches. But if she could somehow get to it...

"You're such a good girl," he said, sliding his hands up her legs. "Not like those other bitches, not like your sister."

"If I'm so good, why are you doing this to me?" she asked shakily, waiting for him to get closer, closer...

"Because it will make her pain even worse."

"Who, Talia?" Rosie asked, momentarily distracted.

"She's always been the one."

The sick flare in his eyes at the mention of her sister spurred Rosie into action. As Eugene leaned forward, Rosie shot her head forward, catching Eugene square across the bridge of his nose with her forehead.

He fell back on his ass and she surged up, her head swimming with vertigo as she made a desperate lunge for the door.

She knew she was doomed before she took two steps. Eugene caught her by the hair and shoved her face-first onto the concrete floor. Pain exploded behind her eye as her cheekbone met the concrete at full speed. He drew back his foot and slammed it into her stomach. She gasped and curled into a ball, sobbing.

"You really think you can get away from me, you stupid bitch?" Another kick bruised her ribs. "I can't imagine why you'd want to leave," he said with a laugh that was like spiders crawling on her skin, "when I need you to keep our guest of honor company."

—∽∽—

Talia spent Saturday night at Danny and Caroline's so Danny could stay at the hospital. She called Danny to check in after Anna went to sleep. Caroline and the baby were stable, but they wanted to keep her in the hospital a few more days, and then she'd be on full bed rest until the baby arrived.

"Anna and I had a blast," Talia reported. "If you need help with her, let me know. I'm happy to take her off your hands."

Danny rang off with a heartfelt thanks and a warning they'd most likely be taking her up on her offer. Oddly, Talia found herself hoping so. She had fun with Anna playing chase and princess and reading fairy tales.

Which got her thinking about her own Prince Charming and what it might be like to have a little princess of her own.

If only life was as uncomplicated as a fairy tale. But with everything between them in such a tangle, Talia didn't have much hope of her and Jack finding their own happily-ever-after.

On that glum thought, she retired to the guest room and spent a restless night missing Jack, envisioning him in his jail cell. The next morning she handed Anna off to her aunt Alyssa and uncle Derek and headed home. On the way, she called Charlie Ferguson, the lawyer Danny had hired to help Jack.

He didn't have much to report but Talia took some small comfort at his assertion that Jack's bail prospects looked good.

A little after two, Susie called and strong-armed her into coming by the restaurant the following morning to talk about her future employment. Talia spent the rest of the day catching up on laundry, paying bills, and grocery shopping. Rosie was supposed to be coming home today, so she called and left a message inviting her over for dinner.

She got a text back from Rosie around six, asking Talia to come pick her up. When she arrived at the dorm, she called Rosie's cell but got no answer. She went to the door, and one of Rosie's dormmates recognized her and let her in. She went up to Rosie's room and knocked. Dana answered in a bathrobe, her hair wrapped up in a towel.

"Hey, I'm here to pick up Rosie."

Dana's brows pinched over the bridge of her nose. "I thought she was staying with you again tonight."

"No," Talia said, slowly shaking her head. "She was in Yosemite with you. She just texted me to come pick her up for dinner."

Dana shook her head, making the towel wobble. "She didn't go to Yosemite. Friday right before we were supposed to leave, she texted me and told me she had to cancel because she didn't want you to be alone."

"She didn't—" Before she could complete the thought, her phone buzzed. "It's from Rosie. 'On my way from library meet me in back lot.'"

What the hell was going on? After everything they'd been through, would Rosie really screw around like this? What reason would she have to lie about where she was spending the weekend?

None of it made sense, and Talia couldn't shake the feeling that something was very, very wrong. She said good-bye to Dana and went outside to the back lot. No sign of Rosie. She called her sister and thought she heard the phone ringing some distance away. But for whatever reason, Rosie wasn't answering.

The call went to voice mail and she immediately redialed. She heard the phone again, but she didn't see anyone around except for a nondescript guy in a black hoodie getting out of his car a few yards away. This time she left a message. "Rosie, I don't know where the hell you are or what's going on, but you need to get over here right now."

The text came almost as soon as she hung up. *Can't. I'm a little tied up right now.*

The picture that came with it turned her knees to jelly. Rosie, her face tearstained and bruised, eyes wide with fear. Her arms bound behind her back, wearing nothing but a ratty T-shirt that barely came to the tops of her thighs.

OhGodOhGodOhGod. He had her. He had Rosie. It was happening again, only this time someone had Rosie.

"Hello, Talia." She turned with a gasp and felt the sting of something stabbing into her neck. In a split second, she recognized the guy in the hoodie as Rosie's physics tutor, Eugene. She told herself to scream but she couldn't make her chest suck in a breath to do it.

"I've been waiting for this for such a long time."

As her vision started to tunnel, she saw the sick light in his eyes as he held up Rosie's phone for her to see.

—⁂—

Talia woke up with a pounding head and a foul, metallic taste in her mouth. Where was she? Fear sent her heart galloping and she tried to put the foggy events back together.

Eugene.

She let out a little cry as she remembered the evil light in his eyes as he'd held Rosie's phone to taunt her.

"Talia?" a voice croaked softly.

"Rosie?" Talia said, turning in the direction of the voice but unable to see anything in the absolute darkness, so dark she thought she must be wearing a blindfold. She lifted her hands to her face and realized they were bound with plastic ties wound tightly around her wrists. She felt her face. No blindfold—the darkness was that profound.

Rosie started to cry, and the burst of relief was swallowed by blind panic as reality fully set in. She was locked up in a dark, cold room, her hands bound and—she shifted and felt the rough floor against the bare skin of her legs—her pants had been removed.

It was happening all over again. And this time Rosie was with her.

Memories of what Nate Brewster had done to her flooded her brain, unimaginable pain and degradation and the certain knowledge of her own death. But at least that time she had taken some peace in knowing that Rosie was safe, that Jack had gotten her away and made sure no one could touch her.

Rosie's sobs sounded very far away as Talia felt a swallowing sensation, as though she were sinking into herself. Pushing the real world away, she retreated to a place in her brain where no one would ever find her. It was what she'd done so many times in the past. It was the only way she could get through this.

No! The same voice that had unfrozen her the other night and urged her to fight, the voice in her head that sounded remarkably like Jack's, snapped her back to reality. *It's not just you this time. You have to think of Rosie. You have to do whatever you can to get her out of here.*

She pushed herself woozily to her feet and stayed along the wall as she felt her way in the direction of Rosie's sobs. The concrete was icy cold against her feet, and her teeth started to chatter almost immediately. After a dozen shuffling steps, she felt her toe hit something that felt like a bare leg.

She sank to the floor and leaned into her sister, sobbing with relief as Rosie slumped against her. "Oh, God, Talia, I'm so scared. I'm so scared."

"Shhh," Talia said. "Tell me what happened."

"One second, I was talking to Eugene about my physics midterm, and the next thing I knew, he was shoving me into the trunk of his car. Then I woke up here. I don't even know how long I've been in here."

"It's Sunday night," Talia said. Or at least she thought it was Sunday night. She had no idea how long she'd been out. "Do you know how long ago he brought me here?" Talia asked. She wondered how long it would take for anyone to notice they were missing.

"Maybe a couple hours?" Rosie sniffed. "I'm not sure because I might have fallen asleep."

So it had probably only been a few hours since she'd been taken. Jack, the only one likely to care if she didn't pick up the phone, was still in custody. A shiver that had little to do with cold shook her to the core.

She and Rosie could be raped, tortured, and killed before anyone even noticed they were gone.

"I think the police were wrong about that Sutherland guy," Rosie rasped. "I think Eugene is the one who's been hurting those women. He has all these pictures." She broke off and Talia felt her tremble against her.

"Has he...did he..." Talia broke off, not knowing if she could stand it if he'd raped her.

"He hasn't raped me..."

Yet. Though unspoken, Talia knew it was only a matter of time unless they found a way out of here.

"He comes a few times a day and he...touches me. It's just like the women described in the news. But it always happens. It's going to happen."

"Shhh, it's going to be okay—"

Talia's pitiful reassurances stuck in her throat as a loud, scraping sound echoed through the room. A split second later, a light switched on, searingly bright. It took Talia several seconds to focus but she knew Eugene was there. Dressed in jeans, a button-down shirt, and Converse All Stars, he looked exactly like the harmless physics PhD candidate he presented himself to be.

But there was a gleam in his eyes, a sick anticipation on his face that Talia had seen in only one other place.

On the man who had tried to kill her.

"I'm so glad you're finally awake. I was afraid for a minute I might have given you too much Rohypnol."

Talia scooted in front of Rosie in a protective crouch. "You can do whatever you want to me, but let Rosie go."

He chuckled softly. "Of course I'll do whatever I want to you. I always do whatever I want." He gestured to the walls.

So focused on him, Talia hadn't noticed the horrific images papering the walls of the chamber. Her stomach churned and she was afraid she was going to throw up, unable to look away from the close-ups of pale, smooth skin carved with deep, bloody gashes.

"Aren't they beautiful?" He sauntered around the room as though studying the walls of an art gallery, occasionally reaching out to run his fingers down one, tracing the pattern of the bloody furrows. "But this one, this one is my favorite."

She didn't want to see, but she couldn't stop her gaze

from following his hand as it traced down the close-up of a woman's back. The picture was different from the rest, grainier and pixilated, but no less shocking.

"This inspired it all. The clean cuts. The sheer perfection." He sounded almost wistful. Then he turned to her and pinned her with his flat, reptilian gaze. "Don't you recognize it?"

Even as she shook her head, she noticed the familiar, honey-colored tone of the woman's skin. The dark red slashes standing out in bright relief. The scars on her back began to burn.

He smiled when he saw the dawning recognition on her face. "I've been waiting for you for a long time."

"Why?" Talia choked out. "Why those other girls if you only wanted me?"

"Practice," he said simply. "Practice makes perfect, right?" He held up his hand, and the glint of the steel blade made the blood roar in her head as her breath came in sharp pants.

He knelt beside her and raised the knife. She tried to shrink away but couldn't escape cold metal as it pressed against her cheek. "And when I finally finish what the Seattle Slasher began, I want everything to go perfectly."

He withdrew the knife. Talia's breath slowed a degree, then went back into overdrive as he moved it to rest against Rosie's neck instead. "But I'll do the Slasher one better. This time you'll get to see firsthand exactly what's going to happen to you when I do it to your sister first."

Before she could react, he grabbed her and shoved her down to the floor to lie on her stomach. He straddled her hips and shoved her shirt up her back. "Oh, God, I've been waiting so long to touch you." His hands traced along her scars in a parody of a lover's touch, making every cell in her body revolt.

She bucked her hips, trying to get him off, then froze as his fingers were replaced by cold metal. Oh, God, he was tracing the knife along the scars. Scraping the oddly sensitive, raised flesh with the razor-sharp tip. She held her breath, waiting for the first slice.

Fight! Instinct took over and she bucked and heaved, trying to dislodge him even though she knew escape was unlikely.

"Stop struggling," he growled.

Ignoring him, she pushed up on her bound hands and threw her head back, hoping to catch him in the face.

He jerked to the side and she felt the hot sting of the knife slicing into the skin stretching across her rib cage. She rolled to a seated position and tried to move her hands to assess the damage.

Blood welled and dripped down her side, but it didn't look too deep.

"You stupid bitch!" The openhanded slap caught her unaware. Pain exploded across her face as her head whipped around and her mouth filled with blood. "Look at what you made me do!" He jerked the shirt out of the way and looked at the slice, shaking his head.

"No, no, no," he moaned. "It's not supposed to be like this. It's supposed to be perfect and you made me mess it up."

He shoved her to the floor and raised the hand with the knife above his head. She heard Rosie's terrified scream and saw her struggle to her knees, as though she could somehow save her. *It was happening again. Except this time there would be no Jack to come to her rescue.*

Tears stung her eyes as his image filled her head and she braced herself for the fatal blow. At least she would die knowing she'd been loved by the best man on the planet. Her only regret was that Jack would never know how much she'd loved him back.

But to her shock, she didn't feel the icy pain of the blade sliding across her throat or stabbing into her chest. She looked up and saw Eugene slumped in a corner, the knife hand hanging loosely at his side as he muttered to himself. "It's okay, it's okay," he was saying. "We'll fix it. We'll fix it and when it's fixed, we'll start over."

Without so much as a backward glance, he turned off the light, plunging them once again into complete darkness. She snuggled up against Rosie as she heard the door shut and the lock slide home.

"Are you hurt bad?" Rosie asked.

"No." Her head throbbed and the cut on her side stung, but Talia clung to the pain. It meant she was still alive. And as long as they were alive, there was a chance they'd make it out of here.

Jack was arraigned and had posted bail by 1:00 p.m. Monday. He called Danny to score a ride back to his hotel only to discover his friend had spent the weekend in the hospital at Caroline's side. She was coming home today, but he would need to pitch in at home for the next several weeks.

"I'm going to need everyone to pick up some slack at the company," Danny said around a yawn. "Unless I can get some new hires, we're going to have to put the Seattle expansion on hold for a bit and have you stay here for a little while longer."

"You sure you want someone who's just been charged with murder working for you?"

"Ah, that bullshit will be cleared up in no time," Danny said.

"Let's hope so. In any case, I'll stay as long as I'm needed." Truth was, he was in no hurry to get back to Seattle. Not when things were so unsettled between him and Talia.

As though he'd read his mind, Danny said, "Talia was great, by the way. She took Anna Saturday when Caroline went into the hospital, spent the night, the whole deal. Maybe she's worth all the trouble after all."

"Yeah, now all I have to do is get her to talk to me."

With Danny unable to pick him up, Jack decided to take a chance and call Talia. The call went straight to voice mail like she was on the other line. He left a message to let her know he'd made bail and was hoping to see her later.

He finally called a cab to drive him back to the Four Seasons, where he showered and changed out of the suit his attorney had brought him for the arraignment. Despite Danny's assertions, Jack wasn't so sure he'd be able to get out of this murder charge so easily. The surveillance tapes showed him entering the hotel around the time Sutherland was killed.

But in the ten minutes he'd spent in the hotel, the surveillance cameras on Sutherland's floor had inexplicably stopped working, so there was no footage of Jack leaving the building. And since he had no alibi and so far the cops had no other suspects, they were going to do their damnedest to take that surveillance footage all the way to trial.

Jack went to the Gemini Securities offices, where he could use their state-of-the-art technology and connections to dig deeper into Margaret Grayson-Maxwell's dealings. He'd already found several links showing payments to Sutherland. The woman wasn't nearly as good at covering her money trail as her husband had been. He'd forwarded all of the information to Cole and the Seattle PD, confident they'd have the old harpy back in jail where she belonged in no time.

Still she was denying she'd sent Sutherland and denying she'd sent anyone else to finish Sutherland off when he decided to roll over on her. But so far Jack hadn't been able to uncover anything in her records to support that theory.

He worked for several hours until he finally gave up in frustration.

Even more frustrating, Talia hadn't returned his call. Was she avoiding him? She'd freaked out again after they'd gone at each other like animals on her living room floor. He got it. She didn't like to lose control, and some deeply scarred part of her was convinced that if she let down her guard too far, she'd find herself trapped again, living under the thumb of another man.

Jack couldn't prove her wrong if she wouldn't even return his damn calls. Irritated, he sent her a text. *Understand you might not want to talk. But msg me back so I know you're OK.*

He went out to get a bite to eat and was back at his hotel by ten. Still no message from Talia. He was starting to get that tight feeling in his gut like something wasn't right. He was grabbing the valet ticket for his car, ready to drive to her house—to hell with the fact she might be pissed off at him checking up on her—when he finally got a reply.

Sorry. Just need some space. Talk soon.

Jack's mouth pulled in a tight line. Just two days ago she'd been tearing at his clothes, as desperate for him as he was for her.

He'd told her he loved her again. And she told him she needed space.

—⁓—

By the third day, at least she thought it was the third day, Talia was nearly mad from hunger and thirst. She and Rosie barely moved from their same spot in the corner, huddling together to provide some semblance of warmth. Every cell in her body ached with the cold, and she felt like the hard concrete floor was grinding her joints down.

Eugene came a few times a day to provide small sips of water, but she and Rosie were given no food. He gave them a bucket in which to relieve themselves and checked on Talia's knife wound. Shortly after he'd left that first night, he'd returned with first-aid supplies. He'd carefully cleaned it with hydrogen peroxide, and when she'd gasped and jerked in pain, he'd scrubbed roughly at the wound with a piece of gauze and told her the pain wasn't even close to what she deserved.

He pulled the sides together with butterfly bandages and covered it with gauze. "Now we just have to wait for it to heal."

It was the only reason they were still alive, she knew. Or at least, it was why she was alive. Eugene wanted her "perfect," unmarred except for the existing scars when he finished her.

But every time he came, she was terrified this would be the time he killed Rosie, just to make Talia's suffering more profound. Yet he hadn't made a move, and Talia decided he was planning to wait to kill them together. She knew he would kill Rosie first.

That's why she'd immediately ripped off the bandages and reopened the wound. She would keep it open, festering into eternity if that's what it took. To give them a chance to be found.

But the plan had quickly backfired. When Gene saw what she had done, he very deliberately took off his leather belt and walked toward her, slapping it against his opposite hand. As he brought it up, Talia swallowed hard and braced herself for impact. But at the last second, he turned and brought the belt down hard across Rosie's bare arm. Her shriek filled the chamber and Talia threw herself across her sister, trying to deflect the blows.

Eugene picked her up and slammed her against the wall, and while she lay there, stunned, he bound her ankles and then looped another tie to join them to her wrists, hobbling her and making it impossible to move.

As Talia screamed herself hoarse, he pushed Rosie to her stomach and brought the belt down over and over until her bare skin was covered in ugly welts, some of them beading with blood.

Eugene stood over them, panting, as he slipped the belt back through the loops. "You pull anything else and she's the one who will suffer, got it?"

Talia nodded and sat perfectly still as he rebandaged the wound, and she didn't move until well after he'd gone.

She'd left it undisturbed and now, what she was pretty sure was sometime on Tuesday, it was still raw and prone to reopening if she wasn't careful. It would take a while to heal. Although, she thought morbidly as Eugene came in to give them each their paltry ration of water, by that time they might be dead of dehydration and starvation. It would serve him right if they died before he got around to killing them.

It wasn't her first choice for an ending, but she'd take it over the violence Eugene had planned. Though she tried to keep her hopes up, the ending where someone—Jack—found them and came to their rescue seemed to be slipping further and further away.

Chapter 23

By Tuesday morning, Jack decided Talia had had all the space she needed. He called her and, predictably, it went straight into voice mail. He grabbed a coffee to go and headed to her house. If she got pissed at him showing up unannounced, too bad. He didn't want to risk warning her and having her take off before he got there.

The idea that she would flee stuck in his craw, and some rational part of his psyche thought maybe this was a sign. When the woman you loved was avoiding your calls and you had to practically stalk her just to get her to talk to you face-to-face, maybe that was a sign this wasn't the relationship he should be pursuing.

Nevertheless, ten minutes later he pulled up in front of her house and was knocking on her door. No answer. He went to the garage and, after a moment's hesitation, keyed in the alarm code and opened the garage door. There was a small sense of relief when he saw her car wasn't there.

Nice to know she wasn't hiding in the house, refusing to open the door while he stood there like a loser. He checked his watch. This was around the time she went to Gus's for a workout. He climbed back into his car and drove over. He didn't see her car in the main lot, but she sometimes parked on the street and went in the back entrance.

Jack jogged up to the entrance, dialing her number as he went on the off chance she'd pick up. She didn't, and he didn't see her anywhere in the gym; the only place left to check was the locker room.

The uneasy feeling was building. Even as he told himself he was overreacting, he started to pull up the tracking application that linked his phone with Talia's. He'd resisted using it before, knowing she'd been upset when he'd tracked her with it the other day. But something was off here.

As he started to log in, he heard a woman call his name. His heart skipped even as he turned and saw that it was Susie, not Talia, waving to him from across the gym. He waited as she stripped off her gloves and jogged over.

"Hey," she said when she reached him. Her skin was shiny with sweat and she was breathing a little hard. She dropped her voice to a whisper. "Is everything okay? Philip told me they arrested you."

He nodded. "I made bail, so for now I'm a free man."

"You're not working out," she said when she noticed his jeans, boots, and T-shirt.

He shook his head. "I'm trying to track down Talia. I figured this time of day she'd be here. Have you seen her?"

Susie's eyebrows pulled together in concern. "I haven't seen her since Saturday. I ran into her here. But she was supposed to meet me at the restaurant yesterday morning and she never showed up."

The dread was amping up, coming to a head. "Did she call you and tell you why?"

Susie shook her head. "I called her but she never got back to me. Which is not like her at all, but I thought maybe with everything happening she needed a break from everyone or something."

"Talia is all about accountability. The way she keeps tabs on Rosie there's no way she'd let someone worry."

"Do you think something happened?"

Jack took out his phone and reread the text he'd gotten from her last night. It sounded enough like her, but anyone could take a phone and send messages with it. "I don't know. I'm going to check in with Rosie and see what's going on."

Rosie didn't answer either. While that wasn't completely out of the ordinary, it did nothing to settle the churning in his gut.

"I'm going to call Philip," Susie said. "Maybe he can help."

He left with a promise to call her as soon as he knew anything and headed to his car. Before he left, he finished logging into the locator for Talia's phone and clenched his jaw when he got the *Unable to locate* message indicating the phone had been turned off.

He felt slightly better when he clicked on the last known location and it showed that she'd been at Rosie's dorm, but that relief quickly fled when he saw the time stamp. It was from 10:13 Monday night, right after she'd sent the last text to him.

He covered the distance between Gus's and Rosie's dorm in record time. He waited until one of her dormmates was leaving and caught the door before it closed. Ignoring a voice asking who he was, he took the stairs two at a time and pounded on Rosie's door.

"Are you looking for Rosario?" a female voice called from down the hall. It was Dana, Rosie's roommate, and it was all déjà vu of the night last week when they'd come looking for her. "Because she's not here."

"Where is she?"

Dana shrugged. "I have no idea," she said, sounding a little miffed. "First she totally lied about ditching the Yosemite trip to stay with her sister, and now she says she is staying with her sister but she won't call me back and tell me why. I mean, if she's mad at me about something, she should just tell me right—"

Jack cut her off. "What do you mean she lied about the Yosemite trip?"

"Friday, right before we were supposed to leave, she sent me this text saying she couldn't go on the trip after all, and she was spending the weekend with Talia."

"She didn't spend the weekend with Talia." Dread rippled through him.

"I know," Dana said with an exasperated eye roll. "When Talia came to pick Rosario up—"

"When was that?"

"Sunday night. She was all, 'Rosie wasn't with me. She told me she was going to Yosemite.' Then Rosie texted her to meet her outside and she left."

"You haven't seen Rosie at all?"

Dana shook her head. "No, not since Friday."

Jack forced down the cold knot of fear that threatened to choke him. He had to stay cool. But holy Christ, it was

Tuesday afternoon and Rosie hadn't been seen since Friday and Talia had been gone since Sunday.

They could be anywhere. Anything could have happened to them.

He forced aside the horrible images pushing at the edges of his consciousness and focused on the here and now and gathering all the information he could to help find them.

"Let's start with Friday. When exactly was the last time you saw Rosie?"

"Breakfast. We were walking back from the dining room, and for some reason her physics TA was here and wanted to talk to her."

"Eugene," Jack said, picturing the younger man in his head. His bland, unremarkable features. His wiry body.

Always there, hanging around on the sidelines, observing everything, listening to every word. So easy to overlook.

He'd insinuated himself into Rosie's life and Jack hadn't even given him a second look. Jack had no idea what his angle was with Talia or his connection with Sutherland, but somewhere, deep in his gut, he knew Eugene had them.

And Christ, if Sutherland hadn't been lying about sending the DVD to Talia...that meant...

He had to swallow hard to keep from vomiting right there in the hall.

He could only imagine how terrified Talia must be, for herself and Rosario. Memories of the last time he'd pulled her out of a basement...the blood, her screams. What if he was already too late?

The thought left a gaping crater in his chest, and he

knew, if Talia and Rosie were dead, there would be no getting over it.

He took a deep breath and forced the blackness aside. Later, he could beat himself up for not realizing it a week ago, but now he had to focus on finding Talia and Rosie before it was too late.

He left Dana without saying good-bye, whipping out his phone as he sprinted to his car. His first call was to Toni, asking for a complete location history for Rosie's phone since Friday and a home address for Eugene Kuusik. Then he called Detective Nolan and left a message to let him know the scoop.

By the time he got back to the car, Toni had sent all of the information to the iPad he'd stashed in his glove compartment. He did a quick scan of the GPS locations—most were on campus, and it also showed the phone being taken to an address in Palo Alto that matched what Toni found for a home address.

Rosie's phone hadn't traveled far and he hoped that meant Talia and Rosie hadn't either. He started his car, intending to go to Eugene's house, but thought better of it when he glanced at the clock. This time of day, Eugene was likely to be on campus, teaching class or working in the lab.

He made another call to Moreno. "I need you to get Novascelic and do me a favor."

"Yeah, and I'd love a blow job from Katy Perry—"

"Talia's missing," Jack said curtly, "and Rosie too." He gave him a brief rundown of all the particulars and who he was pretty sure they were dealing with.

At that, Moreno went all business.

"I need you to go to this address, find anything and

everything that might show us where he takes them. I'm going to try to run him down at his office."

He sped across campus, mentally cataloging everything Nolan had told him about what he'd done to the girls, where he'd kept them. None of them had seen the surroundings but they all described a place that was cold, damp, with concrete walls and floors.

It had to be isolated and well insulated, where no one would hear the screams. Like a basement or an underground bunker. He called Toni again and asked her to pull up the blueprints for all the campus buildings and see which ones might have underground facilities. It was a long shot and would take hours, but it was the only thing he could think of.

He sped across campus to the new Clark Building, where Eugene did his PhD research. As he walked through the entrance, he could feel the rage building at the prospect of seeing the man he was now certain had kidnapped the woman he loved.

He forced it back, reminding himself he needed to treat this like any other mission. Keep a cool head. Don't miss any details. Do not let emotions take over and make you fuck up.

The facility was immense, and it took him a few minutes to find the lab. He walked in, and a small Asian woman looked up, startled, from her microscope.

Jack did a quick scan of the room. There was a main work area with tables full of high-tech machinery he didn't recognize, and beyond that were several cubicles. "I'm looking for Eugene Kuusik. Is he here?"

She shook her head.

"Do you know where he is?"

Another head shake.

He nodded at the cubicles behind her. "Show me his desk."

She jumped at his harsh tone and looked him up and down warily. She gave him a wide berth as she walked back into the cubicles and pointed at the one in the corner. Jack followed her. The desk was dominated by a large computer monitor, and folders stuffed with paper were piled high.

He picked up the first file folder and started sifting through the papers, but found nothing but a set of lab notes.

"Hey, you can't just go through his stuff," the girl said. "This is proprietary research."

Jack ignored her and grabbed another folder. Inside were a series of pictures from what looked like the 1950s or '60s of men in lab coats working in rooms full of giant computers and pages of what looked like building plans for a lab facility.

Something about it made the back of his neck prickle. "What is this?" he asked the girl.

She squinted at the page, started to shrug, then caught sight of something on the bottom right-hand corner. "It's pictures from the old particle accelerator, before they built SLAC."

At Jack's questioning stare, she said, "SLAC, you know, Stanford Linear Accelerator Center."

"I'm familiar," Jack said impatiently, "but what does that have to do with this?" He gestured with the drawing.

"Back in the forties, before they built SLAC, the university built a particle accelerator underground. Gene is always talking about how crazy it is that they used to smash atoms underneath the physics tank."

Holy shit. That was it. Underground. Concrete. Close. "Where's the physics tank?"

She looked at him like he'd grown a horn in the middle of his forehead. "It doesn't exist anymore. It was leveled ten years ago so they could build the new Bio-X facility."

The building where Jack was presently standing. His mind racing, he used Gene's computer to pull up a browser and did a search on "Stanford Underground Accelerators."

Hundreds of results popped up, but the one that caught his eye read, "Stanford Underground: A Guide to the Campus's Most Hidden Spots." He clicked on it and, hallelujah, the page included a map of the tunnel system underneath the university. Including an access point yards away from the back entrance of this building.

Jack stared at the diagram for several seconds, committing it to memory, then sprinted for his car. He popped the trunk, took his Glock from its case, and checked the magazine before tucking it into his waistband. He took his knife and tucked it inside his boot. He riffled through his equipment, cursing when he realized he didn't have his night-vision goggles in the car. He'd have to make do with the Maglite.

He shut the trunk and called Ben. "I know where they are. I'm going in."

⚓︎

She was losing her. Talia sat propped against the cold concrete, Rosie's head in her lap. Her voice was hoarse from talking and singing into the thick darkness. She told stories from their childhood and sang every song she knew from the radio, but Rosie had stopped responding hours ago.

Talia knew she was alive because she could feel Rosie's chest rising up and down. But she wouldn't speak, hadn't moved even an inch for hours. Worse, the last two times Eugene had come to check on them, Rosie had refused water.

Though she loathed the dark, the sight of Rosie in the harsh light had shaken her to her core. She was draped across Talia's lap, her skin chalk white, her full lips cracked and peeling. Her dark eyes were open in unseeing slits, and if she hadn't felt her sister breathe, Talia would have thought she was dead.

If someone didn't find them soon, Talia knew they soon would be.

Every time Eugene came in, she feared this would be it. Though her wound wasn't healed, she could feel Eugene's excitement growing, his control slipping away. This morning when he had come, he had pushed Talia onto her back and run his knife along her belly while he squeezed her breasts hard enough to leave bruises. Then the knife slid lower, catching the waistband of her underpants with the tip, dragging them down far enough to expose her.

Hours later, the memory brought a surge of bile to her throat. The coldness of the blade against her most vulnerable part. The shortness of his breath and the gleam in his eyes as she braced herself for the first cut.

Instead, as he had each time, he'd withdrawn. But she knew the end was coming soon.

It would be so easy, Talia thought, to close her eyes and drift away just like Rosie had done. Retreat to that deep dark place inside her that no one had ever been able to reach. But she couldn't. If she had any hope of surviving this, she had to stay strong.

But goddamn it, it was hard, especially when she hadn't eaten in days and she was lost in a darkness so consuming there were moments she wasn't sure if she was awake or in the middle of a horrific nightmare.

"Please, Rosie, please don't leave me alone in here." At her sister's lack of response, Talia started to sob. She tried to remind herself that as long as they were alive there was hope, but as the hours and days ticked by, she had to accept that this time Jack Brooks wasn't going to come riding to her rescue.

Her sobs choked in her throat at a sharp boom, like a gunshot outside the room. Then the scraping sound as the door opened and she braced herself for the burst of light that would blind her.

And the rest…

To her shock, instead of the overhead light, her eyes locked on the beam of a flashlight. Heavy footsteps, and then a voice whispering into the darkness.

"Talia?"

"Jack?" This had to be a hallucination.

But then the flashlight beam hit her and within seconds hard, muscled arms wrapped around her and a desperate mouth found hers in the darkness.

"Thank God, thank God," he murmured, covering her face with kisses she eagerly returned. One last, hard kiss to her mouth and he knelt down beside her. "Let's get you two the hell out of here."

— ᨊᨊ —

Eugene barely spared Molly a glance as he walked through the lab. In his hand was a bag full of additional first-aid supplies, including some vitamin E oil the woman at the pharmacy had assured him would help Talia's cut heal faster.

It had to heal. He couldn't wait much longer. He was starting to get that itchy feeling like his skin was too tight for his body. His entire being hummed with anticipation. He couldn't wait to watch her face when he fucked her precious little sister in front of her and cut her skin to ribbons.

And then, finally, he would have Talia. He almost came in his pants just thinking about it. He threw his head back against his chair and his hand started to reach down with a will of its own.

At the last second he realized Molly was talking to him. "What?" he asked sharply.

"Some guy was here looking for you," she said.

"What guy?"

She shrugged. "He didn't tell me his name. He was kind of big and mean looking."

Gene's blood ran cold. Jack was supposed to be in jail. Gene had seen news of the arrest himself.

Idiot, you never checked to see if he'd made bail.

He mentally kicked himself. God, how many times had he told himself not to let his excitement get in the way of staying on top of every detail? But in his near delirium over having Talia under his control at last, he'd lost track of Jack.

He took a deep breath, warned himself not to panic.

Just because he'd been here, looking for him didn't mean he knew what he'd done.

Even if he suspected, how would he ever figure out where they were? Still, he needed to go check on them, now. He pushed up from his chair, and that's when he saw the diagram that had been called up on his computer screen.

You can't take him. You're an idiot, a weakling, his mother's voice taunted him beyond the grave.

The beast roared back at her reminding him of how long he'd waited, how hard he'd worked for this. There was no way he was going to let Jack Brooks ruin his perfect moment. He picked up his bag, did a mental inventory of the contents.

Confidence surged through him. There was nothing to be afraid of. He had everything he needed.

———※———

Jack thought he was going to start bawling like a baby when he heard Talia's voice answer him in the darkness. As certain as he'd been that Eugene had taken them to the former lab facility when he shot the lock from the door and shoved it opened, he'd known it was likely he was going to find Talia's and Rosie's bodies.

He found them with the beam of his flashlight, anger surging to mingle with his relief as he saw their bound bodies, only partially dressed. He couldn't dwell on what might have happened and how he was going to exact personal, painful revenge on Eugene.

Now he had to get them out of this hellhole. He tucked his gun into his waistband and gathered her into his arms.

He'd never felt anything better than Talia in his arms, the feel of her mouth under his as she half laughed, half sobbed in relief. He made a mental vow. Now that he had her, he was never letting her go, and he didn't give a good goddamn whether she liked it or not.

"Let's get you out of here."

Positioning the light so he could see, he slipped the knife from his boot and cut through her bonds, then Rosie's.

Talia shook out her hands and gave Rosie a little shake. "Rosie, come on. Jack's here. We're safe now."

But Rosie didn't move. He shined the light over her face. She didn't look good.

"How long has she been like this?"

"Hours, a day?" Talia said, stress raising the pitch of her voice. She tried to pull Rosie to a seated position but she kept flopping around like a rag doll. "I don't even know what day it is anymore."

"It's Tuesday," Jack said.

"He didn't give us any food, and barely any water," Talia said. "He kept her longer than me. Is she dying?"

"She's gone into a catatonic state, and the lack of food and dehydration aren't helping. Our first priority is get her out of here and get some fluids into her."

"Okay."

The catch in Talia's voice broke his heart.

"You hold this," he said, and handed her the flashlight and lifted Rosie's limp form from the ground. He laid her over his shoulder, fireman style, and slipped his Glock from his waistband. "You okay to walk?"

"For miles if I have to."

Jack smiled. "Once we get of here, it's only a few

dozen meters. But watch your step. There are a lot of things to trip on. And stay right beside me. There are a couple of forks before we get to the exit."

"Where are we, anyway?" Talia asked as she followed him out the door. She curled her fingers into the fabric of his shirt and pointed the flashlight in front of them.

"There's a system of tunnels and lab sites underneath campus. Eugene was keeping you in part of what used to be an underground particle accelerator."

He felt Talia shiver next to him. "I thought we were going to die down here."

"Don't think about that. You're sa—" He felt the air near his head stir a split second before the pipe made impact, stunning him. His head exploded with pain and he sank to his knees even as a voice in his head urged him to keep his feet and fight.

But Rosie's weight kept him off balance. He heard Talia scream and saw the flashlight beam go tumbling. He fumbled for his gun, desperately trying to get his bearings.

He tried to tune out the pain and stop his head from swimming as he honed in on the sound of heavy breathing and started to raise the gun.

"Drop it, or I'll cut her throat."

Talia, Jack thought. The small whimper in the darkness sent ice coursing through his veins.

But the flashlight flared to life again and lit on Eugene, the top half of his face covered by what Jack knew were night-vision goggles. He had his hand fisted in Rosie's hair, the blade of a knife pressed against her carotid.

"Do it, Jack," Talia's terrified whisper called from a few feet behind him.

To prove his point, Eugene dragged the tip of the knife across Rosie's throat. A thin line of crimson appeared against her pale skin.

"Please, Jack," Talia cried frantically. "Please just do what he says."

Jack dropped it and kicked it in Gene's direction. He heard a scuffing sound and then the metallic skitter of his gun disappearing in the darkness.

"Get the light off me," Gene barked.

The light shining in his face would make the NVGs useless. It was something they could use to their advantage....

"Bring it over here."

Jack sighed inwardly as Talia obeyed immediately.

"Back to the room."

They felt their way through the darkness, Eugene taking up the rear as he dragged Rosario with him. It would be easy to turn and charge Eugene and overpower him, but not when he had the advantage of sight and he had a knife to Rosie's throat.

He walked as slowly as he could back to the chamber, weighing his options with every step. When they entered the room, Eugene barked at them to go stand in the corner. As soon as they did, light from an overhead fixture flooded the room. Jack blinked against the brightness, trying not to let his satisfaction show.

Eugene had just given up his greatest advantage and he didn't even realize it.

He was sweating, Jack saw, and his hands shook as he pulled something from his pocket. He tossed them at Talia. "You, sit down," he said to Jack. To Talia, he said, "Tie him up, hands behind his back."

Talia's frantic gaze met Jack's and he gave her a subtle nod as he sank to the floor. She took the ties and tied his wrists behind his back. "I'm sorry," she whispered.

"It's okay," Jack said, and flashed a cocky grin for Eugene's benefit. "I've gotten out of jams a lot worse than this. No way this little punk is going to take us down."

"You, shut up!"

Jack could see a vein pop out on Eugene's forehead. Good. Get him angry, get him careless.

"Legs too," Eugene demanded to Talia.

Talia crouched down in front of him and started to wind the flex ties around his ankles. "My boot," Jack breathed so only Talia could hear. He bent his right leg so his pant leg pulled up just enough for her to catch a glimpse of the knife handle.

Talia met his eyes and, making a big show of pulling the bindings tight, managed to slip the knife into the waistband of her underwear. When she stood up, the oversized T-shirt hid it from view.

"Now come here," Eugene said, running the tip of the knife teasingly along Rosie's cheek.

Talia obeyed, crossing to him on shaking legs as she wondered how they were going to get out of this. With Jack secured, Eugene let Rosie slump to the floor. Relief flooded her veins. With Rosie out of the way and Jack's knife in her possession, she might actually have a chance of taking him down.

Eugene circled her. "You know I never wanted to fuck

with an audience," he said as casually as if he were discussing the weather. "But fucking you in front of your boyfriend, I think that will be fun."

He lunged for her, and she heard Jack's roar of anger as Eugene knocked her to the ground and put his knee into her chest as he fumbled for another set of ties. She knew if he tied her up again, she was finished. She squirmed out from under him enough, adrenaline surging through her. She caught him with a knee to his chest with enough force to knock the breath out of him.

He staggered back and she surged to her feet. Without hesitation, she reached under the shirt, grabbed Jack's knife, and charged full speed ahead.

At the last second, Eugene ducked and dodged, his hand chopping down on her forearm with blinding force. The knife slipped from her numb fingers and clattered to the ground.

Eugene snatched it from the floor before Talia could make a move. "You stupid bitch. You think I wouldn't know he had another weapon hidden on him?" He chuckled and launched himself at her. Weak from the days without water and food, Talia wasn't fast enough to avoid being tackled to the floor.

Her head hit the concrete with enough force to make her see stars. She could hear Jack's voice but it sounded very far away. She saw Eugene's mouth, open, snarling in rage. His knees dug into her biceps, pinning her to the ground. He gripped the knife in two hands and raised it high above his head. Though she bucked and strained with all of her strength, she knew it wouldn't be enough.

The knife started its descent and there was an inhuman

roar and suddenly Eugene's weight was gone. She rolled to the side and saw Eugene flailing with the knife as Jack somehow maneuvered his bound legs around Eugene's neck.

The knife sank deep into Jack's upper thigh but he didn't even flinch as he flipped Eugene's body over onto the floor. A snapping sound echoed through the chamber and Eugene went completely still.

"Is he dead?" she whispered.

"He should be, since I snapped his neck," Jack said, grunting as he pulled the knife out of his leg and handed it to Talia.

Talia reached out with a shaking hand and cut the ties around Jack's feet and hands.

"Oh my God, your leg." Blood was pumping from the wound at an alarming rate and Jack's face was pale as he looked down to assess the damage.

"Shit. Looks like he nicked an artery." He took off his shirt and pressed it to the wound. "Gotta stop the bleeding."

"You can't die, Jack. You can't die for me. Please, I love you. I love you," she sobbed.

His blue eyes flickered and she thought she saw the ghost of a smile on his face. She heard masculine voices shouting at the door, but she kept her gaze glued to Jack's face. Frantically she pressed the cloth against the flow of blood, tears streaming down her face as she felt it soak her hands in an unrelenting flow.

She had a flash of Jack pulling her out of Nate's basement, knew in that instant how sick and helpless he must have felt as he desperately tried to stop the blood from pouring from her body.

And now that she finally understood who Jack was and what they could be together... "Please, please, don't leave me," she sobbed as his blood saturated the cloth and coated her hands. "I love you, I love you so much. You can't leave me like this."

Chapter 24

Jack coded twice in the ambulance on the way to the hospital. When they arrived, she barely had time to breathe before all three of them were whisked away for treatment. Talia squirmed impatiently as the doctors rebandaged the cut on her rib cage and cleaned and dressed the raw wounds circling her wrists from the FlexiCuffs.

Rosie was being treated two doors down, and the nurses assured Talia she was going to be fine. But no one would tell her anything about Jack. Not whether he was in surgery, if it was going well.

If he was dead.

Oh, God, she wouldn't be able to stand it. But there had been so much blood, and he'd been so pale ...

When the nurse brought in an IV, insisting Talia needed to be treated for dehydration, she convinced them to take her to Rosie's room instead of trapping her here for however long it took for the plastic bladder to empty.

Her heart squeezed in her chest at the sight of her sister in the hospital bed. Bruises showed luridly against her pale skin, and like Talia's, Rosie's wrists were wrapped in gauze bandages.

Her lip curled at the thought of the man who had done this. That was the only bright spot to her day, that Eugene was dead.

"Hey," Talia said as the nurse moved a chair next to the bed and set up the IV pole next to it. Talia winced as the heavy needle slid into her arm. She reached over and covered Rosie's hand with hers. One small bright spot in the day's events was that Rosie had started to come out of her self-induced stupor during the ambulance ride. Unfortunately, it also meant she became acutely aware of the abuse her body had suffered. "Feeling okay?"

"Never better," Rosie said sleepily.

"We gave her some Percocet for the pain," said the nurse, a plump bottle blonde in her fifties. "She may be a little out of it."

"For the bruising?"

"That, and tendons in both of her shoulders were severely strained from having her wrists tied behind her back for so long."

Talia swallowed back a sob and brushed a lock of hair from her sister's cheek. So much suffering. So much pain Rosie didn't deserve.

The nurse told Talia to call her when her bag was empty and left them alone. Rosie's eyes were closed and Talia thought she was asleep, when she said, "Jack okay?"

"I don't know."

Rosie slid back into her Percocet haze. By the time Talia was almost finished with her dose of fluids, Susie arrived, bringing with her a bag stuffed full of clothes for Talia to choose from. "How did you even know I was here?" Talia asked, shocked and touched that Susie had rushed over.

"Alyssa called me—she's on her way but she wanted to wait for Derek to get here."

"I know everything will be falling off you," Susie said as she handed Talia the bag, "but anything is better than having your ass hanging out."

"You are the best," Talia said, and pulled out a pair of yoga pants and a T-shirt. She started for the bathroom and paused to give Susie a fierce hug. "Thank you."

She quickly got dressed and went with Susie back to the desk to see if she could find out any more information about Jack. Ben and Alex slouched side by side in orange plastic chairs, their long legs sprawled out in front of them. "Any news?" she asked hopefully.

They shook their heads in unison.

Though she knew it was futile, Talia approached the nurse on duty. "My friend who was with us, the one with the stab wound? Can you please find someone to give us an update on his status?"

The nurse shook her head and politely but firmly told her she was not at liberty to share the information at this time. The police, who were nice enough to wait until she was finished with the doctors to pepper her with questions, took her statement about the events of the last few days.

She recounted the experience in a flat, matter-of-fact tone. Almost as though it had happened to someone else.

She knew from brutal experience that it would all hit her soon enough. The nightmares, the panic attacks.

But right now, all she could think about was Jack.

She listened as Alex and Ben gave their own statements, both in regard to how they'd found Talia, Rosario, and Jack, and also what they'd found when they'd gone to

Eugene's house. Namely, the body of a woman stashed in the garage freezer.

As the police wound up their questioning, the waiting room filled with all the rest of the Gemini employees and spouses, except for Danny, who was home with Caroline. "I'm keeping this line open," Danny said when he called. "Let me know as soon as you have an update."

"I will," Talia said, her voice cracking. She hung up and dissolved into sobs.

"Hey," Ben said as he wrapped her in a tight hug. "Jack's a tough mofo. No way a little weasel named Eugene is gonna take him out."

Talia let out a watery laugh and took the tissue someone offered to dab at her eyes and nose. Susie slid her arm around her shoulders and guided her to a chair. "Sit down for a second and eat something." She pressed a Diet Coke and a granola bar into her hand.

Though she hadn't eaten for days, she couldn't choke down more than a bite of the bar. But she couldn't gulp the Diet Coke down fast enough.

Finally, hours later, a doctor appeared and asked who was with Mr. Brooks. He looked a little surprised when all eight of them, including four men well over six feet tall and built like comic book superheroes, stood up.

"He made it through surgery," the doctor said.

Jack was alive. The relief nearly knocked her to the ground.

"But he lost a lot of blood and he's still in critical condition."

Talia choked down a sob as she digested that piece of information. "Can we see him?"

"As soon as he's out of recovery, we'll be moving him

to ICU. Once he's there, you'll be able to see him during normal visiting hours."

Talia nodded and went to check on Rosie. Though she was mostly out of it, she gave Talia a bleary smile at the news Jack had pulled through surgery.

By the time Jack got out of the recovery room two hours later, Talia was nearly tearing her hair out with impatience. Visiting hours in the ICU were very strict, she quickly learned, limited to a maximum of two people for half an hour at a time, with the last window at 10:00 p.m.

It was now 9:36. Finally Jack was moved and they were allowed access. Most of the group had gone home or, in Susie's case, back to the restaurant. Only Moreno and Novascelic stayed. It occurred to Talia that maybe she should let them go in first, the two who had carried their fallen friend out of that bunker and fought beside him on so many missions.

She dismissed it nearly as quickly as it formed. As much as she respected their friendship, that was the man she loved in there. The man she was going to marry, now that she'd finally gotten her head on straight and realized the truth that had been staring her in the face forever: Jack Brooks was the best thing that was ever going to happen to her, and if she wanted any chance of happiness, she would grab him with both hands and never let go.

And if she didn't get to see for herself right now that he was alive, she was pretty sure she was going to break with reality.

In the end it didn't even come up for discussion. A few minutes after they arrived on the ICU floor, a harried-looking nurse came out into the waiting area. "Are you Talia?"

Talia nodded.

The nurse gave her a wide-eyed look. "He is very anxious to see you."

She hurried in, and tears flooded her eyes at the sight of him. Propped up in the hospital bed, an oxygen mask covering the lower half of his face, he looked pale and exhausted.

And alive. Beautifully, perfectly alive.

She took the seat next to his bed and took his hand, unable to speak for several moments as she held it to her face. He said something to her, his voice muffled behind the oxygen mask.

"What?"

"I'm sorry," he said, "that I didn't protect you and Rosie."

Her head snapped back in shock. "Are you insane? If you hadn't almost died saving my life, I would punch you right now." In that moment, it all came flooding back, the darkness, the fear, the cold, the pain, the horror of witnessing her sister's suffering.

But none of that had been as terrible as holding Jack's bleeding body and thinking that she'd lost him. "If you died, I wouldn't, I couldn't—" she gasped, unable to form the words. "And because of me." She gripped his hand in both of hers and held it to her lips. "I don't think I could live after that. I know that sounds ridiculous and melodramatic—"

"It's exactly how I feel. And I will never forgive myself for leaving you vulnerable, no matter what you said or what we thought was going on. When I realized he'd taken you, that I'd failed you all over again..."

She wasn't about to let him shoulder that guilt. "And

I can kick myself into eternity for having the magical ability to attract a serious kind of crazy. You don't have anything to feel guilty for." She felt her mouth pull into a rueful smile. "Once again, I owe you everything."

He grimaced behind the mask and she felt his hand stiffen in hers. "It's not like that, dammit—"

"So now it's time to name your price," she said, ignoring him. "What will it be? Hot sex every day for the rest of our lives? Maybe a kid or two somewhere down the line? Boys or girls? You get first choice, of course, but I'd really love to have a big, strapping boy who's as handsome and noble as his daddy."

The corners of his eyes crinkled in a smile and his fingers curled around hers. "I want a gorgeous, tough little girl who can take care of herself like her mama." He reached up and pulled his mask aside. He curved his hand around her neck, urging her to lie against his chest.

She nuzzled against his hospital gown, felt his sure, steady heartbeat against her cheek. "I love you," she said.

"I love you too," he said, his rumbling voice warming her all the way to the tips of her toes. "But for this to work, you're going to have to accept that I'm going to be protective of you. I'm always going to want to look after you."

"I know. And I can see, finally, that there's a big difference between you wanting to protect me and you wanting to control me. Besides," she said, lifting her head with a little grimace, "I think we've established Rosie and I require some amount of looking after. And if you ever tell anyone I said that, I'll flat out deny it," she added with a mock glare. "Deal?"

"Deal."

—w—

Three Months Later

Jack pulled his car into Talia's garage—no, it was *their* garage now, since he'd officially turned the Seattle operations of Gemini Securities over to Alex Novascelic and permanently relocated to the home office two weeks ago.

He felt his mouth pull into a smile when he saw that Talia's car was here. It was only five-thirty, and in the past few weeks she'd been staying late at Suzette's as they pushed to get the final touches finished on the repair and expansion.

Apparently she'd taken his grumblings that he'd barely seen her lately as the hint he'd meant them to be. Not only was she working all the time, but also lately she'd been exhausted, stumbling to bed minutes after she walked in the door.

He climbed out of the car and unlocked the door that opened into the kitchen, his smile spreading wider as he reached into his pocket, reassuring him that the small velvet box was still tucked safely inside.

Jack wasn't overly superstitious, but he took it as a good omen that the ring he'd had made for Talia was ready on the one evening she'd decided to come home early. This was it, he realized with a jolt. The night he was going to ask Talia to marry him.

Earlier this afternoon when Alyssa Taggart had delivered the ring she'd custom designed, Jack's brain had started spinning with different scenarios of how he'd propose. He had no experience with these things, but he knew that women made a big deal out of it, so he needed to do something special, unique, something that let Talia know how amazing she was and how much he loved her.

All of that slid away as he opened the door to their home. He knew in that instant that Talia didn't require any elaborate setups or an expensive dinner that ended up with the ring at the bottom of her champagne glass. There would be no better place or time for him to ask her than now, in the modest house where they'd fallen in love.

Despite his certainty, he felt a layer of cold sweat film his skin and his hands shook a little as he closed the door, and the fear that had plagued every other man who had ever proposed popped into his head.

What if she said no?

Jack shoved it aside. He loved her. She loved him. They belonged together. End of story.

That didn't stop him from taking a deep, bracing breath before he called out her name when he didn't immediately see her. "Talia?"

When there was no answer, he called again, the anxious knot in his gut tightening when he registered that not only was she not downstairs, but also the house was eerily quiet, no hum of the TV or music she liked to listen to breaking up the heavy silence.

He ran up the stairs like he had wings on his feet and burst into the bedroom, relief pouring through him when he saw that she was sitting on the side of the bed. She looked up with a startled gasp and his relief disappeared when he got a good look at the expression on her face.

She looked stricken and pale, her eyes puffy and red and damp with tears.

"What is it?" he asked, immediately crossing to her to sit next to her and wrap his arm around her shoulder.

She immediately turned her face into his chest. "Is it Rosie?"

She sniffled and shook her head. "She's fine. She's at Caroline and Danny's," she replied in a muffled voice.

Jack felt his tension ease a degree, knowing that Rosie was safely at work—she was spending the summer working for Danny and Caroline, helping with Anna and their new baby boy.

"Did something happen?" he asked, careful to conceal the rage that bubbled up at even the thought of anyone daring to fuck with her again.

He felt a damp huff of breath against his chest. "You could say that."

"What exactly happened? Why didn't you call me immediately?" he asked, gripping her by the shoulders so he could look into her face. "Did you call the police?"

"It's not like that," she said, and sniffed again. A fat tear rolled down her cheek as he watched. "I'm pregnant."

Her voice was so soft he wasn't sure he'd heard right. Even so, he jerked as though she'd punched him. "Pregnant?" he asked, barely able to hear himself over the roaring in his ears.

She nodded mutely.

"How?"

"How do you think?" she asked.

At the sharp, sassy tone, Jack snapped from his fog, the initial shock replaced by a warmth that centered somewhere in his chest and spread outward to his entire body.

"No, I mean, how, if you're on the pill," he said, his gaze irresistibly drawn to her belly, still flat beneath the soft cotton of her shirt.

He half listened as she said something about missing

a couple pills during all the craziness, the hospital stays and after, as she got Rosie settled in with a good therapist and went back to work. But it was hard to focus when the one thought echoing through his brain was, *My baby. Our baby.*

This sharp, sassy, beautiful woman who he loved more than his own life was growing his baby inside her. A wave of happiness hit him with such force he felt his own eyes sting with tears.

"I swear to God I didn't do this on purpose to, like, trap you or push things along," she said, looking at the floor as her fingers knit into a tense ball.

Jack moved to kneel on the floor in front of her and cupped her cheek in his hand, tipping her face up until she met his gaze. "I know that. But just so you know, I was already planning to push things along at a pretty good clip." At her puzzled look, he pulled the velvet-covered box out of his pocket.

Talia gasped as he flipped the box open, revealing a stunning three-carat square-cut sapphire solitaire set in a delicate platinum setting. Her gaze flew to his face. "Is that... are you—"

Jack plucked the ring from the box and took her left hand in his. "I want to be with you for the rest of my life. Will you marry me?"

Her only answer was a squeak, but he took the frantic nodding and the enthusiastic way she threw herself into his arms as a yes. He hugged her back, silent for a few moments, his own throat suspiciously tight. "I love you"— he slid his hand down low on her belly—"both of you."

Her breath caught. "Really?" she whispered. "You're okay with this?"

He pulled back so she could see him. "Okay? I'm ecstatic." *And a little scared*, he admitted silently.

"It's so soon."

"It's what we both want, unless you were telling me what I wanted to hear back in the ICU."

"Of course not, but I wasn't going to hold you to something you said under the influence of morphine."

He smiled, brushed his thumb against the silky skin of her cheekbone. "Fine, this is me, stone-cold sober: Talia Vega, I can't wait to marry you and have a baby with you."

Her swollen mouth stretched into a shaky grin and warm color replaced her pallor. "Me neither. But I didn't really expect things to go quite like this."

Jack bent his head and covered her lips with his, savoring the taste of the woman he loved. Soon to be his wife, the mother of his child. His everything. "If there's one thing I've learned, when it comes to us, things rarely go as I expect them to. And so far that's worked out pretty damned good."

"Better than good," she murmured against his mouth, her lips parting to welcome him inside. "Perfect."

When Megan Flynn fell in love
with Detective Cole Williams, she
thought he was one of the good
guys...until he arrested her brother
for a murder he couldn't possibly
have committed.

Now, with her heart broken and
her brother's life hanging in the
balance, Megan will risk everything
to prove his innocence...

Beg for Mercy

Please turn this
page for a preview.

Chapter 1

It wasn't quite over yet, but Megan Flynn was 99 percent sure this was going to go down as one of the best days of her life.

And judging from the molten look Cole Williams was giving her across her tiny kitchen table, her perfect day was about to glide seamlessly into a perfect night.

"That was amazing," he said, leaning back in his chair, relaxed after a day spent on the water, followed by a home-cooked meal of fresh-caught local salmon accompanied by a bottle of Columbia Valley Pinot Noir. His plate was so clean he might have licked it, and Megan felt a ridiculous spurt of feminine pride in having provided a meal he'd so obviously enjoyed.

Megan traced the edge of her wineglass with her finger and gave him a sly smile. "So maybe next time you make salmon you'll listen to me and not cook it down to a fine dust?"

Cole laughed and leaned across the table to refill her wineglass. "My mom always said you had to cook it enough to kill the bacteria." He set the bottle down and took her free hand in his, his thumb tracing slow circles in the sensitive hollow of her palm.

Megan took a swallow of wine and smiled. "Since you grew up in a landlocked state, I'll let you off the hook. But from now on, leave the seafood to us natives. Deal?"

"Deal. I'll grill the steaks; you do the fish."

Megan tried not to let herself get too carried away with fantasies of a lifetime of quiet dinners like this and wiped what she knew was a completely moony look off her face.

But it was impossible for her not to get carried away with Cole, all smoldering and intense across the table from her. With his dark eyes, dark skin, and bold, almost craggy features, Cole was a little too rough to be classically handsome. But when his full lips pulled into that sexy smile, Megan felt like she was going to melt into a puddle and spill right off her chair.

He pushed back from the table and kept hold of her hand as he walked the few steps to the couch. He settled against the cushions and she sank down next to him, her legs folded under her short skirt.

The short, flowered halter dress was completely inappropriate for a day out on Puget Sound on Cole's boat. Even in early June, the temperature out on the water didn't get much above sixty degrees. But when she'd gotten dressed that morning, she'd chosen the dress as a key part of her mission.

Namely, to finally break through Detective Cole Williams's ironclad control.

Up until tonight, every date with the broodingly sexy detective had ended the same. With a kiss. Then more kisses that started with soft pecks and worked their way up to deep, wet, tongue-sliding, lip-sucking, blood-boiling kisses. Kisses that got Megan hotter than she'd ever been with any other man.

But no matter how hot she got, he never pushed it past hot kisses and light caresses, leaving her humming and thrumming with unsatisfied desire.

She was done with taking it slow. She wanted Cole, she wanted him now, and judging from the way his dark gaze kept straying down to the curves of her breasts swelling over the neckline of her dress, he was finally done too.

He tucked a lock of her hair behind her ear. "I missed you these last couple of weeks."

He looked a little worn around the edges, and for good reason. Cole was a homicide detective for the Seattle PD, and his latest case had him working such long hours that she'd hardly seen him.

"You sound a little surprised by that."

"I am," Cole replied, then held up a hand at her look of mock offense. "I didn't mean it like that."

"Then how did you mean it, smooth talker?" Megan gave him a playful swat on the leg that left her hand resting on the top of his thigh.

The lines around Cole's deep-set eyes crinkled with his sheepish grin. "Usually when I'm head down in a case, I'm totally focused. I forget to eat, forget to sleep, everything." He leaned in closer, close enough she could feel his warm, wine-scented breath tease her lips. "But I couldn't forget about you."

"I missed you too," Megan whispered right before his mouth covered hers. She parted her lips willingly, eager for the heat, the taste of him as his tongue thrust in. Pushing her back against the cushions, he licked, sucked, nipped, until Megan was clutching at him, practically shaking with need.

Please let tonight be the night.

As though he heard her silent plea, his kiss turned fierce and demanding. There was something different in his touch, in the way he kissed her. Like he was starving and she was the most delicious thing on earth.

Megan struggled to catch her breath as he pushed her back onto the couch. She'd known there was passion simmering under that stony cop surface, but nothing had prepared her for this.

Megan slid her hand up Cole's back, dragging the hem of his T-shirt from the waistband of his jeans. She purred in pleasure at the feel of his hot, smooth skin, the sound swallowed up by a sleek thrust of his tongue against hers. She traced her fingers up the hard slabs of muscle, her mouth moving eagerly under his as she sought to drink in every touch, every taste.

Cole pulled the strap off the other shoulder and tugged the bodice of her dress down to her waist. His groan of satisfaction rumbled through her core, sending a pulse of heat between her legs. He held himself still above her, muscles quivering as his hot, dark eyes locked on her naked breasts. Her nipples were hard, aching and tingling, begging for his touch.

A vivid flush rode his sharp cheekbones. His mouth was kiss swollen, his lips parted as his breath came in hot pants. "Jesus Christ," he said in a low, strained voice. "I've been thinking about this from the second I laid eyes on you, and even then... You're so goddamn gorgeous I don't know how I kept my hands off you this long."

He tugged his T-shirt the rest of the way over his head. Megan was treated to a glimpse of a wide, defined chest and rippling six-pack dusted with fine dark hair before he settled himself back on top of her. She let out an "ooh" at the first brush of skin on skin, a little surprised not to see sparks flying from where their bodies touched. He settled between her thighs, letting her feel the rock-hard ridge of his erection straining at the fly of his pants, leaving no doubt as to how much he wanted her. He kissed her again, his tongue thrusting in deep, lazy strokes that had her aching and shifting against him in an agony of need.

Megan kissed him back with everything she had, her heart twisting in her chest with the knowledge that sex with Cole was going to be amazing. Momentous.

Sex with Cole would change everything.

But that was okay. Because she was in love with Cole Williams. It had taken some convincing on her part to get him here, but she was pretty sure he was on his way to being in love with her too.

As scary as the idea of love was, Megan knew that with Cole by her side, everything would be okay.

Riinnnnnggg.

Cole jerked in her embrace, his lips stilling against hers as the harsh ring pierced through the sound of fast breath and wet kisses.

Megan tensed. A cop to his core, Cole never let anything get between him and his sworn duty. Even on his day off. She closed her eyes and started to count to one hundred, trying to cool her body and bring herself back from the edge as she prepared for yet another night on the razor's edge of sexual frustration.

To her shock, the cell phone kept ringing. Cole curled his fingers more tightly in her hair and resumed kissing her with that almost primitive intensity. Wow. *Cole must really want me if he's ignoring it.* A thrill rippled through her at the thought.

A second after the ringing stopped, it started again.

"Fuck!" Cole roared.

Exactly what I had in mind, she thought. "I guess you better get that," she sighed.

Cole nodded and let out a string of curses as he pushed himself off of her and grabbed his cell from the end table. "Jorgensen, why the hell are you calling me on my afternoon off?"

It was his partner, Nick Jorgensen. Megan sighed and tried to swallow back her disappointment. If she really wanted a relationship with Cole, she would have to get used to the demands of the career he loved.

Party's over. Megan sat up and pulled her dress back over her breasts and tugged her skirt down to cover her legs. Cole was silent for several seconds, his dark brows pulling into a tight frown over eyes that were losing their sensual haze.

She could make out a little bit of what Jorgensen was saying on the other line, but not enough to figure out exactly what was going on. Something bad, she guessed, from the grim look on Cole's face.

"I'm off today," Cole said. "Why don't you handle it—"

Jorgensen answered loud and clear. She heard every word. "This is a slam dunk, asshole. Get over here now."

Cole's broad shoulders slumped, and he clawed his fingers through his hair. "Fine, I'll be there as soon as I can." *I'm sorry,* he mouthed to her.

Megan gave him a feeble imitation of an understanding smile, her sexual glow dimming by several watts.

"What's the address?"

Megan's stomach seized as she heard Jorgensen give Cole the number and street.

She had to have misheard.

Cole disconnected the call, zipped up his pants, and reached for his shirt. "I'm sorry, Megan, but I have to go—"

"Did he just say the address is Forty-five Appleton Street?"

He didn't confirm. His face was cold and wiped clean of all expression.

"Cole, that's my brother's address. What's going on?" Panic roared through her veins, stealing her breath, replacing the heat of arousal with the cold bite of fear. Cole was a homicide detective. There was only one reason he would be called to Sean's house. She sprang from the couch and grabbed his arm. "Is my brother dead? Did something happen? You have to tell me!"

Cole grabbed her in a brief, fierce hug. "I don't know the details. I'll call you as soon as I can." He pulled away, and when she looked up, she saw that he'd gone into full-on Robocop mode. He reached for his phone and his jacket. "Just stay here and wait for my call."

The door hadn't even closed behind him before she grabbed her phone and dialed her brother's house. Straight to voice mail. "Sean, pick up!" she yelled, even though she knew he couldn't hear her. She yanked on a fleece pullover and stuffed her feet into flip-flops, dialing Sean's cell phone as she rushed out the door.

Her call went straight to voice mail and she left another message.

She slipped on the damp wooden stairs that led out, barely catching herself before she tumbled down the last two to the paved driveway below. She took a deep breath and gathered her trembling legs under her before continuing.

Please, God, let everything be all right. Please let Sean be okay. Sean had done ten years in the military, including his last tour in Afghanistan. He couldn't have survived that only to return home and...

She wouldn't let herself think it. Her fingers shook so hard she could barely get the keys into the ignition. She made the drive in five minutes flat.

Her heart seized in her chest as she pulled over. Flashing lights from an ambulance and two Seattle PD squad cars created a swirling eddy of blue and red in the twilight. Cole's Jeep was parked behind a black-and-white, but he was nowhere in sight.

Neither was Sean. Megan sprinted across the street, hearing the harsh catch of her breath and the pounding of her heart in her head. The ambulance blocked the driveway. She skirted around and saw two EMTs standing by the back door.

"What's happening?" she said. "Is someone dead? Is my brother dead?"

"Hey, you can't be here," one of them said.

"Somebody tell me what the hell is going on."

Neither responded, but the two men shared a look.

She didn't realize she'd started screaming Sean's name until a uniformed cop got right up in her face.

"Hey, this is a crime scene." The cop, with his blond hair sticking out from under his cap and ruddy cheeks, looked barely old enough to shave.

"This is my brother's house," she yelled, and tried to shove past him. "You have to tell me if he's okay."

The cop grabbed her by the shoulders and gently but firmly made her move. "Back it up."

"Get your hands off of me!"

"Is there a problem, Officer Dicks?"

Megan whipped her head in the direction of the familiar voice just in time to see Cole's partner, Nick Jorgensen, rounding the ambulance.

"Megan?" He motioned for the cop to let her go but caught her as she attempted to sprint up to the ambulance. "You need to get out of here."

"Is my brother in there, Nick? Is he dead? You have to tell me."

His closed, careful expression didn't provide any reassurance. "Megan, go home. Wait for someone to call you—"

"Not until I know—" She stopped when she saw Sean appear in the doorway. The constant strobe of emergency lights made him fade in and out. He looked out of it, like he didn't know exactly where he was.

"Sean," she yelled, a half sob, half laugh, so relieved to see him alive she almost fell to her knees. Sean's head turned at the sound of her voice. He took a step toward her, his leg nearly buckling under him as he stumbled on the first step.

Someone jerked him hard from behind, halting his fall. Then Sean staggered forward a few more steps as though someone was pushing him, his hands cuffed behind his back.

Other details became clear in that split second, her brain registering them in a series of high-definition freeze-frames. *Snap.* She saw that her military-neat brother was wearing a torn khaki undershirt stained with reddish brown streaks. *Snap.* Her brain registered those same streaks on his pants. *Snap.* A spattering of it across the part of his arm she could see with his hands handcuffed behind him.

Oh my God. Blood.

Snap. The man walking behind her brother, shoving him down the sidewalk, was none other than her would-be lover, Detective Cole Williams.

Megan leaped from her frozen stupor. She tried to shake off Nick, but he held her arm in an iron grip. "Sean, are you all right?"

Cole's dark eyes locked on her for a fraction of a second. He didn't make a move in her direction, but instead steered Sean to a squad car. Sean's mouth moved, but the words were obliterated by the din of radios squawking and shouted orders. Neighbors came out to their front stoops to gawk.

Megan's stomach lurched as she watched Cole with her brother. She had been at the scene of enough arrests to recognize someone being Mirandized.

"Let go of me!" She shoved at Nick and yanked until her shoulder threatened to pop from its socket, but he wasn't about to let her go anywhere. "Cole, tell me what's happening."

He shoved her brother into the back of a black-and-white and slammed the door behind him.

"Cole, answer me!"

His wide shoulders were vibrating with tension as he stalked up the lawn toward her, giving a nearly imperceptible nod at Nick. The grip on her arm eased.

She ran, not toward Cole, but to the squad car where Sean waited. She could see his face in the window, panic in his eyes. "Sean, Sean, it's going to be okay." Strong arms wrapped around her waist before she could reach the car. "No, let me go! I need to talk to him!" she screamed. In another second the squad car pulled away from the curb.

Megan wheeled on her captor, shoving at Cole's chest. "How could you? How could you arrest my brother?"

"I told you to stay home—" he started, his low, too-calm voice kicking her fury higher.

"Fuck you! You can't expect me to stay home and wait by the phone. You should have told me what was happening—"

"Megan, I can't give you details—"

"I told you this was my brother's house!"

"I have a job to do. I can't break the rules. Even for you."

His eyes were flat, black chips of ice. Megan stepped back, unable to believe this was the same man who had spent the day laughing and flirting with her. The same man who less than half an hour ago had his hand up her skirt and his mouth on hers, holding on to his control by a thread as he slid her panties down her legs.

Right now he stared at her as though she was just another freak who'd showed up at a crime scene.

Rage dissolved into fear, leaving her desperate. "You have to help me, Cole. Help me get him out of this."

Cole's look thawed a degree, but his mouth stayed in a straight, bitter line. "I don't know what to tell you. Sean's in big trouble."

"No! There has to be something you can do."

He shook his head. "You really want my advice? Get a damn good lawyer."

She went numb.

Cole looked over her head and spoke to someone behind her. "Get her out of here."

"Come on, miss, let's get you home." Male hands gripped her arms, pulling her toward the street as the man she loved turned his back and walked away.

THE DISH

Where authors give you the inside scoop!

From the desk of Stella Cameron

Frog Crossing

Out West

Dear Reading Friends,

Yes, I'm a gardener and I live at Frog Crossing. In England, my original home, we tend to name our houses, and the habit lives on for me. Some say I should have gone for Toad Hall, but enough said about them.

Things magical, mystical, otherworldly, enchanting— or terrifying—have occupied my storytelling mind since I was a child. Does this have anything to do with gardening? Yes. Nighttime in a garden, alone, is the closest I can come to feeling connected to the very alive world that exists in my mind. Is it the underworld? I don't think so. It is the otherworld, and that's where anything is possible.

At night, in that darkness, I feel not only what I remember from the day, but all sorts of creatures moving around me and going through their personal dramas. I hear them, too. True, I'm the one pulling the strings for the action, but that's where the stories take root, grow, and spread. This is my plotting ground.

In DARKNESS BOUND, things that fly through tall trees feature prominently. Werehound Niles Latimer and widowed, mostly human, Leigh Kelly are under attack from every quarter by fearsome elements bent on tearing them apart. If their bond becomes permanent and they produce a child, they can destroy a master plan to take control of the paranormal world.

The tale is set on atmospheric Whidbey Island in the Pacific Northwest, close to the small and vibrant town of Langley, where human eyes see nothing of the battle waged around them. But the unknowing humans play an important part in my sometimes dark, sometimes lighthearted, sometimes serious, a little quirky, but always intensely passionate story.

Welcome to DARKNESS BOUND,

Stella Cameron

From the desk of R.C. Ryan

Dear Reader,

Ahh. With QUINN I get to begin another family saga of love, laughter, and danger, all set on a sprawling ranch in Wyoming, in the shadow of the Grand Tetons. What could be more fun than this? As I'm fond of saying, I just love a rugged cowboy.

There is just something about ranching that, despite all its hard work, calls to me. Maybe it's the feeling that farmers, ranchers, and cattlemen helped settle this great nation. Maybe it's my belief that there is something noble about working the land, and having a special connection to the animals that need tending.

Quinn is all my heroes wrapped into one tough, rugged cowboy. As the oldest of three boys, he's expected to follow the rules and always keep his brothers safe, especially with their mother gone missing when they were children. In tune with the land he loves, he's drawn to the plight of wolves and has devoted his life to researching them and to working the ranch that has become his family's legacy. He has no need for romantic attachments...well, until one woman bursts into his life.

Fiercely independent, Cheyenne O'Brien has been running a ranch on her own, since the death of her father and brother. Cheyenne isn't one to ask for help, but when an unknown enemy attacks her and her home, she will fight back with everything she has, and Quinn will be right by her side.

To me, Cheyenne is the embodiment of the Western woman: strong, adventurous, willing to do whatever it takes to survive—and yet still very much a beautiful, soft-hearted, vulnerable woman where her heart is concerned.

I loved watching *the sparks* fly between Quinn and Cheyenne.

As a writer, the thrill is to create another fascinating family and then watch as they work, play, and love, all the while facing up to the threat of very real danger from those who wish them harm.

I hope you'll come along to share the adventure and enjoy the ride with my new Wyoming Sky trilogy!

[signature: R. C. Ryan]

www.ryanlangan.com

♥ ♥ ♥ ♥ ♥ ♥ ♥ ♥ ♥ ♥ ♥ ♥ ♥ ♥ ♥

From the desk of Bella Riley

Dear Reader,

When my husband I were first married, one of our favorite things to do was to go away for a romantic weekend together at a historic inn. We loved to stay at old inns full of history (the Sagamore on Lake George in the Adirondacks), or windswept inns on the Pacific Ocean (the Coronado in San Diego), or majestic inns made of stone in the middle of a seemingly endless meadow (the Ahwahnee in Yosemite Valley). Now that we've got two very active kids, we have slightly different requirements for our getaways, which are more active and slightly less romantic...although I have to say our kids put up with "Mommy and Daddy are kissing again" pretty darn well! Fortunately, my husband and kids know that my favorite thing is afternoon tea, and my husband and son don't at all seem to mind being the only males in frilly rooms full of girls and women in pretty dresses.

As I sat down to write the story of Rebecca and Sean in WITH THIS KISS, I immediately knew I wanted it to take place in the inn on Emerald Lake. With those pictures in my head of all the inns I've stayed at over the years, I knew not only what this inn looked like, but also the many love stories that had been born—and renewed—there over the years. What's more, I knew the inn needed to be a large part of the story, and that the history in those walls around my hero and heroine would be an integral part of the magic of their romance. Because when deeply hidden secrets threaten to keep Rebecca and Sean apart despite the fireworks that neither of them can deny, the truth of what happened in the inn so many years ago is finally revealed.

I so enjoyed creating my fantasy inn on Emerald Lake, and I hope that as you're reading WITH THIS KISS, even if you aren't able to get away for a romantic weekend right this second, for a few hours you'll feel as if you've spent some time relaxing...and falling in love.

Happy reading,

Bella Riley

www.bellariley.com

♥ ♥ ♥ ♥ ♥ ♥ ♥ ♥ ♥ ♥ ♥ ♥ ♥ ♥

From the desk of Jami Alden

Dear Reader,

Who hasn't wished for a fresh start at some point in their lives? I know I have. The urge became particularly keen when I was starting high school in Connecticut. Not that it was a terrible place to grow up, but an awkward phase combined with a pack of mean girls eager to point out every quirk and flaw had left their scars. Left me wishing I could go somewhere new, where I could meet all new people. People who wouldn't remember the braces (complete with headgear!), the unibrow, the glasses (lavender plastic frames!), and the time my mom tried to perm my bangs with disastrous results.

In RUN FROM FEAR, Talia Vega is looking for a similar fresh start. Granted, the monsters from her past are a bit more formidable than a pack of snotty twelve-year-olds, and the scars she bears are physical as well as emotional. But like so many of us, all she really wants is a fresh start, a new life, away from the shadows of her past.

But just as I was forced to sit in class with peers who remembered when I had a mouth full of metal and no idea how to wield a pair of tweezers, Talia Vega can't outrun the people unwilling to let her forget everything she's tried to leave behind. Lucky for her, Jack Brooks, the one man who has seen her at her absolute lowest point, will do anything to protect her from monsters past and present.

And even though I got my own fresh start of sorts

when I moved across the country for college, I sure wish someone had been around to protect me from my mother and her Ogilvie home perm kit. I don't care what the commercial says—you CAN get it wrong!

Jami Alden

www.jamialden.com

Find out more about Forever Romance!

Visit us at
www.hachettebookgroup.com/publishing_forever.aspx

Find us on Facebook
http://www.facebook.com/ForeverRomance

Follow us on Twitter
http://twitter.com/ForeverRomance

NEW AND UPCOMING TITLES

Each month we feature our new titles
and reader favorites.

CONTESTS AND GIVEAWAYS

We give away galleys, autographed copies,
and all kinds of exclusive items.

AUTHOR INFO

You'll find bios, articles, and links to personal websites
for all your favorite authors—and so much more.

GET SOCIAL

Connect with your favorite authors, editors, and
other Forever fans, and share what's important to you.

THE BUZZ

Sign up for our monthly romance newsletter,
and be the first to read all about it.

VISIT US ONLINE AT

WWW.HACHETTEBOOKGROUP.COM

FEATURES:

**OPENBOOK BROWSE AND
SEARCH EXCERPTS**

•

AUDIOBOOK EXCERPTS AND PODCASTS

•

AUTHOR ARTICLES AND INTERVIEWS

•

**BESTSELLER AND PUBLISHING
GROUP NEWS**

•

SIGN UP FOR E-NEWSLETTERS

•

**AUTHOR APPEARANCES AND TOUR
INFORMATION**

•

SOCIAL MEDIA FEEDS AND WIDGETS

•

DOWNLOAD FREE APPS

BOOKMARK HACHETTE BOOK GROUP
@ WWW.HACHETTEBOOKGROUP.COM